IN AN AGE OF TREACHERY AND INTRIGUE ... THE COURT

"Kiss me," R[...] will. Now."

"You do not know what you ask!" Kat said with a gasp.

"Or what it means to you? No, lady, I do not. You have not told me. But I am well aware what it means to me." Slowly and gently, he pushed at her skirt until the hoops were out of his way. Then he rubbed his hips against hers so she could feel the solid weight of his arousal.

"The queen—"

"Is not here. This is between the two of us. There's no one else to fool or impress or mislead. Only Kat and Robin. Kiss me."

Traitor's Kiss

Joy Tucker

AVON BOOKS NEW YORK

TRAITOR'S KISS is an original publication of Avon Books. This work has never before appeared in book form. This work is a novel. Any similarity to actual persons or events is purely coincidental.

AVON BOOKS
A division of
The Hearst Corporation
1350 Avenue of the Americas
New York, New York 10019

Copyright © 1992 by Joy Tucker
Published by arrangement with the author
Library of Congress Catalog Card Number: 92-90431
ISBN: 0-380-76446-6

First Avon Books Printing: January 1993

AVON TRADEMARK REG. U.S. PAT. OFF. AND IN OTHER COUNTRIES, MARCA REGISTRADA, HECHO EN U.S.A.

Printed in the U.S.A.

RA   10 9 8 7 6 5 4 3 2 1

For my sister, Mary Dee Reilly

Contents

Part One: Stranger's Kiss   5

Part Two: Traitor's Kiss   183

Part Three: Lovers' Kiss   265

Thank you to Undine Concannon, archivist, Madame Tussaud's Limited, for information about Elizabeth Tudor's physical appearance.

Prologue

"**W**ho is he?"

"The big blond man?" A passing servant slowed, darting Kat Preston a glance that showed the whites of her eyes. "The queen's rat catcher."

Kat looked again. The "queen's rat catcher" didn't have the bent shoulders or downcast gaze of a scullion. Nor was there any of an upper servant's oily eagerness in the way he had his back turned to the Earl of Aftondale. She knew how the blond man felt. Aftondale was a notorious lecher, and she and every other decent person in the court at Whitehall did their best to avoid him.

"Are you certain he's no more than a—"

She couldn't repeat it. Not that she was too fine a lady to admit rats existed and someone had to catch them, but the name didn't fit the giant with the rumpled golden curls. He dominated the middle of the room—as if he, and not Elizabeth Tudor, owned it.

"That's just what her majesty has started the gentry folk calling him. He's a nobleman, one of Walsingham's agents who gathers information for the queen. And no one suspected! Not until today. Her majesty was so excited when she heard he had broken a plot against her—she called out God's blessing on Robin Hawking, and then the whole court knew his game. You watch out for him. That one's not safe for a young lady like you to know."

"A spy?"

"Aye, my lady. Trapped a lot of silly young men who thought they were going to murder our Queen Bess and

1

put that Scottish whore Mary Stuart on the throne. Saw through their tricks, he did. He's been called to court to get his thanks in person."

Kat craned for a better look. A clerk in dark robes cut off her view. Edging around him, she was rewarded with another glimpse of the tall, carelessly dressed man. He was handsome—so handsome it was daunting. A golden arrow-point beard emphasized his strong chin. His feet braced themselves against the floor and his hands were perched on his hips. Apparently he had a swashbuckling nature and didn't care who knew it.

The indications of arrogance caused troubled lines to mar her smooth forehead. He flaunted his virility like a cloak. Such striking masculinity was impossible for a woman to ignore. Men like that sometimes took it for granted that all women were theirs for the taking.

Kat had run afoul of a man who took without asking—once. She had no intention of running the same kind of risk again.

But this man had more than just a confident manner.

"He looks clever, do you not think so? A man other men would willingly follow," she said, noting the crush of courtiers and government scribes surrounding him. "Resourceful. Hardened by cares. Like an eagle beset on all sides."

The maid dropped the bundle she was carrying and settled in for a good gossip. "Never go getting any soft ideas about Lord Robert Hawking, my lady. 'Tis a rarity for him to come to court. He dare not show himself among God-fearing people." She nodded sharply. "Not even the queen's favor can whitewash *his* reputation."

Yes, he would be a favorite with Elizabeth, Kat realized. The queen liked men to be brawny and bold.

"I imagine that one would dare anything," she said to herself.

"O-o-o-h, they say he dares plenty with *some* women."

"A cocksman," said Kat with flat distaste.

"Not only that. He will not touch a real lady with kin and friends to protect her, for fear the truth about his—tastes—will get about."

Kat's brown eyes widened. "What tastes?"

"No one knows. Not for certain sure. But for years it has been known he tortures people. Your ladyship has heard how all manner of folk use the Tower of London. It holds wild animals and an armory and barracks, as well as royal apartments and prison cells. Lord Robert has been seen and heard there."

Kat had never been to the Tower, for the simple reason that Whitehall Palace was in Westminster, several miles from the capital.

"If many folk have seemly business in the Tower, why not Hawking?" she asked impatiently.

"Because when he goes into a room, screams are heard coming out. Oh, yes, he tortures. They say that's not all he does when 'tis a woman he gets on the rack." The servant inched closer and her London-flavored voice dropped to a hoarse whisper. "Some of the ladies—highborn ladies, too—giggle whenever his name be mentioned. About how many ways this hangman can employ his ropes ..."

Repelled, Kat turned away and barely noticed when her informant picked up the bundle and scurried off.

She shook her head to clear it of the woman's disgusting hints. It was impossible to believe that cleanly masculine face hid the kind of nature that took pleasure in pain. The fellow might well be a womanizer. Judging by his height and handsomeness, Kat would have been astonished if he were not. He must have opportunities.

But as for other, more sinister qualities ... well, she need not concern herself with what he was, she thought. Nervousness flickered and she suppressed it. All that mattered was that he was an agent of the queen. A solver of riddles.

Kat had a puzzle that needed deciphering. It had been gnawing at the back of her mind for nearly a week as she went about her tasks as a lady-in-waiting. Although she'd only been in attendance on the queen for two months, each day made her more familiar with the workings of the court, which meant she no longer had to concentrate every moment lest she make mistakes. Yet she hadn't been able to make up her mind about her problem. It was more than slightly out of the ordinary. This Robert Hawking would do to help her, she decided. He would do very well.

As long as he kept his desires, whatever they were, to himself.

Just then his gaze swept the room. Kat's gown was dark and she was standing in shadow; there was no possible way for him to pick her slender form out from the throng of brilliantly garbed ladies and gentlemen. But as his eyes moved over the crowd, she drew in her breath. They were beautiful, as pale and bright as silver rubbed to a high shine. She'd never seen eyes so empty of feeling.

Her resolution wavered. A hot shiver licked the base of her spine.

Then common sense asserted itself. There was no reason to fret about Lord Robert and his reputed way with women, not when he looked to have all the warmth of a snowbank. Whatever the truth of his reputation, he didn't bother with gentlewomen; the maidservant had said so. Even if he was dangerous—and he did look dangerous—he wouldn't force himself on a dowdy and well-bred girl who wanted only to talk business.

Which was all to the good, because explaining her problem and what she wanted him to do about it would require privacy.

Very carefully arranged privacy.

Part One

Stranger's Kiss

Chapter 1

His chamber should have been empty.

Robin Hawking tensed, alert to signs which shrieked to him that he wasn't alone. A lifetime ago he'd learned to read the tracks left by predators, whether they were political or merely murderous.

Ten years *was* a lifetime in the service of Good Queen Bess. Drunk or sober, he knew when a bright rug had been shifted on a chest. Or the freshness of perfume disturbed the scent of wax candles.

A sharp, animal awareness crawled over his scalp. He could feel the presence of a watcher somewhere beyond the circle of flickering light provided by the candelabrum. It nagged at Robin that he was more drunk than he would have liked.

A bed curtain quivered.

His dagger barely whispered as he eased it from the sheath of oiled leather at his waist; a man used to stalking the shadows kept to safe, soundless weapons.

The soles of his shoes were silent leather, too. His mind was sufficiently clear to note that his body was balancing itself well, if not with the ease it displayed when he was sober. He shrugged. At least he wasn't weaving. Carefully, he stepped against the slight tilt of the floor.

Stupid to drown the aftertaste of a hellish day with too much sweet wine, he thought coldly. And Robin Hawking wasn't usually a stupid man.

The curtain had been slung over a bedpost to create a hiding place between bed and wall. Padding closer to the drapery, he could see a bellying in its embroidered folds. The tip of his poniard poked at the widest spot.

"Show yourself, knave!" The red and blue flowers of the pattern bobbed in agitation, and his queasy stomach lurched. Weakness in himself infuriated him. Harshly, he said, "I warn you, I am drunk. Drink makes me— impetuous." He prodded the hanging again. A slit grew under the razor-sharp point.

The voice which answered was muffled by the fabric. "I am not knave but friend."

It was pitched too low to reveal anything about its owner.

"Friends do not lie in wait like verminous, scuttling things afraid to be seen in the light."

On the last word, Robin swept the curtain aside with a violent motion. At the same moment he thrust with his poniard. Its edge stopped just short of the smooth neck showing between a pleated ruff and a small, firm chin.

Robin froze. "God's grace, woman, why are you skulking like a thief in a black corner? I could have pricked you prettily before I saw you were a—a lady."

"I *am* a lady," she said quickly, standing erect, her chin rising almost imperceptibly.

Unmuffled, the young woman's voice was deep for a female's, with a breathless, murmuring quality that appealed to him very much. It was overlaid with a soft country accent.

"A lady by degree, possibly." Robin had often found that an insult produced more information than courtesy. He was very curious about how she would explain her presence in his bedchamber. "But what would a lady be doing here?"

Her chin came up higher. "You are offensive, sir."

"How? It is not *I* in the wrong bedchamber." Resheathing his weapon, Robin leaned an arm against the post. He ran the eye of a connoisseur over her form. "Let's weigh the evidence. Your birth might be respectable. Your ruff is a paltry—what, three inches?—and your gown somber for my taste. However, serving maids rarely wear material sown with seed pearls. Or with such a gleam of—damask? Your skirts hang in the old, narrow style, but

I will not complain about that. I may not be able to tell where your hips are; I can see where they are not."

"I do not follow your reasoning."

Big brown eyes regarded him with a simulation of haughty astonishment he found amusing in a girl who couldn't be more than—eighteen? Nineteen? Robin wasn't sure if other men would call her pretty; he only knew he liked looking at her.

With a dignity she probably meant to be freezing, she said, "You become too philosophical for me."

He patted the rear of her skirt. "I cannot abide a thick-bottomed wench," he explained.

"M-many ladies still wear the slim Spanish fashion."

Curious, thought Robin. Though she was trying to ignore his brash behavior, his mysterious lady hadn't made a move to escape his touch. Of course, he noted fairly, she had nowhere to go. She was like a hunter trapped in her own covert.

"The queen much favors the new drum hoops from France," she persevered.

At a mental picture of the queen, Robin grimaced. Abruptly, he wanted more wine.

He had no body-servant. Of course not; there was no one a man in his position could trust. During his infrequent stays at court, he depended on the palace servants for personal service, and, glancing around, he saw they hadn't failed him. A full cup rested on the chest.

Robin kept one eye on the young lady, whose shoulders untensed a little as he removed his hand. Abandoning questions, he strolled over to pick up the cup. Women assassins weren't unheard of, but they rarely used violence and this dewy, serious-eyed specimen seemed an unlikely murderess. Unless . . .

"You have not by chance," he asked, "put hemlock in my wine?"

Her fair skin flushed. The color was so vivid that it was clearly red, though she stood outside the small circle of light. Her quiet voice swelled with anger. It reminded him of someone . . .

"I have not," she retorted. "Do you want me to taste it for you?"

Grinning faintly, he held out the cup. She had to come out of her corner to take it. After a quick, deep draught, she handed it back.

Their fingers collided awkwardly. She looked at him with eyes that seemed to ask him a question. They were beautiful eyes, he decided judiciously. Their shadowed lids and long fringes of dark lashes fascinated him. As chary of his own judgment as he was right now—damn himself for swilling the better part of a cask of wine!—he was sure anyone would call a girl with such eyes pretty.

What did it matter why she'd hidden in his bed curtains? She was here. An unaccustomed sense of irresponsibility made him grin again. He was drunk enough to be reckless and enjoy it.

On the heels of that thought, desire jolted through Robin. Ordinarily he would have been able to control the blood that ran hot and thick through his veins. At least he took care to do so during his infrequent visits to court. This sudden desire for a court lady filled him with surprise.

Robin was aware of the ugly rumors that circulated about him. His reputation had grown willy-nilly, like a seed dropped by a bird in the fertile ground of court speculation. From the very beginning of his employment by the government, his superior, Walsingham, had ordered him to keep silent about the work he did. And unfortunately there was a great deal of work for a queen's agent to do. Elizabeth's reign had been dogged by attempts to unseat her. So what were Robin's old friends to think when he began attending torture sessions in the Tower of London or disappeared for months at a time, returning haggard and dissipated-looking?

Unable to explain, he'd accepted it stoically when they avoided him. He understood the power of whispers. Who would want to claim friendship with a man who supposedly indulged in unspeakable enjoyments?

Dutifully, he had kept secret his dealings with traitors and their dupes, and the informants who battened off both. Now the secret was out. Bess herself had acknowledged him and his service.

Robin thanked God for her hasty Tudor tongue. The

queen's one incautious remark ought to end his career; how could a spy ply his trade if everyone knew what he was?

He was free. Free of prison cells and the stink of terror. Free to be his own man, except for the little matter of earning a living. Time enough to think about that tomorrow.

A shame his good name was already in tatters. His brief hope that the gentry would accept him had died a quick death earlier in the day, when that evil old man Aftondale had approached him with an offer of "entertainment." The court still thought of him as a moral leper. Fleeing, Robin had attached himself to a group of heedless gentlemen whose only purpose for the night was to get drunk, and had stormed out of Whitehall to do the same.

He'd meant to find a woman, too, but none of the town slatterns appealed to him. He liked the freshness of country girls. Milkmaids and innkeepers' daughters had been the object of his sport since he'd become—what cursed name had Bess given to his profession?—ah, yes, a queen's rat catcher.

At least rustic inns and hedgerows offered chances for snatched ecstasy with a willing woman. All it took was the expenditure of a few coins or a little charm. But it was obvious, despite her soft Midlands accent, that the girl in front of him was not the kind a man tumbled in the uncertain privacy of a ditch.

Drinking slowly, he continued his inspection. Her small pink tongue came out to lick a drop of wine from her bottom lip. Moisture continued to glisten on the ripe curves of her mouth. It was little but shapely. So was her proud, arched nose. The pride seemed interestingly at odds with her sweet face, which was heart-shaped. Russet hair grew from a widow's peak, and was coiled under a simple headdress contrived from gold threads interwoven with a few more tiny pearls.

"Who sent you?" he asked abruptly.

"No one. I came of my own free will."

She was here of her own free will, he repeated to himself. There was only one reason for a comely woman to be in his chamber. Pleasure flowed through him.

"We are both of us in luck this night," he announced with a grand sweep of his arm. "I have no prejudice against willow-thin girls."

Her big eyes grew bigger. "My lord Robert, you misunderstand—"

"Robin. No one calls me Robert except my cousin of Burghley."

He swigged another drink. When he had been younger and less wise, he'd counted the relationship with his mother's powerful family an advantage. At the time it had seemed so; it had gotten him his present employment. He looked into the cup. Its pewter bottom shone dully back at him.

He'd been a child when his father had sent him to live in the household of William Cecil, Baron Burghley. The Hawkings were long on nobility but short of fortune, and glad to be rid of a younger son. The years from boyhood to young manhood passed. Burghley ignored the fosterling. At home, even his parents seemed to forget him. His father died. His brother, the new earl, did not inform Robin until after the interment. It was then that Burghley noticed him, and offered him a place in Walsingham's service. Determined to make a life that would be *his*, Robin became a spy.

Today of all days, he didn't want to think how he had earned the silver in his purse. "Your waist is slender as a reed," he said under his breath. "And you smell of summer flowers."

"I would say it is midsummer moon with you, except the month is already September!"

But she did smell like flowers. Desire, huge and aching, moved through him again. His body hardened with it.

No doubt part of his arousal was the wine, he assured himself. He was half-ashamedly aware the other part sprang from the bitterness that had been building up in him for years. It had come to a head today like a wound ignored so long it had gone morbid. He wanted to lance the festering resentment, to give himself over to a cleansing flood of physical release and sink into the softness and heat he sensed in this girl.

However, wariness had become so ingrained he couldn't

help but wonder why she picked *his* bed to favor. There must be plenty of men willing to accommodate her with a quick tumble. Why had she chosen a stranger?

"Do you know what men have begun to call me?" he asked.

A fleeting smile drew him with its promise of warmth as she said, "Women, too." The smile vanished. "You are called the queen's rat catcher, Lord Robin. You are supposed to be clever and ruthless." The way her voice trembled over the last word told him someone must have poured the worst of the stories into her ears. "That's why—"

He stopped listening.

If she had heard those rumors, then it was his reputed skill with interesting forms of brutality that had gotten the damask lady into his bed hangings. Disappointment almost as strong as his desire chilled him.

"The queen's rat catcher is a hero today." *Here's the proof of what you have become,* he thought. This soft-eyed girl had come to his bedchamber to sample the embrace of a vicious, half-human thing. Hero? He knew better. "Her majesty gave me her hand to kiss. And for what?"

"You broke a ring of traitors." She had gone back to her soft voice, but now it sounded soothing. Was she humoring him? "They are saying you are an agent of the queen, so discreet no one suspected for years. Is it so?"

"Oh, yes, lady, it is so. My great act of heroism was diddling a flock of doltish popinjays—to their deaths, no doubt."

Robin stared down at the hand which was holding the cup. It trembled. He glared at his hand in affront. Devil fly away with this idiotic attack of sentiment. It had led him to drink too much, and even a mild white wine like sack could befuddle a man if he drank enough of it.

A small ocean of the stuff was all he could remember of tonight's progress through Westminster and London's taverns with his pot companions. With drunken curiosity, they'd wanted to hear every toothsome, grisly detail of Robin's part in the arrest.

He shrugged. "It is twenty years since Elizabeth locked her cousin Mary away so the Stuart bitch could do us no harm here in England," he said to the bottom of his cup. "Yet there are still plots to free the queen of Scots and place her on the English throne. Tony Babington's conspiracy, the one I stopped, is the third plot in three years. Tell me, damask lady, would you welcome a war? It would take one to settle once and for all who should rule. Our stubborn, spinsterly, Protestant Bess or contrary, Catholic Mary."

"I have no love for Mary Stuart." Her protest came promptly. It sounded honest. "The realm had its bellyful of war before old King Hal's father brought us peace. The Tudors have not done so badly by England. Surely every thinking man—and woman—celebrates every time Mary fails to win free."

Robin hadn't been celebrating tonight. But he'd definitely had a bellyful—of wine and of treason. And also of foolish lads who willingly hopped into treasonous plots under the spell of Mary Stuart. Why hadn't the memory of Anthony Babington trying not to scream on the rack been dulled by the drink?

"I learned to know Tony's band of traitors while I pretended to be one of them. A more inept collection of conspirators never drew breath." Robin teetered on his heels, and came down on the balls of his feet just in time. "I discovered a liking for them. The kind one feels for pleasant, hapless creatures who need protection from themselves. They thought I was their friend. The lads were so trusting, they were willing to befriend me. Not many are." He smiled terribly. It must have been terribly because she recoiled.

"Perhaps you should not be telling me this," she whispered.

A laugh caught in his throat. "Why not? It is hardly a secret anymore. Queen Elizabeth has sung my praises far and wide. Mine was the hand to pluck poor, stupid Tony's letters to Mary from hiding, mine the finger pointing out each traitor in turn. Mine the voice ordering all seven into prison where the torturers were waiting."

No amount of sack could wash those memories away. Nor could wine dilute the shrill echo of Elizabeth's voice demanding that he invent a more exquisite form of execution for Tony. Hanging, drawing, and quartering the primary traitor wouldn't quench Elizabeth's fury over this latest challenge to her reign.

The queen had actually believed Robin Hawking, second son of an obscure but proud family, would bend his mind to such a task. After all, what was he? Merely one of Walsingham's creatures. The kennelmaster of England's pack of spies was not renowned for squeamishness, and the agents he chose to do his stalking couldn't afford over-developed consciences.

"Do I look to you like a man who enjoys inflicting pain?" he demanded thickly, the wine working in him.

Her thin eyebrows drew together. "My lord, I think you have been drinking. I need your clearheaded attention, so perhaps we could come together another time. Only I do not know when or how to arrange a private meeting—" Her voice broke off in what sounded like disappointment.

It had been a day of horrors capped by insults, but this was too much.

"Lady," he growled, "I am not so drunk we cannot come together."

He had never taken pleasure from the anguish of others, in bed or out. He was seven-and-twenty years old, long past the age of innocence, and today he was heartsore for its loss. Robin threw the cup to the floor. The pewter rim thumped among the rushes. If the lady was seeking the unhealthy thrill of bedding a satyr, then the least a gentleman could do was provide it.

Her gasp was swallowed up in a kiss so savage their lips flattened against their teeth. He picked her up—she weighed nothing—and rolled backward and sideways to bring her under him on the bed.

His damask lady didn't make a noise. She certainly didn't fight. And her slender curves felt good underneath him. Robin was sure once he peeled her down to bare skin, she would be soft and pliant and very, very willing. He groaned with excitement.

Her hands curled lax at her sides. "Touch me," he urged.

Kat Preston lay frozen with horror. She stared into Lord Robin's not-quite-human eyes. Up close, they were a

strange combination of colors, silvery gray with a gold
ring braceleting the pupil. Hawk's eyes.

They were no longer cold but hot. He would take, and
she couldn't stop him. That was how things were between
some men and some women. She'd learned the lesson
young.

It was an old nightmare come horribly to life. A big
man, full of a strength that made hers puny. A strength she
couldn't combat. She didn't try, but her stomach churned
with anger, self-pity, fear . . . above all, fear. Fear so large
it was terror. She'd bungled everything.

All she'd meant to ask for was help, a tiny, disbelieving
voice said inside her.

Kat knew what would happen next. She waited for it,
the poking and the plunging, the theft of her small store of
self-respect.

It didn't happen. Instead, Lord Robin groaned again.
"No?" he muttered, circling her wrists with his fingers.
Her fragile bones disappeared into his grasp. Sweeping her
arms above her head, he transferred both of her hands to
one of his. His long, muscular limbs and his grip on her
hands reduced her to helplessness.

"Is this what you want?" His smile had become oddly
sad. It quirked down at the corners, changing the outline of
his untrimmed mustache and beard. His unoccupied fingers clenched in the cambric partlet that covered her upper
bosom from the top of her gown to the ruff under her chin.

With a hideous tearing noise, he ripped the cloth away.

The strange silver-and-gold eyes blazed as he ran them
over white flesh pushed up by the rigidity of her bodice.
The partlet had provided her with modesty. The gown itself began precisely where her nipples began.

"Slight but full," judged Lord Robin, "like little, firm
apples."

He drove two fingers inside the damask and scooped
one of her breasts out. Kat couldn't even produce another
gasp; her breathing had diminished to short and insuffi-
cient pants. Her senses swam.

His tongue lashed the areola without the pretense of a
kiss. Then he sucked, drawing her hard into his mouth and
using predatory, punishing teeth on sensitive skin that re-

sponded with an ache that was neither pain nor pleasure. The feeling was so intense that she finally whimpered under the assault of sensation.

He released her breast. Air struck cold on the puckered nipple and she writhed.

Lord Robin sighed.

She felt some of the tension in him uncoil. He shifted her arms to set them around his neck. Kat seemed to have lost control over her hands—nerveless, they sank into his collar. Starch crackled.

"Must it be rough, sweet heart?" he asked. He had a mellow voice when it wasn't harsh. It sent an unexpected throb through her. "I thought I could give you what you desire, but ... it would be so much sweeter to find— comfort in one another."

He lowered his head. This time his mouth didn't crush hers until she felt obliterated. This kiss ... it was a honeyed brush of flesh on flesh, and it stunned her with its gentle intensity. Her eyes stayed open, roaming over the wooden canopy. A warm odor of wine came from him, as well as a hot smell that was heady and male. Like his mouth, his scent was neither pleasant nor unpleasant exactly. But it overpowered her in the same way. She tried to twist away from it. From him.

It was impossible, of course. Lord Robin must easily be twice her weight, and all of it hard bone and muscle. There was no point in flight or resistance. It didn't even matter whether she chose to surrender or not. This raffish, handsome, drunken lord would take what he wanted from her, as easily as he would strip fruit from a tree.

"Lady," he breathed. He shifted onto an elbow and took some of his weight off her. With a lazy gesture, he began to untie the pieces of her bodice with one-handed expertise, rubbing a thumb gently over her nipple at the same time. "You are a fountain of delights when you let yourself move against me. I pray you, kiss me back."

"Nay." The weak protest was the best she could manage. But it was more than she had expected from herself. Her heart had been thudding with frantic, sickening blows. Now it bounded with hope. Katherine Preston, lady of Priorly, didn't have to be helpless ... did she?

"Ah, poppet. Say aye. Come, say aye and make it all the sweeter between us. We need no rough games."

He proceeded to demonstrate while Kat thought, *That* was what he believed? This—this nobly born oaf imagined she had come sneaking into his room *hoping* to be raped?

Numskull, blockheaded, addlepated *ass*.

Did she mean Lord Robin or herself? All Kat knew was that she was about to be ravished by mistake. Pressed by who-knew-what weights on his soul, Lord Robin might even be a reasonable man driven to unusual villainy—though she didn't believe it for an instant. Whether or not he stayed away from the company of lechers like Aftondale, Robin Hawking swashbuckled through life without a backward glance. Besides, mild men didn't possess such terrifying eyes.

"You are a silent puss," he said teasingly.

Familiar bonds were the hardest to break. Kat struggled against the habit of silence. *Never tell. Never complain. Stay still and quiet.*

Her bodice fell open. He cupped her other breast.

"So sweet and fresh," he murmured.

A disquieting and unfamiliar emotion prodded her to move restlessly. Lord Robin smiled at her as if she were an apt pupil. "See, poppet, that is better." He covered her breasts with more kisses.

Kat tried to think. Did she want to learn to enjoy this, the kissing and stroking? Not initiated by force, that went without saying. But . . . sometime, somewhere, with some man? Kat's whole body shook, then tingled, then shook again at the idea. If some strange sensual alchemy could work so fundamental a change in her, then anything was possible.

Astonished at her thoughts, she stared at Lord Robin's yellow hair. It trailed across her breast. A curl wound loosely around her nipple, imprisoning it in a neat circle.

Robin Hawking was an oddly reluctant rapist, it seemed to her, with his talk about the delights of cooperation. Perhaps he needed the fiction of willingness from women he pinned down and held helpless.

No. Not helpless. She refused to be that.

Kat endured the wet slide of his lips up to the soft spot

under her chin which he had menaced with his dagger. Finishing with the ties that attached her bodice to her skirt—oh, mercy God, he'd have her naked in a minute—he moved his hands to her ruff.

"What lack-wit invented these?" he growled, searching for the closure of the wire and lace.

She would speak. She *would*.

"Not any more lack-witted than a would-be lover who mistakes an honest maid for a slut," she forced out.

His mouth still smiled, but puzzlement creased his brow under the tumble of gold curls. "What, sweet heart?"

She pushed at his chest, which had no effect at all on the rock-hard slab of muscle. The only thing her shove gained her was that he did look at her more closely. Louder, she repeated, "I said, you have made a mistake, Lord Robin. I am not a pigeon for your plucking." She gave an angry pull at her open bodice. "Nor am I a turtle-dove to provide you with a cozy roost for the cockerel you keep between your legs."

Using his open palm, he scrubbed one cheek until it glowed under the growth of wheat-colored stubble. Apparently the action sobered him somewhat. From behind his fingers he gave her an ironic glance. "Not cockerel, madam, but full-fledged—"

Kat's eyes skittered away from the hem of his short doublet, where it was all too obvious he spoke the truth.

"Was it not enough," she rushed on, "for you to threaten to prick me with that?" She thrust her chin in the direction of his dagger.

"You have no turtledove's gentle manner, at any rate. A fine pricking is what I have almost given you, not once but twice." His thick, arched brows met. "Let's understand each other. If you seek to—prick—me so I will hurt you into feeling pleasure, you are out of luck. It sorrows me if that's the only way you can enjoy a man, but I find I have no taste for it tonight."

"Nor have I. Tonight or any night. Have I spoken plain enough for you?"

"Oh, beautifully plain. Indeed. Yes, lady."

She felt him watching her as she sat up and struggled to put her clothes to rights. His thin smile stretched into a taunting grin when she picked up and then dropped the ruined partlet as a lost cause. Lounging back into the shadows of the bed, he seemed able to ignore the state of his body. It had not diminished in the least. Kat hated him.

While she tried to push escaping russet curls into her headdress, he murmured, "The only matter not yet clear— since you have not sought out my chamber for the pleasure to be found in my company—is why we are both still in the bed the chamberlain allotted to me. In token of the queen's gratitude for my service, you see." He added the final, ironic comment as she scrambled off the high mattress.

Kat held her hand over the tops of her breasts. Her heart still knocked and she was afraid he could see the fast, betraying pulse. Those very knowing eyes had gone from hot back to cold, and they were laughing at her. God knew she needed help, the kind of help she had assumed one of Elizabeth's agents would be happy to provide, but her impulse was to flee while he seemed willing to let her go. Despite the casual way he lay among the pillows, danger continued to crackle in the air. His gaze never varied from her, as if he really were a hawk and she had become, not her feline namesake, but something small and particularly tasty.

She couldn't help another darting glance below his doublet; his codpiece hadn't stopped swelling with the pressure of aroused flesh inside. His smile broadened. He had full, well-cut lips. Cecil lips, she realized. He had said Burghley was his cousin. She'd seen the queen's treasurer, William Cecil, Lord Burghley, often enough to recognize the resemblance.

The Cecil features and the pillows decided her. They were real feather pillows, not the mere blocks of wood that had to satisfy ordinary people. A sure sign of how high he stood in the royal esteem. Robin Hawking was a discreet man, adept at digging out secrets and keeping them. He had powerful connections in the privy council.

"Your service is why I came to you," she explained.

He tsk-ed mockingly. "Not came, damask lady. We have neither of us come. If you would but allow me to service you—"

"Can you not get your mind onto higher things?"

"It *is* on a high thing," he told her. "In faith, I disremember when it has been so high."

Clearly defined by hose that fit snugly over muscle, one leg bent at its shapely knee. Since he was lounging on the bed, the gesture frankly revealed the insolent bulge of masculinity barely contained by his codpiece.

Kat spun around and faced a wall. "You are not—kind."

His voice changed. "Lady, if you are in my chamber looking for kindness, you are certainly the first to do so."

A very dull tapestry showing nameless ladies in languid dalliance with effeminate gentlemen hung on the wall. She studied it with desperate attention. If only Lord Robin were like those gentlemen. If only she could handle the problem that had brought her here by herself—but she couldn't.

Her home was being rifled, invaded, *used,* and she didn't know who was doing it. Priorly was worth putting up with this horrible, hot-and-cold man. Although Hawking wasn't a satyr, he was a womanizer, just as she'd supposed. That the rumors about his—indulgences—hadn't stopped her from entering his chamber only went to prove how desperately she desired his aid. Her mistake had been in thinking she could tell him of her problem before he could act on his outrageously lusty nature.

Well-a-day. Now was her chance. A trifle late, but precious nonetheless.

"My need is not what you thought." She felt her shoulders sag. "I need help and—and I am afraid."

Chapter 2

S traps creaked as leather protested his vault from the bed. Robin saw the girl stiffen again, although she wouldn't turn away from the damned wall.

As he walked over and stood directly behind her, she ducked her head defensively. She was tall for a woman; even with her long, vulnerable neck bent, the top of her head reached his shoulders.

God's grace, she smelled good.

He put the thought aside. "Who are you? Have you a name?"

"Kat. Katherine Preston. I am a maid of honor."

A tidbit of gossip rose to the surface of his mind. "Ah. What is it are you called? The queen's mirror."

She whirled to face him, big eyes flashing. "Aye, Elizabeth is pleased to call me her mirror. Just as you are called her rat catcher. How does the charming royal habit of assigning pet names sit with you?"

"Not well," he admitted.

Little as he liked the distasteful nickname he'd been dubbed this afternoon, Lady Kat must loathe the one saddled on her even more. It could hardly be palatable to the girl. After all, her tight young body had little in common with one that was more than fifty years old, despite the queen's claim that they looked alike.

Any resemblance was slight as far as Robin could tell, and all to Lady Kat's benefit. Kat's coloring matched Elizabeth's. Or it might have, before time and smallpox reportedly robbed the queen of most of her hair and all of her complexion; no one except her most trusted ladies had seen her grace without an elaborate wig and mask of face paint for two decades. The dark eyes were the same. Eerily, just now Kat's held an expression he had seen in the queen's—wise and sad, like those of a child who knew too much at too early an age.

It was the strongest similarity between the two women. If he'd had to describe his damask lady, he would have said Kat was a fair image of what the queen might have been thirty years before—had Elizabeth not had the misfortune to be the eighth Henry's daughter.

King Hal's treatment of his wives and family was famous for being erratic, to say the least. In consequence his younger daughter, who was as brilliant as a diamond, was as hard as one, too. Compared to the second Tudor queen to sit on the throne in her own right—the right Mary Stuart disputed—Kat Preston was much more soft, more appealing. A promise of wild honey beckoned from under the tart wit.

He frowned suddenly. "Now that I look at you properly—"

"You mean as more than just a nest for your cockerel—"

His quizzical glance made her blanch. "As you say," he confirmed smoothly. "Now that I look at you again, I think we have met before. Where did I make your acquaintance?"

"Nowhere. Well, you may have seen me this afternoon outside the privy chamber."

"Of course. I recall now. I thought, 'What beautiful, sad eyes that girl has.' "

"I had not believed you saw me," said Kat—resentfully, it seemed to Robin. "Little gets by you, does it?"

He bowed. "I flatter myself it does not. So we are fellow sufferers," he went on. "I can see how you might become weary of being called Elizabeth's mirror. The name's not just. There's a look of her about you, but not so much that you should be stripped of your very self."

Some of the vexation faded from her expression. "You do understand. She's an astounding woman, and I am sworn to serve her, but when she bellows for me as if I were a nothing, a reflection in a pond, sometimes I want to snatch her bald!"

Robin laughed.

She shook her head. "It is not only I, in truth, 'tis not. All of us she gives names to—she does it to show us we are only what she allows us to be."

"You are severe." He retained a bare hold on his own caution. "Surely you do not spread such insights through the open court."

Some things were too dangerous to say. Among them the supposition that the hennaed locks under the crown were anything but Elizabeth's own hair.

"Indeed—"

Pursuing his thought, he continued, "Tudors, you know, have all possessed the fascinating quality of being wise, wily, and petty at the same time. You would do well to consider the revenge Good Queen Bess would take on one of her ladies who speculated aloud about the . . . ah, the original owner of the royal hair. Especially in her current mood. No one has ever called her Gentle Queen Bess."

Robin had his own reasons for resenting his monarch, but he would never harbor a grudge against her. In a way, he supposed he loved the queen, splendid bitch that she was. Elizabeth was a great ruler. But when he contrasted her looks with those of Katherine Preston, he felt rather sorry for her.

"Naturally, I would never say anything damaging where the flapping ears of the court could overhear. But, you see, I thought—I hoped—" Kat's voice again softened to breathlessness. "I hoped you were a safe repository for secrets."

He wondered what sort of imbroglio Lady Katherine was trying to embroil him in. And if there were a chance to save himself from it.

Impatiently, he said, "You should find someone else to share your secrets. I have had my fill of midnight whispers of treason."

"Oh." For a moment, disappointment made her look younger than ever. Then her lashes swept down and her lips closed firmly. The expression belonged to a woman used to keeping her thoughts veiled.

A pity, he thought; she must have been schooled by harsh measures to be so good at presenting an opaque surface to the world.

A vague rippling of conscience—God's grace, did he still have one?—caused him to say, "But your problem cannot have much to do with such an unpleasant subject. What has happened? Has someone stolen one of your jewels?" Thefts occurred frequently in the haphazard living arrangements of the court. She didn't look as though she could afford to lose many valuables. The seed pearls were sober little gems. "Or made off with a lover?" he hazarded.

Robin noted appreciatively that Kat forgot to cover her enticing hint of cleavage with her hand. "I have no lover," she snapped. "Nor do I want one."

"You should not issue challenges like that, Lady Katherine," he said mildly, remembering another snippet of court trivia poured into his indifferent ears by his drinking companions. "You are newly come to court. Already you have a formidable reputation as a scold, damask lady. Several of the gentlemen bewail the darts that flash from your eyes, waking their hearts to love. Or at least to lust. They also complain about the darts from your wit. According to them, you are a citadel that has never been stormed. Any man who tries to conquer you walks away with his head bitten off and handed back to him."

Kat straightened her shoulders proudly. "That's what the gossips say." She added coldly, "They say worse about you."

He rubbed his forehead. His knuckles came away wet. The wine was catching up with him; perhaps he'd be able to sleep. "And yet it is rare for ladies with virtue of such flint-like consistency to risk their maidenhood in a strange man's bedchamber. You did not fight me at first. Why?"

"Mercy God! Do you think of nothing but bed games?"

"In its proper time I do. It is very late. As you may know—or as you, innocent one, may not—midnight is the hour for bed games."

"In your bed, I am sure it is," she said nastily. "However, I sleep with ladies-in-waiting of breathtaking morality."

"How sad for all of you," he commiserated. "How do you plan to rejoin this riotous crew? They do not sound like the sort of merry dames to smile upon dark-of-night escapades."

"I—I shall think of something."

"I am going to sit," announced Robin, and did so. The carved top of the chest prodded him in several places, but it was better than standing on legs which had somehow lost their knees. "Snuck out without a plan for sneaking back in, did you? Well, you have convinced me of your purity. It is clear you have had no goodly amount of experience in pranks like this. Only a virgin could be so sheep-brained."

Her long-fingered hands, which had been busy pleating the folds of her skirt, abandoned the material to clasp each other nervously. "I told you, I need help," she said. "When I heard how good you are at being a—"

"Spy," he said evenly.

"—fortune seemed to be pointing you out to me. Attending the queen is an honor, of course, but I am not used to being ordered around. My home is in the country where I make the decisions. Coming—I mean, finding your chamber seemed natural to me. I am accustomed to *doing*," she added.

His mouth twisted. "And I spoiled your touching picture of yourself as a person in charge of her own destiny? By reacting the way any man would, if he found a young and pretty woman hiding in his bed hangings?"

"I heard you entering and—and I know not why, but I hid."

Delicately, he suggested, "Perchance it occurred to you how the queen will regard our pleasant conversation if she hears of it."

Kat shuddered.

"I see even a country mouse like you knows that she kicks up an incredible fuss over indiscretions by her ladies and her gentlemen. However, I can hardly blame you for ignoring that, when I forgot it myself."

"I meant nothing but conversation!" she burst out. "Faith, I think how men of normal virtue act and how you act are two different things."

Robin leaned his head against the wall. He addressed the plaster medallions on the ceiling. "Lady, had you committed this folly with one of the old he-rams of the baronage, he would have long since had you upended with your skirt over your head. Your maidenhead would have been gone in the first two minutes, lambkin. You would have been tupped before you had time to bleat of your virtue."

His crude comparison caused her eyes to widen in comprehension. Gad, they were lovely.

She planted her fists on the moderate flare of her farthingale. "All this talk of fornicating is because you do not wish to hear me out! You think to distract me. That is it, is it not?"

The effort it took to shrug reminded Robin how tired, and how drunk, he was. "It could be," he admitted. "I am sick of secrets."

"Then I will not bother you with mine. Bid you good eve, Lord Robin." She bobbed a quick curtsy and turned to the door.

"Wait!" Robin got to his feet with really commendable grace, and beat her to the exit by a hair. He slammed a palm against the door to keep her from opening it. "You win. I am your prisoner for the length of your tale."

They were close enough to touch again. Her back was pressed against the panels. The shadow of his arm fell over her face.

He had to force himself not to reach for her. She had fit so nicely against the contours of his body . . .

"But you are a man with so many important matters awaiting your attention! So many hospitable skirts to lift. So many sheep-brained women to—to tup! You must not waste another minute of your midnight hour on me. Time flies on gossamer wings as we speak. Oh, nay, those are moth's wings," she corrected herself, glancing toward the candelabrum. "Alack."

"Time is passing," he said, amused.

"But surely before midnight fades you may still find yourself some lonely widow. Or better still a serving wench who can be bought for a shilling. You will have to look about quick for one with a desperate need for the money. Hurry, my lord! Who can tell when the wine might render you incapable, or the pox make you imbecile?"

"As it happens," he said dryly, "I do not suffer from the pox. And while I must be half-witted to stand here listening to a shrew, if you have decided to discover how capable I am . . . well, I believe I'll be able to prove myself to you."

He crowded another inch closer. Kat tried to melt into the solid wood panels behind her. Her fear was marginally greater than her dislike. Could the man sense how small he was making her feel as he held her caged against the door? She felt no temptation to touch him again.

"Damask lady," he said, "it is you who distract us now. Yet you have gone to great trouble to visit me."

Lord Robin loomed over her. His eyes seemed to bore into hers, causing the fine hairs on her arms to stand on end. Kat wanted to run. She had to get on with stealing back into the bed she shared with three noblewomen. He was right; she was trying to taunt him into letting her go. None of the other ladies was going to condone her flitting about the palace at this hour of the night. *All* of them were going to believe they understood why she had done it. Their answer would definitely include the rumors about the notorious Robin Hawking.

She had worked too hard for a spotless reputation to lose it now. But first Lord Robin had arrived in his chamber late, much later than she had expected, and then he'd been drunk and not what she'd imagined. Worst of all, he'd used up her precious, fleeting time with his lewd antics.

He sighed again. His breath poured over her face. The exhalation made his unbuttoned doublet gape to show his shirt. Thin linen did little to hide the golden hair softening the ridged muscle that stretched across his chest. Nervously, needing something else to look at, Kat lifted the round pomander that swung at the end of her girdle. There was barely room between their two bodies for her to do so.

It was no longer round. Dimly, she wondered just when in the proceedings on Lord Robin's bed its tinsel sides had gotten crushed.

"Stop frowning. It ill becomes you. And look at me, not

at that toy. It is ruined beyond repair, anyway. I will help you—back to your own bed, at any rate. But if I am going to be damned for a fool I want to know why. What made you seek me out, Lady Katherine?"

The note of steel in the caressing voice decided her. She wasn't aware of her expression changing, but he nodded briskly. "Yes, it will take less time to tell me than to try escaping," he said.

Could he read her thoughts? "Does anyone escape from you?"

"Not unless I allow it," he answered coolly. "Now, tell me."

"I must beg a promise." It took a considerable amount of determination to meet his eyes. They weren't hot or cold or amused, or anything now. They simply waited, with an implacable patience that sent icy fingers walking up Kat's spine. She must be sheep-brained, she acknowledged. She had to be to have involved this strange man, with his frightening eyes. "You may not reveal what I say to anyone else."

He snorted softly. "No matter how innocent you are, you know better than that, damask lady. In affairs of state, I do whatever must needs be done. I swear to lies, I cheat babes, I betray secrets by the cartload. But calm yourself. The privy council will have scant interest in a stolen jewel or—no, we have eliminated the stolen lover."

Kat would have ground her teeth at him, but time was running out.

"I wish I were complaining to you of some little crime or imagined slight. But I am afraid I have stumbled across—treason."

He grabbed her. His fingers bit into her arms through her full sleeves. A nearly inaudible noise, the kind an animal might make if it were unlucky enough to be snared in the jaws of an enemy, rose and died in her throat.

He ignored it. "Treason?"

"Aye," she said faintly. "I know you do not want to hear it—"

"You may disregard my feelings. Have you not done so all through the night? What treason?"

Kat couldn't bear another moment of his touch. Her

sideways jerk caught him off guard and took her a step away from him. His grip remained tight on her sleeves, though; for a moment she thought they would give under the strain and rip. Then he let her go, and she staggered, putting a hand to the wall to maintain her balance.

Her throat was dry. She swallowed. "Have you heard of a castle called Fotheringhay?"

Chapter 3

~~~⟨⟨⟩⟩~~~

"I know of it," Robin replied curtly.

"The Preston property is in Northamptonshire, hard by Fotheringhay. There has been talk in the court—"

His head went back, revealing the strong column of his neck. Tendons stood out like cords. Kat observed the signs of anger in him with dismay.

"I have heard the council is planning to move Mary Stuart from her old prison at Chartley Hall to Fotheringhay. It has been whispered for weeks," she went on. Restless, she began to pace.

"Those plans were supposed to be secret," he snarled. He pounded the heel of his hand, once, hard against the door.

Kat jumped. But for the first time she felt slightly superior to him. "Did you really expect a secret to be kept at court?"

"I was assured *this* one had been. God damn those purblind fools on the council." He stared through her so fiercely she stopped pacing. "Only a special few were to be told. Did that collection of dotards safe in their robes of office remember how many lives were riding on the need for secrecy? God's grace! If the conspirators had found out their plot had been discovered, the councilors' skins might have been in danger. Moving Queen Mary would be the clearest warning! Not even Tony Babington could mistake it. He's a dreamy fanatic, but with surprise on his side instead of ours, he could have changed his plans—"

"Aye." Something cold and heavy settled into her belly

31

as Kat took in the fact that Robin Hawking might have been dead instead of alive. But ... she hated him. Kat shrugged and paced again. It was possible to hate a man and not to wish him dead.

"How did you hear?" he demanded.

"From the other ladies. News oozes from the walls at court. Servants overhear, or men tell their mistresses. The foreign ambassadors listen at half-closed doors. Then they buy meals for hungry young men whose masters' tongues wag about state business. Keeping something hidden from all the prying eyes and open ears is a labor of Hercules."

"Which you have accomplished until now," said Robin, his gaze sharpening.

A moment passed before she realized that an expert at secrets had just praised her. Her hand lifted to push the compliment away. She didn't want his approval. She didn't want his attention at all.

Kat would have gone quietly away if she could. Lord Robin saw too much.

Reluctantly, she answered the speculation in his eyes. "When something I love is at stake, I'll do whatever has to be done. Keep a secret or scrub with my own hands or sleep in a ditch—" Or other things, she admitted to herself.

"And what do you love that requires so much sacrifice?"

"My home."

"That is normal enough. Had I a home," he said, "I would give it a lover's attention, too."

Kat whirled to glare at him. Her gown billowed out around her. "You reduce everything to copulation."

"Why should I not?" he asked reasonably.

"Common decency!"

His *tsk* was chiding. "What's more pleasant than exercising my—passion—in a quick tumble? Or better yet, a long and unhurried one?"

Walking toward her, he grinned when she automatically retreated. Furious, she blazed, "Do not compare my love for Priorly to a horse's affection for his pizzle!"

He halted, but the grin didn't reach his eyes. "And how does Fotheringhay Castle threaten your Priorly?"

This must be how he extracted information from unsuspecting folk who got caught in the claws of suspicion, Kat thought. He overawed a person, then softened the suspect with disconcerting talk, then put the question like a knife going into a cheese to cut out the ripe heart.

"I am not claiming that Fotheringhay is a threat. The boot is on the other foot, Lord Robin. I very much fear Priorly is being used for some evil purpose, but I do not know by whom. The important thing is that my home is only ten miles from Fotheringhay, and if the queen of Scots is going there—"

"The order has already gone out. Her household is being transferred. As you apparently know already. What do you mean, your home is being used? How?"

"I am explaining myself badly." Kat paused to give her heart time to slow its fast beat. Despite the calming breath she took, it kept fluttering as if driven by great, panicky wings.

"I must explain how several things came to be," she said slowly. Or her recital would sound even worse than it was. As she was nervously aware, the trick would be to pick and choose the events to tell him. "My father built Priorly when he married my mother. He was five-and-fifty. She was a second wife, only seventeen, and he doted on her as old husbands do on young brides." Kat moistened her lips. "She was very devoted to the old religion."

He appeared to take it calmly. Everyone knew Lord Burghley and the other ministers surrounding Queen Elizabeth were apostles of the reforms that had been creeping into the Church of England.

Lord Robin certainly didn't act like a man who worried about the day-to-day maintenance of his soul. He might not care about her mother's views. Or perhaps he was just waiting for her to reveal bigger disasters. "Was?" he asked.

"Both my parents are with the angels."

"Mine, too." He studied the sad-colored dress, with so few touches of white. "A recent occurrence?"

"Nay," she denied, startled. "A full seven years ago. I was thirteen."

She had to watch her words more closely, she thought

worriedly. His businesslike questions were luring her into talking about herself. And that would never do.

"To make my mother happy, my father had the builders at Priorly include some unusual embellishments." Peeking at Lord Robin, Kat saw him shrug.

"Possessing a priest's hole will hardly condemn you to the rack, Lady Katherine. Half the great houses in the realm are furnished with them. Loyalties do not change as quickly as monarchs. At least, not in some families," he contradicted himself. His mouth twisted. "Henry wants a divorce—and to transfer the wealth of the church to his own coffers. Farewell to the pope. Edward is raised by reformers who have become rich from the sack of the monasteries. Wise men become Protestants."

"Lord Robin, this is common knowledge—"

He didn't stop. Kat wondered if he could. Bitterness seemed to well out of him with the history lesson. "Mary wishes to bring England back to the old faith, the only consolation she has known in a pathetic and loveless life. An astonishing transformation! Clever families are now Catholic again. But Elizabeth—ah, Elizabeth. Those who are Protestant from conviction and not convenience tell each other Hal's little Bess will carry the standard of reform for them. Even before she's crowned, she learns she's the Protestants' darling. Devoted Catholics naturally hate her for this, and the result? Five-and-thirty years later I flush out a covey of bird-witted boys with the misfortune to have principles, and send them to prison for conspiring to murder their queen." Sweat darkened the curls on his forehead.

"You are overspent," said Kat, wondering at her own twist of compassion.

Caustically, he replied, "You are too polite. What you mean is that I am maudlin."

"How can you call me polite after the things I said to you tonight?" Kat certainly hadn't meant to be courteous.

"Rat catchers are spared the burden of pretending to dainty tastes. We are allowed to be plain, honest Englishmen and appreciate plain, honest speaking. You are a shrew, damask lady, but a pretty one. Despite the fact you have a tongue like the edge of a sword, I find you full of delights."

So much for sympathy. She caught him looking at her breasts again and slapped a palm over the soft, exposed flesh. "I am not!"

"Not pretty?" he asked with a glint of humor.

"Not—" She boggled over how to say she wasn't full of delights. "I will leave you now."

"No, you will not."

This time she had the latch under her hand before she made her move. With a quick jerk she opened the door and then she was free, running down narrow stairs.

Two heartbeats later, Lord Robin had her pinned to a seat in a window recess.

"You are not done with your story, Lady Katherine."

"A more ill-chosen place—"

"It is your choice, lady." His tone was pitched low. There was a rough note in it which hadn't been there before. "Speak quietly and waste no more of my time."

"You are frightening me." The admission was a measure of the depth of her fear.

"I intend to scare you. By hell's open mouth, you are the most exasperating wench I have ever met. You hide in my bed curtains, you hem, you haw. Terror is a tool, you little simpleton." His fingers bit into her arms. "If I do not use the tools at my disposal, how am I to pry the whole truth out of you?"

Was he ... asking pardon? From her? "If that is an apology, Lord Robin, it is a most inadequate one."

"Ah. Good. You have recovered your normal temper. Continue."

"Why has none of your victims slaughtered you?" she hissed.

"Doubtless an oversight."

More likely by the time he was done with his prey, there weren't any pieces large enough left to organize an effective revenge.

"There *is* a priest's hole," she admitted, conceding defeat.

A lamp swinging from a bracket flared and bathed them in its light. Robin raised his brows. Her dress wasn't intended to be the color of mud, but of cinnamon. Orange-red glimmers swam over the fabric as Kat squirmed, trying to shake off his hands. Highlights of the same rich color made sparks in her hair.

"What has happened in your priest's hole that made you come to my bedchamber?"

"I cannot tell you . . ."

He just looked at her. Words began tripping out of her so fast she stuttered.

". . . b-because I do not know! But someone's been using it. I got leave to visit home for a few days last week. In the hole there were crumbs and a smell of occupancy—you know, close and sour, as if a man had spent many hours in a small space. Servants mind the place for me; they live in the house and have seen nothing. I have known them forever. They are completely trustworthy. Yet some of the gold plate is missing, and the silver saltcellar. And clothing stored for . . ." Her voice dwindled, then firmed. ". . . for future use has been broken into and tumbled about. I think garments have been sto—"

His hand clapped over her mouth.

Her breath warmed his fingers as it whooshed out of her, and chilled them as she dragged in more air. "A guard," he muttered, so close to her ear he could taste her skin.

It tasted clean, like soap and cloves. Gillyflowers smelled like that. Robin smiled to himself, listening to the clank-and-creak of armored leather as the soldier trod nearer. This was the sort of predicament he was used to. Playing cat and mouse with a watcher who didn't know that he, too, was under observation.

Their fate depended on the vagaries of luck. If the guard happened to investigate the darkness of the window seat, he and Lady Kat would have an impossible amount of explaining to do. He gave a mental shrug. The outcome was in the hands of God. The Deity could hold them safe in His gently cupped fingers, or He could toss them like dice, turning their lives topsy-turvy in an instant. Robin wasn't much in the habit of praying, but he said a short prayer on the off chance it might be answered. Other than that, there was nothing a mortal like Robin Hawking could do except wait and see.

He allowed himself to enjoy the feel of the woman in his arms. A man could drown in the elusive, sensual odor of gillyflowers. A comparison of Kat to the fragile flower wouldn't really be apt. She was hardly a shy blossom. In fact, she was fully armed with prickles.

But for the moment she wasn't struggling. He concentrated on the delicious ear next to his lips. Sometimes a second-sighted guard could sense when a person was nearby, especially if that person was willing the guard to go away. It was safer, and certainly more pleasurable, to lick his damask lady's ear and think of flowers.

Keeping his imagination confined to plants wasn't an easy task with Kat lying beneath him. She had gone limp at the first invasion of his tongue into the whorls and excitingly secret places. This time Robin didn't make the error of believing she had acquiesced. He'd simply take good fortune as it was given to him.

His tongue didn't falter in its delicate probing until realization struck him with the force of a blow. After just an hour in her company he knew he would take from Katherine Preston whatever he could get—whether she was willing to give it or not.

The knowledge opened a place that hurt in his chest. The place where his heart would be if he any longer had such an organ. He wasn't used to thinking of himself as a raptor.

Queen's rat catcher, he thought. Hell. You *deserve* to be called the queen's rat catcher.

The guard neared, paused, began to whistle softly. Kat was already as still as it was possible for a breathing body to be, but Robin felt tension gather in her. He wanted to reassure her. It annoyed him that he couldn't.

That bothered him further. He couldn't afford to let one of Elizabeth's ladies infatuate him. And even if sometime in the last ten twilight years he'd sunk low, he wouldn't degrade himself with thoughts of rape.

Violence for its own sake had never appealed to him. Like terror it was a tool, necessary if unpleasant. Only . . .

lately its stink had become so familiar he could barely smell it anymore.

He buried his face in Kat's hair. Gillyflowers. What would it be like to forget himself for a night in a woman who smelled of gillyflowers?

Not even his inner turmoil could keep him from noting the retreating noises made by the guard. Finally they faded away altogether. Kat whispered, "He's gone."

"You are observant, lady."

"Let me go!"

Robin sat up, pulling her up with him. Carefully, he placed her as far away from him as the window seat allowed. Sweat came off when he rubbed his palms on his thighs. "Is there anything you have neglected to tell me?"

She didn't answer, just leaned against the window and closed her eyes.

"Must I know more about Priorly before I try to find out if traitors are using it as a base because it is near Mary Stuart's new prison?" he restated his question irritably.

"Nay. I promise, Lord Robin." He didn't believe her; her eyes opened too quickly and gave the lie away. But if there were more secrets to be dug out of her, he'd do it tomorrow. Right now he wanted distance between him and this distracting creature with her summer scent.

"Come along, then. I must get you to bed." He shrugged one shoulder at her gesture of rejection. "Your own bed, duly furnished with sleeping companions of unimpeachable virtue. God give you joy of it."

"It is so black," Kat protested.

"Surely a Kat can see in the dark."

"Well, I cannot. Why could we not get to the state apartments by means of the galleries?"

"Because," he explained with insulting patience, "it is dark here. In the galleries there are lights and guards. Do you wish to be seen with me? Perhaps your reputation could withstand such a beating. Mine could not."

"Lord Robin Hawking is famous for biting his thumb at reputation." But Kat said it thoughtfully.

"Since you know me so well, you will not object to a blameless stroll across the tiltyard."

"In the very middle of the night," Kat noted. "With my hair a target for nesting birds and part of my clothing entirely gone."

He provoked her by laughing.

"It is because I know you that I object to being with you," she added.

"Do you consider the tiltyard more compromising than my bed?" he asked. "If so . . ."

She curved her shoulders and pulled closer the cloak he had lent her. It was good, soft wool, and it smelled faintly of him. She didn't want anything to do with Lord Robin in or out of his bed; contrarily the warm cloth gave her a feeling of safety and comfort. Nothing else had done that in a long time.

"I will take the tiltyard," she said.

"I thought you would." She could hear gritty amusement in his voice.

It hadn't rained lately, although clouds scudding across the sky blotted out the faraway stars. "At least the ground is dry," said Kat. "I have seen the yard when it is a sea of mud, with horses and men in armor struggling to provide the queen and foreign visitors with entertainment. This is better."

"Are you always grateful for small favors, Lady Katherine?"

"A person may as well smile as frown. Sometimes happiness is a matter of will."

"That's an odd thing for you to say."

She bristled. "Do you not agree?"

"Oh, you are probably in the right of it," he said indifferently. "I would not know. Happiness is not a commodity that has often come in my way. But for you to say so—well, a statement like that argues a merry disposition."

"And you judge me dismal?" she asked after a pause.

"A flower liberally provided with thorns, let's say."

His words hurt. Try for logic, Kat, she ordered. You do not care what this whoreson of a hero thinks of you. But she found herself saying weakly, "Has anything happened tonight to make me laugh?"

"Poor damask lady."

He stopped by a tree, and she knew they had arrived in

the orchard which bordered the tiltyard. A limb like an in-
distinct black arm brushed Kat's side. She heard a rustle
and snap, and then a solid crunch as Robin appropriated
one of the queen's apples and bit into it. His teeth, she remembered, had been even and strong. Her fingertips went
to her breasts to cover nipples which suddenly thrust themselves against the rigid front of her bodice. The memory of
his demanding suckling produced an ache that only slowly
subsided.

"I would like to return to my own chamber before
dawn," she said sharply.

"I live only to serve you, my lady," he answered, dropping the core to the ground with a thud. "How could I resist a request given so sweetly?"

Kat's nerves were unraveling. Her voice cut like a lash.
"Are you sober enough to be anything but a hindrance?"

"Now that is an excellent question. I have been very
drunk this evening," he admitted without remorse. "I am
still not as steady on my feet as I would wish to be. But
were it not for me, sweet heart, you would have been meat
for the guards—and then the gossips—long since."

Kat followed him sullenly as he took her through the
trees and then threaded a way through the flowers, bushes,
and statuary of the privy garden. His voice floated back to
her. "Be content. I have said I'll put you back in your bed,
and I will do it—whether you have the sense to pant with
eagerness for my assistance or not."

She hurried to catch up with him. "I assure you, I do
not pant with eagerness for you."

"So you have said, lady. Several times."

"You are a handsome, overgrown knave filled with—"

"You find me handsome?" he asked, sounding pleased.

"Filled with conceit!"

Stopping at a window, he inserted the point of his dagger between the frame and sill. A subdued snick indicated
that the knife had moved the latch. The window swung inward. "In with you. And quiet from now on. Not a
squeak."

Kat nearly did squeak when he raised her in his arms
and lifted her through the opening. The glow from a cres-

set lamp lit a corridor. Her feet found the floor after a moment's groping.

Cold from the thick walls penetrated her clothing. She shivered. This section of Whitehall was a rabbit warren. Kat knew how easy it would be to get lost in the chilly maze of low-ceilinged rooms.

She felt as if she were moving underground, Lord Robin close on her heels. Leading the way, she held her skirts away from the rushes and walls to reduce the likelihood of making a sound.

She supposed, especially in the wake of the Babington plot, the queen's guard would be mustered thickest around Elizabeth's chamber. That was the better part of an acre away. As the least important maid of honor, Kat shared a room with other insignificant ladies, and no one had considered it necessary to place their sleeping quarters near the woman they served. After all, they were at court for the queen's convenience, not their own. What did it matter if they answered a summons gasping, with stitches in their sides?

But—although she and her unwanted escort were far from the royal bedchamber—soldiers patrolled all the buildings of the palace. With a motion that was too quick to see, Robin dragged Kat behind a pillar, pressing her close to take advantage of its shadow. Kat's cheek crushed against his doublet. Her eyes opened wide as she felt the thump of his heart. It was as wild as her own.

Two guardsmen, resplendent in the uniforms of the queen's Gentlemen Pensioners, hailed each other and leaned their pikes against the other side of the pillar. Kat stopped breathing.

"All quiet?"

"No more sport than a penny whore. The devil himself would think before tickling her grace's temper this night. Did you hear her at supper?"

The other man gave a bark of laughter.

"All these royal cousins!" continued the first. "Do you remember when her other cousin, the Lady Lettice, married the Earl of Leicester behind her back? Ah, you are too young, lad. Well, this time is worse. I would not want to be the fool who crosses her next."

The second guard didn't suffer from the talkative nature of the first. He grunted and turned to spit among the rushes. The soldiers tramped off in opposite directions.

Robin eased away from the pillar and took Kat by the hand. "Which way?" he asked in her ear.

Kat drew away from the seductive warmth of his breath. She made an angry vow not to surrender to the old helpless feeling again. The future would have to be soon enough to ponder the effect he had on her; now there was no time.

His hand was warm, too, and firm. It made her feel how cold her own fingers had become. Discipline, however, had been part of her life since she'd left little-girlhood behind. She pulled away from him with only a momentary regret for his body's heat and strength.

She pointed silently in the direction they needed to go, and doing her best to be wraithlike, traced the circuitous path leading to her chamber. At last the hinges of the correct door whined under her tentative push.

They both froze. Heartbeats marked a full minute before Lord Robin nodded briefly. Kat took the slight dip of his beard to mean that in his professional opinion no one was stirring. Unwinding his cloak from her shoulders, she thrust it at him.

His eyes gleamed in the dim light. Bundling the cloth under his arm, he stepped back a pace and swept her a full court bow. The flourish of his wrist would have caused an easily impressed lady to faint. Kat compressed her lips. He was magnificent, even with his slovenly clothes and bawdy talk. Thank God, she was *not* easily impressed.

Lord Robin would have to leave now for the sake of his own skin as well as hers. The only hurdles left to leap, literally, were the tirewomen who slept on trundles and had to be sidestepped. After that she would have her gown to untie in the dark and hide from too-observant eyes which might notice the missing partlet. Only then would Kat be able to slide into bed. She'd have to prepare a story of getting up to relieve herself if anyone belatedly awoke.

A familiar gray shadow caught the edge of her vision. Kat thought, "Grimalkin!" and suppressed the impulse to say the cat's name aloud. Before she could reach down and pick her pet up, the striped tabby crouched belly-down. The ringed tail quivered. With slit-eyed attention, Grimalkin stared at the garters knotted below Robin's knees.

The ends swung teasingly as Lord Robin rose from his bow. Grimalkin pounced at the crumpled ribbons. Lord Robin stepped forward a pace to maintain his balance. His foot came down solidly on Grimalkin's twitching tail.

The cat's yowl sounded as if it belonged to an infuriated banshee, and it was loud enough to raise the dead.

Chapter 4

The next few moments were a confused blur to Kat. Lord Robin moved too fast for her to see. He was there; then he was gone. Someone called out in a thin screech. Grimalkin squatted down on her haunches, maltreated tail lashing. Kat could hear movement inside the bedchamber.

Suddenly Lord Robin was returning, darting along the corridor toward her.

"Now what?" Kat muttered.

His teeth gleamed. He was grinning. He was *laughing*. The amused roar stunned her. His fist cupped her chin.

"Forgive me. You are such a serious thing. I cannot resist," he said, and kissed her mouth.

It was brief, snatched, hard. Both of them breathed loudly.

"I lied," he added after a moment, his face filling her vision. "Nothing could make me sorry for that."

Kat hit him.

He stood like a rock under the blow, an openhanded slap that echoed as the door inched open. Lady Jane Monteshote's stubby but inquisitive nose appeared in the opening.

Jane's sleepy eyes lost their heavy look and brightened with disbelief, then delight. Kat groaned out loud. She and Robin formed a damning tableau, and Lady Jane was a notorious gossip.

Thin lips curled back from little, sharp teeth.

"Jane, do not! Please—"

"Guard!" shrilled Jane. "Where is the guard? A gentlewoman has been attacked—you have been attacked, have you not, dearest Kat? Just look at you, your gown all awry and—zounds, the monster has torn the clothes from your breast! Who is he? I shall fetch a candlestick to hold him off. Guard!" The high-pitched tones faded into the chamber.

Turning to Robin, Kat snarled, "Go!"

"I'll not leave you to face—"

"Now you turn considerate? Do not be a fool! She does not recognize you."

"I have kept my back to her." This time his laugh was shaken. "I am more drunk than I believed. Or else you have dazed my wits."

"Lord Robin, my folly will become a nightmare if Jane discovers I committed it with you. She talks."

Robin's eyes glittered. "I see. You have a notable talent for making things plain to the meanest intelligence. A kiss from me would damn you in the court's eyes? Then I'll spare you any more of my company. Fare well, Lady Katherine."

And he was gone again.

Sighing with relief, Kat went through the door. Candles were being kindled inside, and as their lights bloomed her gaze met that of Margaret Treland—not two feet away.

Small and plump, Margaret had a forthright manner and an unabashed preference for the crowded conditions at Whitehall over the luxury of life with her rich husband. She accepted a wrap from one of the serving women, drawing it around her voluminous smock while she pursed her lips at Kat.

"Robert Hawking?" asked Margaret.

The look on Kat's face must have been answer enough.

Margaret continued forcefully, "And you seek to shield a man like that? He should pay for his sins. From the state he has left you in, they are grievous ones. A little penance will do him good." She raised her voice, ignoring Kat's frantic shake of the head. "Our poor Kat has been mauled by that wolf-bitch's son Robert Hawking."

Jane let go of the heavy candlestick she'd been trying, not very convincingly, to lift. "The rat catcher?"

"Do not call him that!" Kat cried. Appalled, she put her fingers to her lips.

At the hint of even more delicious scandal, Jane twirled and hugged herself. "What cat was out prowling tonight? There are two to choose from. A Kat and a cat. What was the she-cat seeking? A likely tom?"

"Hold your tongue!" Margaret snapped. "Such enthusiasm for bad news is unseemly. Can you not see Kat is upset?" She swept the gaping maidservants with a cold glare. "And why do you sluts stand goggling? If you are awake enough to waste the night hours, then we shall have to find you more work during the day." She kept them under a stern eye until most of them had lain down and pulled their blankets over their ears.

A woman with iron-gray braids remained standing. "Shall I help you undress, my lady?"

"That's all right, Maud," Kat said. Maud was her own maid. "You go to bed."

Maud opened her mouth—to argue, thought Kat from experience—but Margaret Treland forestalled her. "You heard your lady. Do as you are told!"

The two Priorly women exchanged glances, then Maud withdrew to her pallet.

With a tight, triumphant smile at Kat, Margaret added, "Come, sit down. Poor Kat."

She means well, but, oh, damn her! thought Kat. And she's hurt Maud's feelings. It would be Kat who paid for that, too.

They moved toward the bed. A rippling snore changed the direction of their steps. Old Cecily Froliot, the fourth lady who shared the chamber, lay on her back, full of the wine that lubricated evenings at court. The racket hadn't made a dent in her peaceful unconsciousness.

By common consent, they chose seats near the hearth where embers glowed from a banked fire. Jane crowded near.

"Has he taken you?" Margaret asked bluntly.

"Nay! I swear it."

"He has taken something. Your partlet at least," observed Jane brightly.

"A man may grab for a pie and get only the shell." Margaret sounded thoughtful.

"Lord Robert Hawking?" Jane's laugh was incredulous. "He's a beast, and everyone knows he has a beast's tastes and cunning. Those arms are like oak. His legs could be borrowed from a Greek statue . . ." Her voice trailed off into a dreamy mumble; then she recovered her usual acidity. "He does not even try to hide his—his preferences. How could Kat fight him off? Assuming she wanted to?"

Margaret regarded her with distaste. "I am sure Kat would not forget her honor in a perusal of his legs. An animal is an animal whether it walks on four legs or two. If you had been attending instead of playing the fool, you would have seen her slap him. That was no light love tap, either. Anyway, it is no matter if he got under her skirts or not."

"No matter—" gasped Jane.

Kat lifted her head and looked at Margaret curiously.

"As long as he hasn't gotten her with child, who will ever care? Except her husband on her wedding night if she ever decides she wants one. And his questions may be satisfied with a tale of sitting down hard on a gatepost or riding too lively a horse."

Jane giggled. "Margaret!"

"Or she can use rock alum from Melos to give her a virgin's tightness if nothing else will do for the sot. Men are such idiots about first and sole possession. She would not be the first bride to make due with such shifts, I assure you."

"And you speak of honor?" asked Kat.

Margaret stroked her cheek. "I speak of survival."

"I could not do or say any of those things. It would be a cheat."

"You are too soft. Men like Robert Hawking will suck the juices from you and spit out the dry husk." Margaret glanced up at a knock at the door. "The guard! Jane, you fob him off with some of your expert flutterings. Let him think we are hysterical females. You'll be able to convince him your feathers are ruffled because a cat yowled. Hurry!"

Still giggling, Jane went to the door.

Kat's shoulders huddled. "Even if she helps me now, she'll not remain silent," she said. "Scandal is meat and drink to her. She will tell, because it will make her important for a minute or two."

"She'll tell for another reason. Three years ago, the queen caught Jane with a man. A gardener." Margaret sniffed. She obviously thought poorly of Jane's choice.

"Jane?"

"The fellow is still in prison. Jane's betrothal was broken off, and her parents will never be able to arrange another unless they bribe some lawyer's clerk or farmer to take her, soiled reputation and all. The queen keeps her at court to torment her, I think. She is the one Elizabeth always sends for flowers. Jane has become bitter. She's thrilled to see someone else about to suffer the same fate."

"And you? Why did you say Hawking's name so loud?"

"Did I do wrong by you? I meant no harm. We have grown fond of one another in the weeks since you came to Whitehall. I thought—you have said you intend to remain unencumbered by a husband. The rumor that Lord Robin wants you will protect you from those who find a woman's virtue a challenge. Few would take the risk of annoying Hawking."

There was something lacking in Margaret's explanation, but Kat couldn't put her finger on it.

"You do not understand!" The desperation in her own cry startled her; she took a firm hold on her composure and started again. "The queen—"

"Is too busy with her own problems to interest herself in yours," said Margaret bracingly. "Now, let's get you undressed and into bed. You look as though you need your sleep, poor darling."

Kat wasn't sure she'd ever sleep again, but she let the other woman deal with ties and hooks. The kirtle collapsed onto the floor in stiff folds, followed quickly by her farthingale.

"You are so slender. So graceful," Margaret said, smoothing Kat's smock. "I am a cow in comparison."

Lord Robin didn't object to her slenderness. The memory crept up on Kat and she scowled. Few saw beauty in slight curves. Lushness was the fashion, not a lithe, boyish figure. Why did a lecher like Robin Hawking have to be the first man to look at her nearly naked figure and call it sweet? Being admired by him was hardly a compliment. The best she could say for the man was that he hadn't forced her when he had the chance.

"What's wrong, Kat? Do you have a pain?"

Kat fixed a smile on her stiff face. Despite Margaret's unfortunate meddling, the other woman was one of the few court ladies who had been kind to a newcomer, and Kat normally liked her robust common sense.

"I feel fine. I suppose I am not used to talking about my body. You will think me silly and countrified."

"Not at all. There's no great wonder to it, especially if you have been fighting off a man. 'Tis to your credit if you are modest. Men—oh, let's avoid an unpleasant topic. There, Jane's gotten rid of that guard at last. We may all breathe again. Into bed with you."

Clambering in next to Lady Cecily, Kat made a tired face at Grimalkin, who jumped onto the bed and stared back at her with feline impassivity. The animal kneaded the blankets several times before curling into a soft weight on top of her ankles.

She remembered that Margaret had made a self-deprecating remark. "You are not a cow. You are just—"

"Far too plump." Margaret pushed off her night robe, letting it fall to the floor. The smock underneath was cut full, but it had to stretch in order to fit over large breasts as yielding as round, fluffy clouds. The linen molded the flesh into loaves just as air could press clouds into whatever shapes took nature's fancy. Margaret grimaced in humorous resignation. "See?"

Kat made herself as small as possible to give Margaret room on the mattress and at the same time avoid touching the obese lump that was Lady Cecily. Whiskers twitching, Grimalkin settled more firmly over her feet.

Perhaps Lord Robin would rather have spent his evening touching a bosom like Margaret's. Soft and full. Not firm and small. A pox on him, she cursed silently, resenting the man for intruding into her thoughts.

"Bold charms are usually thought to be the most alluring," she said.

"Tch. You are a dear girl, Kat."

Like little, firm apples, he'd said, caressing her. Lord Robin, Kat told herself, probably approved of all breasts, no matter whose body they were attached to. He was also a lunatic. Imagine risking so much for a kiss.

She repressed an impulse to stir. The whole world was filled with sensuality. She'd spent her growing-up years blind and deaf to it. Putting all her energy and love into her estate, she'd done her best to ignore the budding of her figure into slim womanliness.

Now within a few hours she'd been handled by Robin Hawking and heard Jane's—Jane's!—voice go avid and then sleepy with desire. Even man-hating Margaret was comfortable in her body in a way Kat envied.

Jane joined them on the other side of Lady Cecily, throwing one of Kat's shoes at a maid to encourage the woman to get up and smother the candle flames.

"Do not worry," Jane said, her chatter a thin thread in the darkness folding over them. "I fooled the guard . . ."

It does not matter what she says, thought Kat. She'll tell. Pity for Jane and the gardener made Kat's heart ache.

Worry troubled her, too. What exquisite punishment would Elizabeth think up for her? Would she become as petty and small-minded as Jane?

The queen's mirror, who was supposed to reflect Elizabeth's perfect purity—caught being kissed by a man. A man whose lustiness was exceeded only by his reputation for cruelty. The court would find new names to call her. *Hawking's woman. Hawking's whore.* A shudder ran through her.

"Are you chilled?" Margaret asked.

"Nay. Just—nay."

Kat Preston couldn't belong to any man. She belonged to Priorly.

Finally, Jane's excited exposition of her own cleverness rambled to a halt, and a second set of snores ripped through the quiet.

"Are you asleep, Kat?"

"Aye." Kat blinked wide, dry eyes.

"Have I done you a bad turn? I was so angry to see you

all rumpled and torn about. It seemed right that he should pay."

"I thank you for caring. But it is always the woman who suffers. Always," said Kat out of the depth of her experience.

In the darkness, Margaret's sigh sounded like the sigh of every woman in the world. "Yes. I knew that. I did not suspect you knew it, too."

"Her majesty requires your presence. At once!"

Kat rolled over. The fact that she could move unimpeded by bedmates caused her to pry open one eyelid. Except for her the bed was empty. Its hangings were drawn back in the daytime position. Unless her cat was hiding in the covers somewhere, even Grimalkin was gone.

She kept the eye open long enough to verify that it was Maud who was shaking her shoulder.

"Anon."

"Not in a while—now! Lady Katherine, you must be up and about. Here, I have brought your black kirtle and bodice, and the black sleeves pricked with green. Please, please hurry. Everything is in an uproar."

Reluctantly, Kat climbed out of bed. Patting back a yawn, she allowed the maid to dress her. "I could not get to sleep till very late. Oh, Maud, bring me a fresh smock at least. I have been in this one a whole day and night. And I want a wash."

"There's no time for your everlasting washing today! The tittle-tattlers have been busy while you slept."

"That's not a surprise."

Maud snapped, "That Jane Monteshote. I could—well, if I got my hands on her and forgot the difference in our stations, she would be sorry, that's all I can say!" Unceremoniously, Maud pushed Kat's chin up to tie a ruff into place.

"Is this yellow? The queen hates yellow starch," warned Kat. After a few painful mistakes, she'd learned that getting along at court depended on paying attention to ridiculous little things.

Maud's fussiness had the odd effect of calming her anxiety. The middle-aged maid was her own servant.

When a stiff, imposing courier had arrived at her country home, carrying an equally stiff, imposing summons ordering Kat to court, she hadn't been able to leave her old nurse or her tabby cat behind.

And see what bringing Grimalkin along has caused, she thought.

Muttering, Maud ripped the ruff away from Kat's neck and ran to a chest to get another. "Your only other clean one is flat," she said, clucking distressfully. "There's no time to heat a poking stick or send it out to a starcher—"

"None of my clothes are fashionable." Kat shrugged. "A flat ruff will hardly make me more a figure of fun than I already am."

"I cannot bear it!" exclaimed Maud, tying the circle of lace rapidly before setting to work on Kat's hair. "You are bonnier than the lot of them, the great ladies who look down their noses. Such skin, and the loveliest hair. At least usually it is, although today 'tis more like a mare's tail. I beg pardon for tugging. I would have plaited it for you last night but Lady Margaret shooed me away. What was I saying? Oh, and your big eyes and sweet ways—"

Kat chuckled. "And my skinny body and long shanks! Do not bother arguing. Denying facts will not change them. I am no beauty. Nor am I noted for sweetness." She thought of Lord Robin's comments, wincingly, as if probing a sore tooth. "You and Lady Margaret have an entirely false picture of me. Most people call me a shrew."

"Most people see only what they wish to see, and not what's there. They are fools," said Maud defiantly. "Even the servants attached to the court know better, and they are almost as proud as their betters. You made sure Gillian got some rest when she had the influenza and gave Bridget medicines for the cracked skin on her toe. The Lord Chamberlain's servants say you are the best of the queen's ladies. You take no offense at being asked to do difficult tasks and never try to shift them onto others."

Kat's fears trickled back. "So many honeyed words make me suspicious. The plain truth, Maud! How loudly is the court clacking about me this morning? What are the rumors?"

Maud's lips closed in a straight line. "I would not repeat such filth."

"If you do not, I'll have to go before the queen unprepared. How busy has Jane Monteshote been?"

Contradictory stories came out in a flood. Hawking had ravished her. She had seduced Hawking. He had chased her naked through the palace. They had been seen by four separate witnesses coupling behindways in the rushes like dogs. She'd begged him to tie her up, to do things to her he'd learned supervising the punishment of wretches in the Tower . . .

"They are saying he *what?* What kind of mind could invent such vile twaddle?" Kat asked in astonishment. "Nay, I am being silly. I have been at court long enough to know how many prefer an amusing lie to the boring truth."

"He is a demon from hell!" whispered Maud. Her hands fumbled with a headdress. "No woman is safe from him. He takes his pleasures—" A long shiver ran through her. "—his pleasures far away from gentlefolk so none will accuse him. Oh, my lady, my lady, if his eye has fallen on you—"

His eyes *had* fallen on her. Both beautiful, strange hawk's eyes.

Kat turned and took Maud's shaking hands in hers, sparing a thought for the irony of the situation. She was defending someone she hated. "He is only a man. Not kind, nor a person I want to meet again. But a man. His desires are all straightforward ones, I assure you."

"You—you are supposed to be abed. They say the things he did to you left you too weak to get up and—and in any case, you dare not let people see the bruises he gave you."

"Am I marked?" Kat asked gently. "Do I move stiffly? Do you smell a man on me?"

"Your arms are bruised," Maud pointed out.

"Then let's hope Elizabeth will not command me to show them to her." She squeezed Maud's fingers in reassurance. *"He did not have me."*

A burst of talk greeted her entrance into the reception room. It died down to an unusual silence as she walked steadily toward Elizabeth. The queen had dressed to awe today; but then, she usually did. Ropes of pearls swung past the thin Tudor waist, and on her gown sapphires vied with the paler blue of topazes from Muscovy. Kat fell to her knees.

Out of the jumble of gemstones came a harsh bark. "Well, young madam! What do you have to say?"

The toe of a narrow shoe with a very high heel tapped in front of her. The queen was tall for a woman and strove to be taller. Kat took the chance of looking up into eyes like raisins, set in a face coated with white ceruse as perfect and smooth as sugar on a sweetmeat.

"I am accused by many, Your Grace. Does a single person step forward, so I may confront my accuser? I would like to know who claims to be a witness to my 'vile acts.' Acts it is impossible for anyone to have seen."

Elizabeth squinted, causing fine cracks in her complexion. "You have a good deal of faith in yourself! Impossible, eh?"

"My faith is in the truth. No one saw something that never happened."

"There are several somethings being mumbled over," Elizabeth said, her voice rising. "Did we invite you to court to disgrace us? We have shown you favor. We even matched your name with ours, made you an example of purity to shine like a pearl in our crown. A pearl fit for the dunghill! You have been exposed for the bawd you are. Look at you, so demure, so modest. If your appearance matched the interior of your heart, you would be covered with filth from the gutter. We'll have no whores attending us!"

"If you do, Your Grace, I am not one of their number." Somehow, Kat's quiet voice cut through Elizabeth's ringing tones.

Several of the listening courtiers and ladies shifted uneasily.

Elizabeth's mouth worked. "You deny that Lord Robin Hawking attempted you? That he had congress with you?"

"I deny he succeeded."

"A frail reed like you?" The queen's laugh grated. "He could break you between two fingers."

Kat remembered Lord Robin's strength. There wasn't

any point in saying he'd tried to be gentle after the first few brutal minutes. Or that he had stopped short under the counterattack of her sarcasm. No one here would believe her.

"Lord Robin did attempt me. Then he stopped. You see, I had something he wanted more."

"Robin Hawking? More than a woman? What?"

"Information."

Elizabeth's breath whistled through her teeth.

Kat had already decided the queen would have to be told about Priorly's priest's hole. It was the only reason she could give for going to see Hawking. And it had the added benefit of being honest. Anyway, the agent had as good as said he'd pass her tale on to others. The queen might go easier on the estate if she heard the first hint of trouble from the owner. Otherwise, the official reaction to suspicious happenings so close to Mary Stuart's new prison might be confiscation.

Kat hoped her fear didn't show in her face.

Her discreet, sidelong study of the chamber didn't reveal a giant with blond curls. Of course not, she thought. Her senses would have picked up his presence. Kat didn't care to analyze that thought.

If Lord Robin hadn't yet made an appearance, it was reasonable to assume Elizabeth knew nothing about the occurrences that had drawn Kat into the path of his erratic lust.

"You may speak, Lady Katherine."

The muscles underlying Elizabeth's face were buried too deep under cosmetics to suggest subtle changes of expression, but Kat shrank back on her heels. Her empty stomach congealed. The flash of Tudor temper wasn't over, just reined in temporarily.

"Here, Your Grace?"

Elizabeth acknowledged the prudence of Kat's tentative protest by saying, "Get up! It pains our neck to bend it far enough to watch you grovel."

"I thank you, Majesty," said Kat, not pretending gratitude.

She rose gracefully and unaided, since none of the courtiers came forward to lend her a hand. Waiting to see which way the royal breath would blow, she thought contemptuously. Well, she was doing that herself. Please God, she hadn't put Priorly in deeper danger with last night's stupid adventure.

She had to put these horrible rumors about her chastity to rest. The Preston honor came first. Priorly next. They were linked, a burden Kat had carried day by lonely day ever since she'd been left alone to represent the family.

Elizabeth led the way to an alcove which emptied swiftly at a lift of plucked brows. Gritting her teeth together to maintain an appearance of poise, Kat followed. The queen turned to face her, and Kat tried not to notice that the raised eyebrows lengthened the queen's white haggardness into a death mask.

There would be a new crop of heads greeting visitors to London Bridge sometime in the near future. She'd never seen this traditional sight of London, and she never wanted to. It wasn't only her own honor at stake here; Kat didn't think she could bear it if anything she said to Elizabeth resulted in more trophies being added. Not even if the heads came from strangers who were defiling Priorly by breaking in, taking without asking . . .

"Have you nothing else to say?" the queen asked.

The low heels on Kat's shoes forced her to look up at her sovereign. Otherwise they were almost of a height. "Your Grace, do you never wish for the freedom to do as you please?"

The raisin eyes registered guarded appreciation. "Constantly. Princes are more hemmed in by custom than the lowest yeoman. Not that the yeoman would believe it. Do you make a point?"

"I must beg your grace's patience. I did search out Lord Robin yesterday. It was a blunder. But I swear—I swear—I did it in innocence, thinking to set a problem before him. It was foolish. I see that now. He—he assumed I was there for a different reason. My only excuse is that I am unused to court ways. Life in the country is different. I was mistress and master of my own destiny at thirteen—"

"A most unsuitable state of affairs. As soon as it was drawn to our attention, we called you to us at court."

Who? Who had tattled to the queen about her and her quiet, busy existence at Priorly? To whom was she so important that it had been necessary to ruin her life? It *was* ruined, or at least altered beyond mending.

"I was much honored," she muttered hastily. Kat did so hate the vast amounts of oil which had to be poured over Elizabeth's vanity to keep conversational waters smooth.

For just an instant, the painted lips twitched. "Information," Elizabeth prompted.

"I am sure Lord Robin has told the people he reports to about it by now," said Kat. "They could explain the case better than I."

"If that is your wish." The queen's startled tone reminded Kat how few subjects would enjoy having their affairs mulled over by the chief spies of England.

She didn't look forward to it herself. But she had no choice.

"My wishes are not important." Kat's sudden rueful smile made the dawning good humor hovering around Elizabeth's mouth fade. "All that matters is that it please your grace."

"God's wounds, do you mock us, girl?"

Kat couldn't understand why the carefully applied flattery caused another explosion of fury.

Elizabeth spat, "Innocence is easy to claim, not so easy to prove."

The sudden anger, when she wasn't expecting it, made Kat feel dizzy. She hadn't slept well, once she'd slept at all. It would be pleasant to faint. Furry dots danced welcomingly between her and the too-bright, sparkling mass that was Elizabeth. She could join the dots . . . and convince Elizabeth and everyone else that she had something to hide. Physicians would be called; she would be carried away so they could pry for proof of her chastity. Such examinations weren't uncommon. The queen herself had submitted to one years ago.

Kat flinched from the idea of learned men with long beards peering between her legs. She gulped saving doses of air. The dots disappeared.

"I am innocent," she repeated. "I have not asked for a

man's attentions. And I cannot help the absurdities others imagine about Lord Robin."

"Fah! That nonsense. Do not speak to us of it! At least he is a man! He does not shirk his duty, even when it takes him places others are too frightened to go." Elizabeth was both fierce and vulnerable. "If we had more subjects like him, there would be more who would love us as we love them."

"Your Grace—" Kat hesitated.

If the other woman had been one of Priorly's tenants, she would have known how to offer comfort. But what could she say to a woman who was threatened with assassination? Who forced even new acquaintances like Kat to dislike as well as admire her?

If Kat was Elizabeth's reflection, didn't that mean the queen was also hers? Would Kat reach old age equally full of venom and melancholy, craving and yet unable to accept affection?

They stared at each other. Satisfaction briefly puckered Elizabeth's eyelids. A cool nod acknowledged and dismissed the compassion in Kat's parted lips and upward-cupped palm. Kat's hand dropped to her side.

She felt used. Elizabeth had asked for her emotion, she was sure of it. Then the queen had rejected it, leaving Kat feeling empty and foolish.

Not Gentle Queen Bess. An echo of Lord Robin's mellow voice sounded so clearly in her mind that she glanced around for him. He still wasn't there.

Elizabeth noticed her quick glance, and disastrously drew the correct conclusion. "Robin Hawking is not your lover? We shall see." She stepped outside the alcove and addressed the throng of courtiers and ladies in a bellow. "Where is our rat catcher?"

Chapter 5

Robin shouldered his way through a huddle of minor hangers-on, who were clogging the threshold of the gaily decorated audience chamber.

"There you are. Come with me."

"Good day, cousin." Robin followed William Cecil out again into another room as beautifully appointed as the one they had just left. Baron Burghley liked the splendor that came with his position as the queen's most valued minister.

"Call me 'cousin' softly," Burghley said, settling himself into a chair with the series of stiff motions required by his aging body. "I am not sure I wish to claim you today."

"Neither would the greater part of mankind. I find even *I* join you in that sentiment." Robin matched his kinsman for dryness. So . . . he had been recognized last night.

His lingering headache twinged. He ignored it, knowing he deserved worse.

Burghley studied him. "What is this woman to you?"

Training he'd had from this man, among others, held firm. Robin looked politely inquiring.

"Do not act the dullard!" In his deliberate way, Burghley was more furious than Robin had ever seen him. "How could you be so stupid as to go playing with a maid of honor? If you had to indulge your lust, why not find yourself some whore who would lay with you without making a scandal of it? God knows Westminster and London teem with them."

"I regret to say that I have not played with any woman of late. Not in the sense you mean."

The desire for what he had *not* had of Kat produced a memory so strong he could feel and taste the freshness of her breast. Soap and gillyflowers.

Robin had been standing, which was appropriate for a younger man in front of an elder kinsman. Abruptly he sat, crossing his legs. He had no intention of letting Burghley see that his body had reacted to the mention of Kat Preston. The thought of a woman hadn't possessed this power over him since he'd been a lad learning to use the capabilities of his developing manhood.

He would see her soon, Robin swore to himself. When he inspected her in the light of a cold and sober day, he'd find her strong, fey charm no more than a product of his wine-soaked imagination. Without the sweetening glaze of drunkenness, she would be nothing to him.

Nothing.

But he had hurt her through no—well, little—fault of her own. And her home was ten miles from Fotheringhay. He couldn't walk away from her any more than he could allow her to escape from him.

"Do you so far forget what you are, and what I am, that you imagine me a fool?" asked Burghley. "I know how you are with women. Your randiness has served to explain your absences from court, but—"

"I assure you, cousin, my *randiness* has never interfered with my duty. Since your memory is excellent, I'll not remind you how the rumor about a preference for the—unusual—in regard to women was started." God's grace, if William Cecil had come to believe the story when he of all people knew the truth, then no wonder others did as well.

"I have no time to salve a wound to your tender feelings. What of the woman?"

"She's nothing to me," Robin said dully.

"Good. Is her virtue intact?"

"You care?"

"Not at all. But her majesty does. Think, man! Never have I seen someone squander the queen's goodwill so quickly. Do you want to be dismissed from her service? Have you no loyalty to your mother's family? Do you owe me nothing? Do not forget it was I who placed you with Walsingham." Burghley bit out the name with an incongruous mixture of respect and dislike.

"To report on his doings," Robin countered.

"It is necessary. Otherwise I would not have the means to advise the queen wisely. He goes too far with his secrecy and his arrogance. Without a check on him, he would—"

"Trick babes like Babington into full-blown treason? Yes, I know Walsingham smelled out the conspiracy when it was only a few mutterings. I wonder, would it ever have crystallized into real action without his interference? My interference?"

"That hardly matters now."

"It matters to me. My orders were to push for clear statements of intent, and to create opportunities for like-minded idiots to plot together. Had I not been planted among them like some poison tree, providing shade for the saplings of treason, those suckling babes would never have gone beyond whining and mewling."

"You waste your pity on traitors. Save it for yourself. The queen will expect you to explain your actions regarding this woman."

"Lady Katherine," snapped Robin. Then, more softly, he said, "Kat."

Burghley leaned forward with an almost audible creak. "You are *sure* she is nothing to you?"

A reminiscent smile tugged at Robin's mouth. "Not quite nothing, perhaps. It is irrelevant. I have not had her and have no intention of taking her. We kissed and . . . not much more. This matter of the queen's goodwill . . ."

If Elizabeth punished him with an enforced rest, he could make a holiday out of it. Get away from the queen's sight so she forgot she wanted him to devise tortures for his erstwhile friends. Perhaps look about for a likely property. A place of his own.

The familiar longing swept over him so strongly his cousin's face blurred. Robin wasn't yet rich enough to buy the kind of estate he wanted. Nothing huge or baronial, just a tidy house with sufficient land attached to pay its own way. It would do no harm to look. Reluctantly, he put the thought away.

He brushed a piece of lint from his good doublet. Elizabeth liked to see men well-dressed. "I had hoped the queen's favor might extend to punishing me with an absence. However—"

"Leave? For what purpose?"

"A whim. A space to myself. It would be pleasant to breathe air that does not stink of the torture chamber."

They were true answers. Just not complete ones. Although Burghley might guess at his modest ambition—property was every man's dream—Robin had no wish to give his powerful cousin a club to hold over him. Even less did he want to betray the slightest interest in Kat's fate. Only God knew what Burghley would do with that weapon. Share it with Walsingham, maybe, though the two men were rivals. When it came to manipulating others, they were two peas in a pod.

Played properly, the consequences of his being recognized last night wouldn't be onerous—for him. For Lady Kat they would be a calamity. Not only would Elizabeth take relish in punishing Kat, but the gossips would chew Kat's reputation and her chances for marriage to a decent man into nothingness.

If Robin were very, very careful how he went about it, he might be able to stave off that fate. Why he wasn't sure, but it seemed vital for Kat to go to a kindly husband who would treat her well. There would be a husband, he knew. Despite her protests, the body that had lain beneath his last night had been soft and flexible. The lips that had refused to open for his tongue had been ripe. There would be a husband.

Burghley sat back. "Stop scowling. I cannot spare you."

"That's just as well," said Robin. "I find I do not desire to leave court after all." A nebulous plan was taking shape in his brain.

"We'll have to find a way to deflect the queen's wrath," warned Burghley.

"I may already have that." Robin repeated Kat's tale of the objects missing from Priorly, and her conviction that the priest's hole had been occupied. "The place is too close to Mary Stuart's new prison for comfort. Anything odd happening there has to be investigated. It sounds as if Mary Stuart's friends would have to be deaf not to have heard she's being moved to Fotheringhay. From what the girl said, while I was busy with Babington the whole court was buzzing with the news," he finished with a flash of anger.

"The court is not a locked box." Burghley gave an old man's hoarse snort. "If I can track the hints and whispers, I will, and the first pair of lips that prattled will be silenced ... after treatment that ensures they have told all they know—to us. Will that satisfy you?"

"It would accomplish nothing of importance. The news is already out."

"I agree. But an example must be made. You are getting soft, Robert. Womanish. There may be another tongue which does not wag in the future because the proper amount of remedial—persuasion—is applied now."

Stroking the two halves of his neatly divided beard, Burghley stared into space. Robin watched his cousin, glad for once he'd never felt any affection for the dessicated man in front of him.

More than just a generation separated them. At times like this, Robin couldn't believe they shared a common humanity, let alone a bond of blood. He'd met men who took frank pleasure in torture, and some who vomited at the thought of it. Burghley and Walsingham were the only men he knew who regarded it with indifference.

"Preston," Burghley said at last. "I have not taken much notice of the girl, but the family is known. A trifling estate in Northamptonshire. The Prestons were clerks and merchants a hundred years ago, and then they were jumped up by the seventh Henry. Well, the name hardly belongs to the old aristocracy."

Robin controlled a smile. The wars that put Henry the Seventh on the throne had thinned England's nobility. Few great families had ancient roots nowadays. Burghley himself had been plain William Cecil before he made himself indispensable to a young Elizabeth Tudor.

Occasionally Robin wondered if the old man resented

his more nobly born relatives by marriage, the Hawkings, and relished turning one of them into an outcast.

"Lady Katherine's mother adhered to the old beliefs," Burghley went on. "That is known, too."

Robin had thought it would be.

Grudgingly, his cousin added, "But the daughter says her prayers in the proper way. The rest of the Prestons are no trouble. They are dead or as good as dead."

Robin displayed an impassive countenance which hid the small contraction along his spine. "Good as dead?"

"For so recently elevated a name, it already has a reputation for tragedy. The uncles, aunts, and cousins died of this and that. Their line came down to this Lady Katherine's parents, her brothers, and her. A flux or a fever took the parents some years past. Only days later, the brothers—there were two or three, I believe—went boating with a neighbor. The craft capsized. The neighbor's body was recovered."

"And the other corpses?"

"Never found."

Serious Kat, with her fragile neck and tense mouth—all alone? Though she'd mentioned her parents' deaths, he hadn't expected her to be completely without family.

"So she has no one to stand up for her," Robin said.

Burghley shrugged wizened shoulders. His rich robe gleamed in the watery light from a window. "No horde of relations, at any rate, who will storm up to you demanding restitution for her stolen maidenhead."

Distaste for his cousin hardened into disgust. "Yet marriage would be the honorable outcome if the lady's name is dirtied because of me."

Burghley's voice cut like a knife. "She has neither power nor wealth. I will not allow you to marry her. I will take steps—"

"She would not have me," answered Robin curtly. "Nor am I looking for a wife." Marriage was a road to wealth he'd never been inclined to take. He'd earn what was his. Or would be his, someday. "Still, it seems to me that people will expect me to wed her."

"Unless they know the queen's—" A veined hand waved in the air. "—little prejudice on the subject. It pleases Elizabeth to believe no man looks at another woman when she is by. Love matches at court never sit well with her. Such a matter would have be to handled tactfully to gain her blessing. You have not been tactful, Robert."

"And I mean to be even less so."

"Where is our rat catcher?"

Robin heard the bellow the moment he and Burghley returned to the audience chamber. He felt a frown pinch the skin between his eyebrows, and erased it. A diplomatic smile lilted on his mouth.

"Here, Your Grace."

Light cascaded off Elizabeth's jewels as she rustled toward them. "So there you are, rogue. We are pleased you could find us." Her anger shot as many sparks as the crystals bobbing on the veil behind her head. The wired contraption resembled huge insect wings.

It wasn't to Elizabeth that Robin's gaze went. He bowed swiftly. "I had only to seek the center of the court."

"A statement which shows how rarely you condescend to visit us. We do not always receive our friends in this particular chamber."

"Where a lady of such beauty is will always be the center of the court." His gaze remained steady. Katherine Preston was standing a little behind the queen.

"My young cousin is graceless. The center of England," corrected Burghley.

"Of England," Robin agreed softly.

"Cozening knaves, both of you." The jibe in Elizabeth's voice had softened noticeably. "We would speak to you and Walsingham. This foolish mirror of ours claims you have something to tell us."

Kat returned his look with a straight one of her own. The only sign that she suspected Robin's praise had been intended for her was a slight blush. The rosy color deepened under her pale, clear skin when he continued to stare.

He couldn't help it. *Not a nothing.* Whatever else she was, this girl could never be a nothing. She wasn't a woman to be used and then left behind, forgotten. Her composure was a film of ice over an enchanting vulnerability. A fierce, bright spirit lived in that slim body. There was character stamped on her face, fresh and unlined though it was.

Robin shook himself slightly. He couldn't afford to admire her, let alone to like her.

"Are you coming, Robert?" Burghley asked impatiently.

"Yes, cousin."

"Do you join us, Walsingham?" said the baron, turning toward a third man with a woodenness that revealed his animosity—to Robin, anyway—as plainly as a shout.

Walsingham smiled. He had the long, fine-drawn face of an ascetic, and the turning-up of his lips failed to give an impression of warmth. "Certainly, with her grace's permission."

"Granted."

"Lady Katherine?" Burghley asked.

Elizabeth's thin lips snapped together like a vice. They barely opened to say, "Our mirror has other duties. The high table has yet to be set."

Kat said quickly and softly, "I have my usual duties to attend to. This lord is aware of anything I could tell you."

She wouldn't even speak his name. Robin regarded her again thoughtfully.

Her dislike was all to the good. Perhaps it would help cool the inappropriate fever in his brain. His plan for the lady's immediate future was inspired by the need to do his duty and, a little, by his passion for justice.

Any other kind of passion could not be indulged.

Inside the privy chamber, Walsingham tapped the fingers of one hand on the back of the other. It was the only sign of impatience he showed. Robin recognized the stance. His master would listen quietly until those fingers had a firm hold on all the facts of the case.

Burghley stooped before the queen. Obedient to a hand signal, Robin ranged himself behind his cousin.

"—a Christian court and we will have moral order—"

"Of course, Your Grace. Robert assures me—"

Elizabeth kicked her skirts out of the way as she strode around the room. She was Maypole-thin, and the solid, flat-footed strides were like a man's. Could she really believe she possessed the same subtle sexuality Kat did?

"—a plague on all cousins! Our poor, faithful friend, you suffer in your ties of blood, as we do—"

"If I may beg your grace's indulgence, perhaps I could explain how Robert's encounter with Lady Katherine could be regarded in the light of a happy accident—"

Burghley hardly needed his help dealing with the queen. Robin let his thoughts wander. Kat looked at a man as if—as if against her own will she were inviting him to drown with her in sweetness.

"—so few miles from Fotheringhay? That murderous bitch is only just housed there, and already her supporters take up their positions—"

"It is not yet sure who is using Priorly, madam, nor why—"

The limp costume Kat was wearing ought to have made her insignificant next to Elizabeth's sparkling display. The queen's mirror. Instead, it seemed to Robin that Kat was the real woman, and Elizabeth the sham.

"—God's wounds, is there no end to the mischief our cousin tries to cause?"

"Apparently not."

The full stop in Burghley's voice made Robin twitch with awareness of the tension in the air. Walsingham leaned forward.

The thin chest behind the padded bodice rose and fell. A memory, like a lightning bolt, made Robin picture Kat's taut breasts with their small, true-pink nipples instead.

Then Elizabeth spoke and catapulted him back into reality. "Robin, we will have the servants out of this Priorly and put to the test. See to it. A night spent bedded on the rack should free their tongues. We shall find out if they know more than they admitted to Katherine. We were wrong in our judgment of her. She possesses not even a pale imitation of intelligence." Her gaze whipped, from Robin to Burghley and Walsingham and, ominously, back to Robin again. "The girl must be a silly drab. Any rogue armed with a likely story could bend her to his will."

Francis Walsingham spoke for the first time since entering the room. "All shall be as you desire, of course. But perhaps we should consider whether there's a chance here to catch bigger fish than a few servants who may be able to reveal little of value." Yes, he had been listening, Robin thought.

The cheeks under the paint caved in. "More?" she croaked, and for once Robin believed she wasn't acting for the audience she always kept around her. "You know of more of our subjects who want to kill us?"

"Only idiots misled by foreigners. Unthinking fools who fail to realize their actions would reduce England to a client state of the Spaniards or the French," Burghley said ponderously. "Your true subjects know your true worth, madam. You are England."

"It is not yet sure there *is* another plot brewing," added Robin, before Burghley could spout more courtly commonplaces or Walsingham could wade in. Kat didn't deserve to have her people broken and maimed. "Torture might produce an item or two of interest. But many persons will say anything under the influence of pain. The threat of it, even. Information extracted by means of the rack or the bastinado is dubious at best. Its value must be set against the certainty that torturing the servants would warn away any real conspirators. They would only set up camp in a location we are not aware of and do their mischief anyway. That must not happen."

"Must? You say *must* to us?"

"By your leave, Your Grace." He shrugged, although sweat began to trickle down the insides of his arms. "You have called me your rat catcher. I am good at my business. It would be failing in my duty to you to speak less than the truth about a consequence clear to anyone who practices my trade."

She cawed inelegantly. "The only trade you practice is lechery. You'll not even grant the little boon we asked of you. How hard could it be for a man of your talents to devise a new method of execution? We want Babington and his rabble to suffer."

"By your leave, Your Grace," put in Walsingham. "If done properly, the traditional way can be a very pretty punishment indeed. The traitor is hanged, cut down still living, castrated, gutted, and then the rest of the body is pulled apart by horses. It will assure the most exquisite suffering. I promise you."

"This is England, not Spain," Burghley said. "Let the Inquisition keep its reputation for horrors. Good, simple English ways are best."

"Hawking speaks sense regarding these people at the estate near Fotheringhay, also. After all, there's always time for torture when other methods fail." Walsingham's cool smile didn't part his lips.

"Your Grace believes me to be as licentious as a buck hare, and as brainless as one, too." The muscles around Robin's mouth felt stiff. "Therefore the silver you put in my purse yesterday was unearned. I shall return it and resign from your service."

Burghley made a futile, abortive motion. Elizabeth exchanged expressive glances with her ministers and then changed moods, smiling widely. "My sweet Robin," she said, descending from queen to woman, "how can you imagine I would ever let you go?"

The expression revealed yellowed teeth. Robin's belly contracted in horror. A rat catcher . . . forever?

In spite of his revulsion, the moment was right to press his idea. "It is my greatest wish to serve your grace." In this matter, he amended privately. "A discreet inquiry into this Priorly could answer all our doubts and, handled correctly, do it without alerting any of Mary's adherents who might be using the place."

"And what sort of handling do you judge to be correct?" Elizabeth's question was too honeyed. "The people there cannot all be desirable women."

Robin answered slowly, as if he were thinking the plan out for the first time. Even a hint that he had discussed it with his cousin earlier would offend her in her present mood.

"Say that I am seen speaking with servants of the Cecil household, who then travel openly to and from the area around Fotheringhay. They spread the tale I have sent them to cast an eye over Priorly. After all, property belonging to a lady the whole court supposes me to lust after . . ." He spread his hands gracefully. "The logical conclusion—"

"Is that a land-hungry man is making sure of his heiress's fortune," said Elizabeth thoughtfully. "People might even conclude that he has deliberately placed the heiress in an awkward position. One in which a maiden might be expected to desire marriage as soon as possible to cover her shame."

Robin didn't care for the assessing look she threw him, but he plowed onward. "All that's needed to assure the story's plausibility is for a sufficient number of witnesses to remark how zealously I tag at Lady Katherine's heels."

"You will make an unlikely lapdog," she warned, but with genuine amusement.

"Will that not be the cream of the jest? Who does not enjoy seeing love create fools—out of other people?"

"It would be as good as a play!"

He bowed. "Especially if your grace lets it be seen that your wit has penetrated my poor scheme. Here I'll be, an unmasked spy of dubious reputation. My clumsy strategems to keep my intrigue secret from you will be obvious. So will the fact I am not fooling your grace. And in the meantime, I'll keep an eye on Lady Katherine and my cousin's servants will have their eyes on her estate."

She nodded decisively. "A fine entertainment. We shall act in your farce. Do not forget we'll be watching, however. Take care you do not try to hold what you catch too long or too fondly. Lady Katherine is under our protection."

Bowing themselves out, the three men paused on the other side of the door. In an undertone so practiced it didn't carry to the guards standing with pikes at the ready, Walsingham asked, "There are Cecil servants competent to do this task?"

"Of course." Burghley's tight lips showed that the insult had been recognized and resented. The spies set to watch Priorly would work hard to uphold the Cecil honor. Of course, honor was the wrong word, thought Robin.

The spymaster asked, "Robin, you are positive you are so well-trained a hawk you can swoop down on this woman and refrain from gorging on her charms? Your indiscretion last night—"

Just as inaudibly, Robin answered, "—can be used. If there are traitors at Priorly, we'll flush them out. Lady

Katherine will make an admirable screen. I assure you I feel no hunger for any charms she may possess."

Sweet, succulent Kat. The lie came easily. He was used to lying.

Chapter 6

"**H**e is here," Margaret Treland whispered.

Kat froze midway through the third curtsy she was making toward the public royal table where Elizabeth would *not* be eating dinner. Even though the queen was dining privately today, as a maid of honor Kat was required to show the gold plate reverence. Of all her duties, this was the one she loathed the most.

"Finish your curtsy," ordered Margaret. "There are visitors to the court observing us. By the way, the rat catcher is watching, too."

Bobbing a curtsy, Kat was unable to resist peeking around for a glimpse of Lord Robin. The impulse to look was disconcerting. There he was, towering over a group of short Dutchmen.

Quickly, she faced the table again and began to back away in the approved manner. "I cannot believe that we are two women grown, making ninnies of ourselves, bowing as we back away from an empty table."

Margaret shuffled backward next to her. "The ritual shows how high England has risen."

"Do not make me laugh or your important visitors will be shocked. All we prove is the depth of the queen of England's vanity. Subjects can show a ruler respect without bowing to the table where she eats or the pot in which she—"

"Do not you make me laugh, either," Margaret implored. "Look. The scullions are bringing in the food."

"You are sure no lady-in-waiting has died tasting the queen's food for poison?"

"None, I promise. If today's the first time some assassin spices the soup with dried foxglove, it is too bad it wasn't Jane's turn to do the tasting," Margaret said with dry humor.

With mealtime approaching, the hall teemed with people. Kat decided that she should stop walking backward before she knocked someone over. She came to a halt, and Margaret stopped, too.

Like all the state apartments, the dining hall was huge. The cavernous size was necessary. Not only courtiers and ladies, but also foreign travelers and common Englishmen were welcome to eat at Elizabeth's expense.

"I have no objection to doing things that have a real purpose," she said, sidestepping to avoid a boy. Comically, he was clutching a small keg so high it hid his face. Someone must want beer, Kat thought vaguely. "I do not wish the queen poisoned, just—oh, why does she make it so difficult to like her?"

"Some people do not know how to inspire true liking, Katherine."

The outline of Margaret Treland's plump face hardened, and Kat wondered if Margaret was thinking about her husband, Sir John Treland.

"Why do men have to be so—so—"

"Necessary?" asked Margaret. "It is a quandary. If it were not blasphemous, I would say the way procreation has been arranged is a sadly mismanaged business." She gestured toward a row of manservants drawn up and waiting for the two of them. Each servant carried a platter or serving dish in his arms. "Let's see if anyone has put hellebore or nightshade in the pudding."

"Hellebore might be beneficial," Kat said.

She walked with Margaret to the food, which would be served at the coming midday meal. She was speaking at random, waiting for Lord Robin to say or do something. He wasn't the sort of man to sit back and let events unfold without the benefit of his intervention.

Margaret picked up a spoon and poked at a piece of fish. "How would hellebore help?"

"The white kind cures fits," she replied.

Margaret stifled a chuckle. "It was not too bad a fit, Kat. I have heard worse tongue-lashings from the queen. You must not let yourself be bitter. It will drive you to do something foolish and hurt you in the end. Or make you like Jane, peevish and nasty-minded."

Easy for Margaret to say when her interference had helped bring the queen's wrath down on Kat's head in the first place. Kat's small burst of resentment died quickly. The advice was good, and Margaret meant well.

"Your pardon, ladies," said Lord Robin right behind them. Rich and smooth, his voice flowed over her. Already tense, she tensed even more as she glanced haughtily over her shoulder. He was very big, very cool, very sure of his welcome.

"Go away," she snapped. "Have you not done me enough harm?"

As if she hadn't spoken, he said, "Lady Kat, if you are free, I crave a few moments." Looking at Margaret, he added, "Alone."

It was Margaret who flushed poppy-red. "If your desire is to be solitary, my lord, we are happy to oblige. You may go be alone to your heart's content. Neither of us shall stop you."

Silently, Kat applauded her friend's resistance to Hawking's sheer good looks. He'd been handsome last night, rumpled and unshaven. Today his beard was barbered to a neat point, his curls tamed into waves. With a doublet and fashionably short, full breeches of tawny velvet setting off his fair coloring, he looked like a blond god.

"Perhaps the lady should make up her own mind," Robin suggested with a gentleness that wasn't really deceptive.

Feeling like the bone of contention between two dogs, Kat tried to ignore both of them and stepped up to the first serving man. He tilted the bowl he was holding so she could inspect the contents.

"Oysters with brown bread," said the bearer.

"A galantine of mutton."

"Pike with Dutch sauce and leeks."

"Roasted blackbirds . . ."

Kat took a small portion of each dish. There were so many that even though she ate only tiny bites, by the time she arrived at the sweets her stomach was stuffed. Margaret was still squabbling with Lord Robin. Kat pulled on her sleeve to get her attention.

"No more arguing," Kat said firmly. "You need to help me with the tasting. I cannot face another bite."

"My dear, have you tasted all of the main dishes by yourself?" Pointedly, Margaret turned her back on Robin. "I shall do the rest while you convince this simpleton he's not wanted." She gave a brittle laugh and patted a waist even whalebone cinched tight didn't make slim. "Eating too much is not such a burden to me as it is to you. What have we here, stewed quinces?"

Robin regarded the row of dishes with a slowly deepening scowl. The expression would have terrified Kat if she had been the sort of woman who could be cowed by a frown. As it was, she swallowed and dug her toes into the soles of her kid shoes.

His fingers bit into her wrist. Anger pulsed from his skin into hers.

"I thought you were nibbling before dinner," he said. "But you could barely force that food down, could you? When I made you taste for poison yesterday I never guessed Elizabeth would force you to do it again. In reality, instead of as a jest."

Kat was puzzled at his irritation. If he wasn't upset with her, why did he look so black? What a disturbing, unaccountable man. She tugged against his grip. "Kindly let me go."

It tightened. "I knew the queen would be peevish over our—adventure. But that she could be vindictive enough to set you tasting for poison—"

She stopped pulling in her surprise. "Tastings are long-established custom. All the maids of honor take turns."

Robin's roar echoed in the rafters. "Is she mad? Why not use dogs or pigs for such a foul task?"

Margaret swung around, her jaw dropping to show a mouthful of almond tart. A startled hush spread over the crowd waiting for the meal. One of the servers fumbled with his tray. It tipped and the contents slid wetly to the floor.

"The pike," said Kat. "It was not very good, anyway. Do not fear," she added to the manservant, who'd gone green. "We'll be witnesses for you that the spilling was not your fault."

Robin's voice drowned her out. "Are there so many ladies-in-waiting one or two are not missed when some lunatic takes it in mind to poison the queen's pottage?"

"My lord!" She jiggled the wrist he held to get his attention. "Her grace is not so prodigal with her maids of honor. None of us has ever died from the tastings, though I have heard several complain of indigestion. Wise poisoners choose not to waste their wares. They must know they would only accomplish the murder of a few mere ladies."

His bellow diminished only slightly. "You can scarcely depend on that theory, comforting as it is. What if there are assassins not acquainted with the customs of the court?"

"Since it seems even a famous spy like you has not heard of one of them, you may be right. But tasting is my duty as—other things are yours. I am not at court by choice, but while I am here I'll do my duty."

"Not this one. Not while I watch."

Flinging her hand away, he grabbed the spoon from Margaret's lax grasp. He went along the line, cramming in mouthfuls at prodigious speed, swallowing immensely at every third or fourth dish. Neither Kat nor Margaret told him he was eating foods they'd already tasted. Kat put her fingers to her lips to hold back a guilty giggle.

Unwillingly, she was impressed. How could he stuff himself like that after last night's drinking? His innards must be made of iron.

Margaret pushed at her. "Now is your chance. While he's busy. Go!"

Recovering her wits, Kat said, "Make sure the steward is told that man did not ruin the fish through his own fault." A door leading outside stood invitingly open and she sped toward it. Margaret was right. Robin Hawking might have come searching for her, but that didn't mean Kat had to stand still and be caught.

As she reached the door, a loud crack of thunder boomed. Peering outside, she couldn't see any flashes of lightning or drops of rain, so she inched out. If a storm threatened, she could see no sign of it. Above, the heavens were milky with thinly spread clouds. A few tears in the cottony white showed blue sky. Mild sunshine bathed the garden spread out in front of her. Its hedges and painted columns ought to provide sufficient places to hide from a man who wasn't often at Whitehall. Dismissing the thunder she'd heard, she lifted her skirts and ran.

Gardeners sat back on their haunches at the sight of her headlong dash, and ladies and gentlemen out for a walk before the meal paused to look down their noses at her. She slowed. Thanks to Lord Robin, she was already an object of fun. Kat felt no desire to give people more to snicker about.

She strolled, keeping to herself and glancing around frequently. It was to her advantage, she thought smugly, that Lord Robin's appearance was so striking, while hers was commonplace She'd see him before he noticed her.

He'd been remarkably free with his compliments this morning ... and they were both fortunate Elizabeth hadn't noticed that the rogue was addressing them to the wrong lady. All that wrathful indignation over the tasting certainly seemed to spring from concern ... but now that he was no longer drunk, why should he feel anything at all toward her? She felt nothing for him except clean, pure hatred.

Kat's conscience produced a pang. *You are lying to yourself,* she thought.

He wasn't a man she could feel nothing for. Something forceful in him had its match in something soft and feminine in her. She cursed softly. Her years of managing an estate had given her a vocabulary as earthy as Lord Robin's. By every stable oath she knew, she couldn't afford feelings for the man.

Keeping to those side paths lined by bushes which could be ducked behind at need, she finally halted under a flag. It rippled in a sputter of almost-autumn breeze.

Briefly, she wondered again about that odd clap of thunder, and then shrugged. Perhaps the weather in this part of the country was different from what she was used to at home. At any rate, she had to find out what the hour was; she couldn't just disappear for the rest of the day, much as she might like it.

The rest of the people had drifted away. All of the paths were now empty. The midday meal must be prolonging itself even longer than usual, she thought. Court meals could go on and on. She padded cautiously in her flat-soled shoes to the middle of the garden.

A sundial stood in the garden's center. It was part of a fountain, but the water was a bare trickle, so there was no danger of being splashed. Leaning over the edge to tell the time by charting the shadow on the dial's face, she heard a savagely pleased "Ah, Lady Kat. Here you are at last."

Before she could bolt, water leaped out of the sedate rivulets. A frothing stream caught her in the eyes, nose, and mouth, and drenched her hair. She stumbled backward before her clothes became worse than spotted. The spray shut off as unexpectedly as it had erupted, and she stood shaking and wiping her eyes.

"You bastard, whoreson devil!"

"And my father always said I was his own get," Lord Robin replied, covering the ground between them in a few quick steps. "Not that he was too pleased about it. As for the rest—yes, that describes me. You would do well not to forget it. Do not run away from me again, lady."

His hand came out in an imperative gesture. Retreating from him, Kat put her own hands behind her back. His eyes hardened. Without warning he reached around her and captured one of her wrists in a hard grip. He did it with such ease she remembered all over again that he could break it like a piece of kindling.

Fear sharpened her tongue. "Of all the ridiculous—what did you do, bribe one of the gardeners to operate the fountain?"

"My lady, where's your spirit of adventure?" he asked mockingly. "I bribed him to go away so *I* could turn the waterwheel. It gave me a great deal of satisfaction."

"I would show my ladylike good temper by laughing," she retorted, "but someone has drowned my sense of humor. Why play such a silly trick?"

"It got you standing still," he pointed out. "Join me. There's something you need to see. And take this." Impatiently, Robin pulled a handkerchief from his sleeve and thrust it at her. Then he walked quickly down a path. His clasp was still firm around her wrist; she had no choice but to follow, staggering slightly.

"How did you know I would be in the garden?" she asked sullenly, dragged along by his long strides. Why did he have to vary his commands and general unpleasantness with good-hearted gestures? The handkerchief's small size helped her hang onto her resentment. The square of linen was barely large enough to dry her forehead and cheeks. Drops continued to roll down from her hair.

"I was not certain you would be here. It only occurred to me that if you were playing 'all hid,' the garden would be a logical place for you to fetch up. A lucky guess."

Wanting to hurt him, she said, "Overmodesty does not become you. Be honest, I pray. It was the rat catcher's expert knowledge of the—"

"*You* are too modest," he rapped out. "Calling either of us hard names will not mend what's between us, lady." His mouth was rigid. "You'll not tease me into calling you a wet rat."

"Politeness? From you, my lord? First you drown me and now you try to get me to fall down dead of shock."

"I hoped a campaign of courtesy might make my presence more to your liking. We'll be seeing more of each other."

"You may save your strategies for ladies witless enough to be taken in by them. Surely you do not desire a longer acquaintance. I do not."

"My desires are irrelevant. So, I fear, are yours. You should not make assumptions, damask lady. At least not about what men desire."

Damask lady. "Do not call me that."

The silver in his eyes glittered next to the gold. "What?"

"You know what."

"Damask lady? Does it offend you? Insult you in some way?"

"It is too—"

Intimate. The kind of name used between familiar friends. Or lovers.

He waited but she didn't go on. They rounded a corner so fast her skirts flew out to one side. "Come with me, Lady Katherine. Since our little bite before dinner, I met someone who claimed to carry a message for you," he said. "This way."

He set the pace toward a section of the palace Kat hadn't visited before. "Do they call you Longshanks at home?" she asked, panting.

"They call me misbegotten," he said flatly. "In here."

Guards stood at either side of an entrance. The small room was dark after the brightness of out-of-doors. Peering, she saw that it was bare of furnishings except for rows of weapons hung or propped along the walls. Obviously an armory or a guardroom.

Then the smell of burning hit her, and a stench like a kitchen midden. "Is anyone there?" she asked, unwilling to set foot any farther into the smells.

Brushing past her, Lord Robin turned a bundle of rags on the floor over with his toe. A scream tore out of Kat's throat.

"Do you know him?"

She shook her head blindly.

"Before this happened, he said he knew you. Look again. Here, I'll clean him up a little." Robin wiped away some of the scarlet stains.

Giving the thing on the floor another fearful glance, Kat gasped.

"If you value that pretty skin of yours, lady, give me an honest answer. Have you seen him before?"

"Jack," she choked out. "Jack Miller. His father is one of my tenants. The boy is—was—he was only fourteen years old. Sweet Jesu, what happened to him?"

"He tried to cut out his own tongue."

"What?"

"In the midst of questioning him, I was called by the queen to give a report. Your young Jack—fooling the guards with his beardless innocence—stole a knife from one of them. He said we would never get him to give up sacred secrets and—"

Kat struggled not to be sick. "But he's dead."

"The guard managed that while trying to get his knife back."

From outside the door came a hoarse "My lord, I swear, it was like he pushed himself on the blade."

Robin ignored the pleading comment. "What was Jack coming to tell you, Lady Katherine?"

She shrugged hopelessly. This cold-voiced, cold-eyed man would never believe she hadn't seen Jack for ages and didn't know why the boy had traveled to court.

His face was like flint, but he pushed her out into the clean air. She gulped the good scents of late summer.

"Why was he being questioned?" she asked. Jack Miller's father would want to know.

Strong fingers dug into her chin and forced her head up. "If by any chance you are hiding something from me," Robin said tightly, "I'll kill you myself. And it will not be a quick death like young Jack's there. Do you mean to tell me you have no knowledge that your tenant's son hid himself in the dining hall and exploded a keg of gunpowder directly after you left?"

"The thunder," she said dazedly. "There was a sound like thunder, but no towering clouds. How? Where could something like that be hidden? I saw nothing out of place."

"Pushed under the table near the queen's place."

"Oh, no." Kat stared at him in horror. "Oh, Lord Robin. I saw him bring it in. A boy with his face covered by the keg he was carrying. I didn't recognize him, I swear." She looked toward the door to the armory. "Jack, how could you do this?"

"Your Jack didn't run fast enough when the powder ignited. I caught him while he was still tangled up in his own feet."

"Mercy God."

"If you are hoping for mercy, God would certainly be the best person to ask. No one else is in a mood to supply any."

"Least of all Elizabeth?" The sense of what he'd said soaked in. "Lord Robin, I did not send for Jack. I cannot tell you why he would attempt so terrible a deed. Why he would *dare*. He was a gentle lad, dreamy but quick to learn. When he was hardly more than a babe, he would follow my brothers about. After they—my brothers—were gone, he and I would talk about them sometimes. It helped the loneliness—"

"Keep to the subject, please."

"My maid is—was—his aunt. A few years ago, his family could not spare him from the mill, and I paid for a day laborer to help them so Jack would be free to go to grammar school. He was their best orator ... Cut out—tried to cut out—?"

The world suddenly tilted, and her legs turned to water. Dimly, she was aware of Robin taking her arm. His grip was warm and solid. It felt unexpectedly safe.

"Very well, you have had enough for now," he said from far away.

She drew deep breaths, and the faintness passed. "This is the second time today I have nearly swooned. I do not like it."

"I am taking you to your chamber." His expression was odd; half angry and half gentle. "For the rest of the day, you are not to come out unless I or someone you know to be an officer of the queen gives you permission. Do you understand?"

"I understand," she said numbly.

They went slowly toward her quarters. Water dripped form her hair to her shoulders. Robin shielded her from curious stares as they passed through the garden.

Kat roused herself to ask, "What will happen to Priorly?"

"Try not to make yourself sick with worry," he advised with rough kindness. "Only I and those I report to know that Jack Miller mentioned you."

"How long will such discretion last?"

"Longer if you tell no one. In the meantime, anyone who sees us will deduce only that you were the victim of a jest in poor taste." His eyes rested on her wet hair.

"You must think me very petty and shallow, if you believe I care about *that* when poor, lunatic Jack—How is the queen taking the news?"

"She's upset," he said dryly.

"Am I under suspicion?" she asked.

The trim beard lifted into an assertive angle as he raised his face to the pale sky and whistled soundlessly. She went really cold, all over.

"I have been wondering," he said, not answering directly. "Why did you not go to Elizabeth with your story of strange happenings at Priorly in the first place?"

Her hand had been bunched into a fist in mute protest against the long fingers holding her arm captive so easily. It was hard work, she discovered, keeping herself everlastingly tensed up against him; her tight muscles loosened. Somehow he must have felt that slight relaxation, because his hand slid down to clasp hers.

"It did not seem so great a thing," she said. "What was there to complain of, really, except some thievery in an almost empty house? I believed it ought to be reported, but hoped you could sift it out privately. If it merited higher attention, a man like you would know what to do. After all, it might have proven to be no more than simple theft, and in that case the incident need never concern important personages."

"And then I kissed you."

"And then you kissed me," she agreed, looking at his mouth. When he glanced down at her, she flushed and fixed her eyes on the path. "And that meant *everything* had to be explained to the queen." Without intending it, she clung to his hand. "Now, I suppose, with Jack trying to burn down the dining hall—"

"The barrel of gunpowder was a yard from Elizabeth's seat. I mislike assumptions on principle, but it would be idiotic to deduce anything except a try at assassination."

"Was anyone hurt?"

"By some strange quirk of fortune, no. A great deal of expensive furniture has been blown apart, that's all."

She sighed. "Jack would make an inexpert assassin. How would he know the queen frequently eats in her privy chamber? And if he saw Margaret and me bowing and scraping, he would have been more sure than ever that she was either in the room or expected soon. The incompetence—"

"Yes."

"Jesu, you said it this morning. Prospective murderers are not necessarily well informed about the court."

Her grasp of the situation pleased him more than it should. Robin frowned.

As if she were working out a riddle, clue by clue, she said slowly, "If I, Kat, had prior knowledge of the gunpowder, I would have run away—as I did—to avoid being blown up. But at the same time, I would have warned Jack not to light the keg because the queen wasn't coming to the hall. So this stupid explosion would never have happened today at all."

Kat glanced at him with raised brows, and he shrugged.

"And why," she continued, "if I had known about the plot, would I have pushed myself on an agent of the queen last night? That would have been very foolish of me. There's your problem. You cannot decide if I am as guilty as poor Jack!"

"Treason to some is loyalty to others. It would depend on which royal lady you believe ought to be queen."

"You cannot trick me that way! My oath is to Elizabeth Tudor and I stand by it."

She tried to free her hand. Robin kept her fingers trapped in his. A single drop of water shivered at the tip of a russet curl, then fell, pooling on the shelf formed by the delicate bones at the base of her throat. He could just see the spot inside her drooping ruff.

Unfortunately, no law of nature said traitors couldn't be reed-thin girls with huge dark eyes and kissable lips.

Robin lengthened his stride, causing her to trot to keep up. At least the exercise would keep her from taking a chill. He grunted softly. He was being ridiculous and knew it. There wasn't any logic in forcing her to look at something like the remains of Jack Miller, and at the same time suffering from this concern over whether or not she caught a cold.

He'd been enraged when Jack blurted out her name. Because he didn't like to be wrong, and he'd already decided she was innocent of whatever was going on? Or because he couldn't shake his nagging liking for a woman who seemed to be waist-deep in treason?

Annoyance with himself kept his mouth twisted into a

bitter line. It certainly wasn't his practice to play childish jests with water fountains, either. That kind of humor required like-minded companions, or the intimacy of close friendship. He wasn't familiar with either. Of course, he hadn't been feeling particularly mirthful when he turned the water on her. He'd been deeply, coldly furious.

"What will happen now?" she asked in a small voice.

"I already planned to stay close to you, lady. As close as a lover. You are mine now." The sound of it pleased him, and he repeated, "Mine."

"That is absurd." Her voice shook. "The queen would never allow—"

"Mine, Kat. I will be watching every moment."

"Watching. Oh." Relief flickered across her features.

"What did you think I meant?" Robin wondered what she saw in his eyes. At any rate, she gasped and looked away. He laughed and said, "Run if you like. It will entertain the court, and you'll not get far from me."

Her pallor was too profound to whiten further. If she wasn't used to the sight of violent death, he thought, she probably saw Jack every time she blinked.

"You said—you have planned to stay close to me? I am party to no such plan."

"But Elizabeth is. So is Walsingham. So is my cousin of Burghley."

"You *all* believe I participated in trying to murder my queen?"

He didn't respond immediately. Then he said, "There will be no formal accusation. The official view will be that you merely had the misfortune to employ the family of an unbalanced young man. The queen will not blame you for harboring Jack. He was your man, but in a greater sense, he was hers, too. Her subject. But remember. Elizabeth has blind faith in no one."

"I am innocent!"

"Perhaps. But the Preston men are all gone. Who protects you? It is a frightening world, full of knaves and cutpurses and investigations into treason. And cutthroat old dames whose main pastime is killing reputations. You should be glad we have been ordered to meet often."

Robin decided not to mention that the idea had been his.

Quickly, he explained how they were to behave. "You'll have adequate opportunities to show how much you despise me. Last night's scandal will be swallowed up in tonight's."

"We shall be laughingstocks!" she gasped.

"I more than you."

"At least that's justice. This is all your doing!"

"All?" he mocked her.

"Very well, not all. But the greater part."

Her strict sense of fairness made him smile. "Are you so proud you would prefer to be suspected of treason rather than put up with the scorn of a few idiots?"

"Would not you?"

"How people act and react, what they feel, what they think—or are led to think—those are means to an end. Nothing more," he explained.

"Feelings are no more than means to an end?" she asked numbly. "Lord Robin, men call me cold. But you are ice."

Heat scalded his cheeks. Did she believe he was like Burghley or Walsingham—cold and dried-up, their passions reserved for bloodless things? Pausing by a low door that led into the maids of honor's quarters, he shifted so she wouldn't see the betraying redness. "I am practiced in the art of getting things done. Sometimes that leaves little room for niceties like feelings."

"I pity you." Despite her bedraggled appearance, she had the dignity of a lady. "And I liked you better when you were drunk."

"Did you? I thought you hated me."

"I did. I do."

" 'Tis well to know how we stand. We shall be meeting as often as devoted bedmates." To himself, his attempted note of geniality fell flat, but she flinched, so perhaps it succeeded better than he imagined. "Resign yourself to a little laughter, my lady, and pray to whichever saints you admire that the snickers save you from worse."

"How could anything be worse? You think I may be a traitor, and the whole world is calling me your whore."

"I regret it." At her incredulous look, he added, "Believe me or not as you will. But grant yourself a favor. Do not pity me. Pity is a weapon, too. I will gladly use it against you if you are foolish enough to feel it."

"I thank you for the hint. Not because I need it—to borrow some of your frankness, you will never mean enough to me to hurt me. I am perfectly and imperviously indifferent to you. But your warning reminds me that you are not a man who commits blunders or does penance for them very often. I do not mean that as a compliment. You are not quite human, my lord."

A bevy of ladies brushed past them, skirts bouncing up and down in the way of the wider farthingales. Open-mouthed stares ranged from astonished to apprehensive. But as the women flitted inside, smothered giggles wafted after them.

"My lord." Kat spoke again with stony calm. "You know as much about these strange goings-on as I do. Grant me a boon. Leave me alone."

Her distaste pierced his defenses; he lashed back. "The queen has stated her wishes. We will have to obey. Much as it grieves me to be unable to leave you to your maidenly solitude, the decision is out of my hands."

Kat went scarlet. It was a day of embarrassments, Robin thought. Even he had colored up, and blushes had never been included in his stock of tricks.

But what had he said to bring crimson flooding up from her throat? Many of the words they'd exchanged last night had been more suggestive; as a jibe, his last remark was practically tame. He studied her while the hot color cooled into a rosy flush that went better with the black and green in her gown.

"Damask lady," Robin said. "Damask is a color as well as a fabric, did you know that? A rose, too. The same pink that's in your cheeks."

"Save your cozenings for a time when people are close by to be impressed by them."

"Then I look forward to dancing with you at the masque tonight. A guard's been assigned to escort you. We shall play our roles within roles for the benefit of the court."

"Surely the entertainment has been canceled," she protested. "There was an explosion in the hall. A boy has died!"

"On the contrary. It is her grace's express wish that life go on as if nothing has happened. Anyway, the masque will take place in the banqueting house, not the dining hall."

"You cannot force me to go."

"Be wise, damask lady. Do not tempt me to force you into anything."

Chapter 7

"Close the chest, Maud," Kat said. "I do not need another change of clothes."

"But, my lady, the other ladies are dressed. The masque—"

"Shall go on quite nicely without my presence."

"That guard is still waiting outside the door."

"Let him wait until his feet take root and he grows branches."

She wondered just what Lord Robin would do when she didn't show herself. The man could hardly steal her from her chamber, she comforted herself. At least . . . she didn't think he would.

Thrusting her needle with unnecessary violence into the design of irises she was embroidering, Kat stabbed herself. "Ouch!"

She pushed the embroidery frame away before blood dropped onto material she could ill afford to stain. Grimalkin, who had been napping on the bed, raised her head curiously.

The frame teetered; Kat waved her hand in the air to relieve the pain; Grimalkin leapt for the needle, which flashed as it bobbed in the candle's light.

Instead of the twinkling prey at the end of its yellow thread, the claws caught her mistress's outflung hand. Kat swore roundly. Grimalkin darted under the bed. Maud exclaimed in dismay, catching the frame and setting it upright.

Normally, Kat would have laughed. She couldn't; she

was too heartsore. "That beast! She's too cooped up in the palace. Oh, Maud, we need some freedom."

The serving woman's lined face lengthened.

Biting her lip, Kat held out her scratched hand to be salved. "I am talking foolishly. And acting foolishly, too."

"Then you'll go to the masque." Finishing with Kat's wounds, Maud lifted a gown of green and gold from a chest. "You are lovely in this. It is your best—"

"Two decades out of date, cut down from one of my mother's and showing every year of its age," Kat interrupted. "I have no 'best,' not to compare with the other ladies. Besides, I do not go dancing."

"But you said—"

"I meant talk of freedom is foolish."

Kat adjusted the embroidery frame. Maud had been born into household service. It would be cruel to explain how it felt to be able to choose her own tasks, to run free through her own fields. Not for Maud the bittersweet joy of responsibilities that sometimes seemed too heavy for Kat to bear alone.

"Why cannot Priorly clothe you in better stuffs? It is not as if you were purse-pinched—"

"Maud!"

She tossed her gray head. "I beg pardon, my lady, I am sure. The new kirtle will be very fine when it is done."

"Aye." The blue satin had been the last piece on the bolt a merchant had been showing grander ladies, and after some shrewd bargaining Kat had bought it for relatively little. Still . . . She sighed. "It was an extravagance. You know I put as much of the profits as I can back into the estate."

"That is like you. You lavish your money on others and skimp yourself."

Kat protested, "That's not the case at all. Priorly is mine to care for. It keeps me, and I keep it. Besides, there are upwards of a hundred people who depend on the estate staying in good heart—you among them. Although something made Jack Miller so discontented he—I still cannot believe it."

"He was ever an unaccountable lad." Maud had exclaimed and blessed herself over the incident earlier. But after years as the Prestons' nurse and then as Kat's maid, her ties to her own nephew hadn't been that strong.

"Bad management would leave all of you to starve. I would hardly like to be guilty of that."

"So I said."

"Maud, I swear to you, I am no saint." Kat couldn't decide which was more irritating—Maud, who believed she could do no wrong, or Elizabeth, who claimed she did no right.

Or Lord Robin, whose steel-bright, steady gaze made her muscles turn to butter.

Tucking the unwanted gown back into the chest, her old nurse cast an earnest glance over her shoulder. "I pray you—forgive me for speaking so plain—do not let your love for your lands and people blind you to other kinds of love."

"Of course not."

"There are men at court besides that horrible Lord Robin Hawking. Proper men who would brave the queen and take you to wife. Bairns might follow . . ."

The unaccustomed softness in the older woman's voice made Kat wrap her arms around her own narrow waist.

"I have never known. Did you have children, Maud, when you were young? You never speak of such things."

"Did have. Only the one. Taken by a flux when he was scarce two year. Never a husband, though."

"Oh, Maud."

"Old griefs, my lady. The worst of the hurt is over and done with many years past. But—a woman does not forget the fluttering of a babe under her heart. She remembers the weight of him in her arms, and the first time another creature calls her 'Mam.' Do not cheat yourself out of the good things women can have in this life. There are few enough of them."

A babe under her heart. Kat hugged herself tighter. "You of all people know why—"

The door swung inward without a knock. "A gift from the queen," said the liveried man standing just outside. The guard who'd been there since Hawking had thrust her into the chamber peered around the door frame in curiosity.

"A what?" asked Kat and Maud, almost together.

"A gown from her grace's own collection, for Lady Katherine Preston to keep. Also a mask."

Accepting the treasures reverently, Maud shut the door in the man's face with her heel and turned to Kat. "I think you will be attending the masque, my lady."

Kat didn't need to be told. Elizabeth's action was the equivalent of a royal command.

Astonished, she said, "She never gives gifts unless it is New Year's. Not to someone unimportant like me. A remembrance to a great lord who hosts her while she is on progress, or a portrait of herself to a foreign prince, aye. But this—are those rubies?"

"Garnets," replied Maud after a squint-eyed inspection. "But they are plentiful."

"They certainly are." The huge stones matched the overall color of the dress. They were sewn to large puffs of pink undergarment designed to poke up through slits in the overdress. The garnets resembled clots of blood. It was quite the ugliest gown Kat had ever seen.

"It is a newer cut than your other things," offered Maud as soon as Kat had been tied and hooked into it.

"But not a prettier." Kat tried to flatten one of the raised puffs with her hand. It resisted her effort. "These huge sleeves and the way the skirt sits so far down on my hips . . . I feel like a wooden doll. And this veil on wires. What do I do if it slips or twists or—heavens, how will I be able to tell what the wretched thing is doing? I cannot screw my head the other way round to see it."

"All will be well," Maud said soothingly. "Many ladies wear them without mishap. Indeed, you are very fashionable."

"The shade leeches all the red out of my hair."

"It is called sops in wine, I think, my lady."

"Whatever 'tis called, it is horrid." Wrinkling her nose, Kat added, "There. My vanity is revealed. I'll wager the dress became Elizabeth just as vilely, and she gave it to me for the joy of seeing me vanquished by this dreadful color."

Maud handed her the mask and shooed her out. Halfway over the threshold, a thought struck Kat. Servants swarmed through the palace like bees. Robin had said she would be watched. But would he think to put Maud under observation, too?

With the uneasy feeling she was trying to match wits with someone infinitely more cunning than she was, she leaned away from the guard and whispered, "Are there any likely lads from Northamptonshire way among the servants here?"

"Surely, my lady, a mort of them," Maud answered under her breath.

"Do any have leave soon to go home?"

"Well—well, I believe there's a Will who serves the master of archery whose mother will be lying in again soon. He has leave to go in the next few days."

"Find out if he will carry a letter to Priorly for me. I must get a message to Pettigrew the steward."

"As you wish, my lady. But the dance will be over before you get there unless you hurry. Oh, enjoy it, my lady!"

Trying to raise her own spirits, Kat stuck her tongue through the mouth hole in the mask.

The banqueting "house" was an enormous tent, brightly lit and filled with revelers.

Her quiet entrance attracted no attention. Dancers whirled. A cluster of musicians made loud and—on the whole—melodious music.

The chirping of birds, singing in their cages near the ceiling, drew her eyes upward. Poor little birds. Imprisoned and expected to be happy about it . . . She knew how they felt.

Nervously, she touched the veil winging out over her shoulders. She wondered if Robin had spotted her, was already watching her. Would his eyes be hot or cold? And what was wrong with her, to be thinking about Robin Hawking's eyes when poor Jack was dead, and Priorly was in danger?

She realized the hand-held mask had slipped to chin level. Raising it hastily, she peered through the holes.

Another dance tune struck up. Lines formed for a reel, while the revelers who weren't dancing receded into a sea of masks. It was odd to think that she knew these people, or at least most of them, and yet the masks made them all strangers.

Hawking shouldn't be hard to pick out of the crowd, though, she told herself. There weren't many men as tall and muscular as he was.

Several men towered over the rest of the gathering. None of them had hair as golden, curly, and thick as she feared to see. Broad shoulders filled a number of doublets; they weren't quite broad enough.

Relaxing, Kat let out a breath and played with the gilt handle of her mask. Perhaps Lord Robin wasn't here. She really didn't want to give him the satisfaction of seeing her obedience—even her unwilling obedience—to his order.

A masked man edged toward her. Then another. From behind her own face covering, Kat looked at them warily. A trickle and then a flood of gorgeously dressed men converged in her direction. There were so many of them, they crowded her into a flowering tree. It leaned.

"Do you not dance?"

"Damsel, has no one claimed you? Let me be the first!"

"Pay them no heed. I pray you, dance with me."

Unable to fathom the reason for their interest, Kat peeked over her mask. "Gentlemen, what are you doing? Have you mistaken me for some other lady?"

There was a blank silence.

"You are not the queen," one of them said accusingly.

"Of course not," she answered.

She stood dumbfounded as the lot of them turned with the precision of soldiers performing a military maneuver and marched away.

"I would have sworn it was the queen."

"What lady was that, anyway?"

"Nobody. Hawking's skinny whore. Have you not heard the jests . . ."

Across the tent, the crowd thinned for a moment. A tall, red-wigged woman stared straight at Kat through slits in an elaborate mask. Candlelight wavered; the mask seemed to smile smugly.

A man stepped up to Kat, cutting off her view of the queen. "A beautiful woman should not be all alone," he boomed from behind a blank cherub's face. He set the dislodged tree upright and meticulously smoothed its leaves.

Not Robin. This one was shorter and wider.

However, lurking somewhere must be her nemesis. That was how she'd come to think of Hawking—as an unwanted destiny pursuing while she retreated. Eventually he'd seek her out and persecute her. He'd made that plain.

But—only if he could penetrate her disguise.

She laughed aloud suddenly. Her mask made the chuckle deep and throaty. The queen's sumptuous gown had already fooled a number of gentlemen. Perhaps that was why it had been given to her. Elizabeth's sense of humor must be tickled by the sight of gallants tripping over their feet to abandon insignificant Kat Preston once they discovered their error. The malicious joke didn't matter. Her changed appearance would hide her from the agent of the crown, too.

In the meantime, she could use a temporary swain. Her new admirer's broad inches formed a helpful screen between her and the crowd.

Hurt pride reinforced the decision. She had her share of feminine instincts. Elizabeth would see that Kat Preston could hold a man, at least for the length of a dance.

Kat kept her voice low and teasing. "Sir, I fear you flatter me. Do you practice magical arts? How can you divine whether I am beautiful or not?"

"Ah, to hear the answer you'll have to dance with me, fair lady."

The gallantry was ponderous but correct. That made a pleasant difference from Lord Robin, too.

"You honor me, sir." She curtsied and placed her palm over the back of his dark-haired hand.

Something curdled inside Kat at the touch. She slowed, looking at him intently.

"Do not delay," he instructed her. "We do not want to miss our chance to join the end of the reel."

They took their places in the dance. Two long lines of dancers stretched ahead of them, each couple waiting for a turn to scamper down the middle of the set. The lively music kept feet stepping and bodies swaying.

Kat said hollowly, "Francis."

"You have guessed already! You were ever a clever puss, Katherine. But I had the advantage of you. I saw you lower your mask for a moment."

Kat bit her lip. Francis never failed to irritate her. She couldn't control her shivery dislike of him, and that always made her ashamed of herself. His strong likeness to his father was the problem—Kat had vivid memories of the late Sir Henry Toth, all of them bad. Overbearing Sir Henry and her gentle father had been friends; she'd never understood why.

"Why do you always speak to me as if I were a child?" she asked crossly.

"Have I lacked in respect? I think not. I have waited and waited, far more patiently than most men, I will tell you, for you to make up your mind about my proposal. I want you to wife, Katherine."

She sighed, the breath sounding like rushing waves within the mask. At least he didn't seem to have heard about Jack, or he would be lecturing her about coddling ungrateful tenants.

"My answer is *no.*"

"You cannot mean that."

"I have told you before, Francis. You do not really want me. It is my broad acres and flourishing herds you desire. And you are grave and forebearing with me, just as a man is with children when he has never learned how to talk with them very well. Your—" The muscles in her throat worked. "Your father was like that, too."

"Most of the time," said Francis, with a rare, real glint of humor.

"Most of the time," agreed Kat quietly.

"Well, women are children." The reasonable tone grated on her. "God has created them to be—"

"Lectured by men. Led by men." She sought a vulgarity to shock him. Lord Robin's was the only one she could think of. "*Tupped* by men."

"Kat! Barnyard talk is not fit for the court! Besides, it is right for a woman to be . . . biddable."

"I am not biddable, Francis. And I will not marry you."

"Our estates—"

"Share common boundaries. It would be a suitable

match if mating property lines and stock were the only considerations."

It was their turn to skip down the set. They reached the other end and Kat drew a grateful breath. The Roger de Manderley reel was a vigorous dance; the red dress, weighted with gemstones, was very heavy.

With an earnest attempt at playfulness that was awful to hear, Francis said, "We could improve the bloodlines of our families as well those of the stock, my dear. Toth blood is old and rich. It would marry well with the youthful vigor of the Prestons."

"The Preston line hardly has a reputation of vigor. I am the—no one has heard of anyone else from my branch for years."

"That's right."

Satisfaction. It rang so clear she couldn't mistake it. Of course—if Kat was the only surviving Preston, there could be no male relatives whose claim to Priorly superceded hers.

"I am astonished to hear you take so much pleasure in my kinless state," she said sharply, "since the accident that stole my brothers also killed Sir Henry."

Charles. James. Sir Henry. All gone in one tragedy-filled night.

"Marriage would supply you with a new family," said Francis archly. "The Toths always breed sons. A man wants sons."

She clenched her jaw. "I am never going to marry. I do not wish to put my fate in anyone's keeping. If you were the last bachelor in Northamptonshire, I would not be tempted."

"We shall see."

The man was oblivious. Conveniently failing to catch his hand, Kat fled down the reel.

Lord Robin leaned against one of the wooden columns which held up the ceiling. Edgy anticipation kept his senses sharp. The edginess was because of the banqueting house; he didn't like the overgrown tent or the number of candles that had been lit for the entertainment. The canvas walls could go up in seconds, roasting all the dancers alive. Anticipation bubbled like wine in his veins because one of the revelers ought to be Katherine Preston.

His mask hung from his fingers. He didn't care who recognized him. In a sense he was working tonight. And this was one situation in which it was a benefit to be known as himself.

As the spiced wine sank in the punch bowls, others began to show a similar indifference. *Perfectly and imperviously indifferent to you*—Kat's phrase had lodged in his head and repeated itself now and then. It fit the beat of the music.

Robin pushed the thought of Kat's barbed tongue to the back of his mind and studied the guests who were tucking their masks in their belts or laying them down.

The Earl of Aftondale had dropped his carelessly on the floor. There was a man who proved age was no barrier to lechery. Surface decorum was required at any function graced by the queen's presence, but Robin noticed the old man slyly pinching passersby. Aftondale favored both young women and young men equally. He wasn't really that ancient, Robin recalled vaguely. The lines of evil that crisscrossed the earl's face made him look older than his years.

Margaret Treland extended her mask to arm's length in order to take a hefty pull at a glass of wine. Drink didn't appear to be cheering her. Her mouth was pursed and her eyes flew from person to person, without seeming to find what she hoped for. As Robin watched, her expression lightened. She made her way toward a foppish gentleman Robin had no trouble identifying as the French ambassador.

Since Robin had not yet been dismissed from the queen's service, the sight of anyone seeking out an emissary from an unfriendly country interested him. In fact, Lady Margaret's fondness for French company was well-known. Robin let his eyes slide past those of another gentleman. That man slipped into the wake left in the crowd by the large Lady Margaret. Several agents had been working for months to discover what la Treland and the frogs were discussing together.

Tonight Robin's main interest was Kat. He grimaced

slightly, aware that his desire to see her was not entirely professional.

His gaze lingered on a tall, slender woman partnered with a man whose barrel waist was made even larger by padding.

At first he thought she might be Elizabeth, then he dismissed the idea. The queen wouldn't be dancing with such an obvious rustic. There were other telltale signs. In contrast to her dress, which was the extreme of an ugly fashion, this woman wore her hair simply. Her ears and neck were bare of jewelry. And from her graceful, easy movements, she was also young.

Yet it couldn't be Kat. The hair was wrong, a dull brown.

After his first mistake, the queen was easy to spot. None of the other women boasted jewels as big as the opals creating rainbows on Elizabeth's gown—though the garnet-lady's gems were nearly as gaudy. But despite the mask she was holding over her face, Elizabeth Tudor had not dressed to be mistaken for a lesser lady, at least not for longer than a minute. Her mask was more fantastical than any of the others, and it glowed with opals, too. She'd been dancing. The exercise had reduced her wig to a rubble of stiff curls. Her loud, defiant laugh was the final proof.

Admiration for the magnificent bitch warmed Robin. Two assassination plots in a fortnight, and Elizabeth Tudor was showing the world that England's queen had the courage and stamina to dance until her partners dropped.

"Ah, Hawking."

He shouldn't have let himself become distracted. "Aftondale."

"Now that you are at court, we must find time together for a good carouse. Somehow we never have, have we? And yet our tastes . . . so similar."

"Do they still bait bears in Paris Garden?" Robin had no intention of going anywhere with the earl, and despised bear-baiting, but it was the most innocuous brutality he could think of to suggest. The man wasn't worth the effort to snub.

"Poor sport. There are new whores in Bridewell House

of Correction, and a sergeant with a fine eye for judging how many lashes they can take and ply their trade afterward." Aftondale leaned forward. Robin had to stop himself from sliding around the pillar to get away from such uncleanliness. "A shilling or two will buy the opportunity to handle the whip yourself."

An addictive pleasure, apparently—at least to Aftondale. The earl was becoming visibly excited.

"God's grace," Robin muttered.

"You must visit my little encampment."

Glad for another topic, he said, "You are staying outside the palace? Was the chamberlain unable to find room for you?" He didn't care one way or the other.

"When I am called to take part in the hurly-burly surrounding the queen, I always set up a spot where private pleasures can remain private. You need not fear we would be watched. My people are expert at finding out-of-the-way places that are still near court."

A flash of red caught Robin's eye. The garnet-lady had erupted into full flight. Robin watched her overlarge partner lumber after her.

He grinned. Despite his previous conclusion, that girl was definitely Kat. In their short acquaintance, he'd had ample opportunity to observe how she moved when she was trying to avoid a hopeful lover: at a determined run.

"Excuse me, Aftondale." He scarcely knew what he was saying. "I am finding miscellaneous pleasures pale these days, next to the many responses to be wrung from one special woman."

Robin turned away from Aftondale to walk swiftly after Kat.

Clear of the dancers, she lowered her mask and used the hand holding it to lift her skirt. Preparatory to another bolt, Robin thought. Her exposed face turned from side to side in a hunted gesture. Three quick strides brought him to her side.

Her mask slipped to the floor from nerveless fingers.

He clamped an unobtrusive fist around her hand before he bent to retrieve the pretty thing. It had the style of a face on an ancient statue.

Robin twirled it lazily before he gave it back to her. "Lady—Artemis, is it? A cool Greek goddess."

She thrust the mask up between them like a wall. "I suppose so."

"Most appropriate. But it is a shame to cover up so much beauty. Even with more beauty."

"Oh, take your false compliments and—and swallow them!" She brought the mask down so she could glare at him. "I look like a hag from hell in this repulsive gown. It is too much like blood for my taste." Her voice faltered.

"The red does compete a mite fiercely with your hair," he said carelessly. "If you must have red, try flame-color. Better yet, green or blue or copper or wheat. Or cloth of gold. But not—" He almost said 'blood' again to see if she would mention Jack Miller, and then found himself substituting, "—garnet." Without changing inflection, he added, "Here comes your other admirer."

He could have sworn his tone wouldn't have told the most expert judge anything about his attitude—toward Kat or the heavy man. But she shot him a quick glance. "No fighting!"

"Of course not," he agreed, and put out an arm that caught the country gentleman amidships, knocking the breath out of the man with an audible "Oof!"

Apologizing profusely, Robin helped steady the gentleman. Then he flexed his arm surreptitiously. The fellow was built like an ox composed solely of muscle.

Next time Robin wouldn't try to deliver a blow disguised as a helping gesture. He'd just put out a foot and let the ox trip.

"Lord Robin, may I present to your notice Sir Francis Toth, who is my near neighbor? Lord Robin Hawking, Francis."

Kat called this beer barrel by his first name? She called Robin a whoreson bastard.

Francis bowed. "Sir."

"Sir." Robin inclined his head so briefly it was an insult.

"The dance was not over," said Francis to Kat, as if admonishing a child. "It was very rude to forget what you were doing and run off. These antics make a bad impression."

"Aye, Francis. You are right, of course." She turned to Robin. "Sir Francis Toth is my *neighbor.*"

Her insistence on the point jolted him into remembering Fotheringhay. Reluctantly, he decided he had more pressing duties than the absolute imperative to uncover Toth's nose and squash it. "Ah. Newly come to Whitehall?"

"Today. I am housed at one of the London inns. Westminster is a long walk, so I had to bustle to be ready to take my part in this marvelous entertainment." Mellowing at Robin's sudden cordiality, Francis gave the padded doublet that extended his already-large waist an affectionate pat.

Coxcomb, thought Robin. *Bumpkin.*

Francis went on, "Since Katherine forgot to write me that she had recently visited her home—"

Kat rolled her eyes.

"—I stopped by Priorly to make sure the servants felt the weight of a master's eye."

"Francis! By what right—"

It was Robin's turn to signal Kat, which he did by pulling her a few inches to one side while several ladies and gentlemen wound by them.

She shook off his hand. "All my people have been with the family since before my birth. They have never given me the least reason to distrust them. Most are dear friends. I will not have you upsetting them with your prying, criticizing ways. Especially now!"

"This is precisely the time to get them accustomed to a man's firm hand, Katherine," responded Francis with fatherly reproof. "Before all goes to rack and ruin with no one from the family in residence. When we are wed—"

Kat's knuckles whitened around the stick of her mask.

"Let me show you the foreign flowers over there, *Lady* Kat," suggested Robin.

"Did you know that just two days ago, ghosts were seen haunting your property?" Francis called after them as, with a smooth, twisting motion, Robin put a dozen people between them and the irritating Sir Francis.

"I thought it best not to let you start a brawl," he explained, taking the mask out of her hand. "It would be a pity to break this toy over his head, though I sympathize with the temptation."

"That ass Francis, saying I am going to marry him," exclaimed Kat indignantly. "And ghosts! The house is less than thirty years old! There has never been so much as a whiff of sulphur about the place."

"Which makes a rumor about ghosts all the more intriguing."

Robin felt indulgent. She'd said *that ass Francis* and not *my betrothed, Francis.*

"You mean . . ." She traced the edge of a gold-spangled flower woven into the ivy climbing the walls. Robin watched her finger and felt a tingling along his own skin. "Someone wants to frighten people away with stories of things that are not there?"

"Or explain away things that *are* there and should not be."

Her tongue came out and licked her lips as she absorbed the implications. "Oh, God." She faced him with resolution. "When do your creatures go to spy out what they can?"

"They are well on their way. What did you expect after this morning?"

He spoke absently. Her mouth had gone soft with worry. The dip in the middle of her upper lip was delicately chiseled, the lower lip full and vulnerable.

She drew a breath. "Do not."

"Do not what?"

"Stare at me so."

Robin decided to risk honesty. It was safe enough; this prickly female would suspect his motives, anyway. "I cannot help looking at you."

"I am afraid of your eyes," she whispered. "They are going to eat me up."

He would like that. He would like to . . . eat her . . . right up.

His knuckles ran down the length of her throat. "I was wrong about this color. Your skin is like milk next to it, and it puts little flames in your eyes."

"Stop. Just stop."

Her *stop* wasn't the oblique invitation it would have been from a flirt or bought woman. She meant it.

He pulled his hand back and inspected his nails. "You are right, lady. The scheme is for me to pursue and you to show reluctance. I thank you for the timely reminder."

"I have no need to pretend reluctance. I *am* reluctant."

The muscles around his smile felt tight. "Hate is a good start."

"If it please you, my lord—and even if it does not—I shall carry out my part in your brilliant plan by seeking company elsewhere. Have no fear. I have no gunpowder or ballistas concealed in my skirt."

He wasn't ready to let her go. "A few cold glances from across the room will not serve nearly as well as the sight of you shrinking from my hideous advances. After all, while the ladies and gentlemen are laughing at me for pressing myself on a statue of a woman, they will not be wondering at my choice."

Kat blazed, "You go too far! I may have to accept slights from the queen, but I do not have to take them from you. What are you, anyway? An animal. Your true nature is to do your thinking the length of your leg from the floor!"

"Lady, if my animal nature really extended the length of my leg, you can be sure my services as a lover would be more in demand. Are you so Puritan in your opinions?"

"Nay!"

The answer was entirely too quick and emphatic.

"Religion is politics," he said softly. "Dangerous politics. What do you hide?"

"Nothing."

"You lie badly," he advised her. "Dance with me. Among the others your guilty looks will pass for terror of the devil Robin Hawking."

He swung her into the throng before she had time to protest. The musicians had switched from the reel to an energetic volta.

Thrusting their masks into his belt to free his hands, Robin grabbed Kat around the waist and lifted her high into the air. Her fingers buried themselves in his shoulders for balance; he kept her dangling long seconds after all the other ladies had been returned to the floor.

It would have been easy to keep her suspended above him. She was light and alive in his arms. But the forceful music drove him on. Drums crashed, pipes and horns called. Dropping her lightly to her feet, Robin touched her hand, skipped with her—and lifted her again. He loved dancing. When they danced, people twirled and smiled and clasped hands—and forgot all the things they thought they knew about him.

The next choice was slower. After the last sedate step, Elizabeth shouted, "La volta!"

"Again?" asked Kat.

"It is her favorite. Remember, the court revolves around her, and woe betide the courtier or lady who forgets it."

"You mean we dance to her tune or we do not dance at all." Kat's shoulders curved downward. "I'll go to bed now."

"In your nest of virgins?" murmured Robin. "I think not."

The music began again. He held her close as they danced. Lifting her was a completely pleasurable experience. He enjoyed the stretch and pull of muscle in his shoulders, the solid brace of his buttocks and legs. Yet she was so slender that handling her slight weight made him feel powerful. Her gown revealed nothing of her breasts, but knowing they were inches from his lips created such an erotic pull he almost tried to bite her through the material.

Her lips had reddened from frequent nervous licking, and her eyes had grown wide and stayed wide. The tiny flames in the dark irises flickered when the music ended.

"No more," she said. "I am—hot."

Though he knew she didn't mean it the way it sounded, Robin laughed. "Yes, lady. So am I." His fingers flexed around her waist. "Very hot."

Kat twitched away from him. "If you want me to stay you must talk like a sensible man."

He navigated her to a quiet corner. "I can but try." Even to his own ears, his ironic tone barely covered the hoarseness of desire. From her dubious look, it was failing to convince Kat he was harmless. More lightly, he said, "What shall we discuss?"

"You pursue, but you give me no chances to retreat."

"No matter. A glimpse of your face will convince onlookers you wish me in hell."

"I do not! How can you believe I wish damnation on anyone?" Her long fingers, perhaps not quite as pale as those of the highest-born dames, picked at a garnet the size of his thumbnail. Garnets were not rubies, but the wealth of them plastered to her dress could not have come cheap. The Preston purse must be fuller than he'd thought. "Even you may go to heaven with my goodwill."

"Many thanks, kind lady. I think I'll delay the happy day as long as possible."

"Do not be so flippant."

Robin shrugged, pretending boredom. He'd barely escaped death too many times to enjoy thinking about it. Life was a thin, shining thread, easily broken.

His bored air apparently convinced her. "You do not care whether you live or die, do you?" she asked.

He looked down at her. "You ask too many questions, Lady Kat. Curiosity is not the healthiest quality a young woman in your circumstances could possess."

"Does it not seem possible to you," she said, suddenly serious for no reason Robin could think of, "that we are all intended to reach peace? That it might not matter what we believe as long as we are sincere?"

"God's grace, woman!" He put his face close to hers to keep his intense tone from carrying. "Remember where you are. Confine your unorthodox views to yourself. Or else you shall have reformers and papists both breathing down your neck with instruments of torture."

The point of her chin jutted at a stubborn angle.

Almost snarling, he ordered, "Promise me!"

"What difference can my beliefs make to you?"

He was taken aback, though he didn't show it. "None at all, lady. But if you are taken up for heresy, my hopes for a quiet investigation are blasted into pieces. The noise of a trial interrupting my work would not suit me. I am a peaceable man."

She made a ladylike little sound, half choke and half snort.

"You are unusual, though," he continued with reluctant admiration. "Taking neither side in the battle for minds and souls."

"Why must everything be a battle?"

"Because it is." He wanted to get her away from unsafe topics. Providentially, when he was with her there was always another subject to be explored. "I am glad you are not Puritan. They train their women to be uninteresting lovers."

She started as if he'd flicked her with a whip. Passion was a whip, he thought—though not in the way that pathetic satyr Aftondale imagined it to be. It was a growing, aching, damnable, pleasurable force driving Robin toward this one woman.

My God, he wondered, what is happening to me?

Chapter 8

"**B**ut then, you have had no training in love at all, have you?" he went on despite himself. "My wide-eyed little virgin. Do not look so worried. Innocence has its own enchantment."

He shifted so only his blank back would show to anyone who might catch sight of them in their corner. He cupped her chin. Her jaw trembled inside his hands.

"This is mad," she said. "*You* are mad."

"Yes."

He bit her bottom lip, very gently.

Her eyelids stayed open as he nibbled at her and played his tongue over her lips. He knew she didn't close her eyes because his were open, too; he wanted to see her face. Robin wasn't sure what he was expecting—a latent hunger she would try to deny, perhaps. Anguish. Disgust or fear. Something. A clue to what she felt when he kissed her.

Instead, she showed . . . nothing. Her mouth was soft under the deliberately seductive assault of his lips—but it didn't answer him with any of the passion he could swear was bottled up inside her slender frame. She didn't move even when he ran a palm down her throat and inside the opening of her V-shaped ruff. Other than the fast knocking of her heart, which he registered with the heel of his hand, she seemed cool and unaffected.

"No heat, either to pull me closer or push me away," he said in puzzlement. "No response, favorable or unfavorable. Am I so unimportant to you, lady?"

When she didn't reply, he stood back and let his hands drop to his sides.

"There are fires in you. What I have not yet discovered is whether they burn for me, for another or for some unreal dream of a man you'll probably never meet." Telling himself it was only to see how she would react, he added, "In the end, it will not matter which. I will find your fires, maiden. And blow them into life."

She moved at last. A tremor took her by the shoulders and shook her all the way to her feet. Robin could see it. He couldn't tell if the long shudder was a shiver of delight or horror.

Turning to watch the dancers, he felt himself slip into a brooding mood. Some of those laughing, twisting, carefree people were traitors, almost certainly. Every court had its Judases. Treason was like a dance. Patterns within patterns emerged, melded, came to life in other, perhaps deadlier forms. If Kat was part of one of those patterns . . .

Her crimson-gowned form slipped around him. Taking advantage of his momentary inattention, she brushed by Robin and disappeared into the crowd without a backward glance. Only her elusive country scent lingered.

Another, stronger perfume wafted over him. Without moving a muscle, Robin braced himself. Elizabeth was often a walking cloud of ambergris.

"Well, our rat catcher," she said, fanning herself with her mask. "We see you have been hard at work."

He decided it was safer not to answer.

"You may partner us for the next dance."

Expressing himself delighted, he led her onto the floor. She leaned forward to whisper harshly into his ear. "Just do not let yourself forget. That child had better remain a virgin. You have visited many prison cells. We assume you do not wish to inhabit one permanently."

It had been another long, hard day. The music struck up, and Robin moved mechanically in the gestures required by the dance, too tired suddenly to block out a yearning to be somewhere else. Anywhere else. A quiet and clean place, warm with uncomplicated welcome. Someplace, and with someone, that smelled of . . .

Gillyflowers.

* * *

The masque didn't end until Elizabeth strode off to bed. By then it was very late. Outside, clouds covered the stars.

Francis was openly yawning as he left Whitehall on foot, and gave no sign of noticing the dark-cloaked shadow that trailed him across two miles of country road from Westminster to London. The capitol city had outgrown its gates. Through the mucky, ill-lit streets of the suburbs, into an inn and up the stairs, the shadow followed patiently and noiselessly. Robin needed to see where Francis was sleeping.

He heard a noise, and flattened himself against the side of a large wooden cupboard that cluttered a passage. A man wearing the apron of a landlord trudged past without sensing him.

"Sir?" the landlord said to Francis, who turned in the doorway to his room. "There is another gentleman downstairs searching for lodging. All my rooms are rented. Would you be willing—"

Indignantly and at great length, Francis refused to share his mattress.

That pleased Robin very much. There'd be only one sleep-befuddled man to handle.

Francis slammed the door in the landlord's face, and the innkeeper plodded back down the stairs. Waiting until the inn fell quiet, Robin glided down to the common room, and stretched out on a bench. He might as well get what rest he could.

The bench was hard enough that he didn't have to worry about oversleeping. It seemed to him that his eyes blinked open every few minutes, and finally a darkness only slightly less black than true night insinuated misty fingers through the shutters. False dawn. Real dawn wouldn't even be a chalk mark drawn across the tops of the trees outside.

He rolled to his feet, and eased himself into the stairwell that led up to Francis's room.

It was dark and close. Herbs had been strewn about to sweeten the place. Robin tried not to breathe deeply, wishing to maintain absolute silence. God knew, he couldn't afford to sneeze. Carefully, he took the stairs two at a time; the even-numbered ones tended to creak.

Upstairs the aroma from chamber pots was barely detectable. One of the better inns, he judged. Francis must like value for money and hold himself very high. Only the best for Sir Francis Toth.

A useful item to consider.

Francis's door opened soundlessly under his hand. He was pleased. Cocking his head, he listened. A snore rattled in the silence.

A lighted rush glimmered, showing a bed with all the curtains drawn. Robin tweaked one of them back.

"So, sir, are you afraid of the cold or the light?" he asked pleasantly.

Francis snorted, sitting up.

"I myself never sleep with the curtains pulled to. It permits rascally characters to sneak up on an honest gentleman." He thought of Kat hiding in his bed curtains and smiled.

"Who—? Lord Robin? By my soul, what are you doing here? An outrage—"

"You remember me. I am flattered, sir. Do you know what I am, then? And more to the point, I think, who employs me?"

"There were plenty of people to tell me after you—by gad, after you *stole* Katherine Preston from me at Whitehall," said Francis, breathing hard. "You are nothing but an ordinary thief-taker."

"Rat catcher," Robin corrected. "They call me the rat catcher. An unsavory but necessary occupation. Since you have not replied to my question, I'll answer it for you. I eliminate rats for her majesty the queen."

"What do you here?" Francis repeated, pulling blankets up to his chin like an elderly spinster protecting withered dugs from a critical gaze.

"What am I doing? Why, the queen's business, of course."

Robin busied himself lighting candles. The other man could chew on the implications of that for a while. It wouldn't hurt to let him sweat a little . . . Kat had covered herself, too. If Robin ever got her into a bed again, he'd take care she felt no reason to hide. He'd teach all that passion in her to blaze out ... Realizing he was staring into the clear amber heart of a flame as if it held a clue to Kat's hold on him, he blinked himself free of self-destructive fantasies. Then he glanced over his shoulder. Francis was literally shrinking into a bed post.

"Surely," Robin said silkily, "a loyal subject can have no objection to a few questions. Especially when the answers will benefit the realm."

Francis's gulp was audible. "What do you want to know?"

"Tell me about ... ghosts at Priorly."

"You wake a man in the middle of the night—"

"Tell me."

Francis cleared his throat. "There were hauntings years ago," he said. "At the time so many Prestons met their deaths. The night of her parents' funeral it started, when my own father lay over in the house. Lights appearing and disappearing, strange thuds and odd cries, doors yawning open that had been faithfully locked."

Great houses often attracted bodiless pests which clung to them over the years like barnacles to a ship's hull. But Kat had claimed Priorly was neither old nor especially grand, and that it didn't suffer from ghostly visitors.

Emotionlessly, Robin asked, "What did your father say to all these portents?"

"Nothing." Face lax and more puddinglike than ever, Francis dropped the blanket, revealing his shirt. "He died the same night. So did Katherine's brothers."

"Really." The way Robin said it wasn't a question.

"My father was staying at Priorly to comfort the Preston children—it was directly after their parents were laid to rest. They—my father and Kat's brothers—went out fishing before dawn. My father was ever a kindly man. He must have wanted to distract them from their grief. There was an accident and all were lost."

"And then?"

"Katherine inherited her property, as I did mine."

Inwardly, Robin cursed the fellow's literalness. "What happened to the ghosts, man?"

"To the—odds bodkins, they went away. At least, I never heard tell of them again until now."

"And now they are back."

"A legion of them. Just over the last week. In the house, in the woods—my people cannot be bribed onto Priorly ground. The Preston servants pull their covers over their heads the instant the sun goes down, and refuse to come out until cock's crow."

"Have you seen anything, or heard dead voices calling?"

"I?" Francis's eyes bulged. "I am a sensible, God-fearing man. When ghosts walk, I stay at home. We have no such irregularities at Thorndon."

Robin decided Toth knew nothing. The man's stupidity was transparent. Unless he was playing a deep game, something to do with Mary Stuart ... but if the man was clever enough to mimic stolid fatheadedness to such perfection, there would be nothing more Robin could pry from him tonight.

If, however, Francis was what he appeared to be—an English landowner of the worthy and hopelessly dull variety—then Robin could accomplish one more piece of business. Not for the queen but for himself.

"My congratulations," said Robin, studying his nails, "on maintaining such a regular household. A pity Lady Kat cannot say the same. You have heard about the gunpowder in the dining hall today?"

"An outrage to our gracious queen—"

"The boy who lit the barrel was one Jack Miller. From Priorly."

Francis said weakly, "Katherine does her best. It is as I said. A firmer hand is needful. She is not a man, of course."

"Indeed, she's not. You have excellent taste in women, Sir Francis, if Kat's an example of what stirs your blood. She's not going to have you, you know."

"I know no such thing! There is a longstanding arrangement—"

"Ah, but what you have understood and what the lady understands may be two different things. Odd creatures, women. Impossible to tell just who might take their fancy." Robin grinned with calculated insolence.

Blankly, Francis said, "You are telling me that *you* have taken her fancy? That she'll not have me because she has already had—*you?*"

"Tsk, my dear sir." Enjoying himself, Robin placed his hand over his heart. "I would never stain a lady's fair name by boasting of—intimacies. A gentleman keeps such dealings private. That's how they are most rewarding. Private. Secret and exciting in the dark. Two bodies that writhe and thrust at each other, a woman who is willing to do anything ..."

"Katherine is not like that," objected Francis. Sweat had popped out along the hem of his nightcap where it dipped over his forehead.

No, Robin thought, Kat wasn't like that. But she could be. He was certain of it.

"You have never found her so?" he asked, scratching his neck.

Despite his well-honed skepticism, he was convinced that anyone who believed she was a light-skirt had to be a fool. He drew a mental line through Francis on his list of potential traitors.

Now that his own dislike was declining into genial contempt, Francis seemed to have discovered an active distaste for him. "Since you have completed your errand, my lord," he said with as much dignity as a man in a nightcap could achieve, "I would be obliged if you would go."

"Rest you easy, Sir Francis," said Robin, smiling. "I have finished the business that brought me here."

A mocking groan went up from a small group at the edge of the bowling green. Kat watched as her ball veered to one side of the pins and rolled weakly to a stop by a pair of Spanish cordwain leather boots.

Robin bent and picked up the ball. "If you will allow me to be your deputy, my lady." He sent it crashing into the pins, all of which obligingly fell down.

"I am very bad at bowls," she told him defensively. "The ball would not have landed at your feet had I aimed it there, I assure you."

"Ah, but what was distracting your thoughts, Lady Katherine?" asked a courtier, nudging the fellow next to him.

"The sky," she replied coldly. "It looks like rain, and I do not own so many gowns I can risk ruining this one. I pray you, excuse me while I escape the weather." Giving the group a general curtsy, she moved swiftly away.

Lord Robin matched his steps to hers. Kat gritted her teeth and tried to ignore him.

"That red thing you wore the night of the masque was not bought for a song," he remarked. "Unless you sing extraordinarily well."

She would *not* let anyone, even Robin Hawking, think she'd chosen that ugly dress. "It was made for the queen."

He whistled softly. "Elizabeth gave it to you? It had the look of something she would choose. In fact, for a minute I mistook you for her. A gift from her own wardrobe? You may consider yourself honored."

"Well, I did not want it," she said ungratefully. "And I could do without the worry of wondering why she would give me anything. Not without an ulterior motive, I would swear."

"Almost certainly not. It was a most striking—I have it! She wanted to keep an eye on you. On us. How better than to dress you in clothes she could not mistake? What you usually wear is not so conspicuous."

Kat had no intention of telling him the other reason Elizabeth might have had in making the gift. It would sound as if she were asking for pity. Poor Kat Preston, not worth the gentlemen's time ...

"You mean my clothes make a poor showing at court. Are you prying for information about my fortune, my lord?"

"Just trying to understand why that gown was so fine and your others are—"

"Not so fine." A wave of her slim, long-fingered hand indicated her plain brown skirt of linsey-woolsey.

"Just so," Robin agreed. The unusual meekness in his tone was belied by the glint in his eyes.

"I do not choose to beggar my estate to impress this lot of vain popinjays," she said flatly. "Once I am dismissed from court I will never set eyes on any of them again. Anyway, it would be folly to wear the price of a year's rents *and* the profit from the sheep *and* the cost of new roofs for the cottagers. That's what it would take to make a show here. Even then, I doubt I could compete unless I hung precious stones from every inch of my body, including my nose, as the dark people in Africa do. So why bother?"

Robin's strong features were alight with laughter and something else, something softer. "And are you content to be a crow among so many peacocks?"

"I know how to value the opinion of chattering fools who judge by looks instead of character!" she flashed. She would have loved, just once, to wear something pretty and be a peacock herself, and she had the uncomfortable feeling he could tell.

"Fortunate Lady Kat," he said, stopping near a gate and lifting her fingers to his lips. She snatched them back. He laughed again. "Surely you have no cause to despair. You have both looks and character. What you wear cannot hide what you are. And that is lovely."

"It is impossible to talk to you."

"Really? Yet so often people seem compelled to tell me all about themselves. Look at me. At me," he repeated brusquely, as Kat looked everywhere *but* at him. "The hopeful Sir Francis is sitting on a bench directly in front of us. Do you want me to protect you?"

Kat hoped the gratitude she felt wasn't reflected in her eyes. How did Robin know that sick distaste assaulted her when Francis was near? The feeling was quite different from the edginess Robin inspired. During the past few days, Hawking had stalked her with embarrassingly public persistence; being near him made her heart race, her breath tighten, her moods vary until the other ladies exchanged knowing glances.

It is not supposed to be Lord Robin, she told herself. *If you are actually going to commit the stupidity of lusting after a man, be a fool over someone else.*

"I hardly require protection from Francis. I have known him all my life," she said without conviction.

"I agree he's not much of a man. But remember, poppet,

boredom may not leave gaping wounds, yet still one may die of it." His silver-and-gold eyes narrowed. "Something besides his lamentable conversation worries you, though. What is it?"

"I cannot guess what you mean."

With sudden harshness, he said, "Lady, you should give up lying altogether. I shall always be able to tell when you try to squeak a falsehood by me." Like lightning, his anger flashed and then was gone. He pinched her chin. "You have very honest eyes. They speak the truth whether you will them to or not. Now what frightens you about that bag-pudding Sir Francis? You are not easily affrighted."

"Little do you know," Kat muttered. Lord Robin's bursts of kindness, and his touch, rattled her. "Francis is harmless—unless he decides to do something for someone else's own good. Then he's capable of wreaking all sorts of harm. With the best of intentions, of course. He values his own judgment over—over God's, I think."

"I am sure God and Sir Francis are generally in perfect agreement," he said, smiling again.

"Francis would tell you so, at any rate."

"Then why do you try to fold yourself so small when he's around? Your shoulders are hunched and your back is curved. Your chin is disappearing into your ruff."

The words came out in a rush. "In looks he's much like his father. Sir Henry. When I was a child, the old man terrified me. He was so big, and I so little. My own father was gentle, diffident almost. Sir Henry would visit and stick his nose into everything. He would find fault with everything, too—my mother's housekeeping, our manners, the food on the table. My father would listen to him and grow angry with us, and let Sir Henry carp and criticize in that—that *reasonable* way that made you want to hit him. And—and when Sir Henry would demand a kiss from me, Father always made me give him one."

"Francis sounds like his exact replica."

"No person is another's exact replica. As we both know." She sighed. "Francis is less bombastic and brutal than the old man. But—I cannot like him, that's all. I wish I could rid him of this delusion we are going to be married."

"Is that the whole list of your fears?"

Kat desperately wanted to change the subject. "I cannot forget Jack Miller," she said reluctantly, but truthfully. "Did his head have to go up over London Bridge?"

"That was not my decision," he told her almost gently.

"His poor family. I wish I could go home to make sure all is well with them. Or as well as things can be."

"Walsingham's talking about letting me go into Northamptonshire," Robin remarked. "Shall I take you with me?"

Their eyes met.

Kat looked away. Out of the corner of her vision, she saw Francis raise his head. His heavy face took on a rich color as he sighted them.

Robin grinned slightly. "Here is your chance to turn him down again. You may find him ready to listen to you now," he said, then bowed with all his impudent flourishes and walked away.

Kat sighed. Summoning up the best she could do in the way of a pleasant smile, she strolled over to Francis and dropped him a tiny curtsy. "Are you well today?"

He rose and gave her an even curter bow. "Well enough. And you?"

"Very well, I thank you."

Of course she was fine—except for the odd symptoms Lord Robin made her feel, and the familiar sinking sensation at having to speak to Francis. And worrying about the Millers and Priorly. And the stares and titters that followed her throughout the twenty-three acres of Whitehall Palace . . .

Kat decided on a frontal attack. "Francis, I am flattered—truly, I am—that you came to the palace today to see me. However, I could never be the kind of wife you deserve. I have tried to tell you so many times. You really must seek elsewhere for a bride."

When he wasn't driving her to screaming distraction Kat was almost—not *fond* of Francis—but resigned to him as an acquaintance. He was a familiar shape in her emotional landscape. Hoping Robin was right, and that she'd at last made an impression on his monumental self-satisfaction, she smiled guardedly.

He didn't smile back. "Do you not believe I could have affairs at court unrelated to you?"

"Why—why, of course you could. But since her majesty and her ministers and most of the clerks have gone to Windsor until tomorrow, I assumed . . . well. Lord Robin keeps telling me assumptions are foolish."

"And him you listen to," said Francis. "Yet you brush aside every piece of advice I have ever given you."

Heat burned in her cheeks. Robin was too much on her mind. She tried to guard against letting him into her thoughts, but the effort was self-defeating. Attempting *not* to think about him kept his image firmly fixed.

Air puffed out Francis's cheeks before he blew it through his lips. "You are blushing," he said glumly. "The mere mention of him can make you—ah, talking pays no toll. I withdraw my suit. I had intended to, anyway. Do you believe he will offer you honest marriage?"

"Nay. Nor would I ask it. I have told you and told you—"

He interrupted her. "In that, at least, you are wise. However nobly born they may be, rogues like Hawking are still rogues. Just—do not let him . . ."

"He's never hurt me," she said. It was true, she thought. Even the first time on his bed, Robin had never been able to hurt her.

Francis looked as if he'd bitten into a lemon. "You'll get nothing from that swashbuckler. Except tears. Mark my words."

"Then it is lucky I want nothing from him," she responded tartly. She sought a friendlier tone. After all, Francis would continue to be her neighbor. "How go your affairs, then? Have they met with success?"

"I have been appointed justice of the peace."

"That's good news. I am pleased for you." Kat was able to say it sincerely. With his taste for minor details and his tendency to regard everybody's business as his own, Francis would make an admirable justice. "Are there parts of the palace you have yet to see?" she asked, intending to hand him over to the keeper of the apartments, who frequently guided visitors around the buildings.

He began backing away, talking the whole time. "Katherine, as a Christian I will always think of you as a sister, albeit a wayward one. But you must acknowledge that it will do a new justice of the peace no good to consort with a notorious woman. I hope you have joy of Hawking, although I doubt it. His reputation is not that of an easy man. I know what you have done," he added heavily.

What you have done. She darted forward, catching his arm. "What do you mean?"

He glanced around furtively. "Really, Katherine. Control yourself. There are people nearby."

She shook the arm under her hand. "If you do not wish to be further contaminated by my presence, then explain what you mean. What is it you have—do you think you have discovered?"

Using his free hand, he batted at her fingers, catching them fully extended so pain shot up her arm. Off guard, Kat cried out and staggered back. She bumped into someone. Unfamiliar arms clasped her all too swiftly.

Francis's face crumpled. "The company you keep will ruin me. Stay away from me, do you hear?"

As quickly as dignity would allow, he hurried out the gate.

Kat tried to free herself from the person standing behind her. The horrible reputation she was earning would dog her when she went home. Francis would see to it. How many others would feel the way he did?

"Ah, Lady Katherine," said a husky voice in her ear. "You are well rid of that one. A bumptious fellow. Most unfortunate hat and hose. You do not wish to waste your time on such a person. What is he, a cowherd? Gamekeeper? Come, this happens most opportunely. It is long past time for us to further our acquaintanceship."

Turning inside the circling arms, she went sick with horror. Francis was bad, but this was worse. Lines from prayers tumbled about in her brain. "Lord Aftondale. Release me, please."

"You need not be shy," he told her with a puff of sour breath. "Robin Hawking has told me of your many unusual charms. You will find me most appreciative of your ... abilities."

She squirmed loose. "He spoke of me? To you?"

"In the most flattering terms. Tell me, my dear—" His whispering voice suggested obscenity after obscenity.

Her stomach turned over.

"Ordinarily, my lord," Kat said steadily, "I would pretend polite ignorance of your meaning. But since you choose to be frank, so shall I. I do not want to know you. Should I ever have the misfortune of seeing you even at a distance, I shall walk the other way. If you try to speak to me again, I'll scream for the guard. Do I make myself clear?"

"A woman of spirit. If you like, pretty chuck, we could make arrangements for Hawking to join us . . ."

Drawing back her arm, Kat clouted the earl across the face.

Chapter 9

Oars bit into the water. The clean strokes barely ruffled the surface of the Thames, which ran clear and calm away from the teeming shores of town.

A few swans had chosen to pilot the barge up the river. Kat could trace the outlines of their plump white bodies and the elegant curves of their necks through the distortion of glass portholes.

"'Did you ever in your life dream you would ride in a boat with real glass windows?" she asked idly.

"Never," Margaret answered with a lazy sigh.

"You need not join me in banishment, you know," Kat added. "It is kind of you, but if you would rather be in the other cabin with the great ladies and the queen—"

"God forfend. The fact I can get you all to myself is only one of the benefits to staying out here. We have scarcely seen each other in all the bustle of packing."

Kat smiled gratefully. Few people chose to be with her since the list of her social crimes had grown to include slapping the Earl of Aftondale. It both appalled and entertained her that the high-born of the court regarded her public reaction to his suggestions as more scandalous than any private depravity they imagined she'd committed with Robin Hawking.

The difference, she supposed, between mere vice and the horror of an indiscretion.

Only Margaret and Lord Robin took the risk of being seen with her now. Margaret's company she clung to, and Robin's she dealt with by refusing to speak to him at all.

In spite of her stubborn silence, he haunted her as doggedly as ever. He hadn't gone to Priorly or Fotheringhay after all.

"At least he could not climb aboard the queen's barge and hide among the rose petals strewn across the deck," she said aloud. "Otherwise I would expect him to pop out at any moment, grinning that detestable grin of his."

Margaret gave her a glance that in someone other than a friend Kat would have described as sly. "Mmmph. 'Tis a bad sign when there's but one 'he' to a woman, and she talks about him without even saying his name."

"Lord Robin," said Kat, enunciating clearly, "has the face and figure of a proper man. If I thought him handsome and—"

"Oh, even I admit he's handsome."

"But inside, he is . . . Do you know who told my lord of Aftondale that I was ripe for the hideous games he plays? Robin Hawking."

"I would not have believed him such a fool." Margaret frowned. "Are you sure?"

"Aftondale said so."

She made a noise like a very genteel horse. "Can you believe anything that old reprobate says?"

"I suppose not." Kat looked at Margaret curiously. "Are you defending Lord Robin? That seems unlike you."

Margaret selected a sweetmeat from a tray. "Does it?"

"Very much so. I thought—well, that you had no liking for men in general. And him in particular."

"Bold, strutting fellows are not to my taste. My husband is just such a one." Slowly, she tore the tidbit into tiny pieces. "There's not a wench on our lands with her skirt unlifted. I came upon him once, having at a milkmaid. He saw me—*he saw me*—and he did not even stop. I am his wife, and he could not bother to accord me the courtesy of a guilty look. I decided then and there he would never defile me again."

A smile still lingered on Margaret's lips, but Kat said in a small, shocked voice, "Oh."

"Men in general, however? I have nothing against them.

Some of them even have possibilities. Dark, slight, poetic ones with long-fingered hands."

"You are describing Michel de Castelnau Mauvissiere. The French ambassador." Kat was still shocked.

"No, I like men young. With smooth skin that is pleasant to touch."

"Raoul Mauvissiere. His son. Margaret, you cannot have fallen in love with the French ambassador's son!"

"Kat," said Margaret, lightly mocking, "you cannot have fallen in love with that horrible Robert Hawking!"

"If I have fallen into anything with him, it is hate." Swiftly, Kat changed the subject. "Is the queen's estate at Richmond very grand?"

"Not so large as Whitehall, but much, much warmer. It is no surprise Elizabeth has decided to move the court there. She usually does once the weather becomes sharp." Margaret pulled her fox-lined cloak tighter under her rounded chin. A brazier put out heat, but the air was still chilly.

"I thought we were moving because of the Babington trial," Kat said.

"Now that Parliament is meeting to decide the final fate of Anthony Babington and his friends, you mean?" Choosing another sweetmeat, Margaret tossed it into her mouth, and chewed thoughtfully. "Yes. Richmond is not so many miles from London and Westminster, you know. Close enough for news from the trial to travel in a few hours, and yet far enough away that it will give us all a rest from the unpleasantness. The topic of Anthony Babington puts her grace into a temper."

Into a terror, Kat corrected inwardly, though Elizabeth hid her fear behind blasts of defiant laughter.

"But Richmond is also beautifully warm," repeated Margaret. "Let's not talk politics. Will you not have one of these? They are very good. Cone sugar and rose water and—"

Kat wrinkled her nose. "I thank you, nay. Are there apples?"

"This taste for raw fruit! You will have people thinking you are a peasant. In the Old King's time, physicians forbade the eating of fruits and vegetables completely."

"And look how the eighth Henry died. Eaten alive by ulcers. I will have an apple, please."

"Here's one, if you must have it," grumbled Margaret. "I suppose that Maud of yours sneaked it onto the royal barge."

"Aye. Grimalkin's with her, too, in a traveling basket, though she has no fondness for animals. Maud's a true friend." Sitting tailor-fashion among the cushions, Kat took a healthy bite. "Like you."

Margaret settled herself beside her. "Do you have many friends, Kat?"

"At home—"

"Not servants or villagers or the workers who till your land. Friends of our own class."

It was suddenly difficult to swallow. Kat put down her apple. "I suppose not. Acquaintances, aye, but after I lost my parents and brothers, I was always so busy with the estate, you see. And I doubt I have the gift of making people like me."

"Now that's nonsense. But it is much the same with me. I do not have many friends—at least, not the forever sort of friend who is the only kind worth having." Margaret took a deep breath. "The kind who does not shirk from doing favors. Will you be that kind of friend to me, Kat?"

"You know I want to be your friend, but if this concerns Sieur Raoul—"

Margaret was suddenly brisk. "Another benefit of Richmond is that there are apartments in plenty for the queen's ladies. We can share one without being smothered by Jane or Cecily. Even your Maud can have her own little room. I have it all bespoken."

"She will like that, but—"

"We can share confidences without worrying about Jane's busy tongue."

Rising, Kat went to the door and looked out at the green and silent meadows rolling by. Margaret and willowy Raoul? The sophisticated but very young man scarcely had down on his cheeks. Even if Kat lowered her estimate of Margaret's age by five years for friendship's sake, there was a decade and a half between the mismatched lovers.

Kat's gaze wandered over the barge. The only reminder of the royal presence on board was the circle of pikes that bristled outward at the edge of the deck, held by soldiers standing shoulder-to-shoulder. The armed guard should have made her feel safe. Instead, the pikemen seemed menacing. How sad to be the queen and always need guards.

A heron rose in ungainly flight, drawing her eyes upward. The bird gained grace as it climbed into the cloud-splattered sky. Sighing, Kat watched it dwindle into invisibility, and then a bend in the river hid that portion of the sky from sight.

The sigh didn't give her any inspiration. She'd have to try to talk some sense into normally commonsensical Margaret later.

The new direction of the stream brought an elegant clutter of towers and domes into view. It was Richmond. The barge docked amid a vista of lovely trees and beautiful buildings.

Once she set foot on dry land, Kat was swept up by a harried chamberlain and told to oversee the arrangement of the furnishings brought with the household. It was hard and dusty work. By the time the evening meal was served, she could hardly get her eyes to cooperate long enough to take in the details of the huge mural facing her seat.

Later, in their room, Kat asked sleepily, "Who was that blond barbarian next to William the Conqueror? He certainly was big."

Margaret closed the door behind Maud and the other maid who had helped them strip to their smocks, and leaned against it. "What in the world—oh, the painting in the dining hall? Hengist, I think."

"Looked like Lord Robin." Kat allowed the softness of the feather bed to soak some of the tiredness out of her body. "He never cropped up today. I wonder if . . ."

She meant to say she wondered if something had been discovered at Priorly that cleared the house of treason, despite what Jack had done. Just in time, she realized what she'd almost revealed. Miraculously, the secret of Jack's origins had not yet gotten out. To hide her consciousness of how she'd nearly blundered from Margaret's shrewd gaze, she buried her head in the furry covers.

"Let's talk about Lord Robin," Margaret said.

"Nay!"

"Do not go to sleep yet, Kat. See what I stole from the spicery. Usquebaugh!"

Kat groaned.

"Just a little, Kat. You deserve it after your day."

Struggling out of the furs, Kat accepted a cup of the oily, sharp-smelling liquid. "I'll get beastly drunk. It will be like sleeping with Lady Cecily for you."

"I'll risk it."

The whiskey tasted sweet and burned hot all the way down to Kat's middle. "Are you not having any? I do not see a second cup."

"No." The feather bed poofed under Kat when Margaret climbed on. "Drink up!"

"God-a-mercy, I cannot," Kat handed the cup back. "I am dizzy already."

"Your insides are empty. You did not eat at supper. I saw how you picked at the food." Margaret took a tiny sip, watching Kat thoughtfully.

"Hours on the water and then lifting tapestries and shifting chests when we got here. I was too tired to eat. I could sleep a fortnight."

"It is your own fault, goose. The liverymen are supposed to do the heavy work, not the ladies. We supervise."

Gradually, Kat subsided back into the covers. "So wasteful to wait for extra servants when two more hands could get the work done. I was there. I have hands."

"And all scratched and blistered they are, too. You do not set yourself high enough. The canaille take advantage."

"Prestons were commoners not so long ago," Kat said dreamily.

"All the more reason to set yourself at a proper distance."

Kat giggled. The warmth from the whiskey had spread to her fingers and toes, and the light-headedness had begun to feel pleasant. "Oh, Margaret! When did you become so proud?"

"It is not being proud to know your station and stick to it. The French *aristocratie* treat underlings in the correct manner."

"I suppose Raoul taught you that."

Margaret took another sip. "He has taught me many things."

"Surely—"

"Do not pretend to be so horrified! I have seen how you look at Robin Hawking. At first you shrank away from the brute like a sensible creature, but now . . . your heart is in your eyes every time he's near."

"I am not married to someone else," Kat pointed out muzzily. But she was, in a way. She was married to Priorly. To the past.

"You should thank God fasting you are not wed to my husband." Margaret plucked at strands of fur broodingly. "Do you blame me for seeking happiness elsewhere?"

Rubbing her eyes, Kat sat up straighter. "It is not up to me to judge. What is it you want me to do?"

Margaret looked up eagerly. "Only what you desire for yourself, I warrant. Stop running away from Hawking. Let him catch you before you die from the green sickness waiting to find out how it is to have the man between your legs."

"Distract him, you mean," said Kat slowly.

She felt slightly sick. Was this why her friend had called out Robin's name in the maids of honor's bedroom at Whitehall? To keep him busy with the problems a veteran lady-in-waiting like Margaret had known the scandal would bring?

"Yes, distract him, but not to any ill purpose! We are being watched, Raoul and I. The other spies pose no danger—either one of us could run rings around them. But Hawking is different. His eyes see everything, damn him, and they are so cold . . . How can you stand the prospect of—"

Could she? *Something* drew her to such a dangerously masculine man. "His eyes aren't always cold," Kat said finally.

"Then have him. Do unto him as he would do to you. Use him for your pleasure until the pleasure is gone."

"How can you be so sure it would be pleasure?"

Margaret looked at her oddly. "You knew what he was before you began following him with your eyes."

"Aye." She did know what he was. Kat knew better than any other woman of the court. He was a man who craved sweetness, who was tired of pain. "I will not cooperate in your little conspiracy."

"Only until Raoul can smuggle me into France. Is it so much to ask?"

"Why do you even care if he suspects? You are not committing treason, just adultery," said Kat crudely.

"Because he is a man! And men stick together. He'll tell my husband. And I'll be dragged back to be John's wife again. You do not understand! 'Twill not be adultery. Raoul has an uncle who is a cardinal. I will convert, be granted an annulment—Raoul and I can marry."

"What makes you believe you will be happier with Raoul than with Sir John? Jesu, the boy's younger than I am, let alone—"

"Let alone me," Margaret finished. "He is. Young and handsome and very clever in bed. He's—respectful of my wishes. Slow to take his own pleasure, quick to attend to mine. He say I am like a large, luscious pastry and he feels like ant, gorging himself on every sweet inch of me. Oh, I am not utterly a fool. He's more in love with the fortune I will bring sewn into my gowns than he is with me. But he has wits enough to know mine are better than his. I'll rule the roost, and he will be grateful and always fond of me."

The idea of such a life sent a chill through Kat.

Margaret's voice was hoarse with intensity. "I shall be Madame de Castelnau Mauvissiere, with a pretty and amusing husband who will keep his mistresses decently out of my sight."

"So you mean to run off with him," said Kat. "And while you do this, I am to bind Lord Robin to a bed so he does not notice."

Margaret's giggle was carefree. "From what I hear, that should be the type of entertainment he likes best."

Kat allowed the fury erupting inside her to boil over. "That's enough! How you can—has it never occurred to you that Lord Robin might be a little deeper, a little more decent, than his reputation? Just because he has had to be present at torture sessions hardly proves he relishes them. Or that he uses the—the paraphernalia of torture when he's abed. Does he look to be a man who needs the promise of strange pleasures to lure a woman?"

"Such heat!" Margaret patted her cheek. "A man may have a taste for violence whether he needs it to catch his prey or not. Do your protests mean you have firsthand knowledge of what Hawking likes when he's in bed?"

"I mean I will not turn bawd for you, Margaret. You are a most persuasive whoremonger. Ah, in French that would be *entremetteuse.* Should I be flattered at your estimation of my charms? Why should I stop at Lord Robin? If you and your precious Raoul are afraid, should I not distract Walsingham, too? Who knows how many lovers I could juggle if I just put my mind—oh, not my mind—to the task?"

Margaret recoiled as if scorched. "Are you going to tell Hawking what I have said?"

Kat rolled off the bed without answering. "I'll sleep in Maud's room."

At the door, she looked back. Margaret's smock was plainly made, and against the luxurious furs it appeared frumpish. The figure inside it spread like rising dough. She was plump now; in a few years, saw Kat clear-sightedly, she would be fat. Maybe Margaret knew what she was doing in choosing the mercenary, not very intelligent Raoul.

Wearily, Kat said, "By your way of accounting, now I have no friends." She closed the door behind her.

Exhaustion assured sleep but couldn't make it peaceful. Waking frequently, she tried to imagine comfort into a scratchy wool blanket—no soft furs in a servant's room. She thought of Robin, laughing at her, frowning at her, kissing her. If it came to a choice between believing him or Aftondale, she knew which she'd prefer to take at his word. Did she dare?

It hurt to think Margaret had been using her. She went

about her duties the next day with hollow eyes until a page came to bring her to the queen. Kat followed without curiosity.

The windows of the royal bedchamber faced east toward a mass of trees. The first impression Kat had when she entered was of cool, diffuse light. The next was her usual awe over Elizabeth's bed, which had traveled with the court. Its huge frame was ingeniously constructed of different-colored woods and had been hung with a gallimaufry of painted silks. Why would a woman who slept alone need such an overblown setting for her femininity? Perhaps in some warped way it compensated for a life whose chances for love had all been thwarted.

What sort of bed would Margaret and her little Raoul choose?

The mental picture of an ant reaching ecstasy over a pastry was sad. Kat shook it off. Curtsying deeply, she waited to be noticed.

A circle of ladies had their backs turned to her. "Naughty Katherine," came Elizabeth's voice from inside the group, "what mischief have you been in today?"

"None, Your Grace," she replied, getting to her feet. "That I know of, anyway. People delight in saying so many things about me, it sometimes takes a day or two for news of my doings to reach my lowly level."

With a crow of laughter, Elizabeth pushed through the ladies, causing them to scatter like brightly colored leaves. "Impudence!" Her mood seemed zestful. "That or honest. But we cannot have our mirror appearing so wan and with—what are these? Dark circles under your eyes? God's death, child. Strangers will see you and conclude we suffer from the same poor looks. Let's improve you."

With a cold, dry hand, Elizabeth drew Kat to a table loaded with jars of creams and powders, and thrust her onto a stool.

"If it please your grace," Kat said in alarm, "I am only a simple country girl. These grand things are not for me." The idea of losing her identity behind the pots' greasy contents put a convincing quaver in her protest.

Elizabeth chided, "Humility is proper in young women of low degree. So is obedience. Hold your face still."

The painting seemed to take hours. Kat's skin began to itch; one of the ladies—a peer's wife—knocked her hand away when she lifted it to scratch. Her shoulders ached and her buttocks grew numb.

Elizabeth gave orders like a general. "No, no, the green over the eyes," she barked. She didn't show a hint of humor; this was serious business to her. "Keep the safflower paint low on the cheeks! Where is the cream for the lips?"

At last, two identical faces stared back from the looking glass. Differences in age had been wiped out. The dead-white complexions were brushed with boldly applied color. The faces had twin hooded eyes, high-bridged noses, secretive mouths.

Feeling curiously blank inside, Kat trailed Elizabeth for the rest of the day, imprisoned by the queen's frequent demands for a pillow, a fan, a book, a warming drink.

In the course of her errands she passed Margaret Treland several times. Neither spoke.

Maragaret was standing nearby when Elizabeth said with a sly glance at Kat, "Why has our rat catcher not presented himself today? Katherine? What have you to say?"

"I do not know why Lord Robin does the things he does, nor does he account to me for his whereabouts."

"He's giving testimony at Babington's trial," someone mentioned.

The animation in the raisin eyes clouded a little, then flashed bright again. "Tosh! That was yesterday. We'll hear nothing further about the accursed trial. Music! Katherine! Do you play the virginal?"

A low murmur of laughter rippled through the bystanders.

"Nay, Your Grace. Only the lute." Kat was briefly grateful her borrowed complexion couldn't change.

"She was virginal before she met Lord Robin." The gleefully malicious whisper was just loud enough to reach her. Kat thought it might belong to Jane Monteshote.

"I am as much a maid now as I was before I came to court!" In the startled silence that resulted, Kat realized that she'd unwittingly copied the commanding tones Elizabeth used.

Everyone was staring at her except Elizabeth herself. Of course, Kat thought; most people never considered what they sounded like to others.

"Jane, go find a gardener and see what he can give you. What *flowers* he can give you," Elizabeth corrected herself.

Her nose turning bright pink, Jane ran from the room. Kat swallowed hard. The queen's talent for malice far exceeded poor Jane's.

Margaret spoke up. "I will play, if your majesty desires music." She moved to the keyboard.

The simple air was French. Kat glanced around under lowered lids, but no one seemed to mark the selection as significant. The last tinkling note died away. Despite the becoming light Margaret looked tired and middle-aged, and after she accepted the polite applause she, too, left the room.

Coming to a decision, Kat scratched defiantly at an itch on her chin and took a step after her former friend. Just then Elizabeth decided that she had an urgent appetite for a sweet which was the jealously guarded invention of one particular cook. Kat had to search the eighteen kitchens on the premises to find the baker and repeat the order.

The evening meal was over before she was released to her own devices. The room Margaret had chosen for them was empty except for Grimalkin, who jumped off the bed and meowed as she burrowed under the hem of Kat's gown. The mewling cries changed to a purr when the animal found ankles under the layers of skirts and began to strop herself around them.

"Aye," said Kat severely, "you would like it if you tripped me and I fell to the ground. You think I would spend the rest of the night lying about, stroking you and petting you—"

The comparison to what Margaret had suggested she do with Robin was too pat. Shaking her head, she scooped up Grimalkin and took the cat outside.

Under the dim light shed by the windows of the hall and chapel, she walked around the palace's inner quadrangle.

The evening quiet was lovely. A few servants went to and from the fountain that served the long blocks of courtiers' lodgings with water. Kat exchanged murmured greetings with the ones she knew by sight.

"Good evening."

"God save you, m'lady."

Overhead, clouds knit together to produce a fine drizzle which lay softly in her hair. She left the hood of her cloak hanging down her back. The mist felt good.

"Can you never be near water without getting it all over you?"

"Lord Robin! How went the trial?"

"Badly for the defendants."

His curt tone mystified her. "You of all people know they were guilty. The result was preordained."

"You speak truer than you know."

Robin walked closer. It occurred to her that the quadrangle was poorly lit and lonely, and that an intelligent woman would run inside. Something discouraged in the set of his shoulders kept her from bolting.

"Were the members of Parliament unkind to you?"

He expelled his breath in angry amusement. "Kind? You have a strange idea of what we were doing. Oh, I received many pretty compliments for making the arrests. I should not complain."

Dampness didn't mute the famous chiming sounds made by the golden weathervanes atop the spires of Richmond. Every now and then a crystalline note drifted down.

"You were expected yesterday," she said.

"Tony Babington asked me to stay until he was sentenced."

His bleakness didn't invite comment.

After a few moments, Kat added, "Her grace is waiting for you to attend her."

"Anon. What are you hiding under your cloak?"

To her own surprise, Kat chuckled. Opening her arms, she swept back the wings of her wrap to allow Grimalkin to leap into the dusk.

"Ah, my nemesis from Whitehall. You have an affection for her?"

"She's mine. From home." Kat turned her face up to

him, and said wryly, "How odd that you should call her that. I think of you as my nemesis."

"I would like to be your fate. What have you done to yourself?" A warm fingertip touched the tip of her nose.

She remembered her new face. "It amused the queen to paint me like a doll."

He leaned close to study her in the soft gloom. With an oath, he said, "It is a crime to smear paint on tender skin. There are leachings of lead and all kinds of other foul stuff in the cosmetics apothecaries blend. Let's get this off you before you end up scarred."

Dipping a corner of his cloak in the free-flowing water, he scrubbed at her face until it felt raw. Then he scrubbed some more.

"Why are you speaking to me? It has been days since you deigned to notice I still draw breath," he remarked presently.

"I missed you."

Her fingers flew to her lips, but the betraying admission had already slipped out. He dropped the makeshift washclout and cupped her chin.

"Did you, Kat? No lying now. Tell me true."

She stared determinedly past his left ear. "The prisoner may come to miss the warden after a while, so they say. Especially when there's no one else to talk to. At least you do talk to me. To the queen I am a reflection, to the court a jest wearing thin. Even Margaret—"

"Lady Treland? What about her? Has she tried to involve you in any of her doings?"

Such anger coiling in him. A big, impassioned, determined man. She ought to be frightened, and yet . . . the inside of his palm was gentle on her abused skin. His hand was large, like the rest of him, the warm pressure a powerful reminder that Lord Robin was an ally as well as an enemy.

"You are real," she whispered.

"Did you think me one of your spirits? Or a hobgoblin? Would you surrender to me if I were?"

"Not my spirits!" she corrected automatically. "I mean, you are . . . oh, I do not know what I mean. Sometimes I am so lonely for another human's touch. Not to be grabbed or bed favors sought from me, but for a kiss that's meant as a gift instead of a demand. Arms that embrace and then let go. Company by the fire. Quiet talk at the end of the day. If I ever surrendered to a man, it would be for those things. That's foolishness, I suppose."

"Not so foolish," he answered softly.

The mist was thickening, and it slicked their skin. Drops, trickling slowly down his face, made runnels of light that gleamed uncertainly.

She stirred. "I ought to go in."

"Why do you back away from me? I am not Aftondale."

"The earl has not come to Richmond." Her brow furrowed with sudden suspicion. "Could it be that a queen's agent gave him to understand his presence was unwelcome at court?"

He smiled tightly. "It could be. I had to do something to keep my hands from his throat. By the way, I am not a John Treland, either—in case Lady Margaret has been filling you with tales of how terrible men can be."

His hair had begun to contract into damp curls. Such beautiful, touchable hair for a hard man.

"You know about her troubles with her husband? You and Margaret seem so hostile to each other."

"The queen of England employs me. My loyalty is hers. Bought and paid for," he said with a self-mocking grimace. Then his full lips thinned into a serious line. "But also I am her man because she's truly the only force holding England together in the face of civil war. I can hardly afford to look with favor on an Englishwoman who keeps company with the French."

Kat hesitated, sure she ought to say something, afraid to reveal too much. The familiar predicament, she thought with a spurt of humor.

"Margaret's not a traitor to Elizabeth, Lord Robin. I doubt she cares who rules."

"Then why would she—ah. Not an affair of state. An affair of the heart. Who's she running after in the French delegation?"

"You cannot expect me to betray a confidence."

"Poppet. You know me better than that. Of course I can."

"Well, I will not tell you. Poor Margaret. If Sir John is so dreadful a husband, could you not ignore her seeking comfort elsewhere?"

"In the arms of the French? A maid of honor could pass all sorts of information to the enemy. Do not tell me you pity her. Where's your common sense? At the masque, the woman kept searching for someone. I thought it was probably the French ambassador." Robin turned her chin so she had to look at him. "So she asked you to intercede with me."

"Not precisely."

"What, then?"

"She asked me to seduce you."

He drew a slow breath. "And what did you say?"

"I told her nay. Do you want me to be a whore?"

"In truth, poppet, I do not."

They stood quietly, listening to the weathervanes chime.

"However, I promise not to object overmuch if you decide to seduce me on your own account," he added.

"I? With all the dire deeds you suspect me of committing? Treason and blowing up palaces and who-knows-what-else? For shame, my lord!"

"I desire you." He said it matter-of-factly, as if it were a simple fact of existence like the sun rising in the east. Unchangeable. Immutable.

She choked on emotion, and didn't even know what emotion it was. Robin made it impossible for her not to notice him as a man. "Elizabeth would kill us. Literally. Or make us wish we were dead. She would levy fines that would cripple Priorly and bar you from employment anywhere in England."

"I am aware of it. You'll note I am not hauling you under a cart to ravish you, damask lady." He dragged an impatient hand through his hair. "It is what I would like to do, though."

Her heart lurched. "You do not know what you are saying."

"Oh, but I do."

"You do not!" Her voice sharpened.

He pulled her a few feet into better light and bent to study her expression. "What is it, Kat? What are we arguing about now?"

She looked down. "Would you rape me?" she asked the pavement. "You had the chance once but stopped. I— You frighten me, and half the time you do not believe me. You could have me arrested. But I have built this image of you in my head based on how you behaved the night we met, and I need to hear if I am right. Would you take me if you thought there would be no consequences?"

Silence echoed.

"Is it necessary for you to ask?"

She met his eyes without flinching. "Aye."

"Then no, sweet heart, I would not rape you. I have never raped anybody." His wry expression seemed to accuse her of something. "I admit to persuading a number of women as hard as I could in the past. Not recently. I have not played with another woman since I met you."

Kat peeked up at him. "You are amazingly virtuous for a man of such reputed insatiability."

He reeled back. "God's acorns, madam, do not spread *that* opinion of me about. My cousin of Burghley would be most displeased." Despite his foolery, he was still full of anger; she could tell.

"You are like a player on a stage."

"Sometimes. Generally not." He sat on the edge of the fountain and pounded his fist on his thigh. "Whatever works."

"You coax, or intimidate—or overwhelm people with your tall inches and devil's smile."

"You begin to know me."

"Why would your own cousin want you tarred with such a black reputation?" she asked.

"It was accidental. There was no way to keep secret the fact that I participated in questionings at the Tower. Questionings are not pretty, damask lady. Folk made up their own reasons for why I was there. And Walsingham and Burghley? They were not about to explain that I was under their orders. Even though that particular cat is out of the bag, the stain lingers." Irritably, he added, "Why am I telling you this?"

His asperity reminded her of another issue.

"Perhaps I should not talk to you at all. Just how were you forwarding important matters of state by gossiping with Aftondale about me? And telling him lies?"

Lord Robin's gape-jawed stare was done to perfection. Kat wanted to believe the surprise was real. "Lady, you cannot believe I would discuss you with that piece of filth."

"Why not? You load me down with constant assurances you'll do anything to anyone in order to reach your ends. Why should I not take you at your word?"

"Idiot woman, because—" He stopped. "You are right. Never trust me, Kat."

She couldn't help it. She already trusted him. Almost. "The queen awaits," she repeated helplessly.

"Yes." He rubbed his temples. "I must speak to you, Kat. Tomorrow. This time it *is* about an important matter."

"I cannot—"

"Concerning a boy named Will. And a retainer of yours who, I believe, rejoices in the name Jedidiah Pettigrew."

Her breath caught in her throat. "Where must I meet you?" she asked resignedly.

"Do you know where the Turtle Cage is?"

"Aye."

"At midday." He got up and turned toward the stairs. His feet dragged; every line of his tall body looked soulweary.

"My lord!"

Glancing over his shoulder, he raised his brows.

Kat said pertly, "You did not kiss me."

His eyes took on a gleam. "I am flattered you noticed, damask lady."

"There are some things a woman never forgets to notice."

"So I am unforgettable, am I?"

"You are impossible!"

He laughed, and ran up the stairs with a lighter step.

Kat was glad she'd obeyed the impulse to lift his spirits. But as she coaxed Grimalkin out from a dry spot within a portico, her lips curved downward. The messenger Will and her steward Pettigrew . . .

Chapter 10

By noon the next day a weak sun had burned away the last wisps of cloud. Lifting her face to the brightness, Kat loitered by the enclosure which was home to a large number of turtledoves. Coos and soft rustlings filled the air.

"It is peaceful here."

"Margaret!" Kat shifted her balance from her right foot to her left, trying to see over the other woman's shoulder.

"Are you expecting someone?" asked Margaret. Her lips were pale and drawn down at the corners, giving her a doughy, unfinished look in the unforgiving sunlight.

Kat nodded unhappily.

With a half-smile and shrug, Margaret turned to go.

"Stay a moment. I tried to find you yesterday evening."

"I was with the queen, then at supper." She lifted her chin, giving it a firm line it didn't usually have. "Then with Raoul."

"I told Lord Robin." It came out too loud and fast, but Kat had to get the words into the open before embarrassment stopped her.

Margaret made a small, despairing sound.

"Not about Raoul," Kat rushed on. "All I said was that you are not a traitor, only a woman in love. You do love him, do you not?"

The pale lips writhed. "Oh, yes. I try to hide my motives from myself and claim to be an aging woman buying a bedmate. Pitiful, am I not? How were you able to tell?"

Kat shrugged uncomfortably. "I have had experience

lately sifting real emotions from false ones. You are a kind person—you wouldn't let the other ladies make a jest out of me, even after I refused to sleep with Lord Robin for you. Heavens, that sounds odd."

"Yes," agreed Margaret. "Very odd."

They both burst into strained giggles.

"And I cannot believe any woman really likes to be called a pastry. Only love would put up with that."

"Robin Hawking is not the only one who sees too much. Of course I want Raoul to fall in love with me. But if he does not, I'll make do with what he can spare for the rest of his life. It is better than nothing, Kat. Nothing's what I have with John."

Kat nodded, accepting that Margaret wasn't going to give up her Frenchman. "Then I feel I need to warn you—but I am not sure about *what.*"

She tried to guess Robin's next move, and couldn't. A soft wall of feeling seemed to get in the way of her critical judgment.

Sheep-brained, she thought disgustedly.

She'd been sheep-brained ever since she met him. It was ridiculous. She wasn't even sure she wanted to try lovemaking with the man. Women gave up too much in bed. Look at poor Margaret.

"Lord Robin might do something, or he might sit back and watch without interfering in your affair," Kat said at last. "He has no love for your husband, at any rate."

"That's a point in his favor," Margaret replied grudgingly. "Kat, be careful. Everyone's saying he covets your estate. Trust me, the kind of man who marries property instead of a woman makes a dreadful husband. I know."

"You are wrong," said Kat quietly, after Margaret left. "He wants everything but marriage. To me or to Priorly."

Robin's first impulse, when he got near the Turtle Cage and saw Kat with the Treland woman, was to rush and place himself physically between the two of them. That would have been stupid, which was why he didn't do it. But as seconds dragged past, he wanted to. God's grace, he wanted to. The last thing Kat needed was to be implicated in further treason.

Measured in the slow slam of his heart, the women's conversation was briefer than it seemed. It ended with what was apparently a dismissal on Kat's part; tension drained from him so thoroughly he felt his muscles go as buttery as if he'd been making love.

It took a minute to trace the source of his relief. Protectiveness.

As he contemplated that bit of unpleasant self-knowledge, his brows knit into a letter M and a wave of anxiety flowed over his body. He simply could not afford to make his judgments about a woman involved in so many suspicious circumstances with the equipment he carried between his legs instead of the equipment he carried in his head.

La Treland walked away through the cherry trees. Kat wandered around the cage, making small noises at the doves and shaking her head at them; as she did so, the sun made it seem as though sparks were flying from her russet hair.

Approaching quietly, Robin heard her scold the birds. "I have not brought you any tidbits, so stop pecking at me so hopefully."

At that moment, Robin felt as though he were one of the hopeful turtledoves. But making Lady Katherine Preston into a tidbit for his bed would bring disaster on both of them. So why was his desire for her so great that when he watched her like this, unobserved, his knees melted like wax in reaction?

Robin wasn't aware of having moved or making a sound, but he must have because she whirled to face him. "My lord."

She curtsied. Her voice was soft. Breathless in the way that, despite himself, always made him feel big and powerful. His frown deepened. Any yielding gesture from Kat to him was unusual. He was being a fool, and she was being altogether too submissive.

"What are you playing at?" he asked.

"My lord?"

"Do not lord me, girl."

"If you mean Margaret—"

"I do not mean Lady Margaret. I mean you. What's got you meek and mild all of a sudden?"

Kat smoothed the tiny circumference of her farthingale. One of the old-fashioned kind that became her so well, he noted. "You are the spy," she said. When he waited for a response to his question, she stamped her foot. "Surely your wits can unriddle the puzzle."

As her voice rose, it was answered by a flutter of wings from the caged doves.

"My wits appear to have gone begging." Not unusual around her, he admitted to himself. Irony dripped from his voice. "So, I pray you, explain why the Kat I know has been replaced by this improbably polite stranger."

"Because you have done something terrible to Jedidiah Pettigrew, whose only crime could be that he's my steward! And that messenger, Will. His felonious act was carrying a letter to Master Pettigrew for me."

"You have decided I—what?"

Robin barely conquered the impulse to list for her the brutal tactics used by officers of the law. Even so, his curt tone was too revealing. He was appalled at how hurt it sounded.

Her blunt question—*Would you rape me?*—had torn a chunk out of his self-respect. Stop acting like a sniveling brat, he ordered himself. Why shouldn't the girl believe the old, foul lies? After all, he'd done his best to convince her she ought to fear him.

More quietly, he asked, "What do Will and Master Pettigrew know that the queen's government needs to know, Kat?"

"Nothing." It was a screamed whisper. "They are only little men. It would be pointless to crush them."

"Then why does the mention of their names make you behave like a stranger?"

He pushed up close to her, because she'd made it clear a dozen times his physical nearness rattled her. Her eyes grew into great, dark wells that would drown him if he weren't damned careful.

"I have told you everything I know or guess," she insisted. "I swear it."

Robin backed away from her abruptly. Relief washed over her features.

Being close to her was a source of pleasure, but less and less could he bear the signs that his touch repulsed her. Sometimes she seemed to forget and respond to him naturally, woman to man. Other times . . . He'd changed, and she'd done it to him. It was disconcerting that desire for Kat was ruining him for bought women. A sensation perilously close to shame twisted his frown into something darker. The hurt of believing she was a traitor was minor compared to the pain that came from knowing she was probably innocent . . . and afraid of him.

"I have done your men no harm," he said heavily. "Here. This is for you from your steward."

Taking the folded letter he thrust at her, Kat turned it over without breaking the seal. "You have not read this," she said slowly. "Why not?"

He put his hands behind his head and stretched. The little bones at the back of his neck cracked with satisfyingly loud pops.

"You will tell me what is in it," he responded, with a fine show of indifference.

With a flounce, she leaned against a tree's slim, gnarled trunk. Ripping the seal with so much unnecessary violence chunks of wax flew, she read aloud in a fast gabble. " 'Most worshipful mistress the Lady Katherine Preston, with the court. If ye be well, I be well. The harvest goes apace, with the butchering and salting of porkflesh set for . . .' "

Stripping a handful of late cherries from a low-hanging branch, he bit into sweetness and then spat the pits neatly behind him. Listening to the steward's letter proved boring. Pettigrew was a conscientious man; he listed the harvest-time chores in exhaustive detail.

Pausing, Kat narrowed her eyes. "This is the second time I have seen you make remarkably free with Elizabeth's belongings. You like raw fruit?"

"What's the difference between taking it now and waiting for the cooks to stew it into unrecognizability? The queen is careful of her possessions but not petty. She will not begrudge us a few. Cherries are better this way. Try some."

A stem with two round, glowing fruits spun in her direction. Catching it, Kat nibbled, with a sidelong glance at Robin.

He smiled without mirth. "I knew a lady with spirit enough to taste the queen's food for poison would not balk at a morsel from my hand."

"Raw fruit is one of my favorite foods. Besides, I never feared you would poison me, sir." She cocked her head. "Strangle me, perhaps."

His laugh was short. "How did you guess?"

"I am learning to read the look in your eye. And your fingers keep clenching and unclenching."

Robin stared down at his hands. They were balled into tight fists. He opened them.

"Strangling you has never been the summit of my ambition. I would rather squeeze you in other places," he told her moodily. It was increasingly hopeless to deny the passion he felt for her. Warmth had begun to trickle into his groin the moment her little white teeth sank into the crimson cherries.

"Why is it always rutting with you?"

"Lady, why should it be anything else?" he asked frankly.

"Have you no other interests? Do you hunt? Animals besides men, I mean. Some gentlemen write poetry or go exploring. There is a world full of things to do beyond the limited range of your pizzle!"

"We have discussed this before. Make up your mind. The last time you had me near convinced my—range was limitless."

"You are arrogant. Shameless. Cocksure—"

He crossed his arms and stood taller, suddenly feeling lighthearted. "Yes, damask lady. It is becoming more sure by the minute."

"Puffed up in your own conceit."

"Puffed up? That, too."

"*Insane*. The queen would have your head—and those other appendages you are so proud of—"

"Now that is just like a woman," he said judiciously.

"Believe me, a man does not think of them as mere appendages."

She rolled her eyes, and her gaze fell on the paper crumpled in her hand. She dropped the cherry stems to the ground and smoothed the letter ostentatiously. "I will continue reading," she said with dignity.

"Do," he encouraged, closing the few yards between them. Bracing his hands on branches to either side of her head, he effectively caged her. To his delight, she didn't protest.

Wriggling, she pushed the letter through the space under his arm and peered over his sleeve in order to read it.

" 'Thus the corn was all got in before the rains. As far as young Jack Miller be concerned, everyone hereabouts be shocked and confused, not least his family. Wretched, unfortunate boy, his brain must have turned and none suspected it. In the matter of ghosts—' "

"Ah."

" 'In the matter of ghosts, I wot not what to say to your questions, worshipful lady. I have seen naught, but my own good lady does swear I snore hard through the night. Divers honest witnesses make claim of noises and moving lights. They have not made a difference in the harvest be all I can report. May God protect us from witches and demons and all wickedness that flies through the night. Jedidiah Pettigrew.' "

She refolded the letter. "How did you know my steward would give answers about Jack and the noises and the lights?"

He bent his head so his lips brushed along her jaw. "I said I refrained from reading this letter, lady. I never made any claims about the one you sent him."

"Pettigrew tells us nothing we did not know already."

"True. But Mary Stuart has been housed in Fotheringhay a fortnight. The son of a Priorly tenant tries to kill our queen, and Priorly ghosts continue to walk. The watchers I have put in place are either blind or the strange occurrences have stopped occurring by the time they track them down." Under his arrow-point of a beard, his chin hardened. "I have delayed too long. I am going to have to take a look myself."

She turned her head away from him. The action bared her throat to his light kisses. Her flesh was smooth and firm under his mouth.

Kat moved out of his reach. "Why did you delay leaving?"

"I could not tear myself away."

"Because of my charms," she asked severely, "or because you think I tried to blow up the queen?"

Robin couldn't supply an answer, and she didn't seem to expect one, because she went on, "Why are you torturing me?"

"How? With kisses? To me they are pleasure. Kat, stop and look at me. Is this so unpleasant to you? My hand on your breast." His knuckles grazed the front of her bodice. "My tongue tasting the hollow behind your ear." The light, moist touches made her tremble.

Her dark eyes were haunted more surely than Priorly was. "I cannot give in to you. Pleasure or pain, it does not matter."

"Of course it matters." He pulled her closer and loosened her ruff so he could stroke his fingertips across the nape of her neck. "Your heart beats harder and hotter; can you feel it?" Moving his thumb to the pulse point under her jaw, he kneaded it knowingly until the sadness in her eyes was replaced by a dazed sheen.

"Kiss me," he ordered. "Of your own will. Now."

"You do not know what you ask!"

She had said that last night. "Or what it means to you? No, lady, I do not. You have not told me. But I am well aware what it means to me." Slowly and gently, he pushed at her skirt until the hoops were out of his way. Then he rubbed his hips against hers so she could feel the solid weight of his arousal.

"The queen—"

"Is not here. This is between the two of us. There's no one else to fool or impress or mislead. Only Kat and Robin. Kiss me."

The huge brown eyes, half-shuttered by drowsy-looking lids, caressed his mouth. He felt rooted to the ground, rooted to the tree, bound by ropes of excitement and—and by God, tenderness—to this one too-thin girl.

"Why me?" Her voice was almost inaudible. "Why do you persecute me with your skill at love? What have I ever done—"

"The passion slumbers in you so sweetly. You are like kindling that hungers to burst into flame, too innocent to recognize what you long for. An irresistible temptation."

Analysis was a mistake. A hairsbreadth from his lips, her mouth primmed and pulled back.

"That's not fair. I am not at fault if you cannot keep that lance between your legs from waving about. I have not invited you or anyone else to pierce me."

Robin took a deep breath. His loins ached. Feelings he couldn't put a name to raged inside him. He couldn't think.

"Kat, you cannot blame me for reaching for beauty."

She flattened herself away from him. "I can expect a man to be responsible for his own actions. That's no more than I expect from myself. I will not kiss you, Lord Robin."

"Apparently not," he mumbled. He ran a hand over his beard and down his neck. God's grace, he felt stupid.

"Am I free to go?"

"Go."

"May I take my letter from Master Pettigrew?"

"It is yours."

She slid around him and started off through the trees.

"Kat."

Her steps halted instantly. Robin took his time turning to look at her. His own—relief? satisfaction?—at her obedience annoyed him; he should be able to predict her reactions and not have to worry about them.

Still, his tongue dried up completely at the sight of her slight, valiant figure bracing itself for whatever would come next. Her fear and courage touched him. He pulled a leather purse from his pocket.

"What is it?" she asked, catching the purse as he tossed it.

He rocked on his heels and watched her. Cautiously, she drew the drawstrings apart. The package inside was wrapped in bright green silk. Yellow gleamed when she peeled the silk away.

It was a hollow ball of gold filigree. She touched it with a delicate thumb before holding it out to him.

"Take it back."

He found his tongue. "Lady, has no one ever taught you how to accept a gift?"

"Gifts have not been frequent occurrences in my life. The ones I have been offered recently all seem to have reckonings attached."

"And you account me so lack-witted that I would try to bribe my way into your skirts *after* you refused me? Let me explain strategy. The time to soften a woman with gawds is before she sets her mind against fornicating. This gift is to replace the bauble I sat on the night we met."

"It must be worth ten—twenty—times what mine was."

"Mark the difference up to my pride. I do not choose to make cheap reparations."

Robin didn't mention his sense of guilt at learning she was as poor as he'd first deduced. Or his hunt for a pomander he hoped would please her.

During the past few days, whenever he could escape from the trial going on in Parliament, he had closed his mind to Tony Babington's fate by concentrating with fierce single-mindedness on the shops in the Royal Exchange. In every one he'd hounded the shop girls for a pomander with simple elegance. The overembellished or merely expensive wasn't good enough for Kat.

She wrapped the pomander up in the green silk and threw it back at him.

From across the intervening space, he saw her eyes mist. That startled him. Any woman would covet this beautiful piece of jewelry; without deluding himself about his own taste, he knew it was exquisite. Its delicately chased design, the work of a master goldsmith, was a perfect match for Kat's femininity.

For a woman to reject it as an insult was understandable only because the woman was Kat Preston. She was a contrary thing. But she was obviously miserable over refusing his present . . . and yet determined to do it.

"By Christ's holy wounds, there's no reckoning tied to this gift, Kat. It is for you, because I want you to have it.

I have no sinister motive. Do you hate me so much you cannot accept a simple offering of good will from me?"

"I do hate you," she admitted. "And I—do not hate you."

Robin disliked the question he was about to ask because it revealed too much of the battered state of his feelings. He despised the knowledge that he was afraid to hear her reply. "Is the desire all on my side? I have learned a little lately about the deceptions we play on ourselves when we need to hold to someone." Tony Babington, broken in mind and spirit, clinging to *him*—and he had caused Tony's downfall.

"I have learned those lessons, too." She looked everywhere but at him. "You would be a most foolish choice for me as a lover, my lord. You are too large. How would I hide you? Women follow you with their eyes. Some of them with their tongues hanging out."

A completely unfamiliar sensation, like a knife-thrust but cleansing, sliced through his chest. Was it joy? She was jealous. "I did not think you had noticed," he said blandly.

"You must know better than I the first rule of a successful intrigue is secrecy, and you made secrecy impossible weeks ago," she scolded, ignoring his comment. "Besides, you are an accomplished lecher and I . . . You would grow bored with the clumsiness of—of innocence."

"You are never clumsy. Only enchanting."

She shook her head. "If I linger in your vicinity, I will cease to be innocent, that's a certainty. I might become stark, staring mad. Who are you, Lord Robin? What secrets do *you* guard with such ferocious intensity? One moment you are hard, the next frivolous, the next bitter, the next . . . sweet."

"To the point, Lady Kat. Admit it. You desire me."

"I desire you," she confessed. Dodging him, she danced backward until he could hardly hear her. "For all the good it will do either of us."

"It will be good!" he shouted after her. "I'll fix matters somehow. We'll be together. It will be good, damask lady!"

She flitted away. Resting an arm on a limb, he pulled the pomander out of its wrappings and put it to his nose. It had taken more hours of determined shopping to find her favorite fragrance to fill the hollow ball.

God's grace, he was turning into a doting courtier. He'd failed to extract the location of the priest's hole at Priorly from her. Delivering the letter and finding out the hole's whereabouts had been the excuses he'd given himself for meeting her today. Instead, he'd just crossed some sort of lover's Rubicon, promising her . . . what? To defy the queen and take her?

By any standard, he hadn't crossed a river Rubicon; he'd fallen in and was cheerfully engaged in drowning. Even after he dropped the rejected pomander back into the purse, the scent of gillyflowers clung to his hands, and made him smile faintly at the ripe, red cherries hanging from the tree, ready to fall into a waiting hand.

Kat woke all at once, her brain working furiously. Except for a rushlight pulsing in the corner, the bedchamber she shared with Maud was dark. The air was filled with nothing more ominous than the maid's steady breathing. A sleepy purr rumbled from Grimalkin's direction when Kat sat up.

From her pallet she could see all four corners of the room. Nothing was out of place. And yet something had woken her. Drying perspiration chilled the back of her neck. Her heart still galloped with fear.

A nightmare? The memory was turning into mist, but . . .

She concentrated. The dream had been of Robin. He'd been teasing and gentle. All the hard edges, the bold masculinity and swashbuckling arrogance, had been missing. A pinprick of regret caused her to prop her elbows on her knees so she could cover her face with her hands. Humiliation burrowed straight through her.

Oh, God, she *wanted* the hardness and arrogance as well as the kindness. It would be reasonable to be drawn to a consistently gentle man. But it was Robin—Robin with his scalding heat and icy reserve—who stirred the sleeping womanhood in her. She must be mad.

In fact, craving him was worse than lunacy. Giving herself to him would be the same as taking her own life, for she'd never be the same after letting him use the tool he flaunted ... to remake her into what she would be ... if she invited him to fill her as he filled her dreams ...

Kat slowly subsided onto her pallet. She slept.

The dream was different this time.

He sat comfortably in the cradling boughs of an apple tree. His shoulders were impossibly broad, his waist and buttocks taut. He was nude. Only antique statues had bodies as magnificent as his, but Robin was warm and alive.

His nakedness wasn't a taunt but a promise. Beautiful golden down covered him, clustering thickest under his arms, over his wide chest, and in the apex of his body. Heavy muscles in his thighs quivered with scarcely controlled strength; the long, thick bolt of flesh between his legs stood out. Being Robin, he didn't offer an explanation or an apology for the state of his body.

"Will you take an apple from my hand, damask lady?" His dream voice stroked her skin and she flushed.

"This is the fruit of the tree of knowledge of good and evil."

Bringing up her catechism embarrassed Kat. Who was she to pretend to virtue? Desire and fear and fascination were all mixed up in her. Heat settled far down inside her, sending out snaky, delicious tendrils into her legs, her breasts. Even her fingers and toes. They curled.

"The tree of knowledge is a fine tree," he said.

"I already know its secrets." Was she warning him, or begging him not to believe her? "I do not need your apple."

He took an enormous bite. "It is juicy and sweet. Like you, Kat. Shall I eat you up?"

The fever-heat was already consuming her, and she couldn't fight his instincts and hers anymore. Had stopped wanting to, weeks ago. It was time to find out if loving with him would be heaven or hell.

"Please. Please. Please."

Then he was beside her. On top of her. Behind, above, inside. It was wonderful in ways she had never imagined. His hardness didn't hurt her. It was sleek and smooth and big. He drove into her soft moistness, and she closed around him, tight, tight.

"I did not know," she gasped.

"What, sweet heart?"

Kat had to make him understand. "I did not know it could be like this."

He scattered kisses and bites everywhere his mouth could reach, praising the smallness of her breasts, her boy-thin hips, the slender length of her legs—things she'd always believed to be flaws. Robin called every one of them beauty. He filled her with life; he completed her. Their skin grew dewy with sweat and the wetness gave touching an erotic sweetness. His lance of flesh wasn't a weapon because he used it to pleasure her. Delight accompanied the opening, stretching, burning.

Heat. She was on fire inside and out. For the first time, she understood what he meant when he said *hot*.

Moving enthusiastically against the rocking of his hips, she strained toward some goal tantalizingly just out of reach. The hair feathering his chest brushed her engorged nipples, and she sobbed, "Robin!"

And then, somehow, everything went wrong.

Although she'd just said his name, a moment later she couldn't remember it. Weirdly, she knew that it had slipped her mind, and she had to get it back. She had to put a name to the man working so hard to show her what love could be. What kind of woman would beg someone to do this to her, and not even be sure of his name? Guilt drove the rapturous, life-giving heat away, and cold gripped her in its place.

The shape of the dream changed. A nightmare started seeping in.

There was blackness, a rending, pain. This wasn't the scene under the apple tree anymore; she and the man above her were someplace narrow and enclosed. A bed.

He was too big, too absorbed in his own sensations to care that he was both crushing her and tearing her apart; he was too male. At the same time he talked to her at droning length about—about ghosts. Ghosts scaring the sheep at Priorly.

The absurdity didn't relieve the nightmare, it only deepened it.

There was no longer anything erotic about the proceedings. Rape left room only for pain and fear. These two bodies were not made to fit. Hers was too young for the act of love, more a child's body than a woman's. The heaving, thrusting, and jamming went on until she was too exhausted to weep.

Finally it was over, and everything went quiet and blind. Kat cringed and tried to fold herself small, to crawl away. She couldn't with his dead weight smothering her.

In some alert corner of her brain, she knew the horror had to be a dream. It was familiar. In one form or another, the nightmare had ruined her sleep since she was thirteen years old.

Suddenly Robin was smiling down at her from the tree again. Even dreaming she suspected something had to be wrong. The sweaty weight of a replete male still pressed her down, so how could she see Robin far away? Not even a man as sly and knowledgeable as the queen's rat catcher could be in two places at once.

Robin scratched himself with the unembarrassed frankness of a big bear. "Do you not know me yet, poppet? For shame." His hide must be made of oak. The sound of his nails scoring across his ribs reminded Kat of boots scuffing over a hardwood floor.

The noise grew louder, and drowned out whatever else Robin was saying. He was shouting now, gripping the tree limb so hard that the tendons and muscles on his arms and in his neck stood out like ropes. But Kat couldn't distinguish the words.

Grimalkin meowed.

The weight on her shifted, fastened over her face.

Her eyes popped open to utter blackness.

Kat tried to suck in a breath of relief. The nightmare had been as bad as she could remember it. Worse, in fact, because Robin had been the man in it this time. New was the first, pleasant section where her body had tried to respond with voluptuous surrender, as well as the part at the end. Except for them it was the old terror. Being held down, forced, blotted out . . .

She made a small noise and twisted to see what had happened to the lighted rush. Perhaps it had been inadequately soaked in tallow and had gone out.

"Stop flapping like a landed fish," said a low, gutteral voice, "or the old woman will be gutted like one."

Kat screamed, but all that emerged was a choked gurgle. Her effort pulled a cloth into her mouth; it must have been lying lightly over her face. A horny, callused hand pressed into her windpipe.

"If you want it that way, mistress." The voice altered, as if its owner's head had turned. "Cut the besom's throat first, and then you can . . ."

Kat went still. The pressure on her throat became slightly less brutal.

"That's a sensible lass. We would prefer no killing. Just come along peaceable-like—"

"Without 'aving 'er first?" The protest came from across the room.

"She's not for the likes of you. This one's meant for his lordship's delectation. He would roast your hangers for midday meal if you tampered with his play-pretty. Pry open the old woman's knees if you cannot keep your breeches closed."

Kat moved again, violently. Her kicking heels caught something that gave, and her captor swore colorfully. "I'll have to tie her ankles. Leave the bag of bones alone," he ordered. "You can buy a quarter hour with a drab when we have delivered this baggage."

"But look at 'er! She's clean. E'en 'er 'air. Where d'ye think I could get the price of a clean 'ore?"

"Let's get her wrapped up and delivered, and happen his lordship will be pleased enough to pay for your whore. Hit the other one again. She's starting to stir."

You must not faint, Kat told herself fiercely. Stay awake and listen. There might be an opportunity for escape—or revenge on the lordship who planned this.

The cloth tightened over her mouth. Then the sheet under her heaved and she rolled helplessly onto a wide surface stiff with scratchy yarns. A rug. Anonymous hands bundled it about her loosely, allowing air to flow to her nostrils.

Lifted and carried, Kat said all the prayers she knew and waited for her chance.

Chapter 11

"H old!"
    "Ho there, guard. Terrible time of night to be working," said the voice at her head. "As you would be knowing, I would imagine, sir."

Kat wriggled frantically, and the portion of the rug around her feet slipped from the grasp of the second man. In response to her mutiny, the carpet tightened at the other end. The air cut off.

A jarring motion roused her eons later. She strangled briefly until the hideous dry press of cloth against her tongue reminded her of the gag. Then she remembered to breathe through her nose, and enough consciousness returned for cold ripples of fear to lap at her.

They were still carrying her—on foot, it felt like. The ground must be rough, since they slid and stumbled occasionally. Recalling her glimpses of the land around Richmond, Kat wondered which way they were going. The carpet blotted out her sense of direction.

North away from the Thames lay the orchard, a number of ponds, and hills that sloped every which way. On the other side of the river ran a lane. The path was used by commoners who came to gawk at the tall spires and golden weathervanes of the palace.

Since it was the middle of the night, she doubted there were any secular pilgrims out and about, ready to be a potential source of help.

The green south of the lane was reasonably flat, too, and planted with elms. Walking there wouldn't be difficult.

So her captors were probably taking her north—or east or west, she thought bitterly. They could be taking her anywhere.

Another surge of panic caused the blackness to go brown. She tried to gulp more air than the carpet contained. The brown drifted.

Jolting to a stop, Kat felt a floating motion that meant they were lowering her. Freshness blew into her face as the rug was unwound. Then she blinked at the removal of the material over her eyes.

Her jaw muscles and tongue were so abused she had to spit several times to get the gag to budge even a little. She was working at it when a man's face with sad, ugly features swam above her.

"Here, lass, we shall get that old rag out from between your teeth. There, that feels better, I warrant. Now a cool drink."

It was wine. Very good wine, Kat noted. The lordship who had arranged this outrage must be rich.

"Who?" she croaked when she could. "Who pays you?"

The broken nose and scarred mouth bunched up in an expression of regret. "Spirited thing. I always had a weakness, like, for soft brown eyes. Pity all that flash and fire will be knocked out of you after his lordship is through."

A hand like a ham-hock lifted her so she could sit. The feeling of dependence shamed her, and she shrugged the hand off. "You seem decent." He did, compared to the other abductor. "What is your name?"

"Samuel. This wet cloth will ease the chafed marks around your mouth."

"You kept that other man from—hurting—me. I would not like to see you punished. You would be wise to say who employs you. And even wiser to let me go. I am not some poor girl recruited for your master's pleasure from the street. I will be missed." He must know that already, but Kat thought it worth saying aloud.

"You are Lady Katherine Preston, one of the maids of honor," he agreed placidly, untying her ankles.

"Her majesty the queen will want me back. She would be far more kindly disposed toward a subject who stole me from the palace if he returned me to it. I would speak up for you."

"Cool, very cool," he said with admiration. "I have never met the queen, nor am I like to. But my master would have the skin off me if I let you go."

"I can pay—"

"Have the skin off me," he repeated with almost gentle stubbornness. "I have seen him play at flaying others alive. By your leave, I do not choose to be the object of one of his experiments."

"Who?" she demanded again. *Not Robin,* her thoughts chittered. *Not Robin.* She absolutely refused to believe it could be Robin.

Simple surprise shone from his small eyes. "You keep strange company, my lady, if you know more than one lord who would do such a thing."

Taking a chain, he fastened one end around her wrist, and snapped the other around a chair leg. He went out, pulling a flap down over the opening behind him. Silk draped the slanting walls, and Kat realized she was in a small but luxurious tent.

Like most of the furniture she'd been used to her whole life, the chair was massive, built of foot-thick beams and meant to last a dozen lifetimes. Under its embroidered cushions it was as strong as a boulder, and as heavy as one, too. Repeated efforts to lift it in order to release the chain left Kat with sore arms and joints, as much a prisoner as before. There was a bed, too. After one glance, she carefully didn't look at it.

She paced for a while, until her own movements began to remind her of the animals in the Tower menagerie, who were supposed to stalk, endlessly, back and forth in their cages. Then she flung herself into the chair and tried not to panic. Robin was too deeply and instinctively possessive to let anybody steal his prisoner away from him. He would come to free her.

A quiver of misgiving shook her. She had misjudged him from the beginning, thinking him too cold ever to radiate the heat of passion. He'd said he would "fix" their situation . . .

Kat pounded a fist into the palm of her other hand, willing her common sense to reassert itself. This was silly. Whether she could trust him or not, Robin Hawking was an intelligent man. Only a hopeless ass would bundle a light-of-love into an itchy rug as foreplay to a romp. And surely he had taken her measure well enough by now to be aware that shackles weren't the way to her heart, or her bed.

He liked his women willing, did Robin Hawking. Blows had been dealt to him, probably by that mighty family of his. A father who called him misbegotten. A cousin content to hear him slandered. Robin's natural gaiety had hardened into arrogance, and his fine sense of justice warred with remorse for arresting fools. When he turned to a woman—when he turned to *her*—it was for a sweetness that would counteract the harsh realities of the rest of his life. That much she was certain of, deep down where she kept her faith in God and sunshine and the power of a determined human being to transcend anything.

But she couldn't lift the chair.

Samuel caught her trying again when he brought her a crust for breakfast. He tutted mildly and left her alone. After she finished a bowl of stew at midday, he handed her a chamber pot. His attitude was so matter-of-fact that she was able to use the pot without losing too much poise. Then he smiled and picked up the chair with one hand. In the other fist he gathered Kat's tether. She had to follow willy-nilly to the opposite side of the tent.

"Not much of a change for you," he said cheerfully. "But a little. I was pressed once as a lad. Served aboard one of King Hal's warships. Manned the oars. I got almighty tired of seeing the same crack in the same fat arse on the bench in front of me. Nothing in this world worse than having to stare at an identical view all day long."

With a casual strength that appalled her, he slipped the loop under the chair's leg and plunked the chair lightly back onto the grass floor.

"Here, I'll arrange the flap so you can see out and no one else can see in. A pleasant, sunny day."

"Please stay and talk to me," said Kat before he could go.

He waited. His patience was as good-humored as ever,

and held a terrifying hint of patronization. Samuel evidently felt safe from discovery.

"When is your lord expected to arrive?" she asked. Nervous moisture gathered in her mouth, and she swallowed painfully.

"This evening, belike. Do you desire anything else, my lady?"

"My freedom."

His smile turned down at the corners indulgently.

"Samuel," she said in desperation, and hesitated.

The amiable villain had already refused money and an offer of intercession. Kat had nothing else that might tempt a man. Except herself.

She was scarcely a beauty, no matter how Robin and this other lord might see her. It was difficult for her to believe her body could tempt anyone. But youth and health ought to be pleasing qualities, and the fact that she was gently bred might add to her value.

A clean whore.

She pushed the thought away.

For his part, Samuel was ugly in an almost endearing way. His years must add up to five-and-fifty; the skin on his neck sagged and little pockets of matter clung to the inner corners of his eyes. A layer of fat covered his formidable frame. His jerkin was impregnated with grease. Not a desirable lover.

A strong one, though. His arms were like tree trunks, and she didn't think he would go out of his way to hurt her. Not like the unknown lord who enjoyed flaying people alive.

"Samuel, you—I . . ."

A clean whore. Katherine Preston, lady of Priorly, had come down to using her body for barter.

"I cannot do it," she breathed in enlightenment. "I was going to offer to trade my—my—" She smiled at him brilliantly. "But I cannot turn myself into a bawd."

"I said you were a lass of spirit," he replied. " 'Tis a pity you must— Well." He went out.

"I do not care if you have a warrant from God, my lord, begging your pardon. I'll not take my craft under the

bridge with the water this high, and that's my final word."
The barge master tried an unconvincing smile. "Consider.
After we drowned in the rapids, 'tis in hell we would end
up. A warrant from Beelzebub, now—that might do you
more good."

Robin jerked open the document with its dangling seals.
"Look again, man. Can you read? The signature belongs
to Lord Walsingham. Have you not heard of him?"

Some of the barge master's ruddy color faded.

"I see that you have. Then you know Satan himself
would fear disobeying this warrant. And if you need further convincing, I am Robin Hawking, one of his hunting
birds. Ah, you have heard of me, too. Then understand
that I mean to get to the Tower of London as soon as possible. Not in an hour or two hours or tomorrow. Now."

"'Twill not take long to dock at Swan Stairs and walk
over to the other side." He started to weep. "My lord,
'twould be madness—"

In front of them, the dark bulk of London Bridge cut off
the sun. Nineteen piers crowded together between the
banks of the Thames, shouldering the bridge's weight of
masonry, wooden buildings, carts, animals, and people.
Spaces between the supports formed sluices, and through
them the normally placid river foamed in a torrent.

"All we face is a little water," said Robin genially, fitting his palms over the hilt of his poniard. It felt good.
Solid and familiar. But the handle slipped a little, because
he was sweating. "Surely shooting the bridge will be easy
for an experienced bargeman and his hearty crew. You
have until the count of five. One, two, three, four—"

Perhaps madness did look out of his eyes, for the master
stared into them despairingly and then turned and shouted
to his crew. Robin settled the knife more comfortably into
its sheath. He started to take his fingers away from the
comforting hilt, and then decided to leave them where they
were. Without something to hold, the hand quivered
slightly.

He hadn't been quite sure of his sanity since a mob of
servants had burst into his chamber before dawn. It had
taken time to pry skimpy details from the old woman,
Maud, who seemed to be the only one to possess any facts

about Kat's abduction. She'd had dried blood on her·face. Then more time had been consumed getting Walsingham out of bed to sign the warrant, and sending men out in all directions to search for a russet-haired girl, skinnier than most, with pretty brown eyes.

Why had she been stolen from her chamber? Who would have the nerve? Or the stupidity? Was it something to do with Priorly? With the queen of Scots? With Fotheringhay?

Oars raised in choppy unison.

The thick columns under the bridge rushed up. White water hurled, leaped, overflowed a narrow slit. Spray blinded him; the roar deafened him. Propelled by the force of the rapids, their barge flew into the air and stayed there for a small eternity, suspended by spume. As the vessel smacked down into the river, Robin's feet flew out from under him. He fell. From his back, he saw the barge barely miss a pillar. Then it shot onto level water once more.

Robin stood up unsteadily. Clinging to the side, he didn't wait for the bump that would indicate the barge master had brought them to dock. He sprang for the stairs at the water gate. "Wait for me," he called over his shoulder.

Walsingham's warrant opened all doors, saving him the time-consuming niceties that usually accompanied a visit to the less savory parts of the complex. He already knew the way.

If Kat had been taken by sympathizers of Mary Stuart, Anthony Babington would be as likely as anyone to know who had her.

"Tony? 'Tis I, Robin," he called softly into the gloom of a small cell. "How are you?"

"Not so ill," responded a whisper.

A young man curled, shrimp-like, on a pallet. In his anxiety, Robin scarcely noticed the bad smells rising from the musty straw. He moved forward. Not shrinking from the torn, soiled, and pest-infested shirt Tony wore, he put an arm around the crooked shoulders and ·hoisted the boy into a sitting position.

"I can walk, you know," said Tony breathlessly. "But for some reason sitting up is hard."

"God, Tony. I am sorry."

"Why should you be?" The cracked whisper was would-be blithesome. "The only reason those butchers working the rack did not leave me a complete cripple is that you forced them to stop. Did you think I could not hear you arguing with them?"

That was precisely what he had thought. Tony had been limp and nearly lifeless by the time Robin had been able to halt some of the severity Elizabeth had demanded. That had been the afternoon of the night he'd met Kat . . .

His questions had to be approached gingerly. He sat on the edge of the pallet and wiped his hands on his thighs. His mind went blank.

"The day has been set," Tony remarked after a silence. "My execution is for tomorrow. Will you be there?"

Robin winced. "I doubt I can. There is—a task I must complete." *By Satan's flaming testicles, Kat, where are you?*

"Ah. Well, I do not blame you. I am not looking forward to the occasion much myself."

"Do you recall the time we went whoring together?" Robin plunged in. "That plump armful who sat in your lap at the inn on Turnbull Street?"

"Do I not! Nell." The white lips turned up in a smile of singular sweetness. "I always wondered if she chose me because you told her to."

Robin *had* arranged for Nell to aim her ample charms toward the fledgling traitor. He'd hoped a dose of the buxom whore's cozy good nature and really astonishing inventiveness would cure Tony's taste for more dangerous excitements. It hadn't. But from Nell's subsequent account of the evening, not for lack of enthusiasm on either party's side.

"She gave me the impression she liked you very well on your own account," Robin said gently.

"I am glad. Nell! Thank you for reminding me of her. I am being allowed to make my confession later. I would not like to have forgotten Nell."

"She would be grievously offended if you did."

Getting up, Robin moved restlessly about the cell. Neither of them mentioned that tomorrow, as part of his execution, Tony would be castrated.

"Recounting the number of sins she introduced me to ought to take an hour at the least," Tony said.

"Think of it as a charitable activity. Your confessor will probably enjoy it as much as you."

The bent shoulders shook. Anthony's laughter led to a coughing fit which lasted a full minute.

"What do you need from me, Robin? Oh, do not bother to deny you have a reason for coming. We said our farewells at the end of the trial. Why are you here? Not for the balmy air or the snug surroundings."

"You are keen-witted today."

"The prospect of dying within four-and-twenty hours sharpens the intellect. Are you troubled? I will help if I can."

"There's a girl," said Robin abruptly. "A woman. She has been in my charge, more or less . . ."

It took time to explain the connection between Kat, Priorly, and Mary Stuart at Fotheringhay. Tony's broken back gave out at the end of the account, and Robin eased him onto his side.

"My thanks," he sighed. "Preston? The name is familiar. I have heard of Prestons abroad, but none in England. If my colleagues are planning to use this Priorly, I am not aware of it."

"Tony, think! Can you tell me anything at all? She was stolen from Richmond more than half a day ago."

"I fear I have never heard of the lady before."

"Then . . . it is personal. There's only one person who . . . but is even he that obsessed with . . ." Robin's voice trailed off.

"This Lady Katherine means something to you? You love her?" asked Tony.

Robin's breath came out in a harsh gasp. "How would I know if what I feel for her is love? When have I ever had the chance to learn what that is?" He stopped. Soon his young friend would have no more chances to learn anything. Except whatever surprises existed after life. More quietly, he said, "Take the lust you had for Nell, and the eagerness you give to Queen Mary. Combine them, and I suppose that's a fair description of how I feel about Kat."

"Love," pronounced Anthony confidently.

Robin gestured impatiently. "Can you remember nothing that might lead me to the bastards who took her?"

"I am sorry, Robin."

"I, too. If your people do not have her—hell, Tony, she's got the temper of a fiend. She's going to blame me."

Chapter 12

The narrow triangle of sky framed by the tent opening was the soft, smoky blue of autumn. It didn't vary much as the afternoon wore on. Now and then a streamer of cloud sailed by.

Dusk came slowly, indicated by a darker tinge to the blue and the arrival of the day's last meal. The moon, nearly full, came out. The wind picked up. It pushed the sides of the tent inward, and then suddenly sucked them outward, like the breath of a huge beast.

Kate forced herself to eat bowled fowl. Whatever happened tonight, she'd need her strength.

"May I have a robe?" she asked Samuel, putting down the spoon he'd given her after he cut the meat himself. He had taken care to keep her away from sharp objects. "Or a cloak?" The tent-side rattled, and she shivered. Her thin smock couldn't protect her from the seeping cold. Samuel was lighting candles; the flames streamed.

"My orders are to keep you as you are."

"No clothes provided for me. Does that mean I am not expected to live through the night?" She felt brittle pride that her voice wobbled only a little.

"Nay," said Samuel frankly. "It means his lordship desires to see you without a gown on."

Into the silence that followed, a soft chiming dropped crystal-clear notes.

"How will it be possible to return me to the court after this night's work?"

"I do not ask questions, my lady. Happen it would be better if you did not, either."

After he left, Kat went back to pacing at the end of the long chain. Futile anger built up until it was a huge bubble clogging her throat. Assaulted in her chamber, trussed up like that wanton bitch in heat Cleopatra and carted who-knew-where against her will, chained . . . and all for the possibly murderous entertainment of some lord with an ambition to see her in her smock.

"And out of it, too, no doubt," she muttered. "Well, I do not choose to be gobbled up like a sweetmeat. I will not let this happen. I will not!"

The chain dragged on her arm. With a low, raw sound of pure fury, Kat squatted on the floor and put her shoulders under the seat of the massive chair. Straining, she pushed upward and saw the chair leg rise a hairsbreadth from the ground.

Hope made her whimper. The sound seemed unnaturally loud, and she eased the pressure, shooting a wary glance at the tent flap. It hung heavy and inert. Samuel must be lurking nearby, but she couldn't see him in the almost-blackness outside the small opening. Placing her feet beneath her more solidly, she heaved up with her back, keeping her eyes on the chair leg. The instant it lifted high enough to release the chain, she snatched the metal ring and pitched forward so the chair wouldn't hit her on its way down.

For a few valuable seconds, she hugged the chain to herself and whispered a prayer of thanks. Then she stood and tiptoed to the opening, peeking out. Samuel was walking toward the tent. Running back to the chair, she arranged herself on the seat, shoving the telltale end of the chain underneath the cushion and fluffing out the skirt of her smock to cover the chair leg. Her head bowed.

As he entered, Samuel nodded approvingly at the resigned picture she made. "That's the way to be. Life is hard, and it goes easier when we accept the bad along with the good."

Unable to help herself, Kat retorted, "All of the bad seems to be happening to me."

"Not a man to cross, his lordship," Samuel said. "I did a long time ago, and I learned my lesson well."

"Is that other man with you? The one who wanted to—"

"Nay. I sent him away. Otherroads, I would have spent the whole day keeping him from sniffing around you. You are safe enough at the moment, lass. 'Tis just you and I."

She must lure him into relaxing, Kat thought. That was what Robin would do. "What did your lord do to you?" she asked. With amiable, solid Samuel blocking the exit, the odds were still overwhelming she'd be in this damned tent when the lord arrived to do something to her.

In his eyes, a light flared and died. "Caught me with one of his women. The bastardly toad."

Kat's face flamed. "Oh."

"He took care he would not share a play-pretty with me again. Made me watch while he punished her for sleeping with me. Poor, silly, generous wench. She used to be so bonny . . ."

"Why do you serve him? Why have you not *killed* him?"

"That will not get the wench her beauty back," he pointed out.

"But it could give you your manhood back," Kat said fiercely. "Being a man is more than what hangs between your legs."

Her heart leaped when the fire flashed in his eyes again, but it faded just as quickly. "You do not tempt me like that, my lady. Better a live servant than a dead—"

"You no longer have that choice," said a pleasant voice from the tent flap.

"Robin?"

Her whisper was high, thin, frail. Now that he was here—his hair wild, clothes wrinkled and dirt-streaked—Kat's desire to trust him warred with a lifetime's experience. Experience of men who died, or used or went away.

She did trust him, she did, but . . . Robin's looks were frankly terrifying. His face was wiped clean of expression and the gray of his eyes might have been forged from the same bright, emotionless steel as the knife in his hand. Rescuer or tormentor?

While her mind was still torn, the rest of her decided.

"Robin, I am so glad you are here." She knew her heart was speaking.

Samuel lowered his head and charged.

Robin sidestepped and brought the hilt of his poniard down hard on the back of the older man's neck. The blow didn't quite stun; Samuel's big arms had already closed around Robin's wrist, and both men went down in a tangle of thrashing limbs. The knife flew into the silken draperies.

The smack of fists landing in flesh drew an oath from Kat. Jumping up, she scrambled along the tent walls in search of the weapon. Urgency and the clanking chain dragging on her wrist made her clumsy. She brushed against one of the candles, and it fell. Fire licked at the dry silk and canvas. With a *whoosh* one whole side of the tent went up in flames.

Shrieking, she backed away, stumbling over the men on her way. Her buttocks made contact with a hard back.

"Fire!" she screamed. "Stop, you idiots. Fire!"

They were too lost in bloodlust to listen. Samuel was on top; his thick thumbs gouged at Robin's eyes. Robin had one hand buried in the folds of his adversary's neck and was squeezing with such force Samuel's skin had gone white as bone. Around the ivory areas purple bulged.

The fire blazed. Its ominous crackle brought her hands together to pummel the back she sat on. Repeated blows by her clasped fists failed to bring attention from either man.

"Damn you! Damn both of you!" Grasping the chain, Kat slipped it quickly over Samuel's head and pulled.

The heavy body went lax.

Robin wheezed, "If you get up, we can take our leave."

Kat jumped off, jerking the chain from Samuel's neck as she went. Robin crawled out from under the servant's bulk.

On three sides of them blazed an inferno. Robin shoved her through the opening. He didn't follow immediately, and she realized he must be trying to haul Samuel out of danger. Flames were consuming three sides of the tent, and licked almost to the flap. Throwing the flap up and wide,

Kat hoped it would stay open and darted back into the fire and smoke.

"What are you doing?" Robin yelled. He coughed fitfully. With both hands under Samuel's arms, he'd managed to gain a yard.

"Helping, you ass," she shouted back. Grabbing one meaty hand, she pulled as hard as she could. It wasn't her contribution that made the difference, she realized as they manhandled the unconscious figure halfway through the opening. Robin's coughed curses made it clear that fury over her foolhardiness had supplied him with a few extra ounces of strength.

They ducked into the cold, clear night, dragging Samuel with them. "Is he breathing?" she asked.

"Yes," Robin answered. "You did not mash his throat with your chain. He should come to presently." He cursed one last time and grinned crookedly. "My thanks for your assistance, damask lady. I would never have suspected your prowess at arms."

Relief and pleasure flooded her as clean air bathed all her senses. It sucked the smell of smoke from her nostrils, washing the acrid taste from her mouth and the sting from her eyes. Its coolness felt good on her skin. Her ears gradually separated the roar of the fire from noises that came from the outside world—the whistle of the wind, the tinkling of chimes, and a faraway pounding.

"We are not far from Richmond?" she asked Robin, bending her back to the task of helping him drag Samuel.

"Less than a league," he grunted. "Did you not know?"

"Nay. But I heard the chimes and guessed. Is this a safe distance from the fire?" Robin had sat back on his haunches.

"The last rain was two nights ago, so probably not. The trees are well back, but the grass might catch. We shall have to wait until the tent collapses and then put out the flames which remain with my cloak and your—no, you had better not take off what you have on."

"For modesty's sake?" she said lightly. Happiness and reaction were like whiskey in her veins, making her giddy.

"For the sake of that pretty skin of yours. You have blisters and scrapes enough. The wonder is your smock did not go up like a torch. Here crouch for me, your hem is smoldering."

His boot ground the glowing edge of the muslin into sooty threads.

"How did you find me?"

"Once I realized who was most likely to have taken you, I had a timely word with this person and that. In certain circles his habits are common knowledge. I already knew the old fox considers it convenient to keep a portable lair separate from the court."

"Aftondale?"

"You guessed? Or has he visited you here?"

"Nay! I swear it, Robin. He has not had me." Kat clutched his sleeve.

"Hush, sweet heart. It would not be you I would blame if he did." He slid an arm around her waist. "I have been so fearful for you," he whispered raggedly. "Not sure if fanatics faithful to Mary Stuart were using you as a pawn, or if Aftondale was subjecting you to his unclean ways."

"There's no doubt it was the earl, then?"

"None in my mind." His face might have been carved from stone.

"Samuel said he does such things—"

"Do not think of them. He'll not be doing them to you." The hard chest crushing her breasts rose and fell in a long breath. "I expected you to upbraid me mightily if I ever found you."

His shoulder was the perfect height to make a pillow for her cheek.

"I am not so silly."

He stiffened. "A horse," he said.

The pounding was coming closer. "Help?" she hazarded. "The glow from the fire might have been noticed from the palace." Kat remembered something Samuel had said. "Or it could be Aftondale. He was expected for tonight."

Robin pushed her gently to one side. "My horse is tied to a tree over there. Do you ride? Can you mount without assistance?"

She nodded.

"Go wait next to the horse. One hint that I am losing,

and you get into the saddle and ride for the east as hard as you can. The guards on the gate at Richmond know you were abducted; they will let you into the palace. God's death! I should have brought trustworthy men with me, but I hoped to get you back without any more witnesses."

"Robin, he's a peer," she said urgently. "You cannot just exterminate an earl."

"I am not forgetting his station. But you cannot—poppet, you really cannot—expect me to ignore what he's done to you."

"I do not trust how pleased you look all of a sudden," she told him, and then, obeying his order, made her way to his horse. His restive mare was tall. Kat stepped up into the bole of a young elm to assure that she'd be able to reach the horse's back if the need came.

"My poniard is gone, I suppose?" Robin spoke loudly enough for Kat to hear.

"Unless it survived the fire."

He pulled his sword free of its scabbard. "The handle was wood. It was an old friend. Ah, well. I would rather lose it than you."

Flames still crackled, although large portions of the canvas had been eaten through. Kat couldn't believe only minutes had passed since the candle had fallen.

Hoofbeats thundered into the glade. The fitful light played over Aftondale's open mouth, transforming its expression into a gargoyle's leer. Robin moved in a blur of speed, hauling him one-handed from a stallion that screamed and reared at the sight and smell of fire.

Helpless between Robin and the horse, the earl tumbled to the ground in an ungraceful heap and lay there drawing faint, mewing breaths. With businesslike swiftness, Robin filched Aftondale's knife and sword, throwing them toward Kat. She smiled with satisfaction. It didn't look as if she were going to have to leap onto the mare and ride away from a losing fight. Jumping down from the tree, she picked up the smaller weapon, pushing the sword hilt farther from the men with her toe. It was heavy, but it budged a few inches.

"I am going to kill you," said Robin to Aftondale in a conversational tone.

Words of protest clogged Kat's throat, and stayed there. Aftondale would be no loss to the world. A silent parade of the victims whose misery he must have caused seemed to hold out arms to her, begging for justice. One of them was Samuel. His master was predatory, perverted. The earl displayed the qualities people accused Robin of having. But Robin hunted cleanly. Aftondale did not.

It was a seductive temptation—to let murder be done without saying a word to stop it. But if she didn't say something, Robin would become . . . *less*. Because of her.

"My lord," she said, "he's not worth staining your sword."

"A sound point, damask lady, as always. I would not be surprised if this piece of filth spews dragon's blood that never wipes clean."

"We would certainly not be able to wash off the stain of killing an unarmed man."

"There's so much blood on my hands, I doubt anyone will notice another clot or two," he said with a bitter glance at her.

"You will know," she reminded him. "And so will I."

Robin didn't bother to warn her that dragons, even old ones, were never unarmed as long as they had claws and fire at their disposal. She was reaching for the reins of Aftondale's stallion with a blind hand. Her serious gaze never left him.

The wind from the sky and the wind from the fire combined to twist her smock to her body, outlining its long-legged perfection. Her plaited hair had come loose around her face. Still burning, the fire lit the loose curls into a bright nimbus. The long knife in her other hand reflected orange light. She might have been an angel of the Lord, calling him back from damnation.

If he rid the world of Aftondale, everyone would assume he had done so to revenge Kat's honor. Or out of pique because the earl had stolen Kat's virginity out from under his nose. Murdering the old devil would be satisfying. But it would also be taken as proof that the ancient satyr had raped Kat. Probably with accompanying perversions. Her reputation was scandal-tossed already. This would sink it completely.

Besides ... God, he was tired of being himself. He didn't want to kill. All the stains on his soul seemed to be blood.

Wicked hooves flashed as the horse danced away from Kat's reaching grasp. Robin flicked a glance at Aftondale, who said quickly, "I have not touched her. Ask her. I did not realize you had such strong feelings about the girl. I would never ..."

Frowning in concentration—if he didn't kill the vermin, what was he to do with him?—Robin was dimly aware that Kat was trying for the reins again. He approved. The last thing they needed was a loose horse causing chaos. She swiveled to follow the lashing reins, and she cried out, "Robin!"

The stallion reared in earnest, hooves pawing the air. In the clear space behind the animal, a figure waving a sword moved.

Robin leaped for Kat. A sweep of his arm brought her behind him. Ripping off his cloak, he flapped it at the maddened horse, which screamed and minced backward on two feet, and came down with a wet thud.

"Oh, dear God," Kat whispered. "Dear God in heaven, is Aftondale dead?"

The earl's eyes had rolled up, and the imprint of a hoof dented his forehead. Bone showed through.

"You there," Robin called, clearing his throat. "Your lord is sore injured. Put up the sword."

"That's a lie," came the response from the other side of the now-quiet horse. "There's nothing that would hurt *him.*"

"It is the truth, Samuel," Kat confirmed. "Look and see."

"A trick! You cannot fool me like that!"

The voice was moving, coming from a slightly different direction. Robin pivoted slowly, trying to identify where exactly the man might be headed in the perplexing gloom beyond the fire's glare.

Aftondale's man rushed into the glade, blade waving. The fellow stopped ludicrously short at the sight of his master.

"Your lordship?" he said, his incredulity somehow painful to witness. "Your lordship?"

Dropping to his knees, Robin inspected Aftondale briefly. "Dead."

Kat murmured a short prayer. At its end, she walked up to the servant and took his hand. "Your lord cannot torment either of us again." She sounded as if she were trying to reassure a child.

"Ah, lass. I never thought I would see the wolf-bitch's son brought down. He—I was afraid to stay with him, and afraid to leave. Understand?" He leaned on the sword, looking tired.

With a crack and a roar, the tent supports collapsed. Sparks fountained high and then fell in patterns of deadly beauty.

Robin shouted, "Kat, stay back. Your feet are bare. Here, you, Samuel, if that's your name, get Aftondale's cloak off him and help me put out the flames before they spread. Move, man!"

The distinct order seemed to pierce Samuel's dreamy contemplation of the earl. He obeyed with quick, jerky movements, stealing the cloak from his dead master's corpse and using it to thresh at tiny fires before they could grow bigger. Robin watched him in puzzlement; the servant didn't seem to notice whether the flames lapped him or not.

He shrugged. Beyond a snapped "Have a care!" there wasn't anything he could do, and he had his own share of fires to put out. The grass wasn't too dry. With some luck, the blaze would die for lack of fuel as long as they kept it away from the wooded area.

After a few moments, he realized another worker had joined them.

"God's grace, Kat—"

"It never fails to amaze me," she said, beating down a tongue of flame with her smock, "how prudish you are for a man of your reputation."

"I'll have to exact a revenge for this."

She gave an ostentatious sigh. Her breasts rose and fell. "What imaginary crime have I committed now?"

"Prancing before me naked when I cannot do anything

about it. Here, take my doublet, at least. What a heedless
wench you are."

"Only since I met you," she said, pausing to struggle
into the unfamiliar garment. It skimmed her thighs.

"You shall burn your feet."

"I am hanging well back and taking care where I stand."

"More than your friend Samuel over there. Hell! His
jerkin's afire!"

They both ran to bundle Samuel in their clothes. He
didn't even have time to scream before the flames were
smothered, but he sat down hard and began to cry.

Robin unwound his cloak from Samuel and went back
to work. "Just sit, will you?" he said to Kat. He could see
she was wavering between an obvious desire to comfort
the weeping man and an equally obvious determination to
continue putting out sparks. At least now she was partially
clothed.

She sent him a grimace, while patting Samuel's hand.
"The fire is almost out, Robin, do you not think so?"

"Yes." Robin attacked a last, stubborn line of flame. It
finally flickered out.

Suddenly all was quiet and dark. Embers glowed here
and there, but the glade was safe enough now, he decided,
surveying the wasteland of charred timbers and ghostlike
scraps of ash. Stumbling a little in exhaustion, he made his
way to Kat's side and let his legs fold underneath him.

"My sweet devil Robin," she said, holding out her arms.
"You look as if you have been to hell and back. Rest."

He didn't question the invitation, but simply stretched
out and put his head in her lap. Shuddering, he buried his
face in the doublet where it was buttoned over the hollow
of her belly.

"We cannot rest. This night's work will land us in worse
grief if we do not get to Walsingham with explanations before news of the earl's death is out," he mumbled.

"But surely—the queen or your cousin—"

"Burghley would throw you to the wolves. This is a
scandal he's not going to relish. And Elizabeth would lock
you up so tight I would never get to see you again. Let
alone—" He dropped a kiss on her thigh. "Let alone put
my head in your lap, sweet heart. We'll leave Aftondale's

body at Richmond, report to Walsingham, and ride for Priorly."

He felt the touch of her fingertips on the back of his
neck. Despite fighting a fire, they were cool and gentle.
"Priorly?" Yearning filled her tone.

"I was supposed to go yesterday."

Walsingham hadn't been pleased when Robin insisted
on tracking Kat instead. He lifted his head to comfort himself by filling his gaze with her, and realized they were
alone. "Where is your friend?"

By God, he was slipping. Taking comfort in her welcoming arms and soft lap, he hadn't noticed the other
man's quiet withdrawal.

"Here, my lord," came the answer. "Just checking on
the horses."

Robin looked up at Kat. Her face was interesting from
this angle, he thought. All chin and lips and eyelashes.
"We had best be going before he decides to take vengeance on us for his master," he murmured.

"I doubt Samuel would want to do that," she replied just
as softly.

Getting up first, he held out an imperative hand. Pulling
her to her feet, he regarded her legs in the faint glimmer
from the embers.

She followed his glance. "God knows what Lord
Walsingham will make of me in your doublet."

"If he has any powers of observation, he will notice you
have very well-shaped knees."

"Thank you kindly, my lord." She curtsied pertly. "But
I have no ambition to show them off to all and sundry."

"Good. Only to me." He stated it flatly.

Startled brown eyes flew to his, and he realized he'd
just claimed possession. Permanent possession. Kat Preston was his woman.

After a pause, he continued, "We'll need to find you
some clothes. In fact, I can think of no reason why your
maid should not fetch you what you'll want for the journey, as long as she can be quick and discreet about it."

"Maud? Is she all right?"

"A bit bloodied, but fine." He tossed her into the mare's

saddle. "You, Samuel, you are free. I ought to arrest you. But I will not."

"Samuel has suffered enough," said Kat firmly, arranging her leg around the pommel in imitation of a sidesaddle.

"My lord, my lady—" The hulking man blinked, then turned to Kat in appeal. "I have nowhere to go."

Seeing what was coming, Robin swore.

Tentatively, Kat suggested, "He could lead Aftondale's horse with the earl tied on, and I could ride pillion behind you."

"And then what?" asked Robin wryly.

"Well, Samuel could stay with us. Could you not find a use for a loyal man? He can be very loyal."

Robin looked at Samuel. Samuel and Kat looked at Robin.

"Very well," he growled. "My lady has a soft spot, it seems. I warn you, Samuel, I have no soft spots."

"Of course not, my lord," agreed Samuel stoutly.

The two men hoisted the earl's body onto the stallion's back. When they were done tying him on, Kat scooted to the back of Robin's saddle, and Robin mounted. She put her arms around his waist, and he could feel the pressure of her bare legs against his thighs. He expected to be too tired and worried for desire, but a jolt of it shot through him anyway. A good thing the ride would be a short one, he thought.

He could feel Kat shaking against his back. Lifting one of her hands from his waist, he kissed it. "Do not fret, poppet. We shall win our way out of this coil."

"Th-thank you, Robin."

Something about her tone made him suspicious, and he turned in the saddle, peering at her face. It was convulsed with laughter. "What is so amusing?" he asked sternly.

"We are. You worried for my modesty, me beyond caring, all of us half-clothed." Her laugh choked to a stop. "Oh, God, Robin, why did Aftondale have to die?"

"To spite us." Robin spoke bracingly; she wasn't about to give way to hysteria, not his damask lady, but he didn't like the ragged note in her voice. He kept talking to give her a chance to recover. "Actually, it is as well we have the mystery at Priorly to give us an urgent reason to leave court. Elizabeth is not going to be happy with either of us. And as you said, exterminating earls will not make me popular. Home for you, damask lady. I promise."

She rested her cheek on the broad support of his back. Home to Priorly—and whatever was happening there.

Part Two

Traitor's Kiss

Chapter 13

K at sat bolt upright in bed.

The inn Robin had brought her to after a quick stop at Richmond was pleasant. The food provided had been filling and comforting, the bath she'd taken in the tub still squatting by the cozy fire a deeply felt necessity. Getting rid of the soot and grime had left her pink and tingling.

Now that she was in bed and clad in the luxury of a clean smock, she simply waited. She knew Robin would come.

The door opened quietly. Soft-footed, he stepped into the bedchamber and grinned at her. "You look like a bride, my lady."

Kat wasn't sure how to respond. Or what he expected as a reward for rescuing her. "Do I?"

"A nervous one."

"Well, you look like a smith's apprentice. Black with soot and singed around the edges. Could you not charm a bath out of the innkeeper's wife?"

"She seems remarkably immune to anything but direct threats and prompt payments of silver. Besides, is that not my bath?"

The tingles on her skin rushed together to form a tide of heat. "Nay, sir. It was *my* bath."

"And you will not share with a fellow traveler who needs a good scrubbing? Fie, Kat. By the way, where's that beast of yours?"

"Maud has Grimalkin. We cannot let her loose in a

strange place. And Samuel is sleeping in the stable so he can keep an eye on the horses."

Robin grunted. "Who will keep an eye on him?"

"It is as good a way as any to discover how trustworthy he intends to be," pointed out Kat. "What are you doing?"

He paused, his shirt half-off. Tightly curled blond hair washed over his chest like sea spray.

"I'm undressing," he said ironically. "What do you imagine I am doing? Even virgins must know men disrobe as women do—by removing their clothes."

"My lord, you had better seek your own chamber. In truth, I deserve to be punished for teasing you when I took off my smock to fight the fire—but your revenge has gone far enough." She wished her voice carried more conviction.

With deliberate insolence, he shrugged off the shirt and let it drop to the floor before he sat on the edge of the bed to pull off his boots.

"Let me make myself clear. While your Maud keeps an eye on the cat, and Samuel keeps an eye on the horses, I'll keep an eye on you. I am not letting you out of my sight unless I have you surrounded by twenty trusty men-at-arms sworn to me personally. Since we lack an escort—and because I doubt you would like very many witnesses to your intimate routines—"

"I do not want *any* witnesses," she said. "Especially you."

"I can always depend on you to be frank. It desolates me to have to disregard your wishes in this matter, damask lady."

"Liar!"

His laughter was soft and mocking. It infuriated her.

"Do you have to take off *all* your clothes?"

"I usually bathe nude," he said imperturbably. His hose followed his britches and he got to his feet. "Why do you object? Does it displease you to see a man's body?" He faced her.

She wanted, desperately, to find something to disparage about his appearance. An amusingly light and critical comment ought to discourage his outrageous mood. But he had never been easily discouraged. And there was nothing to criticize.

"You are magnificent," she whispered.

The taunting lilt at the corners of his mouth faded under her stare. The real Robin was different from the Robin in her dream. Then her imagination had inevitably gotten some of the details wrong.

The hair on his body was thicker than she'd realized. It spread not only across the breadth of his chest but in drifts of gold down his upper arms and legs. It was coarser, too. Of course, she thought dazedly, gold wouldn't be soft. It would be strong and wiry. His limbs were heavy with muscle; the male hair didn't obscure how much strength was stored in his arms and thighs. His shoulders were strong, too, although they were smooth. The fair skin was faintly lined with veins.

True to the dream, Robin's hips were narrow. And there, where his golden curls clustered thickest, his body was responding to the stimulus of her fascination. Flesh filled out. It took a definite shape, and rose solid and hard.

"Have you never seen this before?" he asked, with a grimace that was oddly tender. "Arousal?"

Kat shook her head, unable to wrench her gaze away.

"It does not look like a weapon," she said uncertainly.

"Because it is not. Just a tool, sweet heart. For pleasure, yours as well as mine." He lifted his short, pointed beard into a considering angle. "Shall I have to convince you of that?"

She looked away, and he shrugged and turned, stepping into the bath with a slight splash.

"Still warm," he said with a sigh. "Would you like to scrub my back?"

Kat raised her head, intending to pin him with a glare. She discovered a friendly grin on his handsome features, and tried not to melt. He wasn't so intimidating with his long limbs—and disconcerting maleness—stuffed into the oval tub.

Pointedly ignoring his suggestion, she told him, "There's soap left. They had no perfumes or oils. The innkeeper's wife informed me most of the gentry bring their own bathing things."

"Like you, I would rather wash away the stinks than try to hide them under sickly scents." He scrubbed vigorously. "Was the woman trying to insult you? I will speak to her—"

"Nay. We gave her plenty of trouble. How do you know I prefer soap?"

"You always smell good. It is why I wanted you in the first place, I think," he added calmly.

It was suddenly hard to breathe. "Lord Robin, you are flirting with danger."

"I know it." The gleam in his eyes turned hot. "But I am not flirting with you. I *want* you, Kat. Not just in bed. I want your company at all times. Your—your self. If that's foolish, it is foolish. Perhaps I do not talk to you as a man should to a virgin. Truth to tell, I have never had truck with one before."

Stepping out of the tub, he reached for a towel and rubbed it over his chest.

"Robin." Kat couldn't think of what to say. "Robin, I . . ."

"You have yet to kiss me of your own will," he said helpfully when her voice dwindled away. "I have waited for you to do that since you taught me how patience could be an aphrodisiac."

She folded her arms over her breasts. "Robin Hawking, you are a rogue! I never said—"

"You asked for *a kiss that's meant as a gift instead of a demand. Quiet talk at the end of the day. Company by the fire.* You see, I remember every word. I have fulfilled all your requirements, my lady."

Violently, Kat threw back the covers and ran barefoot to him. The towel dropped to the floor. He was still aroused. When he put his hands around her waist and pulled her closer, she waited for him to crush her in his arms, but instead he left a teasing inch between their bodies. She could only just feel the heat from the round red tip of his arousal through her thin smock.

Their faces, though, were very close. "Let me kiss you like a gift, Kat."

She put her lips within a whisper of his. Robin wasn't

a dream—and perhaps tonight he could help her break the spell of her old nightmare.

"I would like that kind of kiss, my lord."

His mouth brushed hers so lightly she wanted to cry.

She intended to watch him as he kissed her. Instead, her eyelids drifted closed by themselves, and a velvet darkness made her as safe as a butterfly waiting to come out of a cocoon.

The gentle touches of lips to lips went on and on. Light, moist, warm, they felt like spring rain after a dry spell. She'd known she was thirsty to be kissed by Robin; she hadn't guessed he was capable of sweetness.

"Marry me." Another soft, moth-wing kiss.

"What?" She struggled out of the haze of sensuality, making it halfway to reality. Though she forced her lids open, they felt heavy. And how could such soft kisses make her lips feel full, and her limbs drugged? "Marriage? You cannot be serious."

His mouth went stern. "Oh, but I am. Say you will marry me."

"Nay! The queen would—"

Robin said something about the queen that was very rude. He added ominously, "I see I'll have to convince you after all."

This time he took her mouth like a starving man. After a single, shuddering breath, Kat was lost. It was another new variety of kiss, a kind he'd never pressed on her before—not hurtful, not langorously exploring, not teasing with a sensuality too experienced for her to counter. This was simple and direct, ravenous. Delicious.

She opened her mouth to let him take, and instead, surprising her, he continued to give. His deep groan entered her and filled a vast, aching place, stirring even sweeter, sharper aches. He gave her hard, sweeping thrusts of his tongue. Impatient bites from his lips. The exciting graze of his teeth.

"Kiss me back," he demanded, harsh with need. "With your tongue. Kiss me back."

Kat whimpered, but delicately ran her tongue over his bottom lip, and behind his upper one. Gradually, exploring him began to waken instincts that craved more than just to respond. She had followed where he had led, but now she wanted to lead, too. She wanted to drive him wild. *Robin is going to be my lover,* she thought—and the conviction brought no shame, only another wave of anticipation. It would be tonight. Now. The suspense would be over.

His mouth opened wider, and she touched the tip of his tongue with her own. Breathing hard, he let her discover the hot, moist top and the soft, strong root. Her fingers were hot and felt swollen at the tips. They investigated the flat tracery of his ears and pulled at the wet curls on the back of his head. A growl rumbled from his chest when she dug into his shoulders in a desperate kneading. Untutored in this activity as she might be, Kat still knew the growl was one of pleasure, not displeasure.

"Time for bed, poppet."

Picking her up, he swung her onto the mattress. With her legs tucked under her, and her eyes soft and serious, she was the fey girl who'd invaded his bed hangings. The rough way he'd treated her then horrified him in retrospect. Robin told himself he had to go slow, give her a satin seduction, do nothing to alarm her.

It was an effort to force his fingers to go slowly about the business of untying the strings at the neck of her smock. Almost reverently, he lifted the voluminous garment over her head and laid it at the end of the bed.

His gaze wandered from the long, white throat to the subtly molded breasts, from the hollow of her belly to her slim legs. Just peeking out from where they were folded beneath her, were long, slender feet.

Kneeling on the mattress, he linked his fingers with hers and pulled her up until they knelt knee to knee. The wrist he put to his mouth tasted of soap and creamy skin. He licked the frantic pulse point and with his tongue traced the veins faintly visible under her smooth skin to the inside of her elbow. She jumped slightly at the nibble of his teeth.

"Take me, Robin." The plea was desperate.

He could have; he was certainly ready. But Kat had gone pale, and although her eyes still looked shocked by sensuality, he wanted to be very sure her body was as ready for him as a virgin's could be. The emotion in her voice ought to be urgency. "Soon," he promised.

Turning her so her bruised back faced him, he ran a finger down her spine. On some women, the long line was a trench, or not distinguishable from the surrounding flesh at all. Kat's was a series of tender bumps ending in the furrow between her tight little buttocks. She jumped again when his finger failed to stop for more than a tantalizing moment at the dimples on either side of her tailbone.

"*Oh.*"

"My lady likes that?"

"Aye, but surely it is not gentlemanly to ask?"

"There's no room for shame in our bed, Kat," he said, as his finger traveled through the tight groove to the very center of her body. He smiled to find moisture gathering there.

With all the skill at his command, he played with her female flesh until additional wetness rushed to lubricate his finger and Kat sagged against him.

"There are places on my body that like to be touched, too, Kat."

She sighed and turned around to face him. Robin felt as if the soft sound had whispered from his own throat. Her small hand trailed slowly, sinuously, down his chest to hover next to the round, flushed head of his lance.

Breath began to pump in and out of his lungs. His manhood was moving of its own accord in excitement.

Hoarsely, he said, "I plight thee my troth."

Her hand curled into a fist and drew back.

"Nay."

It was suddenly important that she say yes. The desire for her "Aye" tore at him as much as the powerful lust flooding his loins.

"Why not? What keeps you from agreeing? God knows it will be years, if ever, before you would have to redeem a promise to marry me. Why not say yes?"

They were again kneeling chest to chest. She sank back on her slim haunches. "Robin, there's too much you do not even suspect concerning me—"

He opened her fist and kissed her palm. "Let me tell you what I know. You are sweet as ripe fruit, bright as a new penny, crotchety when anyone gets close enough to realize your thorns are merely the protection needed by any rare and lovely flower. You are honorable, and I will kill the man who says you are not virtuous."

"But I am not virtuous," she said in a small voice.

"Because of what we do here? Kat, I swear I regard you as my wife."

She pulled her hands away and scrambled under the covers, yanking them up to hide the aroused nipples on her breasts. "Not because of this. Nor for anything a man has ever done to me. But because I am a sham. Pretending, always pretending. Most of the time I am terrified that someone will find out the things I have done and take Priorly away from me."

"No one could do that without a reason, not even the queen." Reasons could be manufactured, as he was well aware, but he didn't say it. Fear for her sharpened his voice. "What have you done, Kat? If you are not involved in treason, why should you be afraid?"

Kat slid down in the bed. Her hair spilled over the comfortless surface of the wooden block provided by the inn in place of a pillow. She put her hands over her face.

Convinced it wouldn't enter the soft heat of Kat's body tonight, Robin's throbbing hardness began to subside. Painfully.

"You are making it sufficiently clear you do not care to finish what we have begun," he said impatiently. "You do not need to hide. Unless whatever it is you have done is a crime. Tell me, Kat. Are you trapped in treason?"

She shook her head.

Relieved, he felt his concern yield to irritation. His disappointment went far deeper than unsatisfied lust, but right now it centered in the area between his legs. He ached.

The fire needed banking, so he got up and banked it. When he'd finished, he climbed into bed, lay down, and glared at the wealth of hair and portion of her back which were the only parts of Kat visible in the dim light.

"Poppet, tell me what's the matter," he said as patiently as he could. "I cannot help you if you will not trust me."

"Stop calling me *poppet*. I am not a doll or a puppet to move at other people's whim."

"Very well." Consciously, he loosened the muscles of his jaw so his teeth wouldn't grind together. "I shall not insult you by calling you that again. But you have to tell me."

"What will the queen's rat catcher do to me if I do not?"

"Now, why would you want to cut me to the quick, lady? To make the questions stop?"

The line of her back, Robin thought, was the definition of stubbornness.

"I could neither threaten you with the usual punishments nor offer you the usual bribes, Kat," he said quietly. "It would kill me to see one hair—one long, lovely hair—from your head harmed. And I do not believe you could ever be bought. You are too honorable."

"Honor." She curled into an even tighter, more defensive ball. "The honor of the Prestons. Oh, God."

Well, she was a virgin, and virgins were entitled to a few qualms. Perhaps her odd behavior was no more than a flutter of nerves. He sat up and manhandled her into his arms. Her body huddled into his lap, with her limbs crowded together and head ducked, like a baby wrapped in its mother's womb.

Feeling large and male and clumsy, he stroked the soft luxuriance of her hair. "It is all right. If the idea of making love affrights you so much, we can wait. We have a lifetime for bed games. I'll not press you."

She managed to scrunch herself smaller. "You would go without—without comfort? For me?"

"For a while," he answered frankly. "Your nature is warm, Kat. It would not be forever. You are already ... curious. Virgins do succumb to the adventure of lovemaking—or else there would be no new virgins."

The top of her head pressed into his breastbone so hard it caused a sharp twinge. "I cannot lie to you anymore. Everyone else but not you. Robin, it is not the prospect of losing my much-vaunted virginity that frightens me. I am not a virgin."

He went still. "Aftondale? Samuel?"

"Of course not Samuel. Not the earl, either. I have not been a virgin since I was thirteen years old. When I was raped."

Chapter 14

He couldn't get any more sense out of her, leaving him to wonder what else, if anything, she hadn't told him. Dry sobs too violent for speech shuddered through her tightly balled body, dwindling to whimpers as she slowly relaxed into his embrace. From there she slid into sleep, abruptly, like a very young child.

Robin held her, waking every time she shifted. Then he listened to her even breathing. Now and then a tremor or a sob shook her. Emotions filled him—awareness of her grieving anger and her sense of loss, his own resurrected rage that anyone would dare harm his damask lady. In spite of the emotional turmoil, his body responded to her slender softness even when he dozed off; several times he jolted awake to discover himself ready again. Ignoring the need took an effort that left him in a pool of cooling sweat, and extremely bad-tempered. Not thinking of Kat meant thinking about Tony Babington. Tony would die today.

It wasn't quite dawn when he woke her.

"Kat," he said. "There's no time to lie abed this morning. We have to be on our way."

She opened blank eyes. "Robin?" Intelligence gradually returned to her gaze. "Did I lie on your arm all night?" she asked. "Is it numb?"

"No," he lied. His voice was short. "Up with you now. We must break our fast and be gone. Do you wish to use the pot first?"

Blushing, she shook her head. Robin hesitated—he was

erect again, this time with the need to relieve himself—and then shrugged. He was a man. He often started the morning in this condition, and Kat might as well get used to the sight of it. The straps under the bed creaked as he got up and went to the corner.

In a slightly better mood, he turned to find her clad in her wrinkled smock, trying to assemble the pieces of the gown she'd worn from Richmond.

"I'll play lady's maid," he offered, and got to work.

She smiled at him over a sleeve with a new shyness. "You are very good at tucks and ties. Have you had much practice?"

"The women I have been with have not been ladies." His fingers tied steadily. "A man hardly ever spends the whole night with a whore or a fleeting light-o'-love."

"Either of which would have given you a more entertaining night than I did."

"Kat." His tone was dangerously level as he yanked a ribbon into place. "Spending the night just holding you meant more to me than a frolic in bed."

"I should hope so. You did not get one."

"Woman, do not tempt me to homicide while I have my hands around your neck." He adjusted her ruff.

"Well, it is difficult to produce other topics of conversation when you are so—so naked."

A hint of mischief sparkled from under her downcast lids. Robin tilted her chin.

"I am fairly sure I am not so magnificent as you seem to think, at least not in the mornings." He caught her hand and held it to his rough cheek. "In fact, I bid fair to be called a ruffian."

"You are always a ruffian," she said, rubbing the stubble. "And a rogue and a scoundrel—with a disconcerting sense of responsibility. What am I to do with you, Robin?"

"Cherish me," he answered promptly. "Say you'll marry me."

"Did you not hear me? I am not a virgin."

"If my plans for you had proceeded as I intended last night, you would not be one in any case. Whether you are a virgin does not matter to me."

"Do you mean a love match? Who marries for love?"

"I did not say love." He shrugged. "I have never known what that is. But I would be a good husband. I value you."

"Not a love match, then." Turning away, Kat picked up his hose. When she turned back, her face was set in an expression of calm control. She pushed the hose into his hands, saying, "Either way, Elizabeth would sooner part with half of England than see a fine, brawny specimen like you dancing attendance on a wife you—valued. And she would never give up an inch of her kingdom."

"We can find a way."

"My lord, I do not choose for you to be clapped up in prison. She did that to Jane Monteshote's lover, you know. Nor would I want to be like the Earl of Leicester's wife. They wed against the queen's will. First Elizabeth banished them both, then she brought him back but not her. The poor woman never sees her husband. They might as well never have gotten married."

"My happiness is not wrapped up in the queen's favor."

"But your employment is. She would dismiss you and see that no one ever hired you again. *And* she would strip me of Priorly. What can we do?"

Kat's reasoning was sound, and he hated it. "Cherish me," he repeated, admitting that the solution was beyond him at the moment.

She stepped back. "I do—a little. Shall I help you dress?"

Stepping into his hose, he said, "Just with the hooks on the sides. I'll remove myself so your woman can do your hair. Nothing fancy. The roads are not muddy, but we have a hard day's ride ahead of us."

Finishing his dressing in silence, he went to the door.

"Robin," she called softly behind him.

He glanced around.

"You make the nicest pillow I have ever slept on. If you still want me, I will be your lover."

He lifted a brow. "Make no mistake. You will be my wife. I do not know how, but I will make it happen."

Biting her lip, she sat on the edge of a chest until Maud entered, grim-mouthed—over meeting her mistress's bedmate outside the door, Kat supposed.

"You can stop staring holes in my clothes," she said

when Maud was done winding her hair in a coil and pinning it. "There are no bruises to see except the ones I gave myself trying to escape from that damned tent, and— Maud. I will have no speculation about what goes on between Lord Robin and me. None. Do you hear me?"

"But, my lady, my lady—"

"My lord was kindness itself to me last night. He did not even take advantage of the fact we slept in the same chamber," said Kat, spoiling the impression by yawning.

She patted her mouth, and only then realized how tender and swollen it was. Red, too, probably, from the narrow glance Maud darted at it. Recalling the wonderful, eating kisses, she felt color flood up into her throat and face.

It should have been shameful to wish that Robin had been less kind, or that she hadn't been so paralyzed over fear of his reaction to her past. But shame wasn't what she felt. There was only a great relief that one secret at least was in the open between them.

Lurking under the relief was anxiety, because there was so much she didn't have the courage to admit. Some of those secrets weren't hers to tell. Kat was terribly afraid she was falling in love with Robin. But she had always loved her brothers, too, and confessing everything would betray their memory.

Tangled in the web of guilt was the thread of a tentative anticipation. Silly to believe she could ever be anyone's wife, let alone Robin's. He kept the queen's peace. The last man in the world she could ask to sanction her murky affairs was an agent of the law. Not after the part she'd reluctantly played one soft summer's night seven years ago, when her innocence was torn from her and the ordered world of Priorly exploded in violence.

She had done her best to put the pieces of her world to rights. The estate was still whole, its people prosperous and mostly contented. Didn't that count for something?

No, she told herself with ruthless honesty. She couldn't expect Robin to overlook her unwilling crimes. If he persisted in this beautiful, heartbreaking nonsense about marriage, she would have to tell him all that had happened so long ago. He would not want her as a wife after that. No man would.

Accepting her cloak from a taciturn Maud, she went to the common room and found Robin gnawing a buttery crust.

"Eat while you can," he told her briskly. "We shall not stop often."

Kat slapped bacon on bread to make a meal. Taking a bite, she saw that he looked the same as he had the first time she'd seen him: driven, annoyed, rakish, and rumpled. Remembering the way he'd thrown his clothes on the floor last night, she smiled as she chewed. She was untidy with her garments herself, so they were well matched in that, at least.

Even if the things other women got—a husband, a family, the serenity of an ordinary life—were out of her reach, she could have Robin. For a while. Kat wasn't crazy or optimistic enough to imagine he would be hers for a lifetime. But she'd had seven years of practice in living for the moment.

"Are you ready, my lady? Let's go."

Snatching a second piece of bacon, she trotted after him.

Both Samuel and Maud rode rawboned horses Robin had coerced out of the stable master at Richmond. The pace he set would have been too fast for mules or a wagon. Samuel sat his mount like a sack of meal, but he stayed on, occasionally calling encouragement to Maud, whose lined face was deeply unhappy.

Now and then Kat heard him trying to explain away the abduction. Once his voice carried clearly. "We were told the lady's maid would be not young. Somebody did not look closely enough." Kat turned her head to hide a smile. Samuel seemed bent on ingratiating himself with the rest of her household, such as it was at the moment.

Robin kept Kat's gelding next to the stallion he rode instead of his exhausted mare.

And ... Kat talked. Whether because the silent man pushing them north had learned that haughty Lady Katherine Preston was really just Kat-with-no-virginity-to-lose, or from embarrassment at what had *not* happened last night, she found herself chattering.

Her one-sided conversation jumped from the dark clouds piling up in the sky, to the condition of the fields, to the health of the sheep that bunched up and then scattered as the riders passed.

"I have been a country girl all my life," she explained. "The state of the land has always been the most important consideration every day to me. Until I came to court. It does not grieve me to be leaving that artificial life. Although there were delightful distractions. Did you see the play at Whitehall by that fellow with the diverting name? Pikeshaker or Spearchucker or something. Oh, wait— Shakespeare, that's it."

"No," he replied briefly.

Kat rattled on. "The Christmas mumming at court is a sight I'll be sorry to miss. Of course, we have our carolers and festivities at Priorly, too. The house is thrown open to anyone who passes by."

By midday, her flood of babble dried up, leaving her depressed, and Robin grimmer than ever. They were skirting a town when the distant, melodic boom of a church bell reached them.

Robin's profile was turned to her. At first she thought he was speaking softly to her, then she realized his lips were moving in prayer.

"Robin?" Alarm flashed through her. She'd never seen him pray before. "What is it?"

He looked at her. Tears puddled in his gray eyes. Her own eyes widening, Kat leaned across the space between their two horses and wiped a trickle from his cheek with a gentle fingertip.

"Tony Babington just died," he said. "At least, I hope he did. May God have mercy on his soul."

He dug his heels into his horse's sides. The rest of their small party gallumphed along behind. There was no midday meal.

Rain started to patter down, making shilling-sized spots on the track. Drops fell steadily, bringing an early dusk. A small village hove into sight. Robin pulled up and studied Kat.

"You are drenched," he observed in a preoccupied way. "I am a bastard."

It wasn't the right moment to offer sympathy, Kat decided. She shifted in the saddle, hoping to find an inch on her buttocks that didn't ache. "I thought we had it settled that a bastard is the one thing you are not."

He frowned, contemplating the sorry-looking collection of cottages before them. "Say that again after we see what our accommodations will be."

The inn was a hovel slightly larger than the others, not too clean and full of warring smells. Robin refused to allow Kat to eat from the common bowl, insisting that a fresh portion of gray meat be brought for her from the kitchen, and when they went to their chamber, he inspected the bed narrowly before he let her sit on it.

Maud hobbled in, crippled from the ride. Kat said swiftly, "I hope you are not here to disrobe me, because you ought to be lying down yourself. Lord Robin will assist me."

The older woman's mouth drooped with horror. "My lady, 'tis not meet—"

"No arguing, for heaven's sake." Because she knew apparent cruelty would work better than cajolery, she added, "The sight of you creaking around will put aches in *my* bones. Go, now, do."

With a doubtful glance, Maud went. Robin sat beside Kat on the mattress and said, "Roll onto your stomach and lift up. I want to raise your skirt."

With a startled giggle, she complied.

"Not for that reason," he said austerely.

"What reason?"

"I would smack your bare bottom, but it has been pounded enough today." A cooling sting drew the pain from her skin and muscles.

"Liniment?"

"Yes. Here, you may turn over again."

"Do I get to return the favor?" she asked.

"You do not. When did you become so forward?"

She sat up, winding her arms around her knees. It would hardly be clever to admit she was trying to tease him out of his sadness.

"Do you wish me to act the proper maiden?"

"God's grace, no. But I need to talk to you, sweet heart, and I cannot do it while you flaunt your legs like that."

Making a face, she pulled her skirt down. "Are you disgusted by what happened to me all those years ago, Robin? If you are, tell me now. It would hurt, but not as much as being bedded out of pity, or waiting and wanting and never being bedded at all."

A huge breath lifted his chest. "You may confidently anticipate being bedded. A husband has certain expectations."

"I will not hold you to your proposal, Robin. Now that you know—if you only repeated it out of decency . . ."

"When have you ever known me to act out of decency?" he asked in exasperation.

"Several times, much as you would like to deny it." She grinned at him, relieved. "Well, it pleases me to hear you plan to fulfill all those threats of lovemaking you have flung at me. You were right in something you said last night. Since I met you, I have developed an intense curiosity about how it feels to lie under a man."

"Any man?"

Her grin faded. "One man."

"Not good enough."

"Thee," she whispered. "I want to make love with thee, instead of being used against my will and thrown away, all bloody and torn, like a rag that's only good once."

Stretching out his full length, he pulled her to his side. Kat didn't complain at the hard grip of his hands.

"Who did it? Shall I kill him for you?"

"Too late. He died long ago." She tilted her head back. His sadness and preoccupation seemed to have lifted. "Shall we get to Priorly tomorrow?"

"If we make the same time we did today. I am sorry to press the pace, but we have to position ourselves on the spot. Yesterday Walsingham told me Parliament has ruled that Mary Stuart is guilty of plotting to assassinate Elizabeth. This is the first time she has actually been named as a criminal."

Scooting her head, Kat rested it on his arm. "Will Mary be put to death?"

"Elizabeth refuses to sign the warrant. She has yet to overcome her distaste for ending the life of a fellow queen. Not unnatural, I suppose. The outcry overseas will be deafening, and besides—"

"Once one monarch is executed, other royal necks will feel the pinch."

"Precisely." He gathered her closer. "So Mary sits in Fotheringhay, waiting for the ax to fall. It seems reasonable to expect she's planning yet another escape."

"And you will be there to stop her."

"So goes the idea, anyway."

"She must feel like a chicken or a rabbit, listening to the farmer sharpen his knife," Kat said, and buried her face in his sleeve.

"The damned woman has brought it on herself, Kat." He sighed into her hair. "And she's not the only one to suffer for her ambition."

"You grieve for Babington."

"Tony was a brave lad," he said. "I am sure he died bravely."

"So much death. I am sick of it."

After a while, he asked, "You know for certain the man who—hurt—you is dead?"

"Oh, aye."

With a strength that was impossible to resist, he rolled her onto her back so he could watch her face. "You are going to have to tell me more than that."

"Why? What difference will it make? As long as you do not mind that I cannot be a virgin for you?"

"Sweet heart, why should virginity matter? You are more than just a maidenhead to me; after all, that is just an impediment to joining. But there are secrets between us—do not look away, Kat—and they have to end here. Now. Tonight. What happened when you were thirteen?"

She should have known he would be able to tell she was hiding more, she thought.

The bed was built into a wall. With Robin's large bulk between her and the room, Kat should have felt trapped. Instead, the solid warmth of his body spelled safety. Very softly, she kissed his mouth.

It remained hard under the tentative caress.

"You cannot distract me that way." In actuality, he thought she probably could. Undoubtedly could, he corrected, as a curious melting took place in his bowels, accompanied by a hardening close by.

"I was not trying to change the subject," she protested. "I was just ... Well-a-day. When I was thirteen, my parents died. None of us children caught the fever, God knows why. My brother Charles inherited. He was three years older than I. Between us came James."

He nodded. "Charles, James, and you. Go on."

"We got through the church service and the laying to rest in the graveyard, and then the whole county surged into the house to eat and drink. I hated it. All of the adults got drunk. Some of them danced. We were supposed to be *mourning.*"

He imagined her at the coltish, sensitive age between childhood and womanhood, drifting through rooms full of revelers who had forgotten the dead they'd come to honor.

"A stranger, a boy not much older than I, cornered me in a deserted alcove and began to kiss me. Ugly, openmouthed kisses that frightened me, and I screamed." She paused, and shuddered, and went on. "Sir Henry Toth found us and made the boy go away. He stared at me, though, as if he'd never seen me before. He said he had not noticed that I was growing into a woman. When he put his arm around me to lead me back to where the people were, I did not know how to push him away. An older man, a man known to the family. In the past my father had allowed him to embrace me in friendship."

"Where were your brothers?" Robin asked through stiff lips.

"Dealing with a hundred guests who did not want to go home. Finally Maud and Charles and James and I got them all settled into guest chambers or stumbling away into the dark."

She wasn't weeping. Kat lay against his side, with her long, fragile neck resting on his arm, not tense but not relaxed, either. Robin wished she would cry, as she had before, so he could comfort her.

"Sir Henry we had put up in our parents' chamber. Sometimes I resent that most of all. We showed him respect by letting him sleep in the room that belonged to our parents, where we had been conceived."

"Is that where he did it?" His voice was quiet and dry, and he almost didn't recognize it as his own.

"Nay. My chamber. My bed. I was asleep, and then suddenly this huge, heavy animal was on top of me. Inside me. Sir Henry. He kept telling me to keep quiet. I tried to scream, though, and he put a pillow over my face. It is hard to remember clearly after that. Just—flashes of blackness, if that makes any sense. And the pain. Oh, God, Robin, it hurt."

"Yes," he said helplessly.

"When he finished, Sir Henry tidied me up and said if I was a good girl and never told, he would give me a present. Beads or a ring. Something. But if I failed to keep 'our' secret, horrible things would follow. Oh, and he would visit me again, because he l-loved me."

"That's not love, Kat. I am no expert in the emotion, but I know that's not love." Her great eyes searched his, and he toughened himself to go on. "I am to take it the next morning's fishing mishap occurred ... ah, opportunely? Francis's father did not die by accident?"

"You are an officer of the queen."

"I am. So?"

"Some secrets do not belong to me alone." Her voice was intense.

"I see. Shall I make a conjecture? Your brothers. They found out what Sir Henry had done. They decided to rectify it."

She curled away from him, turning her back. Stretching a long arm around her, Robin found her hand and enfolded it.

"They killed or incapacitated him somewhere in the house," he guessed.

Her shoulders twitched.

"The noises, remember?" he pointed out. "The guests and servants were too drunk to move or shaking in their nightcaps out of fear that the dead had come back to see what damage had been done during the funeral festivities. No one in the house got up to discover what the commotion was about. Your brothers took Sir Henry out in a boat and dumped him into the water." He paused. "Are you afraid I would expose them after all these years? Silly wench, I would be more apt to drink a toast to them. They did what I would have done had I been there at the time. I am sorry, Kat."

"Why should you apologize?"

"Because I was not there to protect you."

"That's ridiculous." She rolled over and faced him. Her hand remained small and cold in his grasp. "How old were you then?"

"Nineteen, I believe. Nearly twenty. The wrong age to appreciate the woman you were going to become. I had an inexhaustible lust toward older women as I recall."

A wavering smile rewarded his self-mockery. "I'll be a constant disappointment to you, my lord. I shall never be older than you are."

"My child bride." Pulling her hand to his lips, he breathed on it gently to give it some warmth. "Think of it this way. So many years have passed that now you *are* an older woman. At least, older than I was then."

"By a year! If that. It sounds more like a matter of months."

"Ah," he addressed the ceiling of the enclosed bed. "The lady is sensitive about her increasing years."

She laughed and pinched his fingers.

Robin looked at her thoughtfully. "Where are your brothers, Kat? Why did they abandon you?"

Shadowed lids swept down over her dark eyes. Robin could almost see her thought processes. They were both starkly aware that she hadn't yet admitted any of his conjectures were true.

"Can you not trust me?" he asked.

Subdued, she pointed out, "You told me not to trust you. Not to trust anyone."

He scrubbed his upper cheeks with dry palms. "I did indeed."

Swinging his legs over the edge of the wall bed, he rose and walked to the chamber's one small window. The wooden shutter banged as he forced it inward against the wall. Outside, rain lashed at the panes of thin horn. Amber rain on amber windows.

Kat said quietly, "I have never known why they failed to return. I love them, you know. I still miss them."

The stiffness went out of his muscles. She trusted him

this far, anyway. "I thank you, damask lady," he said, turning. "Can you tell me the rest of the story?"

Her face was pale and set. She looked very young. As young as when she was thirteen?

"After Sir Henry went back to my parents' room, I woke Charles and James and told them what had happened."

"That took courage."

"Nay. I was just so outraged that Sir Henry could be such a hypocrite. Maybe he was as drunk as everyone else. He had certainly been drinking." She sighed. "Charles ordered me to go sleep with Maud, but I disobeyed. I was spoiled and willful in those days."

"Willful, at any rate. You still are." With slow, absentminded movements, Robin began to undress.

Kat's eyes followed his fingers as they removed his cuffs. "Both of my brothers went into our parents' chamber. When they left it, they were carrying Sir Henry over their shoulders. His arms dangled, and his feet kept bumping into James's back. On the banister of the stairwell, too. It was noisy, but I never heard that people thought ghosts had caused the sounds. Do you think they were afraid of wounding my feelings?"

"More likely they wanted to avoid the sharp side of your tongue, little shrew," Robin suggested.

She wrinkled her nose at him. "Let me finish before you insult me again. Or else we'll start brangling and I'll lose my nerve."

"Does it take so much nerve to confide in me?"

A stupid question, he thought, stripping off his shirt, and one he didn't really want her to answer. On the one hand, an agent of the queen should expect people to fear talking to him. The time to worry was when they didn't. On the other hand, from anything he'd ever heard, sharing lives required sharing everything, and it bothered him that Kat was still chary of opening her thoughts and memories. Herself.

"You are rather formidable, Robin."

Instead of demanding unconditional surrender, he held out his arms. A quiver ran over her face, like cat-ice over a pond, and she got out of bed and ran into his embrace.

He wondered uneasily what she had seen in *his* face.

Muffling her voice in his naked chest, she continued, "My brothers unlocked a side door and took Sir Henry outside. That's the last time I ever saw them. I waited until it was nearly dawn. Then I went out and searched. They had left the body at the little boat landing we have on the river Nene. Just—left it, sprawled half in and half out of the water."

"And they were—"

"Gone. Vanished."

"So either they started to put him in the water, were startled by something—it would not take much under those circumstances, especially if they had not killed before—and then your brothers bolted. Or Sir Henry did not die in your parents' chamber and they took him to the river to drown him. Then they ran."

She shrugged. The wool of her gown scratched against his chest. She wasn't wearing a farthingale, and he could feel her limber legs through her skirts and his britches. The physical sensations were pleasant, but for once they didn't distract him from the main point.

"Leaving a bereft and abused young girl alone to hide their crime and manage an estate," he continued. Anger and jealousy simmered deep in Robin's gut. "Tell me, Kat, should I lose my temper with them or you? The loyal sister. You made up the story about the fishing excursion, did you not? Staved off an investigation, kept the law from suspecting. You will not accuse them even to me, will you?"

"To do otherwise would be dishonest. I'll not swear to anything I did not see, and *I did not see my brothers kill Sir Henry.* Are you concerned where my strongest allegiance lies? I have volunteered to be your mistress. What more can I do to show that I trust you?"

The touch of his fingers turned gentle. God's grace, she had fearless eyes. Fearless and frightened at the same time. She was still hiding something. He could tell, although how he wasn't sure. Something to do with the loving neither of them knew how to do, perhaps. Was she getting as good at reading him as he was at reading her?

"Anything else?" he asked, running his thumb along the lobe of her ear.

"Nay. Except—someone spoke to the queen about the fact I lived alone at Priorly. In law I have been a ward of the queen since my parents died. But except for collecting her fees, no one ever seemed to remember I was there, and, believe me, I took care not to remind anyone. Then suddenly I received a summons."

His finger paused. "And you think it was instigated by the person or persons who left a smell in your priest's hole?"

"If I quote your wise sayings too often you will get a big head, but—have you not said I should never make assumptions?"

"Some assumptions are reasonable." He began to tease her ear again, his mind on her story. "I am developing an ambition to view your Priorly for myself. Violence, mysterious disappearances, ghosts, treason . . . You have never told your story to anyone else?"

"Maud. I had to tell her. There were reasons."

"But no man until me?"

If he was asking for reassurance, she didn't give it to him. "Telling has too high a price."

The too-old look in her eyes tore at him. The only way he could think of to replace it with joy was lovemaking, but this shabby chamber was hardly the place to try to erase the memory of her brutal initiation into womanhood.

Pulling the pins from her hair, Robin undressed her to her smock and gave her a light spank on the bottom to speed her into bed. It aroused him just to see her between sheets. Deciding to put something a little more tangible than good intentions between their bodies, he kept his britches and hose on. Climbing in beside her, he left a careful foot of space in the middle of the bed.

"My past does make a difference." She said it softly. "That's why I have always protected my reputation. If there was never a rape, then there was never a reason for Charles and James to kill Sir Henry. I wanted to safeguard them in case they returned. And I knew people would have nothing to do with me if my shame were public property. Even you. You are not—hot—for me anymore."

Robin tried to make his neck comfortable on the wooden block. "Lady, I of all men have had experience being shunned. If you need the facts stated plainly, I am so hot the blaze comes between me and my work, and my rest. My body is besotted with yours."

"Truly?" She sounded so innocently pleased he groaned.

Reaching out, she grazed his full, heavy shaft, and even through the double layers of fabric his flesh responded to her soft, inquiring fingers.

"Truly," he confirmed, breathing hard. "Stop that. Thank you. When we come together, it has to be in beauty, Kat. With peace and time and trust enough to get past your specters. Sweet heart, there are ghosts in your eyes. You will need a long, leisurely loving, not a fast grope on a lumpy mattress, with both of us wondering when we'll have to stop to scratch the kisses of the bed's other inhabitants." He flicked at a tiny spot on the sheet, which wasn't moving but might begin at any moment. "Has the landlord never heard of wormwood to drive away fleas?"

Kat smiled at him mistily. "You are using a base trick to make me laugh. I grant you the points about the mattress and the legions of little bedmates, but we have time enough." So gently and sweetly he wasn't sure she was touching him until her palm began to rub up and down, she caressed him again.

"You do not play fair, damask lady," he said with difficulty.

"And you are not playing at all."

"It is no longer a game for me." He pushed her hand away. Slowly, the urgent ache subsided. "You have not yet said you'll be my wife, Kat. You do not trust me completely."

Resentfully, she said, "That's absurd. We'll never be allowed to marry. We are arguing about words—"

"No!" Frustration adding quickness to his movements, he rolled onto his side and caught her hands over her head. "Not just words. I want thee to wife. There will be no secrets between us, no tiptoeing about certain subjects. You'll admit you want me, too, more than just 'a little' . . ."

Her brown eyes stared up into his, and he could feel the softness of her breasts against his chest.

Hell. The woman he'd set his mind on could seduce him without moving or speaking. She'd been able to do that from the start.

Expelling his breath in another groan, he pulled her hands to his mouth and kissed the bent knuckles.

"Go to sleep, my lady. Another day in the saddle tomorrow."

Shifting to face outward so he could at least try not to be aware of her willing body on the other side of the bed, Robin felt her gaze between his shoulder blades. Gradually he drifted toward sleep.

"Robin?"

"Hmmm?"

The resentment was gone from her voice. "I thank you."

Chapter 15

⁓⌒◯◯⌒⁓

Late the next afternoon, the clouds broke up, allowing shafts of white sunlight to form bars from gray sky to gray earth. A rainbow stretched ahead of the small party of riders.

Maud called out, "A good omen, my lady!"

All around them, the landscape was taking on color and life. "Aye," Kat agreed, beginning to smile.

Autumn's golds, reds, browns, and greens gave the spirit more encouragement than the flat, dripping gray they'd been riding through all day. Kat's mood had been uneven. She'd accepted Robin's refusal to make love, and even been grateful for it. After all, her own sensuality was untried and the implication that he valued her for more than her body was reassuring, but still . . . He was masculine and she was feminine and, watching his strong profile from under her lashes, she felt the desire of a woman for a man move in her again. Sitting up straighter and altering her position in the saddle didn't do much to make the melting, quaking sensation go away.

She watched Robin concentrate on the silver river as it tumbled beside the muddy track. When he glanced at her, his eyes were the same shining silver, except for the band of gold around the pupils.

"How long before we reach the road to Priorly?" he asked.

His practicality steadied her voice. "We stay by the Nene. The house is built right next to it."

"It must be damp."

Kat didn't take offense. As far as she was concerned, Priorly was perfect and required no defending. "I have never found it so, but you must judge for yourself."

Though it was night by the time their horses clopped over the stone bridge leading to the Priorly gate house, the moon was full, and Kat tossed Robin a challenging glance. "What do you think of my home?"

There were no lights glowing behind the windows, and the house looked all the bigger for being dark. Robin leaned back in the saddle to assess the four stories. He was so quiet that her confidence teetered.

"Do you dislike it?" she asked.

He shook his head in a gesture so tiny only someone watching closely, or a woman who cared about him, would have noticed. She did care, she thought. More than "a little." Her natural reserve together with a shyness that was new kept the feeling locked up inside her.

Fragile caring and definite lusting—did they add up to the mysterious state of being "in love"?

Besides, she still had a huge secret she hadn't told him, and Robin deserved a whole love, untarnished by things that had to be hidden. He needed a woman who could be everything a lover was supposed to be. It wouldn't be fair to trap him by telling him she might be in love with him— and then have him learn disdain for her. And it would hurt so much.

Marriage was out of the question. In addition to the un-deniable fact that the queen would ruin their lives there was her own past. She was hardly a fit bride for any man.

Longing to be Robin's wife was completely useless. It wasn't going to be. Much better to remember that they were together for now. All she asked was a little time to be with him. Was that too much for fate to grant?

Robin was still staring broodingly at her house. "A handsome building with a good, strong wall around it. Not as large as a royal palace, but commodious and tidy. Brick?"

"Aye," she answered. From his flat tone, he wasn't im-pressed. Perhaps Priorly seemed ordinary to someone who had seen as much of the world as Robin. No doubt Prior-ly's mistress would be just as commonplace to a man used to a variety of lovers, women who knew where to touch and what to tickle. Deflated, she went on, "Pound on the door. The porter sleeps in the gate house and he should hear us."

After a full minute of knocking with his sword butt, a trembling voice fluted, "Who is there?"

"The lady of the house, and she is cold and tired," called Robin. "Open this damned door."

A peephole slid open with a scratchy sound. Kat threw back her hood.

"M-my lady?"

" 'Tis I, Jem," she said soothingly. "Let us in."

Bolts drew back with a shriek. Kat remarked, "It sounds as if I have some housekeeping ahead of me, but the squeaks are music to my ears. Home at last. I could sleep a fortnight."

Robin glanced at her quickly, and then as swiftly focused on the oak slab creaking open. "I have worked you hard, not to mention your other adventures. You deserve some rest."

"That's not—"

Before she could finish, he slapped his reins lightly against her mount's neck, and the horses trotted forward through the gate.

Maud thankfully tumbled from her mount and limped toward the house. Used to Priorly's design, Kat led the men to the stables. Inside the shelter with its good smells of hay and horse, she slid from the saddle unaided and began to tug at cinches.

"What are you doing? Are your stable men too useless to serve their lady?" asked Robin in displeasure.

She shrugged at him over the backs of their horses. "Everyone is long asleep. I do not want to rouse the whole household."

Diffidently, Samuel put in, "If it please your lordship, your ladyship, I'll be more than happy to settle the beasts for the night."

"I am sure you will," Kat heard Robin mutter.

She raised an eyebrow. Arriving at their destination didn't appear to have improved his mood.

A sleepy stable boy stumbled from the loft, clutching a

pitchfork which he obviously intended to use as a weapon if necessary. Robin grunted and pushed the wobbling tines out of his way as he strode out into the open air. The gangling boy stared after him, loose-mouthed.

"That is Lord Robin, Tom," said Kat. "You are to regard him as your master from now on. He has the queen's authority for whatever he does."

The slack surprise changed to awe. "Aye, m'lady. Welcome home, m'lady."

"I thank you. This is Samuel."

The large man greeted Tom placidly.

"He will be employed here at the manor." Although she stated it as a fact, there was a faint question in her voice. The big man appeared perfectly happy to attach himself to her and Robin, despite Robin's disgruntlement, but . . .

Samuel smiled. "I will serve you, by your leave, my lady."

"You have it."

Looking over Kat's shoulder, he smiled more broadly. She glanced around, too, and saw that Maud had come into the stable.

"If Maudie might bring me a bite before she retires—"

Maud giggled and squirmed like a young girl meeting a country squire at the fair.

"That's between the two of you," said Kat, dumbfounded.

Samuel lost some of his aplomb. "I suppose there's naught I need," he muttered.

Maud bristled. "A bite to sup is not too much to ask. I'll be pleased to find you something. The side door has been opened, my lady," she added.

Wondering if she could have imagined the infatuation she saw between the older people, Kat walked rather stiff-leggedly into the stable yard. She also wondered if there were any point in asking Robin if he would rub her with liniment again.

He was leaning against a wall, arms crossed.

"Have you recovered your temper?" she asked.

He straightened, frowning, formidable. "I was not aware I had lost it."

"Not lost, precisely. Mislaid, perhaps. You have Maud

terrified and Samuel—" No, she couldn't claim the large man was anything but his stolid self.

"Kat, you do realize that villain gives every appearance of planning to stick to you for life?"

"What's wrong with that? If he's willing and honest, I can hire him as I do other yearly workers. I owe him a debt."

"Do you? He was rather late changing sides, as I recall."

"Samuel could have done me harm when I was in his power," Kat pointed out. "Not only was he kind, but he kept the other man who abducted me from hurting me, as well."

"The item to remember is that he did abduct you. He's dangerous."

"Not as dangerous to me as you."

"What's that supposed to mean?"

Although she could feel the anger roiling in him, she put her arms around his neck "It means I want to go to bed. Make love to me, Robin."

His shoulders were tense as a bowstring. "This is not the right time."

"Why not?" She pressed herself to him shamelessly.

"You are not ready—"

"Do you not want to help me be . . . ready?" Her hand found one of his, and cupped it to her breast.

"For sweet Jesu's sake, you do not know what you are asking." His breath sounded loud and fast.

"But I do. I am asking for you. Surely you are not planning to deny both of us until we can be wed? That will be never."

"I refuse to accept that," he returned swiftly. "But, no, I am not that much of a fool—or a saint. My lust for you is so great it is consuming me, but I have another lust, too, and I have to get the two of them resolved before we—"

"What is it that troubles you?"

"Priorly." He detached her arms from around his neck, not roughly but with finality.

"You need to find your traitors before we can make love?"

"Of course not, goosecap. Who is to say there *are* any traitors? The problem's not so easy to solve."

"Robin, please. You are speaking in riddles. It is driving me mad and—and I have not much sanity left, after sleeping next to you chastely for two nights in a row, wondering what it would be like to make love."

"Nor I," he muttered. In the moonlight, his face was all sharp, bitter angles. "Lady, seeing this place ... I have nothing except a small savings. You are a propertied woman. I never meant to seduce a fortune."

"There's been precious little seduction going on," Kat told him, melting. "Who would have thought such a swaggering, boastful fellow could be so scrupulous? Is your conscience always doing battle with your circumstances? Tell it to rest easy. Even if we could marry, Priorly belongs to Charles."

"It has been a long time since he and James disappeared. Do you really believe they are coming back?"

She raised her hands, palms up, in a helpless gesture. "I have to act as if they are. Priorly is the trust I hold for them, in return for what they—" Her voice faltered. "What they did for me. But it need not concern us tonight. Now, at this moment, Priorly is just a place your work brings you, and my very great desire brings me."

She held her breath. Desire for him rushed through her, not as sensation but emotion. Her heart ached with it, thrilled with it. Oh, Mother Mary, have pity on me, she thought. Maybe I do love him.

Robin stretched suddenly, with his arms over his head, and her spirits shot skyward.

"The desire is not all one-sided," he said significantly. He swept her off her feet and kissed her. At the demanding rub of his lips, warmth and wetness trickled into Kat's lower body, mingling with the pangs of—love?—until she couldn't tell them apart. When she'd been kissed until she clutched at his doublet with fingers that had lost their strength, he threw her over one shoulder and smacked her bottom loudly. Either her skirts absorbed most of the swat or her flesh simply liked his touch better than the rub of the saddle. It didn't hurt.

"Where can we be alone, wench?" he growled. "I have no mind to share the loft with your stable boy."

"Side door," she gasped; it wasn't easy to speak upside down while giggling.

The bouncing, jiggling motion blurred the surroundings as he carried her past them. Kat glimpsed pieces of scenes: a torch flaring to show sleep-rumpled servants, the narrowness of a hall fitfully illuminated by the lantern Robin swept up to light their way, the outline of her bedchamber swinging in a circle before he settled her on the fur rug in front of the empty fireplace. Somehow the fractured views of familiar objects increased her sense of urgency. An erotic need for the reassuring solidity of Robin's body flooded her loins.

"Is there kindling? I want you warm."

"You can make me warm without a fire," she said.

"Kat—"

Kneeling, she wrapped her arms around his thighs and put her lips to the jointure of his britches.

"*Kat.*"

"I am beyond modesty, Robin," she murmured. "Show me what making love is."

He eased down next to her, so her mouth slid up his doublet, over waist and ribs and chest. His fingers pushed into her hair, spilling the net and pins. "What if I am clumsy? God's grace, I am so afraid of adding to your hurts," he muttered.

"Mine, more than other women's? Because I was raped? That was seven years ago. I do not live it every day. Oh, I admit, I inspect men carefully to judge if they are the kind that takes. I wondered about you. But it must mean something that I went to your chamber anyway."

Resting his forehead against hers, he began to pull the pieces of her riding dress off her willy-nilly. Kat tugged at his laces.

"Enlighten me," he suggested, closing his eyes.

"Vain man. I went because I find you fascinating."

He kissed her, deeply, finding the closures to her clothing by touch alone. Kat strained against his mouth, her hands less experienced in ridding a man of his gear. When her clothes lay in a heap next to them, he helped her drag his britches and hose away from the bar of flesh she could see standing tall in the lantern light.

Opening his eyes, he laughed low in his chest. "It seems you fascinate me, too, my lady. Come here."

"You had to say that word."

"What word?"

" 'Come.' " She blushed.

With a quick motion, he tumbled her onto her side. "It certainly fits the business at hand."

"Tell me I am not just business."

"You know you are not," he said roughly.

A soft gasp escaped her as he ran a possessive thumb over her small, pink nipples. They pouted into buds.

"However," he continued, his eyes narrowing to shining slits, "you are certainly at hand, and I do mean to make you feel everything 'that word' implies—"

"What does it mean?" asked Kat shyly. "To you?"

"My little innocent. Do you not know?"

"Only what others mean when they say it in rude jests. That the loving is over."

Fierce pleasure blossomed within him. Thank God she could call it *loving* and not *having* or some other crudity. That randy old animal Sir Henry hadn't spoiled her for life. "It shall never be over between us. The term refers to the moment of greatest pleasure."

"Pleasure," she repeated, her voice soft and slow. "Robin, I desire greatly to pleasure you."

Her legs moved restlessly, and they brushed against sleek fur and the short, wiry hair that covered his legs. Not sure how to proceed, she pressed herself to him, running one foot up and down his calf. The muscles of his belly rippled and then his legs scissored together, hard, trapping hers.

"I appear to be in your power, my lord."

He groaned deeply, and his demanding touches gentled. "Make no mistake, the power is yours. There's nothing to fear. I'll be as careful as I can."

She squirmed in his hold. "Idiot." The moist, hot, sliding feeling teetered between urgency and tenderness. "Why put fetters on yourself? I do not want you to be careful. I am not glass. I will not break for being loved."

Getting one leg free, she wrapped it around the curve of his buttock. "Love me."

As if her pleading had broken his control, he had her on her back in the furs in a single easy motion. Without her knowing quite how he went about it, her knees were bent up and out, and his rigid length was thrusting into her softness. It was the good part of her dream, but Robin was no dream.

He was big, bigger than her unaccustomed flesh could accommodate all at once. Instinctively she tightened around him the short distance his first thrust took him, making the small channel smaller. Though his weight was wonderfully male, it was a surprise. Strong odors of horse and man filled her head. The intensity of her desire shattered into a hundred chaotic sensations.

Robin groaned, this time in genuine anguish. "Lady," he gasped despite the sexual need clawing not just his genitals, but every fevered inch of his skin, "you are not as ready as you think you are."

"But I want you so." She was panting, too. "Do we—is it that we cannot fit after all? Is something wrong with me?"

"You are perfect. Perfect. So sweet and ripe and flowing with welcome. We just have to wait while your body learns to open to me."

He withdrew and propped his upper body on one elbow. With the broad tip of his lance caressing rather than invading her softness, he played his other hand over her breasts and used his mouth to kiss her into liquid relaxation. But no matter how buttery and slick she grew, when his aching arousal pressed forward to taste the comfort of her warmth and wetness, her tiny inner muscles contracted like a vice.

Her moan of frustration echoed his.

"Do not wait any longer. Please, Robin. It is killing both of us."

"I will not hurt you," he said between gritted teeth, feeling the pain of corded muscles and tendons in his neck.

Desperation aided inventiveness. Slipping his hand down to where russet curls glistened like a chestnut just being shelled, he ran a searching finger through the folds of delicate skin there. Her eyes widened and she arched.

At the same moment, her defensive tightness eased and he thrust his whole length into her.

"Oh!" she said softly.

Controlling himself with an effort that made perspiration gleam on his inner arms, Robin kept himself from pounding mindlessly and selfishly toward satisfaction. "Kat," he muttered to remind his straining flesh whom he was with, why it was important to go slow.

But she wouldn't let him take the necessary time. Instead, she caught his face in her hands so he could see her delighted smile, and then leaned up to put her tongue in his mouth. The slim hips underneath him rocked awkwardly. A smooth, experienced rhythm would have soothed his lust long enough for him to make sure of his partner's response. This excitingly unpredictable bucking sent waves of dark, rich, painful pleasure through his loins.

She tightened around him again, and he was lost. He wasn't even sure which part was Kat, and which was Robin. As the hot tide poured out of him, he felt he was opening to her.

The violent climax left him stunned. He didn't know how long he lay there, wrapped in satisfaction.

"Damask lady," he said finally, knowing his voice was heavy with repletion. "You are all crushed silk." He slipped away from her.

She laughed, a happy, excited sound, and he lifted his head to regard her suspiciously. A hectic flush still painted her cheeks. Her radiance didn't resemble the drowsy well-being of sexual satisfaction.

"Kat? Did I leave you behind?"

Her blink was comical. "I am right here."

"Yes, but—tell me true, now. Do you want more?"

"*Is* there more?"

At her astonishment, he didn't know whether to be insulted or amused. "Of course. Did you think so little of me?"

She sighed as he moved his hips suggestively. Although he'd been drained, a strong flex along the subsiding length of his manhood rewarded his effort.

"I shall never doubt your boasting again. We have established once and for all there's nothing small about you," she teased. Then her hands gripped him. "I was so afraid I would fail to give you pleasure. You—you are pleased?"

He kissed the suddenly too-serious eyes closed. "Rest assured of that. I have never lain with a woman I cared about before. It—makes a difference."

As he wrapped his arms around her, he silently dared queen, fate, or the world to take her away from him. Wanting to feel as much of her as he could, he used his elbows to urge her legs up around his waist.

"Now, my lady, there's the matter of your pleasure to consider . . ."

Robin went rigid in his final release, and then settled her on the fur rug with gentle hands and a grim expression. The bed was stripped, so he found their cloaks on the floor and flung them over her naked body. Then he slipped in next to her.

"Be happy for me," Kat said, stroking his chest.

"I wanted to give you pleasure."

"You did. You do."

Putting his hands behind his head, he frowned at the ceiling. "Tell me what you felt. From the beginning."

"You *know* how—"

"Tell me, Kat."

She wriggled with embarrassment. "You made me hot. And—achy. I stopping thinking. There was only feeling, and your body and my body."

"Both times, at the beginning?"

"Aye."

"So far, so good. Go on, my lady."

"Then you—we—joined. And everything was different. Not in a bad way, not the way I was afraid it would be. I did not feel smothered or—or snuffed out. But I did not feel *hot* anymore, either. There was a little pain, only the first time, and then a floating warmth. It was very nice, Robin."

"That's not pleasure, my lady. Only relief."

"I am sorry—"

Gruffly, he said, "I have failed you, not you me. If an apology is necessary, I should be the one making it."

She buried her face in the hollow of his shoulder. "Do you have regrets?"

"None." With her ear pressed so close to his throat, his mellow voice had deeper undertones. His cheek rested in her hair.

"Are you sure?"

"I shall do better by you next time, sweet heart. Did you know your hair still smells of gillyflowers? My wife who smells of gillyflowers. We'll have many years of marriage to bring each other pleasure."

She looked at him, and his swashbuckler's grin gleamed before it was swallowed in an arm-stretching yawn. This once, Kat didn't have the heart to remind him they'd never be allowed to marry. A pang of grief for the lifetime of loving they'd wouldn't have wrung a small moan from her, but the sound of his yawn covered it and he didn't hear.

"Frequent practice, damask lady," he said. "Resign yourself to frequent practice in the art of love."

Chapter 16

K at skipped down the stairs, leaving Robin wrapped in their cloaks. She was full of energy and, despite her lover's conviction that he had failed to give her something, happier than she'd ever been in her life.

Before the household's morning prayers, there was time for a quick walk around the grounds and brief conversations with several of the workers. They, she knew, would spread the news that the lady was home among the tenant farmers and their families. Questions about ghostly visitors were answered with shaken confirmations or robust laughter, depending on the person.

But even levelheaded Mark the gardener admitted having seen lights in the copse. He discounted the sighting, however.

"The latest batch of beer be usually strong, my lady," he said dryly.

Prayers were being led by Jedidiah Pettigrew when she skidded into the hall, propelled by the realization that she was late.

Her retainers looked sidelong over folded hands at her and a few winked. Kat hid a smile and tried to compose her mind to follow Master Pettigrew's sonorous phrases. Last night's activities came between her and prayer.

Surely, she thought, God would understand the need she felt to be held throughout the night. To give herself to Robin in the ultimate embrace. The Virgin would speak to God for her, explain a woman's loneliness, plead the special circumstances. Well, perhaps not the Virgin. Kat would have to nose out an earthier saint.

Glancing around discreetly, she caught sight of a blond head over the sea of homespun. Robin was listening quietly, his face expressionless, and it was impossible to tell what he was thinking. But he bent his neck for the final amen, waiting until she'd had a chance to greet each of the servants by name before he strolled to her side.

"Are you a prayerful sort of man?" she asked curiously.

The ironic slant of his eyebrows indicated that he wasn't. But he said, "My lady, you and I need all the help we can get."

Her chest constricted slightly as she wondered if he meant her reactions in bed required a miracle, but then his eyes glittered hot. She relaxed. He still wanted her.

The unfairness of what she was doing struck her. Robin felt *married* to her, while she accepted that they'd never be allowed to wed. Not only would Elizabeth take great glee in forbidding the vows, but there was that last secret about herself Kat couldn't bear to tell Robin.

A man wants sons. Francis had said that, and Francis was an ass, but he was right about this one thing. All men wanted sons; Robin, who was both virile and starved for affection, deserved a wife who could give him children.

And Kat strongly suspected that she was barren.

But for now, she'd be his as long as he wanted her.

"The sheep are all sheared," she said shyly, not sure what lovers talked about in the morning, "and the grain ripened early so it was all brought in before the rain started."

"This is fascinating, my lady. Go on."

The linen kerchief she'd thrown over her hair in the country style was falling down her neck; she pulled it straight. "If the weather remains damp, we might have to parch the wheat so it does not spoil in storage. The stock is all sound. The largest, healthiest pigs have been chosen to live through the winter."

"And have the pigs broken their fast?" he asked gravely.

"An hour ago. Do you mean you are ready to break yours?"

"I do. For some reason, I am sharp-set this morning."

"Foolish man. You should have satisfied all your hungers last night." A lingering uncertainty caused her to study him from under her lashes.

How could Kat look innocent, seductive, and anxious all at the same time? Robin wondered. Smoothly, he told her, "My appetites have a way of renewing themselves with great regularity."

The anxious look melted away, and she laid her palm over the back of his hand to lead him to a table set with country fare.

Spreading honey on a thick, brown crust, she said, "Will you need my presence today? There are tenants with complaints to make and favors to ask, and I must speak to Jack's parents about their son."

"You may see the Millers after I do." His tone didn't invite argument. A twinge of his fear that she had the power to make him soft tightened his jaw. "They may be your people, but I have my work to do. Do not dare to interfere with the queen's justice, Kat."

She filled a mug with ale and handed it to him, covering his fingers with her own when he took it.

"I pray you, Robin, believe me. If there are traitors at Priorly, I want them caught, too. Not that it seems possible for anything to be awry on such a lovely day." The shutters were open, allowing pearly sunlight and autumn shells to pour into the hall.

It was an odd place to find treason, Robin admitted to himself. The house breathed normality. Surfaces gleamed with beeswax and sunshine; fresh herbs were strewn among the rushes. More significantly, the servants appeared well-fed and undistressed at having their mistress returned to them. There were no guilty, closed, or sullen faces to mar Kat's homecoming. Or to hint at treachery.

He'd wandered about as soon as he woke, in a seemingly random pattern that took him into every nook and cranny. Built of red brick, with a central block given a Z-shape by towers set at right angles to each other, the house was really a small castle constructed with defense in mind. Perhaps the unpopular opinions held by Kat's mother had led her father to choose a design usually seen in the wild north, where neighbors still entertained themselves with bloody feuds.

The fortified house was roomy. Above the ground story where the windows were few and narrow, it was pleasantly sunlit. The only inconvenience its plan caused was a lack of exits. Robin had found two; the main entrance that fed directly to the central spiral staircase, and the side door he and Kat had used when they arrived.

Priorly was just the kind of estate, with the kind of people, he would have chosen for himself. Rigorously, he banished the thought. All coveting the place could do was sour him and make Kat as well as himself unsure of his motives.

So he drank the thick, bittersweet ale. "This is good," he commented. "Full-bodied. Your own?"

"Priorly brewing, aye." The brown eyes sparkled naughtily. "But you should have noticed I am hardly full-bodied, my lord."

"And you know *I* find you beautiful," he said under his breath. "You are like the stem of an iris, tall and slim and limber. Are you flirting with me, girl?"

"Aye."

"Then flirt while you show me the things that disturbed you on your last visit."

They started in a storage room on the top floor. Kat threw open trunks and explained what was missing. All the stolen articles were pieces of her brothers' clothing, Robin noted, fingering a velvet gown of the kind worn by older men, outmoded but still well worth stealing for its rich cloth.

"Selective thieves," he said absently.

Kat sniffed. "When it came to the plate, they took only the best. I'll show you."

The lock on the strongbox had been forced. From it, too, only certain items had been taken. "The saltcellar was made in Italy," said Kat bleakly. "In the shape of Noah's ark. The lid formed the deck, and it had elephants and camelopard giraffas and unicorns. I can remember sitting on my mother's lap, naming all the animals."

The cover of the box clanged loudly as she closed it.

On the first floor, she paused outside an ornately carved

door. "Here's the chapel. There's nothing missing from it. At least, not when I was last at home."

"Perhaps we had better take a look," Robin replied. He'd already viewed the inside, but habit urged him to observe his lover's face while she opened this door into her past to him.

Color flooded the small, square room. Precious stained glass tinted the windows, and bright rectangles of painted cloth hung between recesses where statues prayed. Flanking the altar, candelabra were filled with fat candles.

Robin saw Kat's cheeks pale.

"What is it?" he asked.

"The candles," she said. "There should not be any candles in the holders."

Striding forward, he put his fingers around the smooth wax. "Cold," he said unemotionally. "But they have been lit. All of them. The wicks are burnt and there are rivers of wax hanging down the sides. Is anything else amiss?"

She shook her head, the kerchief a flutter of white amid the rainbow color.

Robin didn't comment on the evidence that showed the chapel had been used, probably for an outlaw service. "Then let's inspect your priest's hole."

They went up the winding stairs to a withdrawing room paneled in yellow oak. Kat's pallor bothered him; stopping just inside the door, so they were hidden from the maids bustling throughout the house, he tilted her face carefully to one side and pulled her kerchief off. Then he worried her earlobe lightly with his teeth before sliding the tip of his tongue inside.

"There. That's a spot I missed last night."

The heat from her blush washed over his chin and cheek. "My lord, I hesitate to contradict an agent of the queen, but my recollection is that you lavished the most complete attention over my entire body."

He released her, pleased with the blush and the chuckle that accompanied it. Even if her inexperience—or rather, her one terrifying experience—had blocked a complete response to their first lovemaking, her sensuality was burning hot.

Robin had the shrewd suspicion it would grow hotter

still if it was denied any outlet for a while. He didn't think he could stand waiting too long. Say, until nighttime. Feeling her convulse beneath him, hearing her cry out when passion overtook her—those were prizes he intended to have. For both of them.

Planting his fists on his hips, he turned to the panels.

"What is the trick to your priest's hole?"

"Can you not figure it out?" asked Kat teasingly. "An expert like yourself?"

Her naughty twinkle was back. Swaggering slightly for effect, Robin strode to the wall which had a finely carved mantel.

"Hidden rooms are often located next to a fireplace. The chimney provides heat and the thickness of the wall disguises the presence of extra empty space," he lectured, running his fingers over wood varnished to a satiny finish. Though they were trained to sensitivity, his fingertips could find no cracks or minute levers.

"Oh, how the mighty are fallen when they cannot even locate the correct portion of the wall," mourned Kat.

Directing a narrow gaze at her, he caught her staring at his fingers as they slid slowly and deliberately over the golden, silken wood.

Grinning, he pinched her bottom lightly on his way to the other side of the fireplace, and she gasped and aimed an open-palmed slap at his thigh.

"My lady," he taunted, sidestepping the blow with ease, "behave yourself."

"I am tired of behaving myself," she complained. "Until I met you, that's all I ever did. And now—oh, Robin, do you think I am becoming wanton?"

"I hope so, sweet heart." His grin turned menacing. But he couldn't have said if he added just that hint of danger in fun or in seriousness. "As long as you save your wantonness for me."

"Darling." She called him an endearment so rarely, something new and untested inside Robin twisted painfully. "I am overcome with this need to touch you, to feel how real you are. Am I being silly?"

"It is natural. Lovers love with hearts and hands and—

other parts. God's grace, listen to me. I am the last man in
the world to educate an innocent with poetry."

"And you listen to me." Kat put her slim, cool hands on
either side of his face. "I have never been as innocent as
you think. You are the man I want, Robin. I can be just as
arrogant and stubborn and stupid about having what I want
as you can, and do not you forget it!"

"A gentleman never contradicts a lady. To work, Kat.
The priest's hole is on this side of the wall?"

"Aye. There. That board—"

"Shhh. How will you respect me if I cannot outwit a
simple ... Ah. A seam in the woodwork that's not repeated elsewhere in the paneling. Do I press it—do not tell
me—or—I see, it pries open. And as it does—"

Watching a section of the paneling swing outward with
a critical eye, Robin stepped back, putting a hand out to
keep Kat from being struck by the disguised door. His
knuckles brushed across her breast, and he glanced at her
ruefully.

"You are so sweet to the touch. However, it occurs to
me you do not need me to guard you from your own
woodwork," he began. Kat's eyes fixed and widened at a
point over his shoulder.

Her mouth opened, but no sound came out.

A man dove out of the no-longer-hidden door.

Robin crouched to defend himself. It wasn't necessary.
The stranger, neat in trunk hose and a snowy, lace-trimmed
shirt, raced past him toward Kat.

A ringing slap echoed. Kat cried out, her hand on her
cheek, and Robin couldn't tell what she'd screamed because a roar filled his ears and the yellow chamber disappeared behind a tide of red. He shouted her name, pulling
the knife that had replaced his old poniard as he leaped
forward.

The man ignored him.

"Bitch!" he yelled. "Slut!" Then his insults turned into
a gurgle; Robin had the knife at his throat.

Robin's icy control slammed down over his anger. "The
lady is waiting for your apology," he advised. "You may
deliver it now."

"Robin, for the love of God—"

"I take back nothing," the man wheezed.

Robin let the knife scratch him lightly.

The man persisted, "She deserves to be punished. Letting herself be handled like the veriest whore."

There was a scuffling behind him. "Kat?" he asked sharply.

Someone else answered. "My sister seems to misunderstand my intentions. I will help calm Charles if you two will let me."

Risking a glance over his shoulder, Robin saw Kat with her arms entwined around a second slender man of slightly less than medium height. She wasn't embracing him. Instead, her small, determined hands were dragging back on his waist.

"Will you introduce us, Kat?" asked Robin.

"This is James," she panted. Despite the way she was clinging like a monkey to his back, James managed a creditable bow. His dark eyes, so like Kat's, were fixed on the poniard, but he seemed amused. "That is Charles."

Charles, the one under the knife, sneered. "Who's your whoremaster, little sister?"

"I look forward to hearing where you have been the last seven years, Charles, in spite of the fact you did not learn any manners there." Wiping the blade contemptuously on the back of Charles's britches, Robin slid it into its sheath. "Some degree of civility is due my wife's brother. But I warn you, it can only be stretched a certain length."

"I thought you might be married," said James. "Your conversation was so conjugal."

Robin saw Kat wince. When James patted her hands, however, she released him, and let him turn around and kiss her very properly on the forehead.

Her profile showed to Robin; what interested him was the sheen of tears on her cheek, and the way she was now giving James a real, if convulsive hug. The peek she took at Charles was wary but equally brimming with affection. Yes, his damask lady loved her brothers.

"Oh, James. Oh, Charles. It has been so long. I have missed you so much. My dears—"

"Wife?" Charles apparently had no patience with emotion. "You are wed?"

Both Charles and James had Kat's fineness of feature, although neither was as tall as she. Robin wondered if her superior inches had caused problems Kat had forgotten between the three of them as children. The brothers didn't seem overjoyed to meet their sister again.

In the tiny pause, a small, forgiving smile appeared on Charles's face. "Well, sister, I suppose some foolery is acceptable between a woman and her husband."

Kat opened her mouth but no sound came out. She was blushing furiously.

"Betrothed husband," corrected Robin, as if the difference were negligible. "It is a secret within the family."

Charles's smile congealed. "A secret betrothal is usually another name for fornication."

"That's two apologies you owe Kat," remarked Robin. "I think we will hear them now."

All of Kat's telltale radiance had drained away. "You yourself say that Charles needs to say his sorries to me, Robin. Let me speak with him alone."

He surrendered with good grace, hoping she could talk some sense into this ill-conditioned hothead. "If you wish, my lady. As you know, you may command me in—most—things."

James strolled out of the withdrawing room with him, calm as if he were in his own home. Of course, Priorly *was* his own home.

Kat found a handkerchief in her sleeve and offered it to Charles.

"Here. Wipe the blood off your neck. Oh, take it, do!" she exclaimed when he lifted his nose. "The linen is not contaminated with my sins."

"Then you admit—"

"I'll admit that Robin and I are fond of each other," she said coolly. "What is between us beyond that is none of your business."

"I am the head of the family!"

It had been such a wonderful moment when Charles popped out of the priest's hole, she thought. Pure happiness. Even the slap he'd landed on her cheek hadn't destroyed the feeling completely. But his self-righteous cruelty caused her to lash out.

"Welcome home. Where have you been while I have seen to the planting and the harvesting? And nursed the animals and the people. *And* cleaned up the offal you left rotting on the landing when you decided to leave!"

He pressed the linen to his scratch, which had already stopped bleeding. "I cannot believe I am hearing my sister. My sister for whom James and I killed a man, making us exiles. We have suffered for you, Kat, and you complain of a little hard work."

"I never minded the work," she said, softening. Mercy God, this was her long-lost brother, and she was haranguing him like a fishwife. It had never occurred to her to think the things she was saying until Robin said them first. *Robin.* A small core of anger at Charles's ununderstanding attitude caused her to add, "It was a labor of love. For you, for James. Do you have any love to give me in exchange for the love I have used up for you?"

This was all wrong, she thought miserably. Love shouldn't ask for repayment.

"You seem to be prodigal with your loving, sister," he said disdainfully.

"Perhaps," she said sadly. Charles was looking at her as if he hated her.

"I want your paramour out of the house by nightfall," he went on. His accent was different. It had a lilt that might be French.

"And what will you do if that does not happen?"

"Put you out, too."

"So much for ties of blood," she said. "We *are* tied by blood, are we not, Charles? Sir Henry's blood."

"Are you trying to extort a place at Priorly for yourself and your lover?"

"Not at all. Just thinking back to when we were willing to risk anything for each other. We were very young then. But I wonder if I have misread your intentions all these years. Did you—remove—Sir Henry because you could not brook my being hurt, or because pride made you avenge an insult to the family honor?"

"What's the difference?" he asked impatiently. He paced, a few steps away from her, a few steps back. It was the kind of movement she would have made herself, and her heart constricted. Every look, every gesture, revealed how closely related they were. Yet the laughing, carefree Charles she remembered had turned into a stranger. "A Preston female was despoiled. The insult had to be wiped out."

"There *is* a difference." *Despoiled.* To Charles she wasn't a person, just a not-virgin. And Robin . . . in the throes of lovemaking, had he seen her as a piece of glass, handled carelessly, cracked, and now requiring special care? She took a deep breath. "So you killed and then you ran."

"We had to go into exile." His correction was waspish.

"You panicked. You were just scared boys," Kat murmured, not accusingly but with calm kindness. "Robin said it would be something like that."

"Robin? That lout who has caused you to throw away the honor we saved for you? Or was there any left of it by the time you spread your legs for him? How many others plowed the same ground before him? Holy Mary, what fools James and I were, giving up our futures to revenge a slut's virtue."

"He's the only one since that night!"

"A likely tale. He may be stupid enough to believe it, but I am not. Get rid of him, Kat. I will not have him about, reminding me what a jade my sister is." Without pausing for breath, he added, "Robin who?"

"Lord Robin Hawking. His uncle is the Baron Burghley. More to the point, Robin's a queen's agent and neither you nor anyone else can make him just go away. Priorly is yours, and you can toss me out, but not Robin. He's here on the queen's business."

Her brother's pacing stopped. *"Mon Dieu,"* he muttered.

"I would advise you to limit your French oaths around him," she continued sharply. "Is that where you have been? France?"

He didn't deny it. The hatred in his face was augmented by pure dislike. "You have become a shrew."

"Then I am lucky Lord Robin finds shrewishness alluring. Mind me well. When I have needed a protector he has been there."

Sometimes even when she didn't want one, she thought,

and smiled. As she'd said before, Robin was conspicuous—too conspicuous for them to hide the fact they
were lovers within the close confines of the house. Especially since he was refusing to regard their lovemaking as
an intrigue.

She knew the angle of her chin was defiant. "Aye, he
shares my bed. And he shall continue to do so as long as
that's his desire. If you make me choose between you and
Robin, or Priorly and Robin, my choice will be Robin."
She softened her tone. "He is ready to stand our friend
over the crimes we committed seven years ago. You and
James need not skulk in the priest's hole anymore."

"What do you mean?" he asked quickly.

"Why, that you can come out of hiding now that you are
home. He's willing to let the old scandal stay buried."

"For your sake?"

Charles studied her skeptically. Kat's smile turned rueful. Her gown was a clean but simple gray, and although
making love with Robin had made her feel beautiful, it
could hardly have caused her figure to swell into the voluptuous ripeness expected of a Siren. After the last four
days and her sleepless night, she doubted that she looked
like a woman anyone would trouble to keep. Except
Robin. *Hawking's skinny whore.*

"For her sake," confirmed Robin from the doorway, and
she turned to him gratefully. He opened his arms and she
ran into them.

Folding her in a tight embrace, Robin rested his chin on
the top of her head and regarded Charles mockingly. Kat's
brother looked like a small, sharp-beaked, and self-
important bird with ruffled feathers.

"She's mine," he said almost indifferently. Charles
wasn't worth punishing. He'd had to decide that, or break
the nasty little whoreson in two. "And she'll stay mine. Do
not try to separate her from me. I can make your life extremely unpleasant, brother Charles. And your death even
more so. Do you understand?"

"I have heard of you," answered Charles, reddening.
"What is it they call you? The ferret or the hound or
something."

"Rat catcher," he said impassively. "You are well-informed—for someone so newly come back from the grave."

James, who'd entered behind Robin, went to place a hand on his brother's sleeve. "I have been conversing with Lord Robin. He's not an unreasonable man." There was a warning in James's pleasant tone. "So let's not give him any reason to doubt our ... civility."

Your allegiance to the crown, you mean, thought Robin.

Kat's arms were squeezing him hard. Guessing that she was offering him comfort, Robin kissed her hair where it dipped in a widow's peak to show her that Charles had no power to bother him.

"As Kat said, I should be loathe to hunt down either of her brothers for the death of Sir Henry Toth, especially when you saved the hangman a piece of perfectly good rope. Let's hope I have no other reason to go nosing about you."

The other men took his meaning, he was sorry to see. Charles's expression in particular went so carefully blank it would have warned a babe he was up to no good.

Robin's unease was leavened by relief. Not Kat, it had never been Kat who was mired in treason. But these two brothers of hers, so miraculously returning from the dead to a house not ten miles from Mary Stuart's prison—he could smell the unclean odor of treachery they gave off from across the room.

Chapter 17

230   Joy Tweam

Kat showed Robin a shortcut across autumn-gold woods that took them to the mill. It should have been a gentle ramble, a chance to hold hands and laugh over lovers' nonsense. Instead Kat walked in stiff silence, and Robin was preoccupied with the coming interrogation. Maud trailed a few feet behind.

Jack Miller's parents were elderly, illiterate, and terrified at the invasion of a tall nobleman into their floury domain. They were also nearly dumb with grief over Jack, although it had been weeks since their child's death.

Robin spent an hour with them. First he tried to put them at their ease, and then worked gently at pulling facts or speculations out of them. It quickly became apparent that they knew nothing and wanted to know nothing. Their ignorance was equaled by their astonishment at Jack's actions.

Where could a miller's son get the impudence to imagine he could blow up a queen?

Robin bent to avoid the lintel over the mill-house door, and grimaced at Kat. "They are like hedge-sparrows who raised a cuckoo. How should they be able to guess what the changeling in their nest would do, once it grew to be larger than they?"

"May we see them now?" she asked quietly, not quite hiding a spark of anger at being left outside to pace the Millers' small, plundered vegetable plot.

"Of course." He nodded to Maud, who ducked inside.

Catching Kat's hand, he lifted it to his lips without kissing it. "Do not scowl at me."

"I am not scowling," she said with dignity.

"I will not let you participate in questionings, my lady. That's one ugliness at least I can spare you."

Her fingers twisted in his grip and touched the side of his mouth. Then she slipped into the darkness of the mill.

She stayed an hour. Goodwife Miller begged her sister to eat a meal with her relatives. From outside, Robin listened as Kat gently bullied Maud into staying. In familiar surroundings, the maid had discovered more grief for her nephew Jack than she'd shown before. So Kat and Robin began the walk back to the manor house alone.

Although he didn't share it, Robin recognized Kat's distress over the Millers' suffering. Her shoulders were bowed, and her mouth set. He exerted himself to throw off his own oppressive thoughts.

He hadn't really wanted to wait until tonight.

The wood was thick with brush and trees. A willow's trailing limbs conveniently clung to long, spear-shaped leaves; perfect concealment for a man and woman. With a deft gesture, he caught her arm and pulled her inside the circling branches.

"Robin, what in the world—"

Under the willow it was twilit and very private.

"Come here," he said, hooking a toe around her ankles and tripping her. Her body fell neatly into his arms as he lowered her to the ground. "I hear that you are so lost in love for me that you would choose me over your brothers and your home. Did I understand aright?"

Her tongue came out to lick her lips, and he put out a finger so the quick glide wetted him, too. He ran the moist finger over her mouth, smiling at the way it went soft and vulnerable.

"Robin—" The protest was weak.

"Love is perhaps too strong a word?" he murmured. The loose gathers of cambric on the upper part of her bodice slid down over her shoulders at a touch. He liked her in country dress. It was much easier to deal with than her better gowns.

"Love is a comparative word," she said.

The bones in her shoulders were slender, delicate. Robin paid homage to them with light kneadings that oh-so-carefully pushed the material lower.

"If you have more affection for me than for Priorly or your family, I will be satisfied. Can I try again to satisfy you, my lady? Are you too sore?"

Her blush started at the tops of her breasts. Robin watched it flood upward over her chest, throat, and cheeks in the soft dusk. Then his gaze was drawn by the way her nipples pouted outward without even being stimulated. "Nay," she said. "I am not too sore."

He suckled her breasts as he rid her of the remainder of her clothes.

"Robin, do you really not mind that I am not as big as some?"

Engrossed with the erotic sweetness of her flesh, he was honestly confused for a moment. "As big as some what?"

"As—as—you know. No one is ever going to mistake them for melons."

Given the degree of his arousal, her insecurity struck him speechless. He took her hand, which was plucking at the shirt on his back, and placed it where even an innocent couldn't misinterpret the immensity of his liking.

"Have you considered that I might relish apples more than melons?" he asked hoarsely, recovering part of his voice.

"No man dislikes melons," she stated. But her fingers were eager as they swept over him.

He groaned and said, "The ties."

Kat had to use both hands to loosen his waistband. Even those less erotic touches enflamed him; he was a little surprised to find himself so on fire after last night's exercise. He never worried that he would embarrass himself by being unable to perform, but this extravagant heat ... His damask lady kindled an extraordinary blaze.

Once she'd freed his hips from the restraint of britches and hose, he tested her readiness and found her sweetly flowing, like honey. She was ready. Last night left him determined not to allow her time to cool. He tilted her onto her back on a pallet of their clothing and lifted her legs over his shoulders.

"Your doublet . . . your shirt . . ."

"I cannot wait. But I will be as gentle as a man stroking a kitten. I swear. Open to me. No, do not tense closed—ah, good. Very, very good."

Kneeling, he grasped her slim hips and slid into the honey. They'd practiced last night until she'd learned to relax her intimate muscles to allow him easier entrance. He demanded, "Look at me."

Her eyes were dark, soft, excited.

"Perhaps I am not overly concerned with either melons or apples." Robin thrust deeper. Faster. He gasped and slowed to a careful rhythm. "Perhaps the thing I like so much is you. Just—you."

She gave him a smile of such brilliance his heart almost leapt out of his chest, and moved her hips with so much enthusiasm he had to dig his fingers into her bottom to keep her from tipping him into climax. "Slowly," he ordered. "Softly."

"But I can feel your need. I want your pleasure," she whispered.

"And I insist on yours." He'd chosen this position to give himself the most leeway to play with her. His thumb sought through the short, damp curls that brushed him as he slid out. In. "What do you feel?"

Her lips curved up. "You."

His thumb teased. "What else?"

"Warm. Floating. Happy."

"Not aching? Not as if you want to bite? Scratch?"

"Nay, my darling. I was like that before we . . . joined. Now I am just . . . happy to feel you inside me."

Happy that it didn't hurt, he interpreted. Hoping Henry Toth was rotting in hell, he made his touch, his thrusts, even gentler.

It was no use. Although he used every bit of his skill and held out until his seed spilled from him in convulsions that were as much red pain as red pleasure, Kat's release didn't come.

"Who are these people?"

Kat stood beside the gate house, hands on her hips in unconscious imitation of one of Robin's poses.

"Friends of mine," said Charles coldly. Four fortnights of living in close quarters together had not changed his attitude toward her. "See that bedchambers are prepared for them."

"Sweet Jesu, that's Raoul Mauvissiere! What is he doing here?"

"Obviously, he's visiting James and me. If you know who he is, then you are aware Priorly must show him and the others our best hospitality. Get to it."

He stepped forward with an expression completely unlike the glare he'd turned on his sister. Content to be left out of the greetings, Kat hurried across the yard and into the house. Charles and James . . . and the son of the French ambassador?

Robin was leaning against a battlement at the top of the west turret. December this year was warm, with no snow. His thoughtful gaze brooded on clouds left behind by a rainsquall earlier in the day, now hanging in pale pink and purple splendor over the setting sun. Fotheringhay lay to the west.

Kat slowed on the top step.

A little of her reserve around Robin had returned. His puzzlement over her response during lovemaking was plain enough to her, and had brought back all her self-doubts. She was marked by her past, unable to be what other women could be, unable to experience all he demanded of her. He was virile. Accustomed to uninhibited lovers. With her, he had to trammel the power of his sexuality. The magnificent hunting hawk shackled.

She tried to feel the proper sensations. But even his frankly erotic and arousing descriptions couldn't explain how a woman reached them. Each time it was the same. Her body ached, trembled, dampened with astonishing—almost embarrassing—regularity whenever he touched her. But she seemed to arrive at some predetermined point of arousal and then the delicious heat faded into warm embers. Though it was pleasant, Robin's disappointment showed that pleasant wasn't enough.

Ever since he'd loved her under the willow tree, he had tried to conceal his disappointment. That frightened her. How long before he became bored with hiding his emotions? What had she ever had to offer him, except the chance to be himself? Himself, not Lord Robin Hawking, nephew of Elizabeth Tudor's most trusted advisor. Not a suspected torturer, or the queen's rat catcher. Just Robin. A man with strengths and weaknesses and an endearing need to be loved.

Robin didn't need to turn to know Kat was there. He felt her caution.

In spite of the fact he was throttling his tendency to dominate as best he could, she'd withdrawn more every day. Making love with her was—it was ecstasy, he admitted to himself. Guilt nibbled at the edges of his pride, because the powerful climaxes she gave him were as yet unmatched by anything he gave her. Loving her was more than exercising his lance. It was a union, a losing of himself. A blessing. It made him believe in God. And then it threw him back into himself, whole and replete.

It was also incredibly pleasurable.

The irony nagged him. She was the first woman he'd ever cared about pleasing as more than a matter of sexual courtesy. She was the only woman who didn't shudder and cry out in his arms. Her cruel initiation into the mysteries of sex made it understandable. But he wanted more than her surrender—he wanted the success of raising her to a total, mind-numbing, soul-opening pitch of ecstasy.

At least she was always willing. Not once had she said no when he reached for her, as he did night after night . . .

"What is it?" he asked, to save her from having to work up the courage to address him.

"There are visitors."

"I saw them ride in." His curiosity stirred. Not even Charles would be lunatic enough to parade accomplices in front of him. These might be messengers from court. "Who are they?"

"One is Sieur Raoul Mauvissiere."

He said something coarse. Apparently Charles *could* be that mad.

"Robin, he says they are friends. He and James must have met them while they were abroad. What if the French are planning to take advantage of them and use Priorly to stage an escape for Queen Mary?"

"That's certainly a possibility," he said with restraint.

He didn't want to be the one to destroy the remnants of her faith in her brothers. Robin himself had no doubts. There was only one reason a proud boor would allow his sister's lover to sleep with her under his roof, and that was self-interest.

Therefore, Charles had to be committing treason.

Robin used simple reasoning to reconstruct the elder Preston brother's logic—since Charles hadn't given any sign of deep thinking so far. Charles must know Robin wouldn't carry tales about Kat's rape and Sir Henry's death to the authorities. Even if he was too blockheaded to have noticed that Robin was serious about her, the more sensitive James wasn't. In a reckoning over the murder Kat would be blamed along with Charles and James. They had committed the crime, but she had hidden it. That left only treasonous activity to explain why Charles had allowed Robin to stay at Priorly.

No, the brothers were up to no good. Robin only hoped he wasn't the agent who ended up arresting them. Would Kat be able to forgive that?

"I am to ready chambers for Charles's guests," Kat was saying. "Is there anything I should add or forget to add to their quarters? Something the servants should look for in their baggage?"

"I'll do the spying, I thank you, wench. You'll not allow the filth of this business to smear you."

"But I do not mind helping you, Robin, truly."

"I mind. Heed me. Do not even think of it." He spoke harshly.

"Oh, very well. I'll be in the guest chambers on the second floor, then, or in the kitchen."

He waited until only the tip of her kerchief showed on the stairs. "Kat!"

"My lord?"

"Shall we have fruit on the table at supper? I am in the mood for apples."

There was a moment's silence.

"You need not wait till supper," she suggested.

Robin considered. They hadn't made love on the battlements yet. Then he shook his head. The dying sun was stealing the warmth from the air, and part of his campaign to drown Kat in pleasure was to draw out joining as long as he could. She'd be chilled. And neither of them had the necessary time.

"I want you, but on the fur rug in front of a roaring fire."

"I keep telling you, we do not need a fire ..." The words faded as she continued on her way down the stairs.

Supper was lavish. While none of the dishes was as grand as the fare seen at court, Robin thought Kat must have sacrificed one of the animals being held as breeding stock over the winter.

Roast pork steamed next to game birds with crisp skins. Poached in wine, freshwater fish lay beached on frills of cress. Tarts and pies oozed fragrant juices. Bowls filled with some of Priorly's stored fruits and nuts provided color at intervals along the table. Robin thought Kat had done wonders on short notice.

Raoul Mauvissiere poked dubiously at a plump grouse.

"Our English food unsettles your stomach?" jibed Robin.

"Now, my lord, Sieur Raoul is French. He's not used to seeing his dinner so naked," Kat said from around James. Robin sent her a stern look. She smiled at him sweetly and glanced at Raoul. "There was no time to compound the sauces and creams your countrymen use to clothe your meats. If you and your party are staying with us a while, the cooks and I will try to do better."

"Alas," said Raoul, "I am desolated that we must be away on our travels tomorrow."

"I am amazed you could drag yourself away from court in the rainy weather."

"It rains at court, too," he remarked with a fastidious pinching of his nostrils. He had a mole next to his mouth that moved up and down as he talked. "It rains everywhere in this ... delightful nation."

"I have a dear friend with the queen. Margaret Treland. How did you leave her?" Kat went on airily.

What was the minx up to? Robin wondered. He applauded her neat extraction of the information that the visitors were staying only a night. But on the whole he would prefer she keep her long, fragile neck out of trouble. And Mauvissiere and friends certainly spelled trouble.

"Milady Margaret had just welcomed her good lord John when I found myself obliged to come into the country on a trifling bit of business," explained Raoul. His girlish mouth and fashionably orange-dyed beard quivered slightly.

Robin sat back, taking thoughtful bites out of a duck leg. This pretty boy was the redoubtable Margaret's lover? The longer he pondered the liaison, the more difficult it became to repress a guffaw. He took refuge in his wineglass.

As the meal wore on, his glass became useful as a shield for his expression, though he didn't drink much. Others weren't so self-restrained. Charles began a loud conversation on the benefits of enclosure.

"What?"

Kat's faint protest was lost to all except Robin.

"The champion method—ah, the old way of dividing fields into strips for the peasants and letting them use the common ground for pasture, Raoul—never makes the best use of the soil. The benefits of the new methods—"

"Enrich only the whoresons who gobble up the common land," said Kat hotly. "I'll not have my people sent out onto the roads to starve or turn thief to feed themselves."

Charles smiled thinly. "Your people, sister?"

"I have been mistress here for seven years." In the candlelight, her eyes were stormy. "You will allow me the right to feel affection for decent souls in my care."

"Affection, certainly. You may be as doting as you wish. But land management is a topic for men."

James interceded quietly. "Kat has not done so badly from what I have seen."

"A woman's best is never as good as a man's worst." Charles shrugged.

Robin decided to intervene before the storm he could see brewing behind Kat's eyes broke. A public quarrel with the head of her family would make it even more painful for her to remain at Priorly with Charles in residence.

Leaning forward with a lopsided grin, he forced a slur into his voice. "A woman'sh besht—ah ha, that'sh goo', brother Sharlesh. Come along, my little pusshy, you can show me your w-woman'sh besht. Time for bed."

"Robin." Kat looked stunned.

Charles and Mauvissiere burst into laughter. Charles caught James's arm, cutting off the younger brother's gesture of protest.

"Lord Robin has the right idea," approved Charles. "What say you, Raoul? We can find ourselves a pair of lusty wenches."

"Or even just one. What do you English say? Share and share alike. The one who is not occupied can watch." Mauvissiere's lips were fuller and pinker than ever. "What say you, James? Do you join us?"

"I thank you, no."

"No use tempting James," Charles put in. "My brother's a monk al—"

"Good night, everyone," said James quickly, as he stood.

Mauvissiere seemed to have forgotten the others. He smiled sleepily at Charles. "You have such energy. If you are feeling imaginative, it will not be necessary for either of us to pause in our pleasures. By setting a woman between us at the correct angle, we can both—"

James flinched slightly when Robin slammed his goblet down, sending the untouched wine inside sloshing over the table.

"Let'sh go, Kat," said Robin.

She followed him with an adequate show of obedience, but he could sense her seething behind him all the way to the stairs. In the stairwell, even the breath she drew to speak sounded angry. Checking her with a finger to her lips, he tugged her up the steps and into their chamber.

"You may now screech at me with my goodwill," he told her, shutting the door firmly on any listening ears.

Instead, tears flooded her eyes. "Poor Margaret. He's not going to marry her, is he? And that's what she wanted."

"Our precious Raoul? It would not seem so. Anyway, she's already wed. How—no, do not tell me. It is enough to know that particular avenue for secrets going out of the country is closed."

A few of the tears fell, and Robin gently kissed them away. Kat sniffed loudly, and then glared at him.

"You do not smell of wine. That disgusting display of lechery and drunkenness in the hall was just that, was it not? A display!"

"The more our friends discount me as a sot who can be led around by my—what did you call it once? My cockerel? Anyway, the more they count me a fool, the better I'll like it." He grinned fiercely, and Kat shrank a little in his arms.

"You are misleading them on purpose."

"And you, my lady, are not going to betray me." His arms tightened. "Are you?"

"Of course not. But, Robin, could we not warn Charles and James? Mauvissiere and the others must be using them to get closer in distance to Mary Stuart."

"It would do no good, sweet heart. Let us go to bed. If we cannot solve the problems of the world, we can make a world of our own."

Kat crept out of their chamber to see to the before-dawn chores the next morning. Robin was still asleep; he had been very, very thorough as he tried to give her release.

Once again, she had failed him. On her way to check on the milking, Kat sighed. Except for his unstated disappointment, she was happy with what he made her feel during lovemaking; why couldn't he be?

Although Charles had made it clear he didn't want her interfering with the tenant farms, he had no objection to her continuing reign over the stillroom, brewery, bakery, and kitchen. They were the genteel domains of the lady of the house. Dashing by the chapel later, on her way to change slippers which had gotten soiled, she paused in her reflections about how genteel the floor of a milking shed was apt to be. Someone was singing in the chapel.

Pushing open the door, she said, "Good morning, sir."

One of the visitors who had ridden in yesterday with Raoul spun around, his hand still clinging to the altar cloth.

"Lady Katherine. You are out and about early."

"As are you, Sieur—Sieur Paul, is it not? Are you looking for something? May I help you find it?"

The short, stout man glanced around the room, which glowed with color in the first rays of the rising sun. "No, I thank you. I have already found it."

The cryptic reply alarmed Kat. "Sir" Paul had a proprietary air. A priest?

He allowed her to usher him out. Murmuring an incoherent excuse, Kat slipped back into the chapel for a moment. She touched a candle. Warm. It was an effort for her to smile pleasantly at Paul, who was waiting when she came back out. To judge by the expression on her face whether or not she had noticed anything about the chapel? Kat kept smiling valiantly.

They descended to the hall. The other members of his party were gathered there, eating quickly, like men getting ready to ride. Her smile came more naturally. At least they were really leaving.

She caught up with Charles as he returned after bidding them Godspeed. Even if Robin had forbidden her to say anything about the Frenchmen and Mary Stuart, she could offer some indirect advice. Charles might hate her—in fact, she was sure he did—but he was still her brother. She couldn't seem to learn to hate him back.

"We have to talk. To welcome the French—"

"I am master here. I do as I please."

"Should I genuflect?"

He grabbed her arm. "What does that mean?"

She tried to look at him objectively, and saw the hard, pointed chin under his beard, the light of fanaticism in his eyes. It would be easier not to love him, but she did and always would.

"The chapel was in use this day. Those men who just left do not have our kingdom's best interests at heart. Was there a Jesuit among them?"

"Kat, perhaps the men who risk their lives to return England to the true Church do want the best for this realm."

"Oh, dear God, you have followed Mother's faith."

"Is that so horrible? Has your whoremaster corrupted

your mind so much that you have turned against the old ways?"

"I have nothing against the old ways—or the new ones. To be honest, they seem much the same to me. What I cannot bear is to see my country torn apart over questions only God can answer. Do you actually believe *God* wants killing done to bring the old ways back?"

"Yes." As always, he sounded supremely sure of himself.

She tried again. "Charles, you cannot know what you are saying. Queen Elizabeth would have to be murdered; there would be civil war. What could be worth the tears and the blood?"

"The truth." He looked past her. "The truth which has kept me striving all these years. Do you imagine you were the only one to lose a childhood when you were ravished? I gave up my birthright to avenge your honor. I had to leave everything. What was left, except faith?"

"God is love, not hate."

He didn't seem to hear her. "James and I sailed to France as cargo in a stinking little boat whose captain robbed us of the silver that was all we had. But there were other Englishmen in exile. Men like us, who had fled abroad so they could live their convictions. They took us in, fed us, clothed us, introduced us to people from the French and Spanish courts who wanted to see us returned to our rightful places. Do you not see?"

What she saw was that her brothers had fallen in with a group of exiles who had spent years feeding off each other's angry sense of loss. And now Charles and James were being used by foreign governments to put a different queen on the throne of England.

Fleeing from Charles, she went to James. One brother was no more willing to listen than the other.

"But surely you understand what's going on?" she asked in near-despair.

"Yes, little sister." James returned to the book he'd been reading. "Do you?"

Her frustration with the two of them exploded. "Why do you never *talk* to me? Mercy God, James, the things we should have to say to each other after all these years! Yet we share nothing. I feel as if I have to creep about the place to stay out your way. Certainly out of Charles's way."

"That is an exaggeration."

"Is it? Watch Charles look at me sometime. See the hate. He does not just want me out of the house—he would rather I were dead."

James's eyes continued to move over the print. "It would help if you would wed Hawking."

"I cannot ruin his chances of making a living. And . . . there are other reasons."

"Yes, I understand your difficulties with the queen. But as matters now stand, you are sinning, and sinning joyfully."

"Is making love with him a worse sin than refusing to recognize treason when it is under your nose?" He didn't answer and she went on, "Perhaps I believe God is less judgmental than Charles seems to be."

He smiled faintly, but shrugged.

"Kat." Robin spoke from the door. "I want you."

Something must have changed in her expression at Robin's turn of phrase, because behind his book James flushed, and Robin's thick blond brows rose.

I go to him like a compass point seeking true north, she thought as her feet walked her directly to him. "My lord?" she said.

"It is so fine a day for late in the year," he told her, studying James. "Ride with me."

"My dress—"

"I will wait for you."

It was obviously an order, and Kat picked up her skirts and ran, calling for Maud to help her. After she'd scrambled into a more suitable gown, the maid accompanied her down the stairs, and once they were outside, Kat saw why. Samuel was holding the horses by the gate house. He and Maud drew together the instant he handed over the reins.

"Do you think they are . . . well, lovers?" she asked Robin, nudging her light-footed mare to follow Robin's mount. They veered north into the wood.

"Everyone looks good to someone, I suppose," he answered. Behind the screen of oaks and elms, he angled off in a new direction. West.

"Where are we going?"

"Fotheringhay. I am interested in seeing what happens there today."

Kat swayed to avoid a low-hanging branch. It was bare with the stripped-down beauty of December. Sparrows hopped on the ground, searching for forgotten seeds and chirping. Robin often went out riding alone, and she realized she had no idea where. "Have you been there many times?"

"It is not possible for me to tell you everything."

"When will we be done with secrets?" Was anybody ever able to be completely honest? she asked herself. The thing she hadn't told Robin weighed on her. *Every man wants sons.*

"This filthy business does not allow any of us to be honest," he said, echoing her thought with eerie accuracy.

The clink of metal scraping against metal silenced the birds.

"Robin—"

"It is all right. They are my men." He whistled, and a small troop of armed guards rode out of the woods and formed lines behind and in front of them.

"Do we need a guard?" she asked incredulously.

"I cannot take you into Mary Stuart's prison," explained Robin. "And I'll not leave you in Priorly where Frenchmen come and go as they please."

Kat hesitated, and then she lied. Matters were tense enough between Charles and Robin. "Charles snaps, but he would not hurt me."

"Put it down to a whim." He gave an exaggerated sigh at her lifted brows. "You are precious to me. It must be apparent to all and sundry. I am not deserting you where anyone could take you hostage and use you to force me into covering up some crime."

"You would not do it."

Robin wished he could be as sure of his integrity as she was. "There's a clearing up ahead. I sent orders that it be made comfortable for you."

To hide her uneasiness, Kat exclaimed as it came into

view. "Oh, Robin, how pretty. A pavilion, and a table and stools and food. Are you dining with me?"

"I am afraid not. It will probably be several hours before I am finished at Fotheringhay, so enjoy yourself and stay out of trouble, Mistress Mischief."

"I'll try not to attract any perverted noblemen or tumble into any perfidious plots," she said with a wan smile.

"See that you do not."

The track he took through the trees led directly west; he knew it by heart. After a few miles, it petered out in an open space that surrounded Fotheringhay.

The old castle's gray stone walls gave Robin a feeling of oppression; perhaps the place had been chosen as Mary Stuart's prison with just that effect in mind. Mary liked pretty things, and Fotheringhay was not pretty.

He rode in, fighting his way through a tangle of carts and horses in what used to be the bailey. His scowl scattered several plump, well-dressed men, merchants by the look of them, and he stalked into the hall.

"What are all those people doing here?" he snapped at Amyas Paulet.

The warden threw his hands up in a harried gesture. "They come to sell their wares to Queen Mary."

"God's grace, man, surely you do not allow them to see her in person!"

"I pray the Lord," said Sir Amyas piously, "that Mary's life will soon be over. But a queen is still a queen. She must be fed. And clothed. And provided with the comforts that befit her station."

Robin reminded himself that Amyas couldn't help being a fool. "Who has been in her quarters today?"

"Just some mercers so far, selling embroidery stuffs. She is a notable needlewoman. I could hardly deny her the opportunity to buy silks and needles and suchlike."

"Are they still here?"

"What? Who? Oh, the mercers? They departed a few minutes before you came in. What are you thinking?"

"That patience is a virtue," said Robin grimly. "Describe these mercers for me. Was there a young one among them, beardless, with a mole—"

"Next to his mouth?" Amyas interrupted. "Yes. Do you know him?"

"He is the son of the French ambassador. And I doubt very much that he and Mary were talking about embroidery designs."

Despite the gaiety of the furnishings, there was really nothing to occupy Kat's attention in the glade except her thoughts—and they were so worried she would have preferred almost any distraction. Several of the guardsmen sprawled over a backgammon board, and jumped up at her approach.

"Do not let me bother you," she said, withdrawing hastily. Poor men, Robin must have put the fear of God and a lively respect for their charge into them.

The captain of the guard followed her.

"Begging your pardon, madam. Did my rogues treat you proper? Lord Robin said—"

She decided she'd rather not hear what Robin had threatened. "I have no complaint to make," she said, smiling. "Except—do you happen to have a book I could read, or a game you could join me in?"

The board was promptly confiscated, but the soldiers seemed pleased to lend it to her rather than resentful. They clustered around, muttering soft comment on the play. It took a snarl from the captain to get them pacing the perimeter of the little camp.

Kat was forging ahead in the game by pushing her opponent's pieces to the starting point when one of the guards called quietly, "Horses approaching, Captain."

Instantly, she was surrounded by a wall of broad backs.

"Perhaps it is my lord," she said as calmly as she could. But she drew her warm cloak more closely around her neck and shivered.

"Mayhap," came the captain's laconic reply.

A small party of horsemen burst out of the undergrowth. A sarcastic voice boomed, "What a charming sight. Soldiers in queen's livery defending a game of tables. Where's your captain?"

The officer stepped forward, parting the row of backs. "Here, sir. May I know your business?"

The large voice belonged to an incongruously tiny man. He was very richly dressed. "No, you may not. I am William Davison, secretary of state." Davison stared through the opening left in the captain's wake. The pronounced lines in his forehead became even deeper. "What have you here? A lady? My God, you cannot be daft enough to allow the queen of Scots outside the walls?"

"I am Katherine Preston, Master Davison," Kat said swiftly. She had seen him several times at court, and not much liked what she saw. He was one of those men with a distinct fondness for his own opinion.

"And what are you doing camped on the grounds of Fotheringhay, Katherine Preston?"

The captain answered. "We wait on the return of Lord Robert Hawking, sir."

"The rat catcher?" Davison flushed darkly. "I remember you now, madam. Where does that rogue keep his brains these days? In his breeches? He's given a royal escort to his whore!"

Chapter 18

D avison insisted on sweeping together all the men-at-
arms and bringing them, with Kat, to Fotheringhay.
His sharp questions made her head ache. Where was her
family? Who was the queen's justice locally? Did Kat
have no decency?

"I hope I do," she said, rubbing her forehead. "Can anyone claim more?"

"I am sending for your brothers and this—who did you
say? Sir Francis Toth. We shall see what has been going
on here."

Fotheringhay was a dour place, and once the group
summoned by Davison arrived, Kat thought the castle became even less appealing. Tension crackled in the small
room set aside for Davison's use by the warden.

Charles was subdued and silent. James was alert and silent. Francis Toth stared around with popping eyes.

Robin entered last. His eyes flew to Kat, and she shook
her head slightly, hoping he would understand that it
hadn't been her choice to disobey his order to stay safely
in the wood. His answering nod was equally faint, but she
breathed easier. He didn't blame her.

"God's grace, must we sit in the cold and dark?" he
snarled. Striding to the hearth, he poked at the sullen fire;
every controlled move spoke of frustration.

Impatiently, William Davison said, "Oh, let the fire be."
He cleared his throat. "You are called upon to answer for
your actions in regard to this woman, this Lady Katherine—"

A man who liked to hear himself make speeches, thought Kat.

"In making inquiries, I discovered she is the ward of her most gracious majesty, Queen Elizabeth." A quick glare upwards, where presumably another queen was imprisoned. "She is also the minor sister of Charles Preston here, whom I am told was until recently considered to be dead."

Francis joined in. "As justice of the peace, I wish to hear just how Charles and James have come back from the grave."

A pause stretched out unpleasantly long.

Kat peeked at Robin. He kept his face turned to the fire. It smoked, and the wavering light brushed moving shadows on his brow and cheek.

When no one else spoke, he said, "They came to their senses, that's all. Two scared and dim-witted boys witnessed an accident years ago. Idiotically, they expected to be blamed for the death of Sir Francis's father, which occurred while they were fishing together. They ran to . . ." His bright gaze raked Charles. "Where did you go?"

"Holland," Charles produced.

James said nothing.

"Finally, they realized no one was going to blame them and came home to take up their lives. A short and unedifying tale."

"Do you have witnesses to your recent whereabouts?" Davison asked Charles.

Kat heard her voice. It sounded as if it belonged to someone else. "Why should they need to prove anything? They are not imposters. I will swear that they are my brothers."

"England is surrounded by enemies! A journey abroad makes anyone suspect," said Davison bluntly. "Why should Englishmen want to be anywhere but England anyway?"

"They were young and frightened," insisted Kat. It was true, she comforted herself. "Tell him, Charles, James."

"We admit to foolishness and fear. Have we not been

unmanned enough for one day?" But James didn't sound frightened. His question was calm, a little distant, as if it formed a screen around his feelings.

"The Prestons are all foolish." Francis looked at Kat, and then Robin.

"But are they unnatural enough to allow their sister to live openly in an irregular union with her lover?" The attack from Davison shifted to Robin. The secretary of state reminded Kat of a terrier. "And you, sir, borrowing soldiers who are supposed to guard the queen of Scots, in order to entertain your mistress! A departure from duty which—"

"You will find, Master Davison," said Robin coldly, "that I am as attached to my duty as you are to yours. The lady has been the target of an abduction, and has provided useful information to her majesty's agents. I would have been failing in my *duty*, as well as my inclination, if I permitted her to go unprotected."

Davison's eyebrows rose so far they almost disappeared into the furrows carved into his forehead. It seemed to be a habitual response.

"The lady's brothers are not adequate protection?" he said.

Robin contented himself with a small smile.

Not sure why, Kat burst into tears.

In an instant, Robin's arms were around her, and his hands were coaxing her face into the hollow of his shoulder, so she wouldn't have to endure the stares of all these grim men.

"Charles Preston does not object to my presence in his home." Robin's tone was bleak.

"Is that true, Charles?" asked Francis heavily.

When her brother mumbled, "It is true," Kat's tears dried up. She rested against Robin's chest, drawing shaky breaths, unable to find an explanation for herself. Nothing had made her sob aloud like that for almost two months, not since the night she'd told Robin how Francis's father had used her.

Reluctantly, Davison dismissed them. The group stopped at the crossroads where Francis was to branch off for his own house. Long clouds of smoky breath lingered in the air between people and horses; the weather was turning at last.

"There's a storm coming," said Francis, and Kat bit her lip. Poor Francis, always so good at stating the obvious. With his eyes protruding at Charles and James, he looked like a puzzled, overgrown child. "My father fell into the water and drowned, and you just left him there."

James started to speak, seemed to think better of it, and nodded soberly.

The pop-eyed gaze turned to Kat. "I owe you my thanks, Katherine. You were wise. We would not have suited as man and wife. You would not be a suitable mother for my sons. There's bad blood in the Prestons."

Putting out a hand, Kat kept Robin from making more than a quick, angry grab at Francis.

"Preston blood is of a different sort from yours, at any rate, Francis," she said. "Mine is wilder than I ever suspected."

"I did my best for you," he continued, recovering his usual self-satisfaction. "Wrote the queen on your behalf, got you invited to court—"

"*You* did that?" This time Robin had to put a hand on Kat's shoulder to keep her from launching herself bodily at the unsuspecting Toth.

"It turned out ill, but that could hardly be my fault." He flapped the reins. "I will bid you good day. Do not ask me to Priorly in the future. I will not go."

"Thank God for small favors," said James after Francis rode out of earshot, with the first outright and cheerful malice Kat had heard from him. Snow began to dust the track with white.

"That—that pompous bag of air had the gall to arrange for me to be dragged to court! All that loneliness, so much wasted time—"

Rubbing her shoulder, Robin said, "I am not sorry you came to court. We would not have met otherwise."

Kat wanted to go on protesting, but his serious, intent look stopped her. She sat still under his hand, the air she drew in so cold it fooled the back of her throat into tingling hot. His hand was heavy and firm. It somehow had more reality than the horse under her legs or the light snowflakes touching her cheeks with cold kisses.

From a distance, she heard James say, "Let's be on our way, Charles. These two can find their own road home." Hooves thudded on rapidly freezing ground as the two brothers rode off in the direction of Priorly.

Robin's hand fell away. "Is it too hard to say you are glad we met, too?"

Honesty, and something that had a connection with her impulse to weep, forced her to reply, "Our lives would have been easier if we had remained strangers. This game we play, pretending we'll always be left alone to be lovers—it's dangerous. To our sanity, if nothing else."

"Knowing each other is not worth everything?" The graying light robbed his eyes of their glitter; for once they looked flat and colorless.

"We both carry burdens which can only be borne alone."

"Being my wife is a burden to you?"

"Robin, you want me to be a woman I am not. Even when all is sweet between us, you want more, or different. And you keep talking as if we'll someday be married, and making me hurt you by forcing me to say it can never be. I do not enjoy hurting you."

"Would it hurt less if I were not sleeping in your room?" he asked stonily.

Kat didn't know why she was saying these things. She craved his strength, the supple rub of his skin, his weight pressing her into the furs. The prospect of not taking Robin into her body, no longer holding him there while he worked off his passion, made tears well again. But she couldn't stop. "Perhaps."

"Then I shall remove myself to one of the other chambers. I cannot leave Priorly altogether, but I'll keep out of your sight as much as I can."

The sharp air stabbed into her like a knife. The air, or misery. "Oh, do not! Robin, please, I am being female or something. Pay me no heed. I did not mean it. This is just a very unsettling day. Do not let me pick a quarrel with you."

Gradually, he lost some of his stiffness. A glint in his eyes reassured her. "Promise you will not slap me for asking this."

"I promise."

"Are you due for your monthly courses?"

Such a practical explanation for her emotionalism miraculously cured her mood, and she had trouble hiding a smile. But she tried to sound indignant. "Sir!"

"Ah. You are."

"Not at all. My courses have never been monthly. They arrive at very muddled intervals. But that must be the answer."

"There is another," he suggested.

"My lord?"

"I could have got you with child. Breeding women water their babes with tears, or so I am told."

"That's not it." Without explanation, she went on, "I should not have lashed out at you so. And the last thing I want you to do is leave my bed." She pushed her hood away from her face so she could feel the snowflakes. "Although, come to think of it, we have never made love in bed, have we? Why is that?"

Robin would have cut out his tongue—like wretched Jack Miller, he thought briefly—before he admitted to avoiding the bed because he was afraid it would remind her of being raped. So he said off-handedly, "You are very desirable nesting among the furs, damask lady. When I look at you, and feel the silk of your skin and then the softness of the fur . . . You are as sensual as your namesake, Kat. It really is much like stroking a warm, fur-covered kitten. I am a lucky man."

Her look had longing in it, and something else he couldn't quite read. "I would so like to be your wife," she confessed.

He could barely hear her over the rising whine of the wind. There was no point in yelling back how the boot was on the other foot; he had yet to bring her the ultimate fulfillment. At least her unaccustomed nerve storm was over.

The snow was thickening fast; he had to get Kat back to

Priorly. His light slap on the rump of Kat's mare startled her horse into a canter. Tightening his legs, he loosened the reins to get his stallion moving.

Robin was in the stable with a curry brush in his hand.

Watching the Preston brothers was a boring business, and when he wasn't in front of a fire with Kat, or at Fotheringhay in worried consultation with the warden there, he often found some task at Priorly to pass the time. A task which would allow him to monitor comings and goings. The stable was well-situated to do that.

His cloak hung on a peg and his doublet was unbuttoned. A week after the season's first snowfall, the white stuff was a foot deep outside and the drafty stable wasn't warm, but the exercise had made the cold feel good.

He brushed a big bay with long, smooth strokes. Surviving the hurdle of the only argument he'd had with Kat since they had become lovers ought to have cheered him, he reflected with a return of his old cynicism, but instead it added to his black thoughts.

Robin gave the glossy red hide a final stroke with the brush. Perhaps he ought to be on the spot in Mary's prison, instead of waiting for treachery at Priorly.

He was tying the bay's tail into a neat club with ribbons when a nearly frozen horseman rode into the courtyard.

Pulling his cloak off the peg and winding it around him, Robin stepped out into the drifted snow. The rider identified himself as a messenger from the queen, with letters for Lord Robin Hawking and Lady Katherine Preston. His mouth fell unattractively open when the tall man dressed like an ostler said brusquely, "I am Hawking. Give both of them to me."

The messenger went on goggling while Robin flapped the letters against his thigh in thought before striding away toward the brick house.

Kat was in the stillroom. "I have been making up a potion for sore throats," she greeted him. "Would you like to try it? It has honey and usquebaugh in it."

He shuddered. "No. And if this letter for you says what

I fear it does, you will not be here to physick anyone. Read it."

Breaking the seal, she scanned Elizabeth's elegant handwriting.

Robin ran his eyes over his own message. "That interfering fool Davison has been talking. I am summoned to court."

Kat waved her twin order. "I am, too. Mercy God, what will Charles do while I am gone?"

"Do?" he repeated.

"To the place. The people."

Folding his summons small, he tucked it into the wallet hanging from his belt. The woman simply wouldn't believe the worst—the truth—about her brothers. They and Raoul were planning *something* that involved Mary Stuart. An attack on Fotheringhay launched from Priorly, a secret escape—something. He was sure of it.

He snorted softly; he should be grateful for Kat's trusting nature. She wouldn't believe the worst about him, either. "I am going to talk to James," he said.

In response to a blunt warning, the younger brother smiled with a serenity that drove Robin to pound his fist into his palm.

"Do you not understand plain English? I know you and Charles are hatching some crazy scheme. Whatever it is, it will get you killed. In a messy and painful manner," he said with deliberate brutality. "I'll not hide any further crimes for you. And I am not the only queen's agent in this part of the world. I have to report to the queen, but others will stay and watch."

"And have you, or any other agent, proof of this mysterious crime?"

"Damn you, man, I am trying to keep you from *giving* us evidence. Warning you comes near to a violation of my duty. But I cannot let Kat's kinsmen destroy themselves without saying a word to stop them."

Shaking his head slowly, James replied, "There's goodness in you, Robert Hawking. I thought you could not be the besotted dolt you have acted. Kat has not shown good sense in choosing you, but perhaps she has shown good taste."

Robin gave up. James wasn't going to listen. He didn't even approach Charles. There would be no point.

The next day he and Kat, accompanied by Maud and Samuel and an escort of men-at-arms, began the cold journey back to Richmond Palace.

Part Three

Lovers' Kiss

Chapter 19

"I cannot bear this, Robin."

"What, sweet heart?"

Everything in the hall at Richmond appeared normal to Robin. With its enormous paintings and statues, the room was always grand; Christmas decorations did their best to make it cozy with the green of holly and bay, and the waxy white of mistletoe berries. The queen sat by the central fire, throwing dice—probably loaded, he'd found out from experience—and winning from courtiers who in any case knew better than to lose.

"Is something amiss?" he asked.

A delicate flush rode high in Kat's cheeks. "Perhaps it does not bother you that we are never together these days."

"On the contrary." They were facing the room. He slid a surreptitious hand behind her neck and into her hair. Caressing her scalp, he murmured, "Very much to the contrary. But the queen keeps us with her so much—"

"You especially." Her head lolled back, ever so slightly, in response to the teasing fingers, but her voice remained tense.

"Jealous, wench?" he asked lazily.

"Aye. Jealous and—I miss you. I think I have gotten used to—to—"

"The comfort of a man's body?"

"There's no need for tact. We are both aware how thoroughly you have taught me to crave you."

"Are we? Tell me more. Tell me how you feel when you crave."

"Here?"

"Why not? No one is listening. If we cannot do what we want, we can get a little innocent pleasure from talking about it."

A tremor ran through her, probably because she was repressing a giggle. "Innocent? Oh, very well, I—it is as if we have never touched, never been naked together in body and heart. Something is building inside me—some feeling, some pressure. It is tearing me apart. Robin, if I cannot be with you soon, I shall die."

"Do you not know what you are feeling?"

"Of course I know what it is," she said crossly. "Lust."

"But it is stronger, is it not, sweet heart? Deeper, hotter, sweeter?"

"Aye, curse you. And I do not want to feel this way *all* the time. My mind cannot fix on my duties. I think only of you. I see only you. People have begun to reckon me daft."

"My poor Kat. Do not despair. You will think it worth the aching the next time we get a few moments alone. The best moments in love are called 'the little death.' " He tickled her neck. "You should wear a short, open ruff more often. I like being able to get at your skin."

"Be serious," she ordered.

He expelled a hard breath. It was stupid to arouse her, and himself, when they couldn't possibly make love. Not in open court.

"What is there to be serious about?" he asked lightly. "Her majesty has told me not to concern myself any more with preventing plots to free the queen of Scots. Both of us are kept on continual display to prove we can keep our hands off each other—"

"I beg your pardon, my lord, but that's a task at which you seem to be singularly unsuccessful at the moment."

"We all have our failings," he muttered. "You are mine, damask lady."

"Please." The pink in her cheeks had become scarlet. Her curved eyelids were suddenly heavy. He couldn't doubt she was feeling desire for him. She whispered, "You

are cruel to act this way when we cannot . . . And I always seem to be weeping. I cried at the service last night. The story of the Christ Child always affects me, but I do not usually burst into sobs so loud an archbishop stops in the middle of his sermon to see what's the matter."

To give her time to recover from the fever consuming her, he dropped his hand and said, "Why does the Christmas story touch your heart so?"

"Do not ask me that!"

His vague interest quickened. "Kat? Why—"

In the middle of the room, Elizabeth cawed with triumph and swept up a small pile of jewels. "Our luck holds true! Let us have dancing to celebrate! Where are the musicians? A volta!"

"Dance with me," he said. "Before some other rogue tries to take what's mine."

She hung back. "If I dance with you, I'll—Robin, I'll get so hot. I'll betray us."

He made a decision. "I want you that hot," he said with a wolf's grin. He grabbed her elbow. "We need privacy. Come."

She choked on an incredible noise, a wail that ended in a giggle, as he worked them through the moving forest of taffeta- and velvet-clad ladies and gentlemen getting into position for the dance. The members of the court might as well have been tree trunks for all the attention he paid them.

At the room's lower end, under a loft, was nestled a shadowy alcove, cut off from the rest of the hall by screens. Robin pushed her through an opening in the system of arrases with a light hand on her back, and followed so quickly she bumped into him when she turned.

"Damask lady," he said thickly, and kissed her.

"Robin, Robin." She stroked his face. "Can we? Someone will see or hear."

Music crashed behind them.

"No one will hear," he said, bending. His tongue slid around the curves of her ear, and he felt her shiver. "And if they see anything, it will only be dancing."

Her blue skirts were between them, so he crushed them and her farthingale out of his way. A corner of his brain was still working independent of desire. It wanted to know the why of her haunted look. With one hand, he brought her fingers to his mouth, where he nibbled them while his other hand released his codpiece.

"Tell me why Christmas makes you sad instead of happy," he murmured amid quick forays of his tongue between her fingers.

She moaned. "Do not ask. I pray you. Do not."

Leaving her fingers caught between his lips, he pulled her firmly into the cradle of his hips. She rubbed herself against him—precisely like a kitten, he thought with satisfaction.

Taking her hand, he inserted it between them and folded it over his arousal in a tight, wet caress. Her head tilted back, but he didn't take advantage of the length of smooth, white throat.

"No more secrets, Kat. Why did you weep?"

Her eyes were brown and wide and unsurprised. Her hand opened and drew away. "You even use lovemaking as a tool. Just another way to make me talk."

He couldn't deny it. "Perhaps it is the secrets that keep blocking your responses."

"There's nothing wrong with my responses!" When she wriggled against him, he could feel downy curls and the moist, hot slide of her intimate flesh.

"Of course not, sweet. We just need to unlock them." Leaning against a handy pillar, he lifted her, settling her legs around his waist and fluffing her skirts behind and to the sides. "There. Safe from gossips. The music will go on for some time. As far as anyone else is concerned, we are engaged in a private dance."

Rising as if she were in a saddle, she tried to impale herself on his lance, but he had hold of her buttocks and shifted them, deflecting her. He throbbed, and his hips started to thrust of their own will. They met the smoothness of her thigh. The rounded tip of his arousal was so swollen and sensitive, he had to swallow a groan.

"Robin, for pity's sake. I will die of this heat. Let me cover you."

"To put out your fire without coming to a full blaze? No, my lady wife. Tell me why—"

"Because I cannot have children!" It was a faint scream. "That animal Sir Henry got me with child. Two months passed, and my courses did not come. I had just begun to be a woman and they were very regular then. Maud brought me a tisane of herbs to drink. I did not know what it was, I swear I did not know. But it was pennyroyal. Right after that, my flow began with big clots and—and the babe was gone."

Robin wasn't shocked, but he grieved for a girl whose body had been abused and then abused again. "It was not your sin. You did not know. Kat, you were naught but a babe yourself."

"It was a life in my care," she said starkly. "And my courses have never been the same. The charms and medicines peddled by witches and apothecaries to clear the womb have horrible dangers. When they work at all, the mother as well as the child dies as often as not. If the woman lives, she's frequently barren. I am probably barren, Robin. I can be your lover, but I can never marry anyone, let alone—"

His arms tightened reflexively.

"Let alone a man as good and decent as you," she went on. "You deserve to be a father. You would be a wonderful father."

Kat felt his hands, his body—even the way he breathed—go too gentle, too controlled, and she knew he was thinking of her rape.

"Stop," she said.

Misunderstanding her, he lowered her until her satin-shod feet touched the floor. The slow slide of her body against his was erotic, though she could tell he didn't mean it to be.

"You need not worry, Kat. I'll not ask you to make love just now."

Her impulse to bite and kick at his obtuseness translated straight into a tide of restless, aching need. "You had damned well better make love to me. And you are going to stop treating me like some flower too fragile to pick. I shall not die from a bee's stinger . . ." Her nails insinuated themselves through the slit in his clothes and found his lance of flesh, which was tilting downward now. Her fingers curved and scratched him, lightly but definitely.

"Kat?" he said incredulously. Despite his evident surprise, the flesh grew and thickened under her busy fingers.

"It makes me so glad to have this effect on you. And you do not have some paltry bee's stinger."

"Lady, what do you want from me?"

"To make love." She stood on tiptoe, but couldn't make herself tall enough to sink down onto him. A whimper wrung her throat. "Do you not want me?"

"Yes," he answered tersely. Even in the shadows, the glitter of his eyes was feverish. But he didn't move.

"Please, Robin."

The music reached a peak of wails and driving drumbeats. Modesty, embarrassment, even the need to protect herself from rejection, disappeared. Clumsy in her haste, Kat took Robin's fingers and thrust them into her low bodice, and then used her own hands to push up from outside the gown, forcing her breasts out and over the rigid neckline.

When he did no more than cup one of them tenderly, saying, "Sweet heart, sweet heart, slow down, you will get hurt," she sank partway to the floor. She rubbed one tight nipple, then the other, against his arousal. The buds of pink flesh were more sensitive than they'd ever been before, sending pleasure into her loins in splintering pangs. She pressed her breasts around him. She licked him. She used her teeth.

With a groan, he raised her up from the floor and wrapped her so thoroughly in his arms she couldn't move, not even to rub her lips against his.

"Kiss me hard," she demanded fiercely. "Bite me. Fill me."

Just as fiercely, he said, "I will not give you pain. *I do not like it rough.*"

"Neither do I!" she cried. "Act the way you would if I had not been ravished. You have to be Robin Hawking. I do not want you to be—fettered, always fearing I will break in your arms if you let yourself drive too hard or too deep. Every time we join, you think of Sir Henry, not of me."

"That's a lie." His voice was deadly quiet, but it carried clearly over the wailing music.

"Is it? I cannot get close to you with him between us."

His arms loosened their iron hold. Instead of stepping away, Kat pressed closer. Desire ebbed and flowed in her, creating an almost painful emptiness low in her body, followed by a tingling awareness in the tips of her breasts and fingers. Her toes wanted to curl.

"Are you angry?" she asked, catching his face between her hands.

"Because you tell a truth? Of course. Is that not the usual response?" His irony bit, and tears filled her eyes. "But not at you, poppet— God's grace, forgive me, Kat. You do not enjoy being called—"

"Call me whatever you like. I—I am going to call you husband from now on. If you want a childless woman." She waited breathlessly.

"Wife." A swoop pulled her up and poised her hot, waiting softness over his arousal. "My wife."

The brush of his hard flesh sent sensation spiraling through her loins, down her legs. Hooking her heels over his lean buttocks, she drove down on him, gasping with the pleasure of being filled.

He was watching her with raw hunger. "Tell me how it feels."

She did. Short, panting phrases. Soft gasps and moans.

Amazingly powerful sensations flooded her as his mouth tugged at her breasts. His fingers made her feel the softness of her bottom by digging into the twin roundness. His arousal completed her. There was nothing but this, nothing but making love. It was her dream again. But this time the good part wasn't ending.

The music swelled, driven by the impatient drums, and became part of their rhythm. Heavy velvet and sleek silk were more sensations to add to the racing tide of feeling. Robin was part of Kat, Kat part of Robin. She didn't have to worry about the exact degree of his forebearance and the reason for it. This time, he was doing nothing but *feeling*, too. The knowledge freed her to give in to the pounding, pulsing rush that threatened to tear her apart.

She screamed. The high, excited sound mingled with the

last crash of the music. Release left her dizzy, and she came slowly back to herself to realize Robin was still standing rigid, gripped by passion.

"Come, Robin, come," she urged. A sweet languor made her movements lazy as she laced kisses over his jaw.

The exhausted little voice told Robin all he needed to know. Such a spent thread of sound could only be the result of satisfaction. She had been ready, so ready; time had done its work, healing the wounds to her spirit, and the release of giving up her secret had led to another kind of release. He rubbed his face between her breasts, felt her heart beat, and ecstasy poured out of him in huge, slow, easy pulses.

After a sweet, silent eternity, she murmured in a stronger voice, "If any people look in, they are going to wonder why you are still lifting me in the volta when the dance is long over."

It wasn't really quiet beyond the concealing screens. There were ladies and gentlemen out there, servants bustling, tongues wagging. The queen.

Sanity returned in a rush. Every additional moment they lingered was a danger to Kat. He set her down with a thump.

His clipped-back cloak of black velvet striped with silver silk was presentable. He unclipped it, and arranged the folds to cover any wrinkles their violent exercise had created in his black doublet and white breeches and hose. But Kat . . .

"Your satin is creased."

"It is new, too. It took me months to embroider. Ah, well. All in a good cause."

"Here," he said, pulling out a pouch. "Unless we have squashed this one, too, wear my gift and perhaps it will draw attention away from your skirts. You'll just have to retire before any of those love bites darken into bruises," he added, slipping a gold chain made from large links around her waist so the excess trailed down the front of her skirts. At its end swung the pomander he'd tried to give her once before. "And no nonsense about how you do not accept presents."

She stood on tiptoe to kiss him. "Showing me how to

feel so—so—that is present enough. And the pomander is lovely. The chain, too. Everyone will wonder who gave them to me."

"Say that brutish monster Hawking forced you to take them. You resisted as long as you could, but he bit you and finally you said yes."

Smoothing back his hair, he trod quietly to the end of the gallery. "Wait a minute, then slip out the other end," he ordered.

"As you will, my lord," she said demurely. "Oh, Robin, if you truly want me, I will wed you if we ever can. I am glad there are no more secrets between us. I do love you—"

But he had already gone. Feeling foolish, she counted off the empty seconds, then went out through the crowd of revelers and ran to her quarters to be alone with her happiness.

It was very odd, because she'd eaten little and drunk less, but she had to stumble out of bed and be sick first thing in the morning.

Elizabeth posed in front of the windows in her private chamber. The queen had all the tricks of a vain woman in her arsenal, noticed Robin, including the ability to use light to her advantage. Watery sunshine washed over her, making a halo of her borrowed locks and dramatizing her stick-thin figure. Even when her brown teeth showed in a grin, the light coming from behind blurred time's ravages on her smile.

"Are you happy, Robin?"

The question made him wary. This morning he certainly was, but Elizabeth was the last person he wanted to know it. "Why should I not be, Your Grace?" he asked evasively.

"That's so." Her grin broadened, creating dust in the paint at the corners of her mouth. "We have shown you our favor, have we not? Kept you by us in our amusements, asked your opinion in matters of state, seen to your every pleasure?"

Not every pleasure, he thought, and then shifted uneasily. "Yes, madam."

She rustled close to him in her stiff gown. "We have a small task for you to perform. Something well within your abilities. And when it is completed—dear, loyal Robin, there shall be further rewards."

Robin didn't like this at all. Her majesty was up to mischief, or worse, if she approached him directly instead of Walshingham or Burghley.

When he didn't reply, she pouted. "You have been to Fotheringhay. You know its precincts. The warden, Sir Amyas, trusts you."

"I think so." The affirmative was even more unwilling than before.

"*I* trust you."

The hair on the back of Robin's head was rising. A situation was always dire when the queen referred to herself as a person instead of a plural.

"Kill my cousin for me."

Robin's mobile eyebrows rose. He should have seen the command rising.

The idea was tempting. This wasn't the same as inventing new means of execution. As a matter of statecraft, assassination would be a better solution than execution to the vexing problem of Mary Stuart. The damnable woman was never going to stop trying to escape, never going to lose her ability to bend young men to her cause. He thought of Tony Babington.

Elizabeth explained, "For one monarch to execute another would cause an uproar all over Europe." Especially among other rulers, Robin thought. The queen added, "A quiet murder would be infinitely preferable. As long as it is untraceable to me it should soothe my fellow princes and leave England's interests in the Netherlands, Spain, and France undisturbed."

Yes, it was tempting. The reward for doing his sovereign so signal a service would be immense. Riches. An estate. Even his heart's desire.

He could ask for Kat.

Elizabeth's flexible voice was pure seduction. "Parliament, my council, all have begged me for years to sign the order for her execution. I have finally done it. There would be no sin. You'll simply be carrying out a legal warrant of your government in a private way."

"And if I were to be caught undertaking this 'small task'?" he asked.

Her smile slipped a little. "You are better than most at sneaking around on your quests. Although last night you were were not as careful as you usually are, were you, my Robin?"

Horror held him rigid. He and Kat had been seen going behind the screens, or someone had noted her creased skirts when she came out. "I'll have to ask what your grace means," he said woodenly.

She recovered her honeyed sweetness. "Naughty man, you know very well what I mean. But I am willing to overlook your misbehavior in return for this trifling service. If your role in ridding me of my Stuart cousin becomes public, a short stay in the Tower by you would pacify the political busybodies—in one of the more comfortable apartments, of course. The Tower is not all cells and dungeons, I assure you. And afterward, I will still be grateful."

His thoughts clicked on at a frantic pace. The warrant ordering Mary's death might be legal; what Elizabeth was telling him to do clearly stood outside the law. It would, in fact, place her *above* the law. The result would blast away the delicate balance between monarch and parliament. And that fragile sharing of power was all that had prevented civil war since Elizabeth's grandfather manhandled the throne from her grandmother's uncle.

Robin swallowed painfully. *A private way to carry out a legal warrant . . . a trifling service.* By every saint he'd ever heard of, he wanted to do it. *He wanted Kat.* Removing the Stuart bitch from the earth where she'd caused so much trouble would assure he'd never have to run Walsingham's or Burghley's distasteful errands again. Robin would get the woman he desired and an estate of his own to provide for her. He could almost taste the heady flavor of success. Almost taste *her,* the sweetness of her mouth, and the salt and honey of her breasts. In his arms, she had finally been free—free of her fears and his fears, old secrets, old violence . . .

Secrets. Lies. Deeds done in the dark of night. Memories that made love the puzzling pastime of other, more fortunate people. Murder.

One of the long-fingered hands that were Elizabeth's chief beauty reached up to pat his cheek. The caress felt silky on his skin.

"Well, my Robin?"

Her confidence burned in his gut. Fate seemed to be offering him a choice. Kat—and the danger to Kat if he lost the queen's favor—or killing a woman he heartily wished dead. But would Kat want him if he fouled himself with murder? His damask lady actually believed him to be an honorable man.

"Your Grace, I wish I could do as you suggest. I cannot. To obey you in this would make me a traitor to England's best interests."

"*I* am England!"

"Then it would make me a traitor to myself." He said words he didn't mean to say, in a deep, warning growl. "I am not a hangman or a butcher to slaughter women as if they were rats in a cage."

Her fingers turned into claws, raking his cheek. Robin felt the immediate trickle of blood, but he stood like a rock as she spat full in his face.

"Dolt! Honorable idiot! Lecher!" she shrieked in a contradictory flood of abuse. "That horrible Scottish bitch will live forever and I'll never be safe! What am I suggesting that is worse than her plots and counterplots and conniving? My poor England will not have peace as long as she lives."

"Ask me to do something else," he said flatly. "I'll find her a more secure prison, stand guard at her door day and night. I will do anything but slay her."

"Out!" she screamed. "Out of my sight! Away from my court!"

She broke into sobs so heartrending he almost relented. The enormity of refusing an order from the queen of England squeezed huge droplets of sweat from his brow. They dripped, stinging in the deep cuts on his cheek.

No. He couldn't build a life with Kat on a slippery foundation of blood and guilt.

His bow was a masterpiece of flourishes. "By your leave, Your Grace."

Elizabeth waited until his footsteps receded, and the small noises of doors opening and shutting in the outer chamber had faded away. Then she carefully wiped the tears from her painted face, strode out among her ladies, and raised her voice.

"Find us that drab of a Katherine Preston. We shall deal with her next."

"How could you so mismanage the queen?" William Cecil, Lord Burghley, snapped. His ancient body was beginning to wear down, and he was pettish over his inability to get out of bed.

"Her majesty tried to buy me to assassinate Mary Stuart. I am not a pimp to sell myself to do murder, or a bought-boy from the streets to lick Elizabeth's behind."

"So that's why she refuses to let the order of execution be carried out. The fool woman is trying to find someone to murder Mary for her, just as Mary has been trying to kill her all these years." Burghley almost smiled. "Well, the idea has its merits. If the queen of Scots were the victim of a private murder, we could claim that the government was not responsible. France and Spain could squawk all they wanted, but who would listen?"

"The people of England," Robin suggested dryly. "Especially if the two greatest powers in Europe declared war on us."

"It will not come to that." The old man blinked, evidently considering his queen's desire to hire a murderer. "Davison was just here, jabbering at me. He wants the privy council to find a way to force Elizabeth into acting on the warrant in a legal fashion, but by God how can we?"

"If you want the queen of Scots put down, you shall have to find another rat catcher to do it."

"What's the matter with you?" asked Burghley.

"I seem to have found some wellspring of self-respect."

Robin knew where it had come from. Kat. He hadn't even caught a glimpse of her slender figure or russet hair as he stormed out of Richmond. Anyway, it wouldn't do

Kat any good to be seen with him again. When he touched his face thoughtfully, his knuckles came away rusty with dried blood. It was something to have been scratched by a queen, he supposed. Kat had scratched him, too, in their private dance, but that had been . . .

"How delightful for you." Burghley's sarcasm broke into Robin's reverie. The older man continued, "As it happens, I meant that once her grace's mind is fixed, no one can budge it. And she does not wish to be notorious as her cousin's killer."

"She just intends to buy murder in a suitably quiet fashion."

"That cannot be allowed, certainly." The baron sounded wistful. In the first unguarded sentence Robin had ever heard from him, he added, "She would become uncontrollable."

"So *I* thought."

Burghley gripped his long old-man's beard. "You may go do your thinking in France for the foreseeable future. King Henri can use a little watching. I take it you have been dismissed from Walsingham's service as well?"

Robin shrugged.

"I will see to it. The death of Aftondale will suffice for a reason. People are still talking about it," said his cousin. "From now on you'll be acting for the family."

"Lady Katherine Preston."

"Put her out of your mind."

"I cannot." Robin smiled mirthlessly. "You will say I have been foolish. There have been promises exchanged. I mean to keep mine."

"How?" asked Burghley without much interest.

Robin's leg muscles tensed, as if there were something he could do right now to make Kat safe. Deliberately, he untensed them.

"I do not know. I would take her with me, but there's no way for me to support her. I need your aid. Her reputation is in shreds because of me." It was bitter to have to admit it. "Other men may see her as easy prey. How Elizabeth will act—"

"—is what the girl deserves. Her misbehavior has been a scandal." The old, dry voice cracked like a whip. "*She is not for you, Robert.* Her family is insignificant and her honor is tarnished. I will do what I must to keep you apart."

"The wrongdoing was all mine. I . . . trimmed her choices until I was the only choice she had left. She should not be punished for my sins."

"I might offer her my protection in exchange for your promise to forget her."

"Now that is a promise I would break." Robin's warning was deadly soft.

Burghley seemed to weigh his seriousness, then the old man spread his hands. "Go to France. If you really value Lady Katherine, I'll do my best to see that Elizabeth does not maul her too badly. Take a ship from Dover . . ."

Chapter 20

Kat was home.

Looking out a window at the garden, where February winds were scouring the ground clean of dead leaves and snow, she thought, *Life is a very odd business.* She had been given several stunning proofs of that lately. To choose one example, she had never imagined that being sent to Priorly would seem like a prison sentence.

Sometimes the queen's curses echoed in her ears. *Hellbound slut* and *my lady greensleeves* were the nicest things Elizabeth had called her. This time the words had hurt, because this time she was guilty. Not that she believed making love with Robin was a sin in God's eyes—but it was in the eyes of most people. Having willingly broken the rules, she was now going to have to pay. It seemed like a lifetime ago that she'd said, *The woman always suffers,* to Margaret. With a mixture of ruefulness and exultation, she knew nothing had changed.

Unfortunately, Charles's opinion of her was no higher than Elizabeth's.

The worst had happened, and she was living through it. Not the worst, she corrected herself. Robin had not been condemned to gaol. He was free. Somewhere, he was free.

Oh, God, she missed him. The ache of separation was usually a dull depression, making every day gray. Attacks of nausea that had begun right after Christmas added to her leaden feeling. Now and then, though, when she came across something that belonged to him—a boot left behind, or clippings from a haircut that had lain undiscovered under the bed till she noticed the gleam of gold—the loneliness pressed down on her until she wanted to scream.

She didn't, of course. Charles made it very clear she'd been taken in on sufferance, and she did her best not to attract his attention.

Instead, she laid the boot carefully in a chest, and wound the scraps of hair into a bright knot that she pinned under her clothes. That way Charles couldn't see. What he couldn't see, he wouldn't complain about.

And her elder brother obviously wanted to see her as little as possible.

A gasp of surprise ripped out of her when his neat reflection suddenly appeared in the window; he was standing behind her. She swiveled on the window seat, and Charles pushed a piece of paper at her.

"From your paramour," he sneered.

Creases showed that it had been folded and then opened. Obviously Charles had read it already, but Kat didn't mind. She touched Robin's bold, slanted writing with gentle fingers.

Charles spoke loudly to a shadowy figure in the background. "Well, fellow, you have seen me put the letter into her hand. You may tell the Baron Burghley his cousin's whore is alive and well. Now get out."

Jerked out of her contemplation of the unexpected treasure, Kat lifted her gaze. A man, with fat covering his muscle, stood in stolid silence. His unfamiliar livery stretched at the seams.

Kat's eyes grew round. The large man stared at her without recognition.

"Aye, sir. Very good, sir."

His withdrawal left her alone with Charles. Hunching her shoulder nervously, Kat read her letter. *"To my wife,"* it began. A smile trembled across her lips.

Robin wrote that he was trapped in Dover by bad sailing weather, and was still hoping to find a way to make his fortune so they could be together. His damask lady was constantly in his thoughts. He wanted to dance with her again, as they had danced the last time he had seen her.

Why had she not written to answer his first letter? He signed himself *Your betrothed husband, Robin Hawking*.

Kat lifted her gaze. "Robin's first letter? I never received—"

Charles didn't even blush. "I put it in the fire. Which is where this one would have gone, but that damned officious messenger insisted he had orders to see you."

"And you do not want to offend Burghley. Why, Charles?"

"He's one of the most powerful men in the realm, ninny." The answer made sense. And yet there was something in the way his eyes bored into hers that pricked Kat's suspicion.

"Are you sure you are not afraid he'll discover how many French guests you entertain? How can you fool yourself about Raoul and the others? Can you not tell that those men do not come here for the pleasure of your company? They plot—"

"I will not listen to your fantasies again." Charles stalked off.

Kat watched him go with worried grooves between her eyes. Then her glance fell to the letter, and the frown lines smoothed out. She held it to her lips.

"Oh, Robin," she said aloud.

Kissing the letter wasn't nearly as good as kissing Robin would have been, but at least the scrap of paper was a connection, proof that he hadn't forgotten her. The wicked reference to their dance was typically Robin. He wouldn't let those strange, beautiful, wrenching sensations slip from her memory. As if they could.

Maud found her there in the waning light of late afternoon, running the letter through her fingers.

"My lady, my lady," Maud breathed. "Samuel is here! Did you see him?"

"Still here? I thought he must have gone. Charles was not exactly welcoming to him."

"He's hiding on the path to the mill. Do you have an answer to send Lord Robin?"

"Bring me paper, pen, and ink, and I will," Kat replied with a dawning smile. The expression made her face feel strange, and she realized how long it had been since the world had seemed hopeful enough for her to smile at it.

"All of the paper is in *his* chest. *He* will notice if any is gone," warned Maud. Hatred thickened her county accent.

Kat's smile faded. Her maid was right. Charles would notice.

"Bring pen and ink, then," Kat directed, unable to banish a tinge of bitterness from her voice. Robin's note was something she would have liked to keep. "I will use the back of this letter for my reply."

Writing took until full dark. She only stopped because she was running out of space—and she couldn't leave Samuel out in temperatures that dropped sharply, once the sun had been replaced by a skyful of stars that were like hoarfrost, glittering and cold.

Maud took the letter and ran out into the night with it hidden in her woolen cloak. Her steps were quick and eager, like those of a young woman. Love made everyone young, thought Kat.

She wished that once, just once, Robin had been able to say that he loved her.

Moving quietly through the house, she put the bottle of ink and carefully wiped pen back where Charles would expect to find them.

Sneaking around with Charles's things was dreadful, and her skin crawled. The excuse that his actions had forced her into it disgusted her as much as the action itself.

Her guilt turned her steps to the withdrawing room. Someone was in there; loud bumps and thuds were coming from behind the door. If it was Charles, she would try one more time to convince him how foolhardy it was to trust Raoul. Perhaps she'd even bring up the enclosure. He knew the estate folk better now—people with names and faces. No matter how casually he talked about thrusting his own people into homelessness, surely Charles couldn't actually put them out.

Trying to feel hopeful, Kat pushed open the door.

"Charles? There you are. Oh—and James. May we . . ." Belatedly, she saw that the panel which normally hid the priest's hole was wide open. "What are you doing?"

A chair, ornately carved and piled high with cushions, stood half-in and half-out of the gap in the woodwork.

At the moment she was more concerned with the expressions on their faces. Charles looked angry. But then, he always looked angry when he saw her. James's features were screwed up with surprise and concern. For James to display anything but inhuman serenity . . .

"What's wrong?" she asked, coming closer.

"You are wrong," spat Charles. "In the wrong place, doing the wrong things. Holding the wrong opinions. Taking the wrong lover. Holy Mary, why did you have to bumble in here now?"

Her gaze went to the chair. "Who is that for?"

James exchanged a glance with Charles. "Just at the moment," said her second brother apologetically, "I am afraid it is for you."

He pushed the chair completely into the tiny room behind the wall while Charles leaped forward and caught Kat before she could run.

She struggled; it was hopeless. Charles might not have the strength of a Robin Hawking, but he was male and heavier than she was—and she hadn't felt well for several months.

With a hand around her wrist, he hustled her forward. Her heels dragged on the rushes, slowing him only a little. Tears blinded her, not only from fear but because of what the chair had to mean. Her brothers weren't dupes. They were active conspirators.

"You are going to break Mary Stuart out of Fotheringhay and hide her in our house. You sent poor Jack Miller on that fool's errand with his silly keg of gunpowder."

"He begged us to allow him to do it," explained James. "Jack was one of the few we showed ourselves to when we first came home. His passion for the cause burned as ours did."

"Because yours did, you mean. The heroes of his childhood. He looked up to you both. And you are traitors."

James stood to one side in the small space beside the chair in the priest's hole, watching as Kat grabbed the doorjamb with her free hand.

"Traitors to what, sister?" Charles jeered, shaking her to break her grip. "The bastard daughter of a king who made decisions with his loins? We are striking a blow for the true faith, the true line. Mary is descended from the first Tudor Henry, just as much as Elizabeth is. She is legitimate. She has the best claim."

"You have lost your wits!" she said as Charles shoved her hard into the chair. The walls of the priest's hole rose around her. "Elizabeth has been queen for near thirty years. The commons love her. All they know about the Stuart woman is that she helped blow up her second husband so she could marry Bothwell."

Charles slapped her on one cheek and then the other. Her head reeled back, bouncing off the cushions.

"Slut! How can you repeat those old lies about an honorable lady? What would you know about honor, anyway?"

"Let her be," said James. Surreptitiously, he patted Kat's shoulder before backing out of the priest's hole to join Charles in the withdrawing room. "We'll return soon with food and blankets and, er, a bucket. In a few days you will meet the royal lady and judge for yourself."

"I do not want to meet her!" she protested as the secret panel swung into place. "For God's sake, James, do not leave me in here. I thought it could never happen, but I am with child!"

For an instant, the spark in James's eyes might have been pity. Then Charles leaned through the doorway to spit in her face, and Kat jerked her head to one side to avoid the wetness.

The door slammed shut.

The ripe smells of Dover's waterfront clogged Robin's nostrils. In the six weeks he'd been delayed here, waiting for decent sailing weather, the stinks had become familiar enemies. The light application of scent he'd paid a barber for just this morning didn't help much. Even inside the tavern where he lounged with a full tankard, the fishy essence of Dover was strong.

The acrid odor of tar, and the dankness of fish and seaweed, increased momentarily as a beautifully dressed

young man swung through the door. The newcomer
dropped into a seat next to him and took a hefty swig of
Robin's untouched ale.

"Amazing how even the wind and rain cannot sweep the
stink out of a port town, is it not?" Thomas Seyward asked
cheerfully.

"I had not noticed."

"God's acorns, man, lighten your mood! You have been
glooming about ever since you arrived. Have you thought
more on our proposal?" Thomas had been trying to lure
him into a venture for a month.

"A company of adventurers," said Robin, trying out the
sound.

"With a fine ship and the seven seas to choose from.
There's a bilge full of loot out there, Robin, my lad." A
serving girl with black hair squeezed through the space between tables, giving both men a generous view of unbound
bosom as she did so. Thomas reached out an indolent
thumb and forefinger and pinched her nearest buttock to
gauge her charms. "After supper tonight, eh, chuck?" She
smiled an agreement. Seyward turned back to Robin. "And
if you think she's ripe, consider how many dark-eyed ladies are waiting in the Spanish Main to welcome Englishmen between their, er, arms."

Robin merely shrugged. "I already have a dark-eyed
lady."

By every red-clawed minion of hell, was Kat safe? The
letters he'd left for her with William Cecil, Baron
Burghley, had gone unanswered. Perhaps, he thought, he
should cut loose from his mother's relative. He could refuse to spy on France and instead seek his own fortune.
With Seyward, for example.

Where would that leave Kat?

"Ah, but is your lady here?" asked Thomas with a
good-natured leer. "You need to relieve the congestion in
your spleen by a trip upstairs with one of the wenches."

Robin took the ale back and swallowed some of it. "My
spleen will have to keep. But I will talk to you more about
your company. Joining you would be difficult. I have a re-
lation who has half-promised to protect—something I

value. He considers my time his. I would cross him by signing with you."

"Is that the one who sends you letters every week?" asked Thomas curiously.

"The same."

Burghley's letters always contained the same orders. Stay in Dover, sail when possible. Keep away from Katherine Preston.

Concern for her safety might have led Robin to obey. It might have. He didn't have to make the decision. The messages never explained where she was.

And since his slim savings were all he had to live on, he couldn't swoop down and take her away anyway. He had to trust the baron to protect Kat, and hope for the best.

Trusting and hoping didn't come easy to Robin.

"We are receiving a charter of incorporation, you know. 'Twould not be common piracy," Thomas rambled.

"Is gentlemanly piracy any different?" asked Robin. "Sinking other vessels and sacking Spanish colonies leaves people dead whether the queen gives her blessing to it or not." Still, he thought, it must be a more honest profession than spying.

"True," Thomas agreed, his enthusiasm unabated. He winked. "But I would suggest you not say so to John Hawkins or Francis Drake. And where they have gone, there's plenty of gold still sitting in Spanish strongboxes waiting for us to scoop up. Have you no uses for a fortune?"

He did, oh, he did. To make a home for Kat. As if his yearning conjured a vision, the door banged open again and a man in the livery of his cousins, the Cecils, stamped out of the rain and into the Grey Gull Tavern.

The livery didn't fit the fellow's gigantic proportions very well. "Samuel," Robin called softly.

"My lord," Samuel answered. "I have a letter from her."

The table almost overturned as Robin pushed past it and grabbed the folded paper. The first thing he saw when he smoothed it open was his own handwriting; he swore raggedly and flipped the sheet over. Thomas shrugged and went toward the door, pausing to glance curiously at the writing. He said something about meeting again soon, but Robin barely heard. He was reading.

"The queen sent her back to Priorly?" he asked, aghast.

"Aye. I only got to see her the once. She was a mite peaked. Maudie said the lady's been ill."

"I have to go. I have to get her out of there." He added a short, ugly curse. "If I had known where she was, I would not have wasted six weeks without visiting her. My cousin of Burghley must have thought she'd be safe with her brothers."

"I cannot say either of them impressed me particularly. The freemen about the place are all in an uproar. Seems that Charles is enclosing the fields and putting in hedgerows to mark boundaries come spring."

"Kat will be frantic for her people." Running his eyes over his henchman, he said, "You had no trouble along the way? You were accepted as a servant of the Cecil household?"

"This person and that asked why so rich a man as Baron Burghley could not afford enough cloth for my livery. Then they said it was understandable; after all, he would not be rich if he put out the money to clothe someone too big for an ordinary pair of breeches." The large man shrugged hugely. "'Tis too bad we could not steal a more fitting size."

"I am glad we thought to pick up the livery before we left my cousin's house at all. Otherwise Charles would not have let a servant sworn to Kat and me on Priorly ground," Robin replied absently. "Change your wet things. I'll order you a meal. We will ride while there's still daylight."

"If you can call it that," said Samuel, but equably. "'Tis snowing again."

They outrode the storm. It took several days of hard, cold, miserable riding on roads whose ruts were frozen solid.

When they arrived at Priorly, snow had stopped falling, but ice crystals blown through cracks in the stable's walls glistened in the feed at the bottom of the mangers.

"Where are all the horses?" asked Robin sharply of the

foolish-looking stable boy who stood gaping at the new arrivals.

"The master and his guests took 'em."

"Which master? What guests?"

The boy answered the last question first. "Them frogs. They came back. Rode Fotheringhay way again, they did, with Master James. The other servants, they all were told they could go to the winter fair at the village."

"Where is your lady?"

"No one knows, m'lord. But ghost noises been heard by day and night three days now."

Tossing his reins to Samuel, who tossed them to the boy, Robin strode through the courtyard. Samuel followed. The front door didn't budge when he pushed, and no one responded to his loud knocking. The side door was barred, too. If there were servants within, either they had orders not to let anyone in or they were cowering in their beds—at high noon. Had there finally been more ghosts at Priorly while he was gone? In the priest's hole, perhaps? There was no reason for either Charles or James to hide anymore, leaving the question—could someone else suffer from an urgent need for concealment?

"Find me a stout piece of firewood," he said, measuring one of the few narrow windows on the ground floor.

"You want in, my lord?" asked Samuel.

"I want in."

"Begging your pardon, my lord, we don't need a battering ram. The lead holding those bits of glass is not stiff at all." Winding his cloak over his arm, Samuel gave the many-paned window a nudge with his elbow, and glass went crashing inward. Robin spared him a quizzical look. Samuel explained, "Had to get Maudie back in last time I was here after the doors were locked. I was a mite more careful about noise and breakage then."

"Well, I am not as slim as Maud," Robin grunted. "Let's hope I fit."

He did, barely. His henchman was far too large. Robin would have taken the time to unbolt a door for him except that a hollow, eerie pounding was echoing through the empty house.

It might have made others think of ghosts, knocking at

the gate of life to be let back in. Robin instantly thought of the priest's hole. It was embedded in walls that were perfect for conducting sound.

Freeing his poniard, he took the spiral stairs two at a time.

Robin swept into the withdrawing room like an avenging angel; at the sight of Charles Preston next to the closed priest's hole, he stopped so fast he rocked on his heels.

"A good day to you, Charles," he said heartily. This meeting *was* good. Kat's brother would confirm to him where Kat was. Of that he had no doubt. He fingered his knife.

But Charles wasn't thinking of his sister. His lips peeled back from his teeth, and he stretched the rope in his hands so it twanged. "You! Whoremaster. Rat catcher. Well, you'll not catch me. Or her gracious majesty, Mary Stuart, queen of Scotland and England!"

"You talk like a bad play, Charles," Robin said.

"Robin?" The cry was muffled.

"Kat?" Realization had already dawned on Robin. "Are *you* in that damned priest's hole?"

"Aye!" she screamed back. "Can you get the door open?"

"As soon as I remove a slight obstruction," he said, smiling sweetly at Charles. "How long has Kat been a prisoner?"

Charles shuffled sideways, and Robin let him, though he kept a wary eye on a silver candlestick he thought Charles might be making for.

"How long?" he repeated.

"Three days. We have fed her," said Charles sullenly.

"What an excellent brother you are," Robin marveled. "It is sad you are a traitor as well. What is the purpose of the rope? It would not, by chance, be to tie Kat up?"

Halting next to the candlestick, which was tall and heavy, Charles looked down at the rope as if he'd never seen it before. "It was," he admitted. "But it will do as well to use on you!"

With a gesture as quick as a snake's, Charles flung the rope at Robin's eyes. At the same time, he reached for the candlestick, ripping the candle off the sharp, protruding point in the middle. The spike gleamed.

Robin knocked the rope away before it hit him, and his smile became genuine. "Thank you, Charles. Now I will not have to tell Kat I attacked you without provocation."

Flipping his poniard through the air almost negligently, he nodded with satisfaction as the handle struck Charles a solid *thunk* on the temple. Charles slid to the floor.

Working the mechanism to open the panel, he glanced down at his victim. The blow had been hard, but not too hard; Charles was breathing and no blood ran from his nose or mouth.

The door opened, and Kat tumbled out into his arms. She was so stiff, he staggered back a few paces. But his arms went around her fiercely. "Sweet heart," he mumbled in her neck. "God's grace, you are so thin."

"I have always been thin," she pointed out breathlessly.

"But not like this. Let me look at you. Poppet, you are so pale, and a breeze could blow you away. Have they been starving you?"

"Nay. They put bread and a fresh jug of water through the door every day. It is just that I have been having trouble eating." Or at least keeping anything down, she thought—but this wasn't the time to tell him she had been wrong about her ability to conceive. "Every time I heard someone in the room, I banged with my feet on the wall. Is—is Charles alive?" She looked down at her brother's crumpled form.

"I would not kill one of your kin on purpose," Robin answered virtuously.

"Did you have to fight him?"

"He attacked me, Kat, I swear it. We were fighting over you in part. And over Mary Stuart. He admitted his politics. You are going to have to tell me what he and James are up to—and quickly. James has gone off to Fotheringhay with a group of men."

Her heart was going to break, she thought clearly, if she had to choose between Robin, and Charles and James. "They are my brothers."

"Look what they have done to you." Gently, he hooked a lock of unwashed russet hair behind her ear.

"It is true, I would rather not see them again as long as I live," she said slowly. "But I do not want revenge. I cannot stop loving my brothers, no matter how little I understand the men they have become. They are traitors. They are also all the family I have in the world."

"I am your sworn husband—in the sight of God, if not of man. And you are an Englishwoman."

"Has Elizabeth treated either of us so well we need to consider her welfare first?" she burst out. Helplessly, she repeated, "They are my *brothers*. Aye, they are up to mischief and we have to stop them, but then could you not let them go?"

He kissed her as if he were trying to imprint his mouth on her lips. "No, Kat. The situation is too serious. Do you want civil war? I cannot find excuses for them this time."

A moan came from the door. Robin set Kat carefully on her feet. Then he bent and hoisted Charles up.

Her lover's hands were encased in heavy winter gloves. They looked huge as he twisted the front of Charles's doublet and shirt, tightening the cloth into a noose.

"Which path to Fotheringhay have the others taken?" he asked. "James and the rest? I have neither the time nor the inclination to be subtle in extracting information. You will tell me now or I will hurt you badly. Very badly. Trust me, you will tell me in the end anyway. Choose."

Charles gurgled.

"You are *strangling* him," gasped Kat.

"Do you think so, my lady?" Something anguished flashed in addition to the usual glitter of his eyes. She noted that whatever regret he was feeling for her sake didn't interfere with the grip he had on Charles's neck. Or the deadliness of his voice. "Go wait at the stables. This will not take long."

"I'll tell," Charles whimpered.

"Good." Robin's grip didn't loosen; he simply transferred it a few inches down so the smaller man could speak.

Under his crushed ruff, Charles's throat worked. "The loyalists are gathering in the wood, near the wide bend in the brook that feeds into the Nene."

"How many?"

Triumph made Charles's narrow face ugly. "Five there. More inside Fotheringhay itself. Too many for you, rat catcher. *These* are not rats but men. Do you believe I am afraid of you? What can you do except free my soul to be glorified with a martyr's crown in heaven? I tell you the truth so you will feel in your gut that you are too late. Mary will be out of her prison within hours, and when I do not join the others, they'll take her to another safe haven. As soon as the word goes out that Mary is beyond Elizabeth's reach, Ann Boleyn's whelp will die."

"Enough!" said Robin with sudden briskness. "We have better things to do than listen to you blather."

He trussed Charles neatly by reversing the smaller man's doublet, which he wrapped over his prisoner's arms and buttoned down the back. Charles's hands dangled uselessly at the rear. Robin forced Kat's brother to bend at the knees, and then tied Charles's feet and hands together with the rope that had been meant for Kat. Then he stuffed the ruff into Preston's mouth.

"I hope you did not send the house servants away for the whole day. You are apt to get rather chilled before anyone comes back if you did. I am taking Kat with me. With any luck, she'll never have to set eyes on you again. Farewell, brother."

He took off at a run, half-carrying Kat, who was still stiff. Samuel joined them at the front door as they burst through it on their way to the stables.

Kat's loyalty to Charles and James, who didn't deserve it, warred with loyalty to Robin, who did. When they reached their goal, she leaned against the stable wall, panting, while Robin shouted at Samuel to re-saddle the horses.

"Here, you will freeze," he added, taking off his cloak and swirling it over her shoulders. He gave her his gloves, too. Her hands were swallowed up in them.

"It is more important for you to be warm and strong so you can stop them," she said, each word increasing the sickness in her middle. The nausea was the physical result of her confused emotions as much as anything else. Helping Robin meant hurting her family. In addition to the rest of her miseries, pure feminine panic pricked her. It would be awful to be sick in front of her lover.

He didn't give her body time to betray her. "Up with you," he said, throwing her into a man's saddle. "I cannot leave you here, so you'll have to ride with me."

"Your cloak and gloves—"

"Samuel, give me yours. Where's that stable boy? You'll have to make do with his. The lad can cover himself with straw if he has nothing else. It must be done; we are like an army seizing what it needs," he told Kat impatiently, though she hadn't protested. She realized the necessity, too. Robin turned to Samuel and said, "Go among the tenants and find a cob to ride. Then join me at the wide bend in the stream. Do you know where it is?"

"Aye, my lord. But—Maudie."

"You'll have to worry about your woman later."

"Easy for you to say," remarked Samuel steadily. "Begging your pardon. You have your woman with you."

"Where *are* the servants?" Kat asked.

"At a winter fair," answered Robin. "Maud should come safely home with the rest. We need you in this venture, Samuel."

"Very well, my lord," agreed the large man, sighing.

Robin swung onto his horse. "Now, Kat. Ride with me!"

Silence was impossible as they pressed the mounts as hard as they could through the trees. Ice crunched and twigs broke under the hooves. But neither Robin nor Kat spoke until she said reluctantly, "Charles gave in too easily."

He swayed in the saddle to avoid a whiplike branch. "Are you sure?"

"You detest Charles, so you think the worst of him," she pointed out. "He does not lack some kinds of courage. He was misleading us."

"That's what I thought," agreed Robin. "It pleasures me to hear you say so, though. Are you on my side in this, Kat?"

She gave a little sob. "They cannot be allowed to succeed. But do not ask me to choose sides."

His stallion came to a halt on a rise above the house.

She realized Robin had led them to a sheltered spot with a view of both the front and side doors as well as the bridge.

"You were willing to chance the world's censure to be my lover a few short months ago," he observed as he surveyed the vista before them.

"That was different."

"How?"

"Then I was risking only my future and my happiness. Now my whole family is at stake."

"It is my future, too. There he is. I wondered how long it would take him to wriggle out of his bonds. I tied them loosely enough. Ah, a horse saddled and hidden behind the dairy. Let's follow him."

Robin paced his stallion to the speed of Charles's mount. That kept them far enough behind to avoid attention, and yet close enough to get occasional glimpses of Charles and his horse through the tree trunks and winter brush.

Charles took them several miles and then slowed. They were nowhere near the bend in the brook, Kat noted. As she and Robin pulled on their reins to maintain their distance, she studied her lover's profile. He looked coolly interested. The handsome features might have been cut out of marble. Only the glint of his eyes as they swept the woods immediately surrounding them showed any strong emotion. Cold anger. Grim determination.

The hunter at work.

Her sickness returned full force, but this time it took the form of spreading numbness. Kat tried to clutch at the pommel and couldn't feel it under her fingers. Forgetting the need for quiet, she said, "Robin?" and dimly understood that she was sliding sideways from the saddle.

Robin saw Kat begin to fall and snatched at her reins. His stallion bumped into the gelding she rode, and both animals blew loudly through their nostrils. Far ahead, Charles's mare whickered a greeting to the other horses. The bugling of the stallion shattered the winter silence like a trumpet blast. Charles looked over his shoulder and cried out.

He was answered by the whine of a bolt leaving a cross-bow.

Robin heard the distinctive high-pitched twang and recognized it for what it was. One of Charles's friends, waiting for him to join them in the woods, must have shot when he yelled. Robin bent in the saddle in case another bolt was being readied, trying to keep both Kat and himself ahorse.

"Kat!" Hating himself, Robin slapped her. "For the love of God, Kat, hold on to your senses! We're under fire."

"Do not hit me again, Charles," she mumbled.

This time he would kill that whoreson brother of hers, he vowed, and shook her. "It is Robin, sweet heart. Can you sit your horse by yourself?"

Her lovely dark eyes blinked. "I think so. Did I swoon?"

"Just for a moment. Stay here. Something's happening."

No more shots were being fired; ominous quiet filled the woods. A look at Charles made him decide not to ride forward. The eldest Preston was crumpled on the ground with the short arrow of a hand-held crossbow sticking out of his neck. Robin no longer had to worry about eliminating Kat's troublesome relative.

"Kat, turn your horse," he ordered quietly.

"Why—oh, mercy God," Kat said as she bent forward and caught sight of her brother. "One of his own men has shot Charles!"

She tumbled off her mount, causing Robin's startled stallion to rear. The hooves flashed bare inches from her swinging hair. Cursing richly, Robin clubbed the animal behind the ears to bring it down, and then leaned over and hauled her over his saddlebow.

He dumped Kat unceremoniously back into her own saddle.

"Did you learn nothing from Aftondale's accident? Stay out from under a horse's legs! Go back the way we came. Turn west at the stand of willows and head straight for Fotheringhay. Find a sergeant, anyone, and have him bring armed men here."

"But my brother—there's a crossbow bolt in his neck. Let me help him!"

"He's beyond help," said Robin brutally. It didn't take an expert to recognize death; only Kat's hopeful nature could fail to mark Charles's utter stillness for what it was. "So will we be if you do not get us aid. Go!"

His harsh command drove her to kick her horse into cantering a hundred feet. At an equine scream, she turned the gelding around.

Robin's stallion was going down, a second bolt sticking out of its hide. Robin jumped clear and rolled to his feet. His legs braced themselves in a lithe and aggressive stance. He yanked his poniard and sword from their sheaths. Even from where she sat, Kat could see that his eyes were blazing.

Figures impossible to tell apart in dun and brown cloaks were circling him. One of the men worked furiously to re-load the small crossbow. They all maintained a cautious distance, and Kat could see why. Robin held his weapons at a professional angle. It was evident her lover knew how to use them. Even more daunting was the force of his confidence.

His shout echoed off the snow and ice. "Who wants to die today?"

But there were five of them, and one of Robin. Samuel was heading off toward the wrong meeting place on an ill-conditioned cob, assuming he'd been able to borrow one.

Frantically, Kat dug her heels into the sides of her gelding and pointed it toward Fotheringhay.

Chapter 21

T he guard inserted a horny finger inside his helmet and scratched his scalp with a sound like rock being drawn across rock. "Cap'n," he bawled finally, "there's a lass out here with a strange story for you."

Relief made Kat sag over her poor mistreated mount's neck, but she didn't have time to worry about how hard she'd pushed the beast to get to the castle. The captain of the guard arrived, and she repeated what she'd told his underling. "Lord Robin Hawking sent me," she finished. "He's hard-pressed. Oh, please!"

The captain took a minute to make up his mind, but a long look at her face apparently convinced him. As he started roaring orders in stentorian tones, men spilled into formation. At a quick step, they marched out of the castle in the direction she pointed.

The captain remained. "Let me help you down, my lady. That horse is blown."

"Aye," she agreed, accepting his hands and sliding to the ground. It rolled under her unsteady feet, but she shook off his grip. "Do you have another hack I could borrow?"

"I cannot let you leave."

"But Robin's out there." For Kat, the facts were simple and unanswerable. "I have to find out what's happening to him."

"Robin Hawking can take care of himself," said the captain. "And I have a need for you here. Should any of those damned conspirators be in the castle, you'll have to identify them for me."

"I—I could not."

However, the captain's firm tug on her elbow drew her into the hall, where a large number of people were being herded by more soldiers.

Alarmed or curious faces stared back at her. They blended into an impression of hundreds of eyes. "I cannot," she repeated.

"You must." His voice changed, became carefully flat. "Sir Amyas, this is the young lady."

"We have met," came the disgusted response.

She remembered the prim man in the dark, neat clothes from her first visit. Mary Stuart's warden was a Puritan, and he hadn't approved of the woman Secretary Davison had assured him was regarded in court circles as Robin Hawking's whore.

"I cannot tell if I have seen any of these people before or not," she said to him stubbornly. "I am sorry."

"Look again. You are quite safe. There are extra guards at Queen Mary's chambers, and here in the hall. Look into each face."

But if I do that, she wanted to cry out, I might see my brother James.

Too many loyalties pulled her. Charles was a small heap on the ground with an arrow sticking out of him. If James lurked somewhere in this high-vaulted hall, he would be as good as dead once he was identified. Would they be in danger if she had never sought help from an agent of the queen?

What had Elizabeth done to earn a devotion greater than the one she owed the other children of her mother's womb? The Tudor queen had shown Kat the worst side of her character, and Kat admitted to herself she was human enough to dislike her sovereign for it.

Her sovereign. No matter what her flaws or foibles, Elizabeth was the rightful ruler of England. The only person in the whole kingdom who could keep it from erupting into war.

And Robin was out in the woods, fighting for that queen—and his life. Winding her arms around her waist,

Kat thought of everything loving him had cost her. Mercy God, she was sheep-brained, just as Robin had said that first night. Because no matter what she lost, if the opportunity to be lovers with her hunter of men were to present itself again, she'd take it again. Better for both of them if they'd never met, just as she'd told him. Because once they did, nothing could have kept her from falling into his arms.

The thought was terrifying. Her life had been one headlong rush toward disaster since Robin had entered it. And now she had to think for the child inside her. A child who would be a Preston, not a Hawking.

"Have you ever seen any of these men?" Sir Amyas insisted.

She had to control this situation. She had to protect her baby's uncle.

"Nay," she lied steadily.

The warden sighed. "For the story you have told to make any sense, there should be men in here who have been plotting to sneak into the private quarters and free my prisoner. These men should be ones you have seen before. *Look again.*" He dragged a young, blank-faced man wearing the good broadcloth of a small merchant out of the crowd of servants and men-at-arms. "Here, is this one familiar?"

Raoul Mauvissiere stared at her insolently. His beard had been allowed to grow up his cheeks, and hid his distinctive mole. It was enough of a disguise to alter his appearance considerably, but Kat recognized his too-curvaceous lips.

Words caught in her throat. Poor Margaret, she thought.

What would Robin want her to do? While self-righteous Sir Amyas might be avid to expose anyone as a spy, Kat wondered if Elizabeth would be happy about a political scandal involving the son of a foreign ambassador.

As she hesitated, Sir Amyas, not recognizing the fish he'd caught, pushed Raoul back and reached for another victim. "What about this one?" he asked.

Kat tried to keep her features still and her eyes dull as man after man was paraded in front of her. Then a cap was pulled from an auburn head and James's dark eyes met her gaze. Something leaped in her.

"Nay," she whispered.

The captain, damn him, had seen the flare of emotion in her. "Sir Amyas, maybe we had better put this one to the question."

To the question? Oh, God, they meant torture. Desperately, Kat sought words to change their minds. "Sirs, for what reason? You would not use thumbscrews on a poor wretch with no proof!"

"The purpose of the screws is to obtain proof," pointed out Sir Amyas.

"But that's not justice. That's—horrible."

"You have a delicate stomach for a woman who sleeps with Robin Hawking," said Amyas. "Are you sure you have no other reason for favoring mercy?"

"It is not being softhearted to wish to spare another useless pain. Torture *will* be useless. There's no cause to believe this man knows more than anyone else."

"Then we'll let the others hear his screams and make sure they are sufficiently piercing to loosen the tongues of the guilty."

Catching her eye, James shook his head. The small gesture stifled her protests. He stood quietly between the two guards who came forward to flank him.

A horrid silence ran through the hall as people realized what was going to happen.

Then the doors burst open and an excited page fell through. "Sir Amyas, the guardsmen are coming back from the woods!"

A collective sigh of relief replaced the fearful quiet, but Kat could tell not everyone shared it. From James to Raoul to several others flashed a signal almost too quick to see. More guards meant less chance of success—or of escape with or without Mary Stuart. And if Robin was with the group . . .

Oh, Robin, be unhurt.

James reached into his clothes and pulled out a knife. Weapons appeared in the hands of his friends. The plotters formed a tight knot and backed toward the door.

The guards and servants weren't cowards. They pressed

after the intruders as if drawn by invisible strings, shouting, "Treason!"

An arm snaked out as the small pack of conspirators pressed close to Kat. The hand at the end of the arm wrenched her off her feet. She slammed into Raoul. The Frenchman was stronger than his willowy frame looked.

"We have to take you with us, Kat," said James. For once he was bright-eyed and in tune with the moment. He's happy, she thought incredulously. As if he's been saving himself for this one great effort. "We cannot leave you to Elizabeth's tender mercies. She has none."

"You want a hostage against Robin's vengeance, you mean," she said.

Real regret shone in his expression. "Nay, dear—but there's no time to convince you."

The group began to move again toward the exit, slowly. Kat shot a pleading glance at Sir Amyas and the captain; both were standing stock-still, watching. Just watching.

"Robin." She didn't know she'd moaned it aloud until Raoul shook her.

"Be still, slut. And pick up your feet. I will not drag you up and down the stairs."

"Then leave me," she said promptly.

His feminine mouth split in a pretty smile. "With pleasure. But you will not be able to put a name to me if I do."

His knife knicked her rib cage.

"Raoul, you madman, stop pretending you would kill her," said James.

"I am not pretending. What do you care?" Raoul was still smiling.

"She *is* my sister."

"This is hardly the moment to remember it."

Raoul's light remark was deeply insulting. Kat tried to read the truth in James's face. The Frenchman didn't consider James enough of a man to protect his female kin. Was he?

"Sometimes we have to accept allies who disgust us in a good cause," James said slowly. "But this—nay, this is too much."

His fingers suddenly dug into Raoul's hand. Since it was the hand with the knife, the point sliced her skin just above her abdomen. *The babe.* Terror for the child filled her throat and she screamed.

Men whose shoulders and boots sparkled with melting snow swarmed through the doorway. One of them was tall, with a proud, blond head lifted at an alert angle.

"Kat." Robin's furious bellow was wonderfully reassuring.

He started for her, clearing a path by swinging his arms like clubs. There was gore on his cuffs and a big blotch of it stiffening his cloak. Kat saw the red stains and was instantly convinced he had been bleeding.

She cried out, "Oh, God, Robin, what have I cost you in blood?"

Twisting in the hold Raoul hadn't loosened, she punched viciously with her elbows.

The knife at her middle sank deeper; there was a cold sting. At the same time Raoul and James rolled away from her. Then Robin reached her ... and shoved her gently into the arms of the captain of the guard.

Kat wasn't stupid enough to expect more. And yet she wanted only to throw her arms around him and cling. The captain wasn't a good substitute, and she struggled away from him and watched tensely.

Robin reached down and heaved. He stood up his full height, gripping Raoul with one hand and James with the other. His eyes were like bits of ice. Kat felt the cold.

"Drop your knife," he said to Raoul, and it clattered to the floor. He didn't look at Kat, but his voice softened, and she knew he was speaking to her as he asked, "How badly are you hurt?"

The fingers she put to her side came away red, but she thought the cut was shallow. Breathing a prayer of thanks that it was no lower or deeper, she said, "It is nothing."

Robin shot her a glance, knowing Kat was capable of lying from misguided good intentions. At the sight of smeared blood, he went still. Her eyes were huge and trusting. He wouldn't betray that trust by creating more death for her to witness.

He wouldn't let the one who had put cold steel to her white skin go unpunished, either.

Shoving James toward Samuel, he tightened his grip on

Raoul. Slowly, using his now-free hand, he pulled his poniard and slit Raoul's clothes over the ribs. Judging the depth with a fine eye, he ruthlessly cut until he hit bone.

"So, monsieur, let's test how you enjoy the treatment you give a lady," he said viciously.

Blood dripped. Raoul's lids fluttered, his eyeballs rolled back and a wet stain that wasn't blood spread across the middle of his merchant's gown. With a disgusted oath, Robin pushed him away one-handed. The shove catapulted Mauvissiere into a stone wall and knocked the Frenchman completely unconscious. He slid to the rushes.

"Get him out of here," Robin said briefly to a guardsman, "before I kill him. Hold him in a separate cell. His is a special case; Bess will want him handled differently from the others. But—get him away from me."

Amyas began yammering questions. Robin answered them with a curtness he could see offended the warden, and didn't care. He interrupted another of the Puritan's shrill inquiries to order that a chair be brought for Kat, whose pallor worried him.

"Yes, we brought the skulkers in from the woods," he added in a snarl. "But they're all dead."

Kat's voice wasn't even a whisper. He read the word on her lips. "All?"

James paled.

"Sir Robin had accounted for each and every one of them before we even got there," interjected one of the guardsmen admiringly.

The chair arrived and Robin put her hand over his in a formal gesture to lead her to it, but Kat stepped back as if he'd offered her a snake. "Where are the bodies?" she asked more loudly.

Robin was beyond giving a tinker's curse whether they had an audience of a hundred or not. He couldn't let her think . . . "Charles died of the crossbow bolt, sweet heart. I told you that. His soul was gone before you rode away. You just did not want to believe it."

She stared pointedly over his left shoulder. "I want to take my brother Charles's body home."

"Brother, eh?" said Amyas sharply.

The undertone of glee in the remark opened a spring of futile anger in Robin.

"Be silent!" The hard command rang out over the growing whispers of the other occupants of the hall.

Amyas darted him a contemptuous glance. "Coddling your whore will not change the outcome of this day's business. She can take the body if she wants it. It is nothing but dross, anyway. But a traitor's head belongs to her majesty. It will make a fine adornment for London Bridge."

Kat stumbled outside, where she was quietly and thoroughly sick in the snow.

Strong hands held her shoulders while she retched. She didn't need to look to know they were Robin's. The moment she regained her strength, she jerked away from him.

James was there, too, held in a firm grasp by Samuel. "This is good-bye for us, sister. Godspeed on your way through life. My life is apt to be rather short, I fear."

"Why did you do it?" she asked, holding a corner of her cloak to her mouth. "I understand Charles taking part in this insanity but you? You are so levelheaded."

He actually laughed aloud. "I'll soon be short a head altogether. The Almighty will have to give me another one so I can wear my martyr's crown."

"Charles said that, too. About a martyr's crown."

"He had his faults, some of them grievous, but he earned one."

"Shot by your own friends in a mistaken ambush?" said Robin.

It wouldn't have happened if she and Robin hadn't chased him, Kat thought drearily.

"He must have blundered into the meeting place without shouting the password. The whole enterprise was blessed by the Church, sister. No matter what the circumstances of his death, that will count on Judgment Day."

"But you are not a fanatic. How could you?"

Despite wrists that someone had bound, he raised a thumb and traced a sign of the cross on her forehead. "Because I am a priest. That's how I have spent the last seven years, studying—and making ready to join my brother by birth and my brothers in the order in our crusade to bring the true faith back to England."

A priest? Kat gulped the cold air and then let it go, seeing James through the haze of her breath. Awe dazed her; she didn't make the mistake of thinking a priest's life easy. And in James's case, as he said, it was apt to be short. Tinging her awe was disappointment. He hadn't even told her.

"Come back inside, both of you," Robin ordered. "I'll find a place where you can rest until I am done, Kat. James, you will need to answer more questions."

"I will stay outside," said Kat.

"I have no objection to being interrogated by a warm fire," James said, tranquil as ever. "We lost this time, Hawking. There will be other times. Sister, do not be foolish. It is cold and you have to think of the—"

"Let it be!" She put her arms around her waist. The family that had been separated from her for so long was dying around her. Robin was at least partly responsible; so was she. News of the baby would be incongruous at this moment.

Her own failure ate at her. She should have been stronger, braver, smarter, more persuasive. She hadn't understood the depths of her brothers' involvement in this treason; if she had, could she have talked them into giving it up? Reason said no, but guilt said yes.

Robin was close by her side. Without giving her a chance to argue, he picked her up cradle-fashion. "You are going inside before you freeze."

His arms felt safe and half of her wanted to stay cuddled in them forever. The other half squirmed until he had to put her down or drop her. Her soft-soled slippers skidded in the snow, and she grabbed for his cloak to keep from falling.

Embarrassed, she let go. "I will come in and listen while you question James."

Robin said, "No!" and James said, "Nay!" at the same time.

"Then I will wait out here for what I am allowed to take home of Charles." Vaguely, she was pleased that her voice remained cool. "His body will receive a decent burial on Priorly ground."

James blessed her again. "Go with God, then." He

leaned forward and whispered, "Take care of the babe. It will be the last of our name."

Kat was not going to be budged, Robin realized, and he gestured at Samuel to take James inside.

Pausing at the entrance, he asked her, "Are you hating me very much?"

"I do not know what to feel. I am no longer sure who I am. Being locked in a dark hole for three days by people you love makes the world seem different when you finally get out."

At the reminder of James's part in keeping her in the priest's hole, Robin growled softly in his throat and turned to the door.

Kat ran in front of him. "In there—in Fotheringhay—James objected when Raoul threatened to kill me. At the instant it really mattered, he shielded me. Do not let him be tortured."

He walked around her. "I will do my best. If you are bent on returning to Priorly today, a troop of guards will go with you. Be there when I arrive. It may be several days, but I will join you as soon as I can." He turned in the entranceway to frown at her. "You have not forgotten that we are betrothed, have you?"

Sadness made her eyes big and soft. "Nay, my lord. I would not forget."

He wished she could smile.

Inside, it was warm enough compared to the chill outdoors that he shed his cloak. Shouting at Amyas soon worked him up to a sweat.

"There is no reason for torture," Robin stormed. "All of the plotters in the building have been captured. Those in the woods have been killed."

Amyas believed torture would obtain the names of others sympathetic to Mary's cause, but, "All right," the warden said finally. "I will send them directly to London. The experts in the Tower will have the pleasure of loosening their tongues."

A servant interrupted, bringing Robin word that Charles's body was ready for Kat to take home.

"Do not leave Fotheringhay yet," the warden warned him. "There is more work to be done, rat catcher."

Flinging on his cloak, Robin went out and supervised the loading. Otherwise, he was afraid the scullions would simply dump the corpse into the rickety wagon provided for transport. Kat wouldn't have liked that.

Shepherding the wagon into the courtyard, he saw that James and his fellow conspirators except for Raoul were chained together in a long line. One of them fell, and James had to do a jig step to save himself from going down.

Far above in a narrow window, a shadowy figure peered. All in black, it brought a scowl to his face. Mary Stuart was watching another contingent of the young men loyal to her cause dance to their deaths.

He found Kat in a sheltered corner and helped her to sit next to the wagon driver. "Take my cloak," he said, throwing it around her.

"It is Samuel's. You already gave me yours."

"Well, now you have them both."

"Ride over to Priorly soon. I—I have some news for you. Not a matter of state. It is just something we need to talk about."

"As soon as I can."

Stepping back, he nodded to the driver, and the wagon lurched forward.

Samuel appeared at his elbow. Now that Kat had brought it to his attention, he noticed that his henchman's large form was scantily covered by a grimy blanket that smelled of horse. "Lady Kat is a sensible girl," Samuel said as the courtyard emptied. "'Twill all come out right in the end."

Robin grunted. "Only drunkards, maidens, and lunatics hope for happy endings. If I cannot win out of here by nightfall, I want you to get yourself to Priorly and make sure the lady is bothered as little as possible. In particular keep a pompous ass named Francis Toth from entering the house. He once cherished a fancy for her and her property that may grow again now that the place is indisputably hers. The man could hector a saint into a sickbed. She's ill enough over this business."

"As you will, my lord."

Robin trudged back into the hall. Sir Amyas insisted

that he write a report of the day's happenings. They were sitting down to a belated supper Robin didn't have the stomach for, when William Davison entered unannounced.

"I have it, gentlemen," the secretary of state called out. "The warrant authorizing Mary's execution."

Robin let Amyas exclaim and quote Bible verses about vanquishing the unjust. He put down his spoon and studied Davison. A fevered, mulish air gave Elizabeth's councilor an odd resemblance to Mary's adherents.

"I am surprised her grace is letting it be used," Robin said. "When last I heard, she was exploring other ways to remove the queen of Scots."

Amyas developed an intense interest in the wine. Raising a brow, Robin asked, "You, too?"

After another deep swallow, Amyas muttered, "You talk in riddles."

Paulet began to tell Davison about the disposition of the captured plotters. "Fine, fine," approved the little man.

So Elizabeth had tried to get Mary's pious warden to commit murder, just as she'd asked Robin. She'd run mad, he thought.

The stubborn jut to Davison's beard grew more pronounced. "Mary's removal is necessary. No one can deny that."

Well, no, reflected Robin. Not if their queen was growing desperate enough to beg a Puritan to break so serious a commandment. Her normally sound judgment must be disordered.

Amyas was telling Davison about the day's foiled attempt to rescue Mary.

"Did her majesty give you permission to use the warrant or not?" Robin interrupted bluntly.

Davison drank deep. "We will behead Mary tomorrow. It will be a great day."

"Hallelujah," agreed Amyas.

Elizabeth had *not* authorized the execution, then. Robin studied the two men with contempt. Both of them glowed with excitement. Did they actually believe she would thank them for flouting her will? At any rate, he could do nothing to stop them. A trip to London or its close neighbor Westminster would take two and a half days, no matter how hard he drove the horses.

It was too late.

"I will leave you to the enjoyment of contemplating the morrow," Robin said. God's grace, what ghouls. When it came down to it, Mary Stuart was a middle-aged woman who must be frightened out of her wits. A pang of longing for Kat, even a Kat who wouldn't smile at him, destroyed what little appetite he'd had. He stood. "By your leave, I'll be on my way."

"You do not have our leave," Davison barked. "Your presence will be needed as a witness to the execution. The earls of Kent and Shrewsbury will act as observers also. Once the deed is done, we must be able to show the queen that it was carried out correctly."

Robin laughed. Elizabeth wouldn't care how "correctly" she was disobeyed. She was going to be furious.

The hall was crowded and noisy when he reluctantly entered the next day. A scaffold with a block, a stool, and an incongruous, brightly colored cushion waited at one end. People crushed together around a railing defended by men-at-arms. The members of the throng were all richly dressed. With a twist of his lip, Robin realized that the county's gentry must have been invited to the spectacle.

"Was Lady Katherine summoned to see this?" Robin demanded, finding Sir Amyas and breaking into his conversation with a matron.

"Hardly," said Amyas coldly in response to Robin's question. The warden returned his attention to the woman. "Queen Mary will be wearing a black gown, as is her habit, but it will be removed before the ax is used. Her underclothes are all red." His prim mouth and small eyes narrowed in confusion. "Her tirewomen say she chose red so the color will not clash with her blood."

The matron nodded as if this made great sense.

Sickened, Robin stated, "You do not need me here." He waved a hand. "There are witnesses everywhere. I am leaving."

"Davison is a bad man to cross, but do as you please.

By the way, a messenger from your uncle rode in this morning," Amyas told him.

Robin was about to growl what the messenger could do with himself when a stir ran through the crowd.

Walking with the proud, stately pace of a woman who knows all eyes are on her, Mary, queen of Scots, stepped up the stairs of the scaffold. Though he'd always been immune before, Robin felt a glimmer of the fascination she'd wielded over men who should have known better. He'd always considered her self-centered. If vanity could give her this air of dignity as she faced the ax, then perhaps vanity wasn't so bad a thing.

Her bold, dark gaze, rather like her cousin Elizabeth's, swept the crowd. It fell on him, and Mary nodded slightly. He found himself nodding back. They'd met more than once. Now they were two adversaries greeting each other.

After that, somehow he couldn't force himself to leave. The whole ten years of his service to Elizabeth had been a long chase that would end only with Mary's death. He had to stay.

A cleric from the Church of England began a sermon. It seemed to go on and on. Robin wasn't the only one who thought so, apparently, because around him people stirred and muttered. He kept his eyes on Mary. Her long, thin face registered anger—over the clergyman's impudence, Robin suspected. After all, this was Mary's execution, and the parson was spoiling it.

Startling the crowd, the queen of Scots suddenly broke into loud speech. In Latin, a language calculated to annoy her captors. From the "Aves" and "Pater Nosters" sprinkled among words he didn't recognize, Robin gathered she was embarking on a rival prayer. He almost grinned. Mary wasn't the woman to allow a mere clergyman to steal the stage.

The cleric shouted louder. Mary yelled. The people in the throng joined in, bellowing to the Almighty in English.

Finally Amyas quieted everyone. A sheepish silence fell over the hall. Mary's female servants removed her black outer garment. Her smock and underskirt *were* a deep, dra-

matic red. The color reminded Robin of something ...
Kat. The dress covered with garnets.

A few minutes more, and he could ride away from this
accursed place and see Kat.

Mary knelt on the colorful cushion. The scaffold wasn't
high, and Robin was close to the edge. His eyebrows
snapped together at the sight of the executioner's hands
shaking. No wonder the hooded man was unnerved—it
wasn't every day an execution degenerated into a shouting
match, or a queen's neck stretched out on the block.

The ax fell.

It struck off-center, and a groan went up from the
crowd. The second cut did no better. Mary's body jerked.

"This is butchery," said Robin, appalled.

He started for the steps. Mary didn't deserve this; no
one did. In common decency, he would have to take the ax
away from the bungler and do the job himself.

Just then the ax came down for the third time. It sliced
clean.

A round object rolled to Robin's feet. Fighting his rising
gorge, he stepped back, bumping into Amyas, who scurried around him to reach down and lift the dead queen's
head by the hair, for the delectation of the witnesses.

Robin thought he'd never forget the look on Amyas's
face when the warden realized Mary's luxuriant hair was
false. It was the final touch of farce. The head slipped out
of the wig Amyas was holding and tumbled once more to
the floor.

"Yes," Robin said sarcastically, "all in all a very 'correct' execution."

Striding away from Amyas, who was still staring at the
wig, Robin threaded his way toward the exit. He needed
fresh air.

"Lord Robin?"

"I am Robin Hawking," he acknowledged impatiently,
beginning to turn toward the whisper. "What is it?"

"The Baron Burghley sent me to give you this," said the
whisperer.

The first blow caught him at the base of the neck.
Dimly, he was aware of pitching forward. The second

blow was a carefully calculated clip to his jaw disguised by the motions of competent hands that caught him as he fell and lowered him to the floor. He appreciated the expertise even as unconsciousness rolled over him.

Chapter 22

He had been ill.

Robin knew that must be true, because his head pounded and his mouth tasted bad. His eyelids didn't want to open wider than slits. Pain burst in his pupils. Doggedly, he narrowed the slits even farther until he could get a fuzzy picture of his surroundings.

He was seated with his back against a wall amid the rich odors of the Grey Gull, the tavern in Dover. Plump, soft forms on either side of him held him up.

Maybe he'd had too much to drink, instead of being the victim of a disease. One of the barmaids pressing close to his shoulder put her nose to his and giggled. "Me lord, you do have saucy ways. 'Ware your hand now!" Robin realized his hands were full of lush, almost bare bosom on one side and inviting thigh on the other.

But he couldn't remember getting himself into this situation.

"Why am I here?" he asked, slurring the words badly. He ran an uncertain tongue around his lips. They were cracked.

"Why, to sign our charter!" said Thomas Seyward. Thomas belonged in Dover, Robin thought with painful slowness. They had met in the Grey Gull a number of times to discuss joining a company of adventurers ... but when? Not recently. The recent past was filled with visions of Kat, and a roomful of screaming people. Robin wasn't sure of much, but he was sure it was wrong for him to be in Dover.

316

Thomas grinned as Robin retrieved his hands and dropped his head in them. "You entranced these fair creatures onto the bench next to you before ever I arrived. Lucky dog, to be joining a company that will make you rich and sitting in such an enviable position at the same time!"

"A compromising position."

Both women nudged closer until they were sharing his lap. His hands adjusted with no orders from him to catch them around their waists so they didn't topple him over.

One was a luscious dark-haired creature who peeked at Thomas as if asking his permission. Seyward's doxy, he recalled vaguely. The other was a blonde with curls that bounced over large, well-formed breasts, drawing attention to them. At Thomas's nod, the brunette got her leg between his and rubbed suggestively. The blonde pushed her most obvious attractions right under his chin. White flesh, lots of it, brushed his beard.

Too disoriented to push the wenches away or to become aroused by their ministrations, Robin stared rather foolishly at the motherly breasts. His beard was a darker gold than the fair hair mingling with it. It was longer than he normally wore it, too.

Longer. Any yet the last time he'd been in this room he'd just had his beard trimmed.

Priorly. Mary Stuart. The execution. Charles and James. *Kat.*

"God's grace," he said, focusing on Thomas. He felt like a clock that no one had bothered to wind. "How many days have I lost?"

Thomas's grin wasn't quite invincible. It wavered under Robin's gaze. "You are talking nonsense, friend. You have been here in Dover a number of weeks, drinking rather deep—"

Carefully, Robin scooted the lapful of female flesh off his knees. When the women tried to cling, he said, "I hope you received payment in advance, because you'll get no coin from me. Find wealthier pigeons to pluck."

That was a language the quayside had taught them. Without a backward glance, they smoothed their skirts, adjusted their bodices, and swayed away.

A slow, wintery fury crystallized in Robin.

"Who employs you? The queen or my dear cousin?"

"What do you—"

"Answer."

He didn't even have to draw a weapon. Thomas seemed to judge the danger promised by Robin's loosely curled fists and babbled, "'Twas a jest, that's all, a jest. They brought you in a traveling wagon and left you here a fortnight ago. An apothecary has been dosing you. He said you would waken today. I was to make you believe little time had passed . . ." His voice dwindled away.

"Queen's livery or Burghley's?"

"Burghley's."

"Does he employ you?"

"Yes."

Hell, but Robin's head ached. "So he arranged for you to try to bring me into your little company of gentleman adventurers. Why?"

"You are his kin, is what I heard," said Thomas sullenly. "He wants you away from England. Something about a woman he does not want you to have. You did not move heaven and hell to get into France, so he told me to push you in a new direction."

Robin asked the most important question. "What of Lady Katherine Preston?"

"They said you would ask. 'Tis no use you looking for your whore, they said. If you want a drab, man, let one of the bawds here content you—"

Some elemental bit of clockwork became unsprung in Robin. It was pleasant to let go of the constraints of civilization. He hurtled over the table, his fingers steel around Thomas's neck.

The other man's hands pawed ineffectually at his grip, then Thomas's face purpled, his eyes bulged, and his tongue began to protrude horribly.

Above the pounding in his ears, Robin heard a high keening which he gradually identified as a woman wailing. It went on and on.

The sound was irritating. The nearly-dead thing in his hands posed no danger, so he glanced around to roar an order for silence. The black-haired wench shrieked mindlessly.

The woman wasn't Kat, wasn't anything like Kat. And yet . . . He didn't want to be the cause of anyone's tears. Because of Kat, he'd learned the meaning of redemption. He couldn't slip back into the old pattern of eliminating God's mistakes. Robin didn't want to hunt and slay. Not even the same miserable kind of creature as he had been himself.

Releasing his victim so abruptly the half-strangled man fell to the floor and he himself stumbled, Robin kicked Seyward out of his way and went to the door. Then he turned on his heel and came back. A quick search of the trembling body revealed a purse plump with coins.

"I will take it as a given that this was your reward for diddling me. The payment is forfeit. Consider yourself a fortunate man. If it were not for my lady that you call a whore, the forfeit would have been your life."

The contents of the purse more than covered the price of a dependable horse, and Robin left the seaside town while it was still light.

He rode in the direction of Westminster. While Kat might still be at Priorly, he thought it more likely Elizabeth had ordered her back to court, the better to torment her. The estate had been Charles's property, and since Charles was a proven traitor, Priorly now belonged to the crown. Guessing where the court was located at the moment was impossible; it went where Elizabeth chose to go, and in the wake of Mary Stuart's execution that might be anywhere. So he went where Parliament was.

Even in the countryside, he could detect ripples from the upheaval among the realm's great ones in response to Mary's death. A smith nailed a new shoe on his stallion, and passed on the news that Queen Bess was claiming through thick and thin she hadn't meant the warrant to be carried out. Davison had been clapped in the Tower for his part in the grotesque execution. The rest of the privy council was rumored to be trembling for fear of the same happening to them.

Worry for his cousin, Burghley, who was very much a part of the council, didn't bother Robin. He was too angry over the mean trick his cousin had played on him. Besides, William Cecil had outwaited his royal mistress's temper too many times without permanent damage to fail to do so now. The rest of the council could go hang, literally, with Robin's goodwill.

The fear that kept him traveling through the slush of a March thaw was of what Elizabeth might be doing to a scandal-blown lass whose brothers were traitors. And whose lover must have seemed to have disappeared off the face of the earth.

That must have been what Burghley had intended. A junior member of the family had exhausted his usefulness. Having become an embarrassment, with Thomas Seyward's help he'd been nudged toward a future that would take him out of Elizabeth's sight. The same maneuver would keep him away from a woman the Cecils did *not* want to welcome into the family. A neat ending to a troublesome problem.

Robin, however, didn't plan to be disposed of. Not easily. Not at all.

His thoughts were so bleak that the sight of London came as a surprise. The city spread cozily along the still-ice-rimed river, under a blanket of smoke from fires that spoke of warm hearths. The air was chilly, but not cold. His breath no longer spouted in feathery plumes.

An odd conviction of good luck began to buoy him up. He stabled his horse and hired a barge to take him upstream the few miles to Westminster. Parliament seemed the best place to get news of the court. His luck proved true. A little gossip with the barge master revealed that the queen was at Whitehall.

If fortune's wheel is spinning for me, it spins for Kat, he thought with determined hope.

"Bess is not holding court at Whitehall, mind you," said the talkative riverman. "She only came to scold Parliament about the bitch queen of Scots being executed. You'll have heard the hubbub, I imagine? Today, I hear, she's going back to the comforts of Richmond."

"Do you know where the royal dock is?" Robin asked.

"Of course, sir."

"Set me down there."

Respect sobered the riverman's face, and he gave the orders.

The queen's barge was already docked. It was an unmistakable craft, long, sleek, and gilded so the sun twinkled off the sides.

After paying the barge master, Robin went straight up to the first guard who happened to be in his path.

"I must have speech with her grace," he said in his flattest tone, the one that was least likely to be argued with.

The guard was a Gentleman Pensioner he'd never seen before. His travel-stained clothes obviously didn't impress the resplendently dressed pikeman. "So does half the privy council, fellow, as well as the king of France and the pope in Rome. They cannot, why should you?"

Robin let the guard see his eyes. "Because they are not here. I am."

"Begone with you," said the guard, but the jovial contempt in his voice had dwindled and he stepped back a pace, gripping his pike.

With a light push, Robin helped the pikeman over the edge of the water steps. The resulting splash distracted the other guards so well that Robin was able to stride onto the vessel while they were peering into the river.

"What are you doing here?" It was a woman's demand, breathless. For less than a heartbeat he managed to fool himself into believing it might be Kat's. Even before he looked in the direction of the voice, he was aware the hope was false. Every tone of his damask lady's voice, the slightest whisper of her scent were printed on his senses. This wasn't Kat.

Still, he hadn't been expecting Margaret Treland, who had never made a practice of speaking to him.

"Is Lady Kat here?" he asked baldly.

"No," answered Margaret just as tersely. "I do not know where she is. Her family's property has been confiscated. That brother of hers, the Jesuit, is in the Tower."

Robin's quick flick of the fingers dismissed James. "I have to see the queen."

Her ruddy color paled. "Have you run mad? You were at Fotheringhay, were you not? I have heard talk. You'll end up on a rack somewhere, too. How would that help

Kat?" Dark circles ringed her eyes, and he saw that much of her plumpness had melted away since he'd last seen her. She looked older.

"Mauvissiere?"

Her breath hissed in. "Kat told you?"

"Kat does not betray her friends' secrets, nor does she willingly think the worst of anyone. I guessed."

Her shrug was a pathetic attempt at unconcern. "Raoul has been bundled out of the country. He never even sent word . . . Well, he made it plain enough when John came back demanding husbandly rights that he would not fight for me." She grimaced. "I told Kat she had chosen badly when she fixed her heart on you—but her choice was better than mine. At least you have returned for her."

"But you say she is not here," he reminded her. "Can you get me an audience with Elizabeth?"

"If you are sure that's your desire. I'll do it for Kat."

Some of the tension seeped out of him. His luck was holding. "You are a good friend, Lady Margaret."

"Not particularly." She settled her headdress more firmly over her hair and gave him a wry smile. "But Kat is. Perhaps goodness deserves a reward for once. If a reward is what Elizabeth gives you. Follow me."

Several courtiers jumped to their feet as Robin entered the barge's cabin section with Margaret on his hand. Her air of bustling importance—and Robin's expression, which was indifferent enough to belong to a man sure of his welcome—kept anyone from blocking their path. Potpourri had been sprinkled on the deck; it released its ghosts of dead roses as they walked to the inner cabin's door. Robin would gladly have traded the stronger perfume for the scent of gillyflowers.

The door opened and a young, rabbity woman came out.

When she saw Robin, she drew a sharp breath. Margaret clapped a hand over the newcomer's mouth.

"Jane Monteshote," Margaret whispered. "An admirer of yours. I can keep her quiet. But I do not claim to be brave. You enter the inner cabin alone."

"I thank you."

"Do not thank me yet. Wait and see what comes of this. Jane, be still!"

Robin eased himself into the private cabin.

The queen lay at her ease on a broad cushion of cloth of gold. A scarlet velvet rug protected her feet from drafts. The color reminded Robin of Mary Stuart's underclothes. His measuring gaze seemed to prick Elizabeth; without moving her eyes from the book she was reading, she asked querulously, "Who disturbs us?"

"Your conscience, my queen."

Flying up, her eyes went blank with shock for a moment, then she snapped, "We already have one. An inconvenient possession it is, too. Get out!"

"Conscience is not so easily gotten rid of."

"Our gentlemen will skewer you on their pikes and leave you for the crows."

"They can try," he said with an appearance of calm. As if from a distance, he could feel his body responding to threat—blood pumped wildly, muscles tightened, his mind cleared of everything except the immediate goal.

The calculated insolence had its effect. Elizabeth's jaw dropped.

While she was flummoxed into silence, he strolled toward her and dropped casually onto the cushion. Her preference for large, fair, stalwart men was well known. The last one who had successfully overawed her was her father. It occurred to Robin that his faint resemblance to the hero and devil of her childhood couldn't hurt his chances of emerging from the cabin with a future.

"I bring you a bargain, Your Grace."

"Why should we barter with you, Robin Hawking?" she asked sharply. "You were with Davison and the others, deliberately overturning our will at Fotheringhay!"

"I was there keeping fools from releasing your cousin onto the countryside to plague us all. Anyone will tell you that's the truth."

She tossed her head, and the borrowed red curls jiggled. Jewels scattered through the coiffure flashed with the brilliance of stars—all cold fire, no heat.

He deduced that someone had already confirmed his story, because she shifted her attack. "And what is this bargain you bring us as an excuse for pushing your way into our private quarters?"

"A good one. An arrangement that any overlady would be happy to accept since it will benefit her subjects."

"Benefit you and your whore, you mean."

Robin didn't bother to deny that Kat had given herself to him. God's grace, he was proud of it. In awe of it.

"Lady Katherine is innocent of all blame and all guilt. If the world wishes to shout abuse, it should do so at me. I am the man, the elder and more experienced."

"We knew we could not trust you with her!"

"I am afraid your grace was right." He couldn't force fear or remorse into his voice, and could tell the amused pleasure in it grated on Elizabeth. Since throwing himself on her mercy would net him nothing, he lounged deeper into the cushion and smiled at her. "So we both owe the lady recompense, do we not?"

"You dare burst in on us and boast of your lust? Filthy, indecent— *Who do you imagine yourself to be?*"

"An Englishman whose indecencies, as you call them, are all healthy, human ones, I thank you," he replied with icy pride. "An Englishman who refused to do murder at your command, madam."

"You cannot prove—"

"By my word alone? Perhaps not. But how many others received and rejected the same orders? I know that you tried Amyas Paulet, too. If there are others, I can find them. I am good at tracking things down. It is a craft I learned in your service. And once we band together to sing the same song, we will be believed. I think saving my queen that embarrassment might well be worth a small estate and your blessing on a wedding between two persons who would prefer to make little noise in the world."

Her anger was so great she actually choked on it. Her face contorted and a spasm of coughing shook her. The painted-on complexion cracked, and her wig tilted to one side.

Robin waited until her breath wheezed with more regularity. With a courtier's grace, he poured wine and offered it.

He counted it a small success that she snatched the beautifully blown glass goblet and drank off its contents rather than dashing the liquid into his face.

Slamming the cup down, she said grimly, "What do you want?"

"I told you. Recompense for my lady, which will also repair the lives of those who depend for their living on the Preston estate. She's a good overlady. As caring about her tiny piece of England as you are of the whole kingdom, Your Majesty."

"Priorly has been remanded to the crown for treason!" As acquisitive as her father and grandfather, Elizabeth could be counted on not to forget the name of a property, however modest.

"But Lady Katherine committed no treason," pointed out Robin. "In fact, it was her alertness that foiled a plot against you."

"And turned her into a bawd," said Elizabeth with vicious satisfaction.

"And cost her her reputation. For that, too, she must receive amends. Marriage."

"A wedding ceremony will hardly cobble over *her* sins. She had the chance to be perfect in her virtue," muttered the queen, "just like us. She could have been an example of a way of life that leaves women free . . ." Shaking off her reverie, Elizabeth glared at Robin. "Whom do you put forward as the candidate for your slut's soiled affections? Some impoverished nonentity content to take your leavings if we provide a handsome dowry?"

"I suggest myself." He didn't trust himself to say more.

Silence. "So. You have fallen in love with the girl?"

The taut, raw jealousy of a nature that couldn't bear to be second to anyone stretched under the smooth question. This was Elizabeth's sticking point, he thought. Not even the outright extortion he was trying would infuriate her as much as the idea a man had looked at her—and given his heart to another.

Dear God, he wanted Kat, whose lack of vanity was a refreshment to the spirit. His Kat didn't demand love; she scarcely believed she could inspire it. He closed his eyes. Where was she, his damask lady? Did she need him?

He would dredge up another half-lie for Kat's sake. Opening his eyes, he ran them caressingly over the skinny figure in the outrageously exaggerated costume. "Your

Majesty of all women should not need to ask. Could any man bask in the presence of true beauty and fail to feel its fire?"

She leaned toward him, softening, and he barely repressed a shiver. He manufactured another lie. "Men are drawn to your grace's loveliness and wisdom, and then left with empty, aching arms."

"We are England's bride," she said. "Our energy, our ardent devotion, everything that we are we have given to England."

"As all know. But lesser mortals have, er, baser needs."

"She's a substitute?" asked Elizabeth. "For us?"

Robin felt a stirring of pity for the queen. All her life men had turned from her to other women—first her father and then the suitors she'd worn out with her evasions and political maneuverings. England had profited. The vigorous energy that might have gone into service in the bed of a husband or lover instead rained down on the kingdom she loved, making it bloom.

But Elizabeth had withered. She really wasn't anything like Kat at all. He wanted to laugh, to curse, to kick something, but he controlled himself. He hated all this pussyfooting around the Tudor vanity. If he got out of this with his head, and with Kat, he'd never meddle with great ones again.

In a wheedling tone, Elizabeth asked, "How can we be certain we'll be safe from you?"

Robin winced to think he'd reduced his sovereign into making the plea of every victim of extortion. "Madam, you are England. I love my country. Striking at you would make England bleed. Who else could lead us? Your heirs are a thin and sorry lot."

"Call for a clerk. We shall do what we can for you."

"Not a clerk. There's no time. And any document has more force written in your own hand."

Too far. He could see that he'd gone too far from the way her hands clutched at the scarlet lap robe. Then the claws loosened, and she cooed, "So much heat. Are you sure infatuation is not at the heart of your impatience?"

When other wiles fail, he thought, fall back on the truth.

"I have to marry the girl, Your Grace. It is a matter of my honor, not hers alone."

She pulled a small table close and chose pen and paper. "Since when does honor have meaning to our rat catcher?"

"Since the day I performed the questioning while Tony Babington hung on the rack, I suppose."

"What does that mean?"

If she didn't understand, he had no way to explain it to her. Without answering, he directed, "The property returned to Lady Katherine to dispose of as she wishes." He wouldn't steal her estate to obtain his dream. "And your order to her that she wed me with no delay."

The feather of the pen brushed Elizabeth's sharp chin rhythmically. "Why a command? Why not permission?"

"One of her brothers is dead because of me," he reminded her. "The other sits in the Tower awaiting punishment. The lady may not be overly glad to see me riding up in bridal finery."

The rouged lips remained tight but turned up at the corners. It wasn't an expression Robin liked at all. The quill began to move steadily over the paper.

"Here you are," Elizabeth sang out at last quite cheerfully, dusting sand over the still-wet ink to dry it. She handed Robin the orders.

Running his gaze over the elaborate curliques of her handwriting, he objected, "But this gives Priorly to me, not Lady Katherine. And you grant both of us permission to marry where we please!"

"Do you not imagine she will be happy to take you, now that you are master of her estate?" asked Elizabeth softly. Abruptly she turned brusque. "Be content with what we have given you, pretty lordling. Look and see; we have awarded you several other tidy properties, too. You and we are quits. When you remember what you know about us, keep in mind that the memory of princes is also long. Aftondale, a peer of the realm, was killed in your vicinity not so long ago. An inquiry into the events of that night might be enlightening ... and not entirely healthy for those who were there. It is against the law to draw steel within court precincts, were you aware of that? The punishment is cutting off the offender's right hand. You are right-handed, are you not? Yes, I thought so. There's quite a ritual attached, I hear. It is most interesting."

"I can assure your grace I plan to do nothing—nothing," said Robin, with so much charm that the opaque eyes blinked, "that would make my presence at such a ritual necessary."

"Then we understand each other."

He bowed and left.

Going through the outer cabin, he saw that Margaret Treland had the rabbity woman backed into a corner. He veered and tapped Margaret on the shoulder.

"My thanks, Lady Margaret." Remembering that Margaret had called the other woman his admirer, he smiled at—at Jane Something, wasn't it? "I thank you, too, Lady Jane."

Jane's snub nose went pink with pleasure.

"Your talk with the queen went well?" asked Margaret, eyeing the paper clenched in his hand.

"I think so," Robin said. "If I use it properly."

"Did she tell you where Kat is?"

"I did not press my luck by asking. But I know how to find out."

On the dock, the pikeman he'd helped into the river had been fished out and was sitting, shivering, on the water steps. Robin's mood was so good that he gave the guard a hearty slam on the back and said, "You should change out of those wet clothes, friend. The weather is not yet good enough for swimming."

His victim did no more than glare, and one of the other Gentlemen Pensioners haled a passing barge for him.

Robin looked at them reproachfully. "I might almost believe you wanted to get rid of me," he said.

Just because he felt exuberant, he waved good-bye as he boarded the barge.

"Where to, sir?"

"Baron Burghley's house. It fronts the water."

The trip was short; Robin barely had time to decide exactly what he would say. Ushered into the master bedroom, he found himself wondering how long his cousin had to live. The baron wasn't just worn out, he was dying.

Since the last time they'd met, William Cecil's skin had turned pasty, and the strong facial bones they both shared stood out starkly.

Robin's shock must have shown in his expression, but the faded eyes remained as cynical as ever. "Not a very pretty sight, am I? Do not concern yourself over me. Death is an old friend. I will greet it with relief."

Robin leaned against a bedpost. He should have known the tough councilor would reject any sign of feeling.

"You are here, Robert, so I suppose Thomas Seyward was unsuccessful in getting you to join his band of sailors?"

"He was." Robin considered his next words. "You are not well, cousin, and I do not forget that you took me in when my own parents did not want me. To my surprise, I even have some affection for you. I bear you no grudges for the way you had me carted off to Dover." At least, he wouldn't bear a grudge as long as Kat was safe and sound. "But I am not some green lad to be led around by the nose for his own good. In fact, I have become a propertied man. This comes from the queen." He handed over the precious writ.

Actual approval enlivened Burghley's voice when the old man finished reading. "Two rich properties and this Preston place as well. You have done better than I would have predicted. Should I ask how you obtained these gifts from Elizabeth?"

"No."

"Ah. Shall I look about in the time I have left for a likely heiress?"

"Find a rich ninety-year-old or a little girl for someone else. I have my wife picked out. Where is Lady Kat?"

"How should I know?"

"Innocence hardly becomes you, cousin. We both know you have set a watch on Kat, if only to ascertain where she is so you can keep me away from her."

Burghley's sigh was like the rustle of dry leaves. "Staring death in the face has made me sentimental. I find I have some affection for you, too, boy. You will not stop looking for her, will you?"

"I will not stop until I have her." It was a vow.

"She is at Priorly." He pushed Elizabeth's writ across the covers to Robin. "You were the man who dragged down her brothers. Are you sure the lady wants you back?"

"She'll take me whether she wants me or not."

Chapter 23

❦

"Where the devil is Lady Katherine Preston?"

The fussy little man the Crown had installed to oversee Priorly staggered at Robin's shout.

"The young woman is not on the premises, I can promise you, Lord Robin," he said, straightening his cap. "Naturally, I had her put out when I took charge."

A gray tabby cat, swollen with a spring litter of kits, sauntered up to the group by the gate house. Bumping her head against Robin's boots, she demanded to be recognized. He bent to scratch the furry chin. Refusing the attention, the tabby glided toward the patch of woods. When he didn't follow, she looked over her foreleg and meowed with impatience.

Robin relaxed slightly. Kat Preston was around someplace—probably at the mill, which lay beyond the wood—whether the fool of an overseer knew it or not. Even if all cats were gray in the dark, this tabby was certainly his damask lady's, and Kat would never abandon her pet.

"Put Lady Katherine out, did you?" Robin said. "Did she take her cat with her when she went?"

"Of course," replied the overseer huffily. "I recall the lady tried to take a very handsome basket for her . . . cat . . ." He eyed Grimalkin uncertainly.

"Which you denied her, I imagine," continued Robin with false amiability. "How far along has the enclosure gone?"

"Unfortunately it is too early to plant hedges marking off the estate portion from the tenant land. Those who have been offered sections have protested that the fields will not support them. Once spring is truly here they'll be free to go." He tittered at his own pleasantry. The Priorly folk wouldn't just be free to leave. They would be forced by starvation to join the many homeless who roamed the highways.

"Your slowness is not unfortunate. It is very fortunate, because I'll not have to stand over you with a whip while you pull up the hedge plants one by one." Robin's voice crackled.

"Wh-what?"

Robin jerked his head at two of the men he'd hired now that he was propertied. Just now they were hard-faced. His new master of accounts and his new chaplain boxed the royal overseer in on both sides.

"Make sure this scum takes all his belongings away. Do not let him conveniently forget anything that would give him an excuse to show his chitty face here again. And Master Lewes," he added to the chaplain, "hold yourself ready. I hope to have a ceremony for you to perform."

The Priorly servants clustered at his elbows—as soon as they recognized him in the luxurious velvets he wore. A man dressed up for his wedding.

The steward, Pettigrew, spoke up. "Our lady be at—"

"The mill," Robin finished. The listeners bridled in surprise, and he guessed that a new Priorly legend was being born. *No use trying to hide anything from t'new lord, lads; he knows everything, he does.* Keeping his face straight, he prodded, "Go on."

"She be at the mill." Pettigrew offered a timid smile. "Her and Maud. The Millers took them in when that moldy, wizened rogue claiming to be from the queen tried to send them away."

Robin took the shortcut to the mill with only Grimalkin for company. The path was spongy, the trees a-drip with melting ice. Spring leaves were locked up in the buds swelling on otherwise bare-looking twigs.

Hope pumped its intoxicating tingle through his veins. Only fools believed in omens, and yet the sparse signs of the coming season struck him as good. You just want Kat, he told himself ruthlessly. You'd see a good omen in ravens flying counter to the sun around a church's steeple.

A voice broke into his thoughts. It wasn't the voice he heard in his imagination, Kat's soft murmuring. It sounded sharp with a well-honed edge of desperation.

"I have told you already, Maud, I will not put that foul stuff in my body."

"My lady, you will come home by way of Weeping Cross! 'Tis already too late to use the pennyroyal—"

Robin stepped back delicately until he was sure the women, Kat and Maud, couldn't glimpse him behind the leafless underbrush.

"—but the black-spurred rye will rid you of the babe."

"Why can you not understand? I do not wish to be rid of this babe."

"Because it is Hawking's!"

Kat's answer was almost too low for him to hear. "Aye. And for many other reasons. I had not expected to be able to conceive a child. It is almost a miracle."

"A badly timed miracle if you ask me, begging your pardon, my lady. If you bear the poor mite, how will you rear it? Selling your clothes has brought in a little coin, but we cannot live on a few shillings forever."

"I know." Kat sank onto her heels briefly before kneeling again to wield a trowel. He wondered how long she'd been working in that uncomfortable position in her condition.

Her condition.

She said sturdily, "And I cannot ask the Millers to give us living space for years and years."

Both women, he saw, were crouched in the garden with their hands in the dirt. Spring had arrived early in the sheltered corner.

His thoughts ran riot. A baby? No woman had ever wanted his child before.

Kat smiled ruefully at her former maid. "You think I am being stupid and perhaps you are right."

A chill ran through Robin.

"'Tis just that you are gentle-bred," said Maud soothingly. "Ladies and gentlemen do not get the practice in fearing poverty the rest of us do."

"Well, digging in the Millers' vegetable patch is one fate I never foresaw coming my way." Kat held up her hands. Even from a distance, Robin could see blisters forming crescents on her slim palms.

"So you will let me get the seven grains of rye from the wise woman." Maud tucked a strand of Kat's russet hair into her kerchief with tender fingers.

He held his breath.

"Nay."

Air rushed from his lungs and then filled them again.

"Even if I am being cloth-headed, this babe is mine. My sweet responsibility. Oh, Maud, they have taken all my other obligations away. There's nothing left to tell me who I am."

"And what does that mean, I pray you, my lady?"

"It means I need this child because it will need me."

The older woman snorted. "Nonsense. You'll both starve. The truth is you cannot bring yourself to harm Hawking's get."

"I would be pleased to think that was the case," Robin remarked, walking forward. He halted with the elegantly pointed toes of his boots just touching Kat's knees. "However, I doubt Kat could ever willingly hurt anything or anyone that came under her protection. Least of all our child."

"Come back, have you?" asked Maud in a sour tone.

"Rather behindtimes, it seems." He looked down. "How are you, my lady?"

Kat was so surprised she couldn't move. After weeks of silence, her lover had come back. "I am well," she said.

From her vantage point on the ground, he appeared ten feet tall and formidably broad in the shoulders. She gave herself over to the luxury of running her gaze over him.

"Not ill?" he asked, frowning as he took her wrists and hauled her to her feet.

"That was last month and the two before, my lord." It was impossible not to feel shy under his gaze. In the confusion and unhappiness since Fotheringhay, she had relived the heedless love they made at the Christmas dance in countless passion-filled dreams. Now . . . her homespun country dress hung loosely, but not loosely enough to hide the changes in her body. Her breasts were lusher, her belly no longer hollow but rounded. She knew her face had filled out into a new softness.

"When?"

"November, I think. My stomach began playing tricks on me during the Christmas revels. That usually begins in the second month."

"And you did not tell me?" His voice was too even.

"I did not guess myself until later. Well, you know why. Maud realized it first. She—" Glancing around, Kat saw that Maud had withdrawn out of earshot. "By the time I was sure, I had no idea where to send a message. I knew you would return to Priorly if you still desired me."

"I did come to Priorly. In February. You did not tell me then either. For the love of God, Kat. Are we never to be done with secrets?"

"There was hardly a chance to tell you then. And . . ."

"And that was the day Charles died and James was taken away," he finished for her, his frown heavier than ever.

The last day she'd seen her brothers was too painful to be picked over, even with Robin. Especially with Robin, she thought.

"You have changed, too," she said.

"Kat, I swear I have not changed," he replied emphatically. Wrapping her dirty hands in his warm fists, he brought them to his chin.

She closed her eyes against the hot glitter in his eyes; then, feeling like a coward, she opened them. "You *are* different. Grimmer. More established, somehow. Your clothes are very grand. You have always been assured, and now you are—commanding."

His frown softened. "Are you mine to command? Then here is my order. Marry me."

"I wish I could." Kat knew her heart was in her voice.

"I am rich, sweet heart. You and the babe will never go threadbare. We can even keep Priorly."

Her hands jerked in his, and he tightened his grip. "But the queen—"

"Has given it back."

"To me or to you?" she asked shrewdly.

He hesitated.

"To you," she guessed. Disappointment cut deep, but Kat told herself not to be a fool. "You will take care of the place? Keep the workers? The estate can turn a profit without enclosing."

"When we are married, I'll leave the management of Priorly to you. You may make what decisions you please. I'll have my work cut out for me learning to manage the other properties the queen has given me." He kissed her fingers one by one. Kat didn't miss the speculation in his quick glance at her face.

"I can tell when I am being bribed. The lure is appealing," she admitted, biting her bottom lip to keep it from quivering. "You are cruel, Robin. You offer me heaven when you know I should not take it."

He slid her hands around his neck and put his own on her expanding waist. "Why not? What stops you?" His knowing hands roamed. "Do you no longer desire me?"

Her knees almost buckled. She looked around to make sure Maud was still out of hearing distance. "Of course I desire you. You—you make me so damned hot, even the way I am now."

His kiss landed on the tip of her nose. "I like the way you are. I like being responsible for your breeding. A miracle indeed. If we are careful, it should not stop us from . . ." Damp heat bloomed at the apex of her thighs as he ground his hard hips lightly into her soft ones. "You will not mistake gentleness for something else this time, will you? We have gotten beyond that, have we not, sweet heart?"

Her moan somehow encouraged sharp little pleasurable pangs to shoot through the heat and the wetness. "Aye," she confessed before she could stop herself. "But that's beside the point."

Kat could feel him looking at her, and the old feeling that he was calculating how to snatch her up, eat her up, overcame her. This time there was no accompanying fear. Mercy God, she wanted nothing more than to be the focus of his hawk's gaze. To be the woman he sought over all others.

"What about Charles? What about James?" she asked

despairingly. "To marry you would be the same as saying that their fates do not count. One of my brothers is dead, the other close to death. Because I went to you, an agent of the queen! A wedding will not cure the past. No matter how I long for you, I would always feel we were making love on their tomb stones. I cannot be your wife."

"Not to wed me will mean bastardy for our son or daughter. Where does your loyalty belong?"

"You still know how to use all the tools at your disposal to win to your goal."

"There's never been one more important to me," he muttered. A flush stained his cheekbones. "Kat, I would rather you wed me of your own free will. But if you choose not to . . . I have orders from the queen, in her own handwriting. We are to be married, will ye nill ye."

"That's . . ." Improbable, astounding, moon-mad. Impossible. *"Elizabeth* says we must wed?"

His color deepened and his lips thinned into a knife-slash. If she didn't love him, she thought, she would suspect him of lying.

"Are you questioning my word?"

"What have you done?" she asked urgently. "Good God, Robin, what did you do to cause such a jealous, hoarding woman to set you free?"

The stunned look he turned on her made her feel as though her heart had been cut open to drip huge red tears. Shockingly, desire still ached and burned between her legs.

"You have never spoken to me like that before," he said. "Doubting me. Looking at me so."

"I did not mean to insult you." Her whisper was so intense it rubbed her throat raw. "I am frightened for you."

"You looked at me the way other people do. As if I were a butcher. As if I had grown horns and a tail." He smiled bitterly. "Well, maybe you have reason."

Kat didn't know what to say. Breaking away from his hold, she walked to the end of the garden. The riot in her soft and secret places faded, but her breath continued to come fast. Under her heart a series of faint tremors brought her hands to her womb.

The child was her first duty. A wedding would give it

a father and the safeguards of wealth in one fell swoop. And if the bride's brothers haunted the marriage bed?

That wasn't important compared to the baby's welfare. Finally, she said, "The babe's moving."

He stared in fascination. "What's it like?"

"Like moths dancing among the treetops."

"Our babe will dance at our wedding," said Robin. When she didn't answer, he added harshly, "Even if you feel that your brothers still stand between us, you have no choice, damask lady. This is our wedding day."

Kat barely recognized her own old chamber. The bed and walls had been stripped of their hangings. Even the fur rug was gone.

Crates and bales and boxes tumbled every-which-way. Fabrics spilled from them in colorful confusion.

Maud found Kat touching a flame-colored velvet cloth with reverent fingers and a blank face. The maid tsked. "New orders, my lady. This will be your dressing room. You should see the lord's chamber. New hangings, new linens, a fine painting by some Italian or other."

Kat noted that Maud's opinion of Robin had undergone a transformation. The maid hadn't been very happy accepting charity from her lowly cousins, the Millers.

"The lord says there will be no separate lady's chamber," Maud went on. "He insists that his wife sleep next to him."

With the sudden exhaustion of pregnancy, Kat felt her eyelids droop and craved a nap, but couldn't have one because Maud began to strip the homespun from her body.

Tired and obedient, Kat let Maud bathe her with a well-soaped washcloth. Her hair was brushed until it gleamed and then arranged to hang in a russet waterfall.

"Only virgins wear their hair down on their wedding day," she roused herself to object.

Maud shrugged. "The lord wants it this way."

The gown she helped Kat into was ivory satin. Green vines and leaves twined over the skirt and sleeves, matching the tiny emeralds that winked green fire across the bodice. A short standing ruff opened around the bosom and left a tantalizing inch of cleavage bare. The gown was handsome without being in the preposterous height of fashion. Robin had guessed, she thought. Guessed how she longed not to be a crow.

"No one would guess you are breeding. You are beautiful, my lady."

Kat studied her fingers. The skin was cracked and her nails were jagged. Surely all this was another dream.

"I am damned," she said.

But when Maud pronounced her ready to go to her wedding, she looked around wildly. "My pomander, the one Robin gave me. Where is it?"

"Here, my lady." Maud clipped the chain around her waist. The golden ball swung in a flashing arc. "Providential, that's what it is, that you would not sell the thing."

"It was all I had of Robin."

"That and the babe."

At the reminder, Kat laid her palm on her abdomen. The tiny brush of moths' wings rewarded her touch.

Nothing seemed quite real. Robin came to the door to fetch her. The walls wavered and the floor slanted strangely as he towed her to the chapel. A horde of people followed. Though Kat had known most of them her whole life, they were a blur.

The chapel glowed like a gem in the light of tens of candles.

"An accursed den of popery," said a stranger wearing a sober surplice with sleeves.

Was it possible for her head simply to float off her shoulders? Kat wondered. "My mother loved this chapel," she mentioned to no one in particular. "There's always peace in it. God lives here."

"If my lady likes the place, we shall be married here." Robin's tone brooked no argument. "You may begin, Master Lewes."

The clergyman's unmusical voice drifted in and out of her hearing. There was a long pause.

Robin tilted her chin up with a gentle fingertip. "Kat, you must answer now. Repeat what I say. Listen. I, Katherine, take . . ."

The baby moved. Robin's voice, insistent and irresistible, tugged the words out of her.

For better or for worse. How could there be anything better than giving herself to Robin? How could anything be worse than surrendering to her brothers' enemy? *I shall worship thee with my body.* In front of God and man, she was swearing that making love with Robin Hawking was the holiest act of her life.

But how could she once more sleep with the man she had accidentally helped to destroy her family?

The baby kicked, and she realized it would not be the last of the Prestons. It would be a Hawking now. So would she. Katherine Hawking. The only Preston left was James. And he would die a traitor's death.

Robin put a gold ring on her finger and held her hand so tightly the metal bit into her flesh. He walked her to the hall, where trestles had been set up in addition to the table. Trumpets flourished as they entered.

Although Robin must have brought the musicians with him in anticipation of the celebration, the wedding feast was sparse. It was too early in the season for there to be many courses. From somewhere a calf had been obtained for veal. All-too-lifelike suckling pigs lay on platters in rows as if they were nursing. Kat couldn't smell the young meats without thinking of the small life within her. She swallowed hard, sat beside Robin, and ate nothing. Tired fruits and vegetables had been stewed to provide variety, but they didn't tempt her appetite, either.

"It will be good when it is summer again," Robin said, leaning sideways to speak to her. His breath, spicy and familiar, was more real than the tables and the new, unfamiliar silver plate, or the too-quiet throng. "We'll have fresh fruit and a babe to laugh with."

"Children do not laugh right away," she countered. It was a mad conversation for a bride and groom. Perhaps she was going mad. "They have to grow and learn."

"You will be a fine teacher. You taught me the meaning of laughter." Candle flames leaped in Robin's eyes. Watching them, she felt light-headed.

Under his breath, he said, "This is a wedding, not a wake." Pushing back his chair, he strode to a corner, picked up a lute, and tossed it to one of the strangers he'd brought with him. "Play something merry. I promised to dance with my wife."

A quick-paced galliard brightened the mood of the gathering, which had been dampened by the bride's white face. Noise increased as the levels of wine and ale slopped to mere inches in bowls and kegs.

The music slowed to a slow, stately measure. Around Kat and Robin other couples revolved in languid patterns. Robin's hand touched hers, he turned, turned back, and his skin grazed hers again. The heavy satin of the gown he'd chosen for her swung out and then fell into gleaming folds with petal smoothness. Every motion was a caress. Robin brushed against her once more, closer than the dance called for, and she leaned into his strength, needing a little of it.

"Tell your women you would like to go to bed now," he said softly.

Too bludgeoned by emotion and too dazzled by his sensuality to do anything but obey, she found Maud. "My lord says I want to go to bed."

A shout of laughter from those who overheard startled her into blinking. Jolly or leering faces surrounded her. The revelers jostled her into joining a crowd of women going up the stairs, like flotsam carried by a wave. The tide of bodies swept into what had once been her parents' chamber, and left her beached in the middle of the room while eager helpers removed the lovely gown and then reached for her smock.

"Go away," she said, clinging to the garment.

Advice flew from all sides.

"Your husband will expect you naked for his pleasure."

"Gives the men a chance to gawk, but 'tis all innocent-like, my lady. Climb under the covers before they get here."

"'Tis not as if the lord's never seen your tits before. He must like them," called someone else bracingly. The crack of a slap followed quickly.

Maud came out of the crowd shaking her hand, and Kat knew her maid had slapped the would-be wit.

"How many of us have not loved unwisely?" Maud demanded. "Or wished that we had? If the lord and lady were previous in their behavior, well, they have made up for it with holy vows. 'Tis not for such as us to judge. This is a happy occasion."

"The bride does not look so happy."

Maud stared about sharply but couldn't pick out who'd made the remark. She shook Kat's elbow. "Make haste!" she hissed. "Let me undress you."

Kat clenched her fingers in the neck of her smock. "I will not show myself!"

Her pregnancy would be exposed. It was silly to try to hide it; most of the witnesses to the wedding undoubtedly knew already. But an instinct far older than she was held her frozen. She had to protect her baby from jeers and scornful jests.

"The groom is here!" a young girl by the door called.

At the front of his groomsmen, Robin shouldered a path through the tangle of women until he reached his wife. Kat looked besieged. Her head was bowed so the long hair curtained her face. As if she expected a whipping, he thought.

"We tried to disrobe her—"

"My lady is waiting for me to act as her tirewoman tonight." He put an arm around her shoulders. They trembled.

Maud said, "My lord—"

"Time for us to leave them alone, Maudie," said Samuel, pushing through to the forefront.

Robin raised his brows. "Where have you been? No, not now, man. Tell me tomorrow." The need to make love with his wife—his wife who was growing round with his child—rushed through him. "People, you may leave me to manage my lady. Dawn will be here soon. What's left of the night is best spent in bed."

Renewed laughter faded as the household trickled out of the chamber. It seemed to take a very long time. Kat felt good pressed against his side. She wouldn't refuse him, he thought. This wasn't the night for scruples—either hers or his.

Perspiration covered him with a fine sheen and his body was hard and throbbing. Robin shut the door firmly on

Maud's troubled expression and turned to examine his prize.

"Take off the shift," he said, his mouth dry.

Russet hair sifted over her like a sheet of auburn flame as she shook her head.

"Then I must."

The few steps it took to reach her felt as though he were swimming through water. He'd never experienced such a weight of sexual need before in his life. It slicked his skin, burned in his loins, made him drunk with the potent desire to pour himself into her. He had her; he finally had her. Robin tugged the sendal smock over her head. The cool slide of silk on the insides of his wrists was impossibly erotic.

"I feel as though I am opening a New Year's present," he said with a shaken laugh. "But we have more than a year. We have a lifetime."

When her body was naked to his gaze, he forgot to breathe. "You were sweet before." He reached out to touch her ripeness. "Now you are beyond beauty. Kat, you are everything to me."

The tip of his middle finger fell, not on either of her now-full breasts, but on the curve of her belly.

At the tender, barely discernable stroking, she stumbled backward.

He caught her by the elbows. "Do not fall in your haste to avoid the monster's touch, lady wife." Lust and love and anguish combined to make his tongue clumsy.

"You know you have never been a monster to me."

"Then why do you shrink away? I thought at Richmond you learned pleasure in my arms. God willing, we'll be married a long time. You had better get used to performing your marital duties."

"I have a duty to you," she flared. "I have a duty to our child. I have a duty to my brothers. By marrying you I have done what I can for the babe. It will not be a bastard, and I thank you for that. I do, Robin. But somewhere between being locked up, and seeing Charles die and James taken away, and being alone all this time—I have lost the ability to be happy. Or to make you happy."

He reached for her again. "Just being with you is the greatest happiness."

Whisking herself to the foot of the bed, she said, "If you did not believe what I said this afternoon, then I am sorry. I warned you. I will not make love."

"And what of our wedding vows?"

Her big eyes were almost black. "You are the queen's rat catcher, and I set you on my own brothers. How can I romp in bed with you after that? If raping your wife is to your taste, you may enjoy your husband's privileges as often as you can catch me."

He stalked to the pile of his possessions still heaped on the floor, and pulled out the sword he hadn't worn to his wedding.

"My congratulations." Ripping back the bed covers, he threw the weapon lengthwise on the sheet. "You used the one argument that could destroy my lust and keep you safe from my hideous advances. Get onto your half of the mattress and cover yourself, lady wife."

A tiny part of him hoped she'd apologize. He'd be more than pleased with a wife who wept and flung herself into his arms. Instead she climbed into the bed and within a few moments was fast asleep.

Cursing steadily, he got himself out of the expensive bridal clothes that didn't seem to have impressed his bride, and lay down on his side of the blade. Pain between his legs was the legacy of thwarted desire. The candles he had forgotten to snuff provided a dim glow. Despite his frustration, he couldn't keep his eyes from her sleeping figure. Her body was curled, still protecting its little passenger.

Carefully, so he wouldn't wake her, he stretched out an arm across the sword hilt and brushed a curl away from her small, elegant nose. Holy hell, he hoped neither of them rolled over while asleep and sliced flesh on the sharp blade.

Robin wasn't aware of closing his eyes or giving in to the need to rest, so when the dream came it was doubly horrible.

He was watching Kat's face. Light pulsed softly over her high smooth forehead and pointed chin. Her eyes and mouth were closed; she slept. Though he knew it was impossible, he could hear her voice, low and strained, speaking to him. She was refusing to welcome him inside her body. He didn't want to listen to that again. It hurt too much. Each ragged word seemed to cut into his flesh.

When he moved his throat muscles to order her to stop, no sound came out. Trapped and terrified, he struggled to touch her, to ask her for help. And that was ridiculous. He was the man, had been forced to be a man since he was seventeen years old. Men didn't beg. Men didn't turn to a woman for aid. Then something happened to her that replaced the terror of his speechlessness with a new horror.

Her face was glazing over with ice.

Frost whitened her lips and painted her large, curved lids blue. Crystals of it crept from her jaw over her delicate cheekbones and reached the russet tendrils that wisped at her hairline. She was dead, because he had killed her with his wanting.

No, not dead. The blue lids cracked open and amused old eyes looked into his. "She's a substitute for us," said Elizabeth Tudor.

"Robin!" Something was shaking him and he swatted at it irritably. "Ouch! Robin, wake up."

"It was a dream," he mumbled, scrubbing his cheeks as he sat up. His elbow banged into the sword hilt, and he glared at the weapon balefully before turning a thoughtful gaze on Kat.

The candles had burnt down, but dawn's pure light streamed through half-open shutters. Rectangles of the light fell over her where she stood bending over his side of the bed. Both of her hands still gripped his shoulder. The robe she'd thrown over her nakedness gaped to show the line of shadow that divided her bosom into two perfect halves.

"Why are you up?" he asked.

"I could not stay in bed."

"Could not stay in bed with me," he amplified.

When she shrugged, her breasts swayed slightly. His body responded, driving away any impulse to tend to normal morning-time needs. He lay back with a pretense of laziness. The quilt tented up, revealing his state of arousal.

"Is merely lying next to me too much happiness to risk?" he asked. "I am flattered."

He was pleased that she couldn't seem to decide where to look. Her pink flush was a good sign, too, he thought.

At last her restless glance met his. He could tell she suddenly realized what he'd been contemplating, because she shoved the opening of her robe closed and straightened so quickly he could almost hear her back twang like a lute string.

"We are husband and wife, Kat," he said. "Finally. Completely. Beyond the right of church to sever or man to deny."

She flinched. "What was your nightmare? You were groaning."

"Perhaps I was dreaming of us. On our wedding night. Without a sword making a fence down the middle of our mattress."

He won the flicker of a smile before a frown creased her brow. "I hope not. You were crying out, too. Not—not in joy. Please, Robin, tell me."

Deciding he wasn't going to get what he wanted, he got up to use the pot.

Their situation didn't really call for teasing. It wasn't the sword between them, and it wasn't that old bastard Sir Henry. It was Charles and James, and Kat's damnable scruples.

"To be truthful, my lady, I dreamt I was in bed with our most gracious virgin queen."

"That would be terrifying," she said with a stab at lightness.

"It was," he said dryly. "First it was you lying next to me and then it was Elizabeth and . . ."

"What?" said Kat when he didn't continue.

James. "It has given me an idea. Can I buy you, Kat?"

"You already have."

"Not like that. Could you learn how to be happy again if I got James out of the Tower for you?"

"How?" she breathed.

"All the guards know me; I can get into the prison section. It would take . . . no." The idea inspired by his dream of Kat-Elizabeth was too dangerous for Kat. He could make the attempt alone, but not with his wife.

The eager flash in her eyes darkened, and she began to straighten the bed covers. "He cannot be rescued from the Tower. The place is nearly impregnable. Less than a handful of prisoners have broken out in the five hundred years it has been standing. I could not bear for my child to lose its father as well as both of its uncles. Put the idea out of your mind."

"I'll devise something."

She jerked, viciously, on the sheet. "Robin, do not be an ass. Even if you get in, the only person who can go from the Tower at will is Elizabeth."

To keep her from reading the idea in his face, he turned away.

But she came up with the same solution at lightning speed. "You could not bring James out. But I could. That's what your dream meant. I could pretend to be the queen. Oh, God, Robin, together we could save one of my brothers!"

Chapter 24

He argued, he swore, he shouted at her. Only one point budged her. "You would be gambling not only your safety but also our child."

Her arms curved over her belly, but she said, "Robin, think. Not even Elizabeth would put a breeding woman to death. She would wait until the babe was born. Your mother's family, the Cecils, would take care of it, would they not? Your child?"

"God's grace, if you care nothing for your own life, listen to what you are proposing. They are cold people, Kat. You would not want them raising our little one. Take my word for it." The pain in his voice was more naked than he meant it to be.

She touched his cheek. After the briefest of caresses, her hand fell. "Then we'll have to plan so well and do our parts so carefully we live to be very proper, very dull parents."

Exasperated, and scared for her with a fear that sank claws deep into his bowels, he tried again. "What happened to your concern for *my* skin?"

"You will make the attempt no matter what," she said shrewdly. "If I go with you, pretending to be Elizabeth, you'll at least have a chance of surviving. Besides, when I think of sharing your danger, it does not seem as great. Does that make sense?"

"None," he replied bluntly. "Kat, I will not have it. When all is said and done, James does not deserve your taking this kind of chance. He's not unjustly imprisoned. The man's guilty."

"It was your dream," she pointed out. "You thought of this first, you know you did."

"Well . . ." He grinned reluctantly. "It is a splendid plan. But *no,* Kat. I'll think of another way."

That afternoon, he politely changed a laugh into a cough when he came to their bedchamber and caught her removing screwed-up rag scraps from her hair. She put her hands up to hide what she was doing, and he turned in the door, blocking Samuel, who was behind him.

"I was wrong," he said. "The documents I want you to carry to London must be elsewhere. When I find them I'll send for you."

"As you wish, my lord," answered Samuel, as placid as ever.

She'd need more time to get rid of the evidence that she curled her hair, Robin thought indulgently. He wracked his brain for something else to say to Samuel that would delay his own entry into the room and give Kat a few moments.

"Ah, I almost forgot. Why did you bide here instead of searching me out to tell me of the straits your lady was in?"

Samuel looked quietly astonished. "Your lordship told me to stay at Priorly and watch over Lady Katherine. I did."

"It did not hurt that Maud was here rather than somewhere else."

"No, my lord, it did not."

Robin gave an unwilling chuckle and dismissed his henchman.

He knocked before walking in. Mischievously, he said, "Damask lady, I find you enchanting whether your curls are natural or . . ."

He got a good look at her, and the desire to tease her over an endearing bit of feminine frailty evaporated.

"Ordinarily I leave my hair to curl by itself," she said through stiff lips, "but the wave nature gave me is not tight enough to give the right effect. What is your opinion?"

Kat's heart pounded. The illusion was as complete as she could make it.

"That's the way Elizabeth wears her hair. And the ugly gown she gave you. Is that paint you have smeared on your face?" Robin's expression could have been carved in stone.

"Not ceruse," she said quickly. She hadn't forgotten his objections to the harsh cosmetic. "I made it out of oils and powder. The pink for the cheeks and lips as well as the green for my eyelids come from harmless plants. The stuff rubs off at a touch, but I am hoping it will last long enough. Will I pass as Elizabeth?"

"It is uncanny. For a moment . . ."

"We have to go to London and get James out without delay. Soon it will be too late for me to play my part. I am almost swooning in this corset. I have gotten too fat."

"You are not fat. You are pregnant!"

"With a child whose uncle is in prison awaiting a death sentence. Our babe would want to help James, too."

Hands on hips, he strode around her in a complete circle, inspecting her ruthlessly. "Your voice," he said coldly. "It is soft and sweet. The queen's is—"

"Changeable. Sometimes deep and hoarse." Kat spoke with a low, rough edge. "Sometimes crisp and manlike." She barked the words. "Sometimes sugary." The too-dulcet tones of an aging coquette sounded cloying to her.

"Too bad women do not go on the stage. You could make your fortune." His admiration sounded unwilling but real.

"You are all the fortune I ever wanted," she told him in her own voice. "You and a babe."

"I am aware I offered to buy your affections by doing this. Do not remind me." He sounded tired, almost defeated.

"Robin, I am doing this because I am your best chance of success. If you give up this insanity, and swear you will not go near the Tower, I will cut this gown into ribbons and never paint my face again. But if you are going into the Tower, I will do anything to get you out alive."

"Even with you disguised as the queen, our chances are slim."

The baby moved. *I am sorry, little one,* Kat apologized to it. *We must go keep your brave idiot of a father safe. It is your foolish mother's fault he's pushing himself into deadly peril.*

"Try to sneak off and do this without me and I will follow you, Robin."

"And God alone knows what might befall you on the way," he muttered. "You win. Be ready to travel tomorrow at first light. We'll dress plainly and put up at a quiet inn when we reach London. I'll need a day or two to get in, see James, and then acquire a suitable body."

She moistened her lips. They were sticky with rouge. "A body?"

"We have to leave a corpse in James's place. Or do you expect the jailers not to notice that his cell will otherwise be empty?"

"Oh. Oh, Robin."

"And now for God's sake take off that gown and put it away until we need it again. It reminds me of what the queen of Scots wore to her execution." He closed his eyes. Without the pale, alive glance lighting his face, it was obvious that the skin beneath the beard was drawn taut and tense. "The color of—"

He didn't finish, but she took his meaning. Kat, too, had always considered garnet-red to be the color of blood.

A hired barge slid up to the Tower's water gate. The change in the motion of the deck, from smooth forward motion to a gentle bobbing, roused Kat from a light doze. She blinked and remembered just in time not to touch her face, which was stiff with her homemade cosmetics.

An ingenious covered litter enclosed her. From outside it came Robin's command. "Lift your end carefully— carefully!"

The sensation of rising into the air followed, and she knew Robin and Samuel were settling the litter on their shoulders. Robin hadn't told her where he'd found the queen's livery they wore under long cloaks. Or the source of the piteous contents of the rug bundled under her tall-heeled shoes.

The closed curtains were to keep her supposed identity

a secret from the barge crew. Once inside the Tower, she would have to be "Elizabeth"; for now the fewer who saw her the better. Kat took advantage of the interval to whisper a prayer for the poor dead man they intended to leave here. Robin hadn't let her glimpse the corpse, but he'd assured her it would fool the guards.

"They'll expect it to be James, so they will not give it more than a glance," he'd explained, looking grimmer than ever after scouring the hospitals.

A shouted challenge hurt her ears. She twitched the curtains aside and stuck her head out. "Who interferes with our progress?" she shrilled.

Bearded mouths fell open, then snapped shut. A gaudily dressed officer stepped forward and bowed deeply.

Before he could speak, Kat added in a perfect copy of Tudor irritation, "God's death, it matters not. Let us go on."

Whipping the curtains shut, she sank back and put her hand on her chest. Right through the cruel binding that had been necessary to squeeze her ripening body into a thin shape, she could feel her heart beating so hard that for a frantic moment she was afraid it would leap into her palm.

Be calm, she thought. Do not recall the babe in danger of losing its mother. Do not think how Robin risks his lands, honor, and life in a cause that's yours, not his. Just remember that you are Elizabeth, and you have a right to ramble about the Tower of London at midnight if the whimsy takes you.

From the other side of the curtains, Robin was saying, "Her majesty wishes to inspect one of the prisoners. Her majesty does not wish her presence here remembered. Very—unpleasant—things will happen if talkative rogues speak of this visit. It never took place. Is my meaning clear?"

Several strangled-sounding *ayes* answered him. The litter resumed its steady pace. She wondered how long the ambergris which impregnated the gloves that completed her costume would linger on her skin. The scent was almost overpowering.

Not only was the perfume Elizabeth's favorite, but it masked competing odors. She shrank from the rug.

As the litter traveled through the series of buildings and courtyards that made up the Tower, Robin murmured for her ears, "We are leaving St. Thomas's Tower ... going through the Bloody Tower ... by the White Tower ... around barracks ... This is Flint Tower. It has the darkest dungeons and the dankest cells. James is being held here. Hold yourself ready."

Kat redoubled her prayers. Pieces of old rituals mingled with pieces of new. She hoped God didn't mind.

Metal scraped metal and then hinges shrieked as a heavy door was dragged open. The litter sank to the floor with a subdued thud. Robin helped her out.

Her first thought was that rats couldn't live in a place like this, let alone human beings. It was small, cold, very wet, *very* dirty. There was no air, just a miasma of waste and disease.

Samuel blocked the doorway, facing out, and Robin held a lantern over a pile of rags in one corner, illuminating it.

"*God.* James."

Her brother blinked uncertainly. "Lord Robin came yesterday and said you were going to try to get me out, but I could scarcely credit it. Is that you, my dear? I hesitate to wound your feelings, but if you have been using a new beauty treatment, 'tis not effective."

"Neither is yours." No wonder Robin hadn't been worried about matching the corpse to James. His lower face was bushy with beard, and as for the rest of him, one death's head attached to a skeleton would look much like another. But ...

"What of the injuries?" she said to Robin, unable to control the horror in her voice. "How will his keepers miss the fact that they are missing from the—the body?"

"It's been taken care of, my—Your Grace," Samuel grunted.

Robin didn't look at her.

She had to blot tears. It would be a disaster if her powder streaked. No one would believe Elizabeth had wept over a traitor.

Her regret wasn't just for James or the thing they had brought to take his place. It was for her husband.

Robin pushed past her to pick up James's emaciated form and gently place him to one side so he could empty the rug over the pallet of soiled straw. Kat forced herself to look at what fell out. The damage inflicted on James's person had been copied on the corpse. It was her fault that Robin had once more been forced to use knowledge he hated. She shuddered. Glancing away, her eyes accidentally clashed with Robin's. His were empty.

What have I done by showing I hoped James could be rescued? she wondered. What have I done to Robin? He walked away from a brutal profession, and I pushed him back into it. What have I done?

He began stripping the rags from her brother and dressing the body in them. Kat wrapped James in a clean shirt and then crouched next to him until Robin completed his task.

"A moment," James said. "Where did that poor wretch come from?"

"I did not kill him to provide you with a twin, if that's what you imply," responded Robin without inflection. He was withdrawing into that emptiness, Kat thought. "The body came from St. Katherine's Hospital a stone's throw from here. You—and he—may rest easy. He was already dead of a lingering illness when I relieved the grave-digger of the immediate necessity of a burial. It wasn't a fever or pox or plague that took him. Kat's in no danger—from that, anyway."

"I cannot give him last rites, but I must offer a prayer for his soul."

"Do it on our way out of here."

Efficiently, he rolled James into the carpet and deposited the sausage shape on the floor of the litter. Because Kat couldn't get to the bench in the litter without stepping on her brother, he picked her up and plopped her onto the cushion. Her hands fastened on his upper arms and didn't want to let go.

"I am so frightened, Robin," she whispered. For him.

"The rest is nothing. We have only to stroll out and gain the safety of the river. I wish I could kiss you, Your Majesty."

"My face would come off." She had to be strong for

him. Though her heart was breaking, she forced a carefree note into her voice. "I thank you for the offer, though."

She tucked her feet where they wouldn't rest on James, because she doubted there was an inch of him that hadn't been brutalized in some way. Do not think of his pain, or the danger to Robin and the babe, she reminded herself again. To think would be to feel, and she had to be hard and glittering. She had to be Elizabeth. With hurried movements she straightened her skirts and the winged veil that rose behind the hair piled high on her head.

"I am ready. James? How are your accomodations?"

"Delightful," came the faint reply. "A vast improvement over Tudor hospitality."

Robin closed the curtains. "Let's go. No more talking."

As he and Samuel retraced their steps, time crawled with even more excruciating slowness than before, although her heart still beat so fast her fingertips tingled. Her legs ached with the need to keep them braced against the tall baseboard so her heels wouldn't land on James.

As soon as they left Flint Tower, the sound of marching feet joined them; additional guards were falling in, she guessed. The Tower authorities must be all aquiver over this unusual visit.

The noise, or her own nervousness, had the babe inside her in an uproar. There was nothing else for "Elizabeth" to do unless they were challenged again, so she put both her hands to her compressed middle and let herself feel the fusillade of tiny kicks.

The babe's activity was wonderfully reassuring. Her tight corseting didn't seem to be bothering it at all. A strong and healthy child—a boy? Robin hadn't indicated in any way that he would be less pleased with a girl. Her own father had been fair-haired and gray-eyed; with a blond father and grandfather, perhaps this infant would have Robin's beautiful coloring. The litter glided forward, and she dreamed of Robin's child.

Trouble erupted all at once. There was a quick tap of footsteps, which she heard because they were out of step with the marching feet.

"Your Majesty! Majesty, have mercy—"

The curtains dragged open. She heard Robin spit a barn-

yard oath. The frame beneath her hit the floor. Then he
was on the side she could see, wrestling with a much
smaller man.

"Master Davison!"

She was so surprised her exclamation emerged as a
croak. The former secretary of state twisted in Robin's
grasp, staring at her full in the face. One of her husband's
long arms was slung all the way around his opponent's
neck, with his palm over Davison's mouth and his fingers
hard around Davison's jaw. A quick jerk and the neck
would be broken.

It would be an easier death than the one Davison had
condemned James to undergo when he'd agreed with
Paulet's decision to send her brother here. From his appearance, the bombastic little man hadn't suffered any ill
treatment; he was richly dressed. The same fortune that
was keeping velvet on his shoulders and jeweled rings on
his fingers would be buying him tender care from his jailers. For a horrifying, liberating instant Kat hated the man.
His pomposity. His arrogance. His casual barbarism. He
was like Sir Henry Toth in the way he disposed of other
people's lives. It would feel good to watch him die.

Power. This was how power felt. The woman she was
pretending to be had traded love for this dark enjoyment.

Robin said, "Your Majesty?" His coolness reminded her
of things he'd had to do in the world where the maintenance of power meant men had to die. He'd done the dirty
work that kept the dance of power going. At the wrong
word from either her or Davison, he would kill.

"Hold," she said, her voice shaking. "Do you recognize
us?"

Davison's eyes flickered. He knew. She could tell.

"Are you standing in our way?"

Inside Robin's unloving embrace, he shook his head.

So low only Kat and Davison could hear, Robin said,
"Why should we trust you?" He freed the mouth under his
hand by a hairsbreadth to hear the reply.

"Trust is not a common virtue," gasped Davison. "But
you may have trust in me. My loyalty has always gone to
those who take care of me—Your Grace."

Robin considered. He didn't like leaving loose ends that

could be twisted into a noose for Kat's neck. Or his own, for that matter. But snapping Davison's spine would make the eventual discovery that a false Elizabeth had been in the Tower inevitable. And . . . foolish as it was, he didn't want to add to the horrors he'd already committed preparing for the escape. It had killed him, a little, to have Kat see that mauled body.

Slowly Robin let him go.

"By her grace's leave, we'll be on our way," said Robin very quietly. He looked at his wife. "And I for one intend never to return."

The rest of the escape went according to plan. Kat scrubbed off the paint and clawed her way out of Elizabeth's gown while still in the litter, but she didn't breathe normally until the ship they put James on sailed away on the tide.

"Will he live to see France?" she asked Robin, as the masts disappeared into the distance.

"His wounds are bad ones, but I hope so. You did what you could for him."

"So did you. Let's go home, my lord."

"You go. Samuel will take care of you on the road. I think I will inspect the other properties the queen deeded to me."

"Robin?"

She stood on tiptoe to kiss him, but he stepped back from her. Before he turned away, she saw that his eyes were still empty.

Chapter 25

Sawdust choked the air. So did the hearty curses of working men.

"My lady," said Jedidiah Pettigrew plaintively, "are ye sure ye want all this fine oak destroyed? 'Tis wanton waste—"

"All," Kat answered firmly. "Rid me of every splinter."

Samuel gave the steward a buffet on the shoulder before he attacked a paneled wall with an ax. "Breeding women are like nesting birds," he advised. "Be relieved it is just one room my lady wants changed." Since his wedding to Maud he'd grinned occasionally, as he did now.

It was a tiny but genuine grin, full of amusement at life. His wife had turned out not to be beyond childbearing age. Some of the manor folk called Maud's pregnancy witchcraft, others the intervention of saints out of favor with reformers. Horrified by both explanations, the chaplain, Master Lewes, had produced the register of births to prove that Maud was a mere three-and-forty. On this late April day, the center of the controversy stood next to Kat with an arm around her mistress. Her belly was two months smaller than Kat's, but both were noticeably rounded.

"Lord Robin will not like it when he finds the paneling gone," Pettigrew warned.

Kat surveyed the ruin of the withdrawing room with satisfaction. The priest's hole was open to the light. She intended to have the resulting alcove fitted with shelves. They would do to display some of the collection of bowls she'd begun to amass. Fancifully carved wood, shining metal, precious glass. It took a great many containers to hold the fruit Robin liked to find in every room he passed through during the day.

There was something like spring, the season of new life, in using the priest's hole for a pleasant, homely purpose.

"I promise you, my lord will not mind," said Kat.

If he ever came home.

There had been letters. They would have been brief to the point of insult except that they invariably began, *To my dearest and most beloved wife,* and ended, *From thy faithful husband.* Each mentioned where he was writing from, but by the time her messengers went back with her response, he was gone without saying where. In one note, he called her "damask lady," and that was the one she reread most often. It was like hearing his voice.

After supervising the progress in the withdrawing room a while longer, Kat said, "Samuel, be sure to tell me when the last of the paneling is off. I shall want to inspect the walls with the plasterer."

She wandered into the kitchen garden with its rows of herbs and vegetable plants. Spring was here in earnest.

Hidden in the folds of her plain skirt were Robin's letters. Her secret vice, she scolded herself. The way other pathetic creatures craved strong drink or perverse excitements, she pined for the sight of his bold, slanted writing.

It was never enough. Kat knew it wasn't her nature to enjoy being discontented. Everyday pleasures had always suited her temperament, and here she was in possession of more than she'd ever imagined would be hers. Priorly safe, a lovely spring, the delight of a babe kicking—not gently anymore—under her heart. The respect of her neighbors had returned as soon as news of her wedding spread over the countryside. Even Francis Toth had called.

His reason was to inform her of the sad fact that James had been found dead in his cell at the Tower. She'd been on tenterhooks, terrified that the substitution had been uncovered and Francis was taking a typically long time to announce that she and Robin were under attainder for aiding a traitor. But instead he'd eaten all of the sweetmeats hospitality forced her to offer and informed her that he had recently become betrothed. Kat listened to him enumerate his intended bride's rather tedious virtues with patience, and vowed to send the girl a very expensive wedding gift as consolation for getting Francis.

Reestablishing neighborly relations with Francis might not belong on anyone's list of blessings, she admitted to herself, running the ribbon she'd used to tie the letters together through her fingers. At least she was no longer sickened by his resemblance to his father. The old memories had lost their hold.

Robin had done that for her. There were plenty of reasons to be thankful. And surely—surely!—Robin would return in time for the babe to be born. He'd been pleased about becoming a father, awestruck almost. Even if he hated her for her desire to save James, he would come back for the birth.

She remembered his wicked play on the word *come* and her fingers tensed. It had shocked her that as her sickness waned and the pregnancy advanced, she missed love play more, not less. With time the shock faded, but the desires remained to trouble and titillate her.

"Robin, damn you, where have you gone?" she said out loud, scuffing her foot in the grassy walk to relieve some of her frustration.

"Here."

She spun around. He more than filled the arbor that led into the garden, which hadn't been built to accommodate a man of his height. His beautiful clothes were rumpled, as usual. Familiar golden stubble showed on his cheeks over his beard. His eyes were very bright. But they weren't empty anymore. As he stared at her round middle, they shone with fierce feeling.

Because she was at a loss, she said at random, "We shall have to get that arbor replaced so you do not have to bend to enter."

"Am I welcome to stay, then?"

All Kat could do was stand, holding his letters to her breast, and let him wash over her senses. Her breath shortened. Her blood raced. Behind and above his head of unruly curls, the Maypole rose in preparation for the dancing and feasting that were only days in the future.

"I tried to stay away. I know I must disgust you."

"How do you know that?" she asked, still dazed, filling her eyes with him. A gray-striped puddle flowed around her feet, but for once she had no time for Grimalkin.

"Can you think of my hands touching you and not remember what else they have done?"

She walked toward him slowly. He braced himself on the flimsy latticework sides of the arbor.

"My lord, I have always known about the way you made your living. You never lied or hid anything from me. It was I who kept secrets from you. Why should I suddenly make judgments?"

"You had not seen my handiwork before," he said tiredly. Letting go of the lattice, he wavered on his feet.

"You are overspent," she said in alarm. As quickly as the bulk at her middle allowed, she hurried forward to put an arm around his waist. "How long have you been traveling without sleep?"

"Two—no, this is the third day. I was making excuses to myself to stay away, and then I could not anymore and . . ."

"Hush. Do not think of it now." His weight would have overbalanced her as well as him, but he made a heroic effort and straightened until she could lead him to a bench, where they both started to collapse.

Her haven by the feet she knew best disrupted, Grimalkin dashed between their legs into some bushes. Kat sat down with a thump.

"That animal is always underfoot," Robin said, pulling away from her arm but slumping beside her.

"Cats are like that. So are children. Will you mind?"

"I will try to be a better father than mine was. If you'll let me stay."

"Aye. Please."

They sat side by side, not touching.

"Kat, you do not have to cling to me every minute of the day," Robin said with the terrible patience he had shown her ever since he'd returned to Priorly. It reminded her of the unfailing gentleness that had marked the time when he couldn't look at her without remembering her rape. "All is well. Your suitor—"

"Former suitor, I'll thank you to remember."

"Sir Francis haunts the place because he wrongly believes we are in good odor with the queen. He is satisfied that James is dead. More importantly, so is Elizabeth. This letter from my cousin—" He waved it in the air. "—mentions not a word of an investigation. Believe me, if there were any suspicion, he would be quick to say so. Sick or well, Burghley has never been stingy with bad news. There's nothing to worry you. You do not need to chase me with big, sad eyes for fear that the worst is about to happen."

"James is really safe?" she asked, looking down self-consciously.

"He's in France, being cossetted by a convent-full of nuns who consider him a living saint. A message was passed to me in Lancashire where my manor to the north lies." He grimaced.

"What is it?" Kat rose from her chair in the newly plastered withdrawing room and joined him by a window. After four nights' sleep, his strength of body and mind was obviously fully restored. He rode, walked, threw himself into any work on the estate she asked of him. Fully restored, Kat thought—except for the not minor fact that he never touched her.

"I always imagined myself saying *my manor* with pride. I worked so long to become propertied. But the lands are only my reward for burying Elizabeth's secrets so deep that other princes will never discover them. Dishonor piled on dishonor."

"Believe me, my lord, there is no harder occupation than keeping the lands in good heart and taking care of the people on them. You will earn your estates ten times over."

He smiled reluctantly. "Riches do not make up for losing . . . other things."

Kat's hand went out to caress him of its own will. She would have stopped if she could. Every time she made an advance toward him, no matter how innocent or unseductive, the result was the same. He stiffened and avoided her.

It happened again; he stepped back. The movement wasn't obtrusive and it was almost excessively polite. If she hadn't known better—if he hadn't made it clear over the course of several days that he no longer wanted her—she would have assumed he was clearing a space so she could look out the window at the pretty scene below.

Men and maids ran to and fro on the green. The younger people were tying a rainbow of ribbons to the Maypole for the dancing that would accompany dinner, while their elders laughed at them from seats on the grass.

But she did know better. Whatever loneliness had brought him back to Priorly, it certainly hadn't cleansed him of the resentment he must feel for her.

And why should it? she asked herself. It was her fault, all hers, that he'd been drawn into Priorly's treasonous affairs. He could have walked away from bloodletting months ago had it not been for her. Something had brought him back. Perhaps it was no more than the deep, driving need for a human warmth his own kin had never provided. But one thing was sure. It hadn't been love. Despite what he'd said about not being able to stay away, he wasn't even sharing their bed.

"I do not blame you for hating me," she said. "Only, please, I beg of you, do not let your feelings about me affect the way you treat our child. After all, the babe was conceived when we were—easier—with each other."

His thick brows twitched together. "Hate you? Kat?"

"I am glad you no longer have to earn your living in a way you despise. If I am sad, it is because I kept you dealing with treason. And I do not deserve it, but can you at least say you understand why I refused to make love? It was not to force you into helping James."

"Of course I know that. I had hoped if I could give you a life for a life—James for Charles—then the scales would be even and we could live in peace with each other. That was stupid." Hunger, quickly suppressed, flashed in his eyes.

A joy so huge it was absolutely preposterous grew in her. "Stupid? Why?"

"Because to get you James I had to show you the results of my work."

"Robin," she said slowly, "let me see if I understand properly. You desired me, laid claim to me, married me in the teeth of royalty, and now you are positive that I hate you. I underestimated you, feared you, desired you, wed you, and have been imagining you hate me."

"Wench, you are making a mockery of my tenderest feelings," he said. His gaze had narrowed to glittering slits.

"How is it that before I gave myself to you, I was your 'damask lady,' and since then I have been reduced to 'wench'? *Do* you have tender feelings toward me?"

"How could you doubt I have feelings for you, woman?"

" 'Woman' is better than 'wench,' " she told him. "I suppose I have doubts because you never once told me so."

"Well, you have never said it, either!" he burst out.

Her Robin was *so* tall and *so* handsome, she thought with another spurt of that incredulous joy, he couldn't really look menacing even when he glared at her. At least, not to her. Not anymore.

"I did tell you once. You did not hear."

"And you never repeated it?" he yelled furiously.

"Are you shouting at me?"

"I am telling you I love you!"

"And I believe it," she assured him. "Only the truest, purest love could bellow a declaration like that."

He snapped his beautifully etched mouth closed. Below his beard she could see the muscles in his strong throat constrict as he swallowed. "How did this become a jest?"

"A jest of great importance. Do you realize this is the first time since Whitehall you have shouted at me? Normal people do not live in an atmosphere of high drama. They do not tread so lightly around each other's feelings that they cannot tell if the other has any. They argue and make love—"

"Kat, you cannot complain I have never made love to you," he said, looking at her figure. "Nor that we have never argued."

"I love it when we fight." Tears stung and welled over. "I love it when you touch me. I love *you*. If you have stayed away for the better part of two months because you do not know that—then, my clever former agent of the queen, you *are* stupid."

Walking with the careful dignity of a pregnant woman, she went to the door and paused.

"We have both been injured by violence. Not just I, but you also. We both carried our burden of secrets as if they were the most important things about us. The hurting is over, and the secrets are all harmless because we have shared them. I was wrong not to make love with you on our wedding night. But I was not blaming you when I denied you, Robin."

"Are you sure?" He could scarcely believe it.

"It was just—too soon to let go of my grief. I spent so many years holding everything together for my kin. After Fotheringhay, I could not help Charles because he was dead. I had to try to *fix* things for James. As brothers go they were almost worthless, but the habits of love are hard to break."

Feeling as if he'd been butted by an ox, he stared at her. "Do you think loving me could become a habit?"

"It already is. Let me finish. You did only what you had to regarding my brothers and far less than the strict letter of the law," she went on firmly. "The guilt was mine for thinking the past was as important as the future. I let my shame be more important to me than *us*. The only thing there should be between us is love, and it should bind us together, not cut like a sword that keeps us apart."

The light in his hawk's eyes was a hopeful sign, Kat thought. Very hopeful. She didn't try to conceal the smile that was tugging at the corners of her mouth as she continued out the door.

"Where are you going?" he demanded with an edge to his voice. It was the harshness of urgency, and she almost laughed aloud.

"Outside." She didn't look back. "I am tired of making love only in dark and secret places, are not you, my love?"

Going with care down the spiral stairs, she repeated to herself in wonder, "My love. My love. I have a love." Her middle wasn't immense yet, but it sat solidly between her and the sight of the next few steps. She slowed even more.

Under emotional duress, she'd placed the baby in peril once; she wasn't going to do so again.

Quick steps sounded behind her. There wasn't even time for the single flash of fear she felt to rip completely through her before she recognized Robin's footfall. Then he was abreast of her and sweeping her into his arms.

"You came for me," she said triumphantly.

He grinned. "Not quite. Where shall we go to repair the omission?"

Her arms tightened enthusiastically around his neck and her hair tumbled out of its kerchief. The scent of gilly-flowers whispered over him. He stopped at the bottom of the stairs to rub his face in the soft russet mass. "Your hair is like silk," he said thickly. "My damask lady."

Her chuckle delighted him. The assurance underlying it was entirely new in his experience of Kat.

"Your increasingly plump lady," she said. "I hope you are as pleased with me as you seem to think you will be. As I recall, you had hard words once for thick bottoms."

He hefted her. "Ah, but from what I can tell, your bottom is as shapely and sweet as ever." The arms supporting her shifted so he could run his hand knowingly over her upper chest. "Here there are some changes, however."

"To your taste, my lord?" she asked in a suddenly silken voice.

His own gust of laughter caught him by surprise, and he leaned against the wall as he guffawed, hugging her soft body to him. How long had it been since he'd laughed out loud?

"I am not such a fool as to answer that question, except to say you are always and in every way to my taste, Kat Hawking. It is you who compares apples to melons, not I. Now, where shall we go?"

"You'll give me a choice?" she asked, feigning shock. "This overindulgence in one so newly married is very lax. You should start as you mean to go on."

"If I start right here," he threatened with a wide grin, "the servants will have a sight not commonly afforded to them, and one of us will have pleats down the back from being pressed into the stairs."

"Then I choose the soft grass and soft light outside."

Cradling his wife in his arms, Robin strode with a swagger out the side door and into the green freshness. The strumming of a lute broke off mid-melody. The manor folk froze, then shuffled their feet as the master carried the mistress into their midst.

A flush brightened Kat's cheeks. Robin dropped a kiss on her nose.

"My lady and I," he announced in the spreading hush, "require the use of the green. A dinner with delicacies for all is set out in the hall. Open the cellar so the feast may be merry. Enjoy it! The May dancing will take place after."

The grin just wouldn't leave his face, but he watched closely to make sure every serving man and wench, milkmaid, clerk, shepherd, huntsman, brewer, baker, and scullion-at-large trooped away toward the promised meal.

"Robin, you just gave over a hundred thirsty gullets permission to drink the cellar dry," Kat protested.

"Yes, was it not clever of me? It will take them hours." He set her on her feet and walked her backward until her spine met the Maypole.

A breeze whipped ribbons around them in a waterfall of colors. He touched one and looked at Kat thoughtfully.

"Hours?"

"Does my lady object?"

"N-nay." Her eyes grew larger as he took a handful of the ribbons and walked around her. He went in a complete circle, stealing kisses, grazing the tips of her breasts and her belly with the backs of his hands, binding her loosely to the towering pole. "Robin—"

"You were a very, very pretty girl at court," he interrupted. Tucking the ends of the ribbons into a perfunctory knot, he uncoiled her hair and loosed it to the wind. "From the night I had the good fortune to find you in my bed hangings, I could not take my eyes from you," he murmured softly. "But here in the country is your place. Everything about you is exquisite in the way of pure, natural things. Your skin is the damask of roses, your hair the glowing brown of chestnuts. Of gillyflowers." Some of the cinnamon-colored petals clustered near a wall. He picked them and scattered them in her hair. "You are as irresistible as . . . England."

"You have been able to resist me. For two months," she reminded him, but her eyes were roaming his face with the same hunger he could feel in himself. An hot ache had already started low, low in his body. It simmered and made him hard and ready.

"Never for long," he replied. "Are you sure you wish for a true marriage, Kat? I saw you and wanted you and forced myself on you—"

"That's nonsense!" she exclaimed, standing up straight inside the ribbons. "You did not force me!"

"I did not let you go, either, sweet heart," he reminded her.

She ducked her head, smiling. "Aye, well, after a while I did not want you to let me go."

"My reputation—"

"I had barely seen you across the room before I was hearing about your reputation." She surveyed the soft chains that held her. "What are these, you idiot, a test to see if I suffer from curiosity about your prowess with ropes?"

Relief hurtled through him at the amused tilt of her delicate brows. It put to rest once and for all his last lingering doubt—not about her, but about his need to prove his normality. "I do not think we need any trashy adjuncts to make our loving more exciting, do you?" he asked smoothly.

"Nay, my darling. If it is as exciting as last time, I'll be fortunate to survive such pleasure," she answered frankly.

On the word *pleasure,* he kissed her with lips and tongue and nips from his teeth. She laughed and kissed him back, wriggling against the satiny constraints. "Robin, darling, release my arms so I can hold you."

He chose a black ribbon and pulled it from the knot. "This is memory," he said.

Unwound, it fluttered in the breeze.

With deft sleight of hand, Robin slipped the laces to the upper part of her gown out of their holes. "You have such lovely eyes. I knew they were pretty even before I realized how delectable the rest of you is, too." He freed a green

Maypole ribbon. "This is fear. So much fear was bound up in our memories. But we can remember only the good times, Kat. And whatever life sends to frighten us, at least we can face it together."

A red ribbon was anger, a blue one grief. "All our feelings were tied up in secrets," he murmured, abandoning the one remaining ribbon that tied Kat to the Maypole so he could unhook her wide-waisted skirts. The single white ribbon still wrapped around her held the now-detached parts of her gown more or less in place. "We can let them go now."

"Aye," she whispered yearningly. Opening her arms, she pushed the last ribbon away. Every stitch she wore except her smock fell to the grass.

"Oh! Robin, you—you lecher! How knew you how to do that?"

"I have been dreaming of undressing you for weeks."

Her comical outrage was balm to his soul. It didn't distract him from sliding the smock over her head; the pulsebeat of desire was too urgent in his loins. The sight of her body so voluptuous with their child brought him to his knees. He rested his forehead lightly on the roundness that proclaimed the reality of their lovemaking.

He had to finish what he'd started. "Secrets cannot be erased," he said, throwing back his head. "But neither of us has to remain knotted up in them forever. Was it enough to give you a life for a life?"

"My darling, the life I carry inside me came from you. If I had not been half-mad from grief and guilt myself, I would have seen I owe my allegiance to us—thee and me and the babe." Her hand touched his hair. "Are we talking instead of embracing because the way I look now is not pleasing to you? I would understand—"

He groaned and pulled her down so they lay side by side. "I'll show you how not pleased I am, damask lady." His hand led hers to the throbbing center of his need.

The small, happy sound she made in her throat almost undid his resolution to be completely honest. He had to detach her fingers with more firmness than he intended. Kissing them in apology, he studied her face in a sidelong, speculative glance. "There's one more secret to air."

"Now?" she wailed. "Robin, can we not just be happy together for once? Please. The plots and conniving can wait."

Her lips were red and parted, the tips of her breasts pouted at him. Since he'd seen them last, the nipples had grown from little apple blossoms to crowns of a deeply sensual rose. "The rest can wait," he agreed.

He sat up and with jerky, determined movements rid himself of his clothes. As soon as he'd shoved his hose off his ankles, Kat sat astride his hips and ran her fingers over his shoulders, his back, his chest. The hard flesh standing between them strained higher.

"Do you desire to make love sitting?" he asked into her hair. God's grace, she smelled so good. He touched her where he knew she liked it, and she gasped.

"The grass tickled," Kat managed to say. "And the babe . . ."

"Ah, yes, the babe is of such a size we have to be careful." The softness of the curls between her legs was tickling *him,* and beckoned powerfully. Need pounded through him so fiercely he could scarcely talk, let alone hold them both up. He lay on his back in the grass. His fevered skin felt the prickles as increased stimulation. "It will not hurt the babe for you to be atop, will it? Sleep, babe. What your parents do really is not any of your business . . ."

Kat took him inside her.

He tried to discipline himself to enjoy her tightness and heat without allowing the sensations to push him into finishing. Five months' worth of loneliness clamored for release. He concentrated on the ends of the ribbons as they danced around her smooth white shoulders, and he told himself they would distract him enough to keep control. His body didn't believe it. He groaned. Every second was brimful of such raging need he thought his next breath would break into a shout of climax.

She leaned over him, and moisture broke out between their bodies, lubricating the slide of her breasts over the hair that covered his chest. Long russet hair fell across his mouth. He bit it, and even that was unbearably erotic.

Kat wanted the pleasure of being joined to last forever. But her restless heat wouldn't slow down for a long, drawn-out loving. It flared higher, and her hips plunged as the rest of her undulated against him, trying to feel as much of Robin at one time as she could. And then the heat peaked in hot spasms of pleasure that pulled a scream from her before she relaxed, gasping, on his broad chest.

Robin's hands grasped her buttocks and worked them in a furious rhythm that matched the thrusts of his own body. As his pleasure spilled, it renewed Kat's. This time the wonderful sensation rippled through her in warm waves that carried her naturally into sleep.

When she woke, she was lying clutched to his side by one long arm. His other arm pillowed his head.

"Husband?" Kat liked the lazy sound of the word as it left her lips. She smiled at the ribbons swaying above.

"Wife," he acknowledged, turning his head to grin crookedly at her. "Have you taken any hurt?"

"The babe seems to be as boisterous as ever. Look. You can see it kick." They both watched a small bulge appear and then lie smooth. "And certainly I am feeling better than I have in months and months. Should we make ourselves presentable so the May dancing can begin?"

"We must talk, Kat."

She remembered he had a secret still to tell. Sitting up, she dredged her smock from the pile of disgarded garments. "Do not tell me. Let it be. I am afraid of a secret you would bring up when we—at such a time."

"Damask lady, you are the most courageous person I have ever met. I am the one who should be quaking with fear. I have you, Kat." He knelt and took her by the shoulders. "Finally I have you, but this news could make you slip away from me. And I would have to let you go, because I have cheated you."

Her fists clenched in the linen. A little part of her started to die, but she said, "A woman? Or women? I do not like it, but I understand. We were apart a long time and there must have been many temptations to a man as virile as you ..."

For once his eyes were wide and startled. "Kat, I do not want you to be—complaisant. I want you to be a jealous shrew and *care* whether I am faithful. There has not been any other woman. I have not even looked—" A self-conscious expression creased his face. "Well, in Dover perhaps I looked."

"As long as that's all you did ..." she revived. "I suppose you had better explain what is bothering you. Cheated how?"

He released her shoulders and picked up his own shirt.

"I did not do it only for my sake. It was for you. And the child."

"How noble of you, my lord. Did what?" She pulled on the smock and then shook the pieces of her bodice in the hope some of the wrinkles would disappear. If Robin hadn't been romping abed with someone else, Kat wasn't sure she could manufacture concern over his confession. Languor filled her limbs. She felt thoroughly loved.

"Elizabeth did not order us to marry."

Her hands stilled. "We wed without permission? Mercy God, Robin, she'll clap you in the Tower. She'll get some surgeon to make you into a eunuch and send you as a present to the Sultan of the Turks. She'll—"

"We had permission," he soothed.

"But not a command." She let Robin take the bodice and lace it over her sides. "You tricked me!"

He expelled a hard breath. "Yes."

"Well, you must really have wanted to marry me, then."

His predator's eyes met hers. "Yes."

Kat couldn't look away. The queen's—hawk. Robin wasn't a low form of life, was not a *rat catcher*. She was country-bred, and knew that while hunting birds often were satisfied with small prey, they also sought more worthy adversaries. Robin had been determined to have ... her.

"Since you desired to catch me, it is good I had an equal desire to be caught."

A blue ribbon waved close to her shoulder. Pulling it forward, she brushed the end of it over his cheek.

"No more secrets, Robin Hawking."

The silver-bright eyes dazzled her. "We'll live lives of surpassing dullness. I promise you, damask lady."

She laughed at him, while the ribbons danced on the wind.

Avon Romances—
the best in exceptional authors and unforgettable novels!

LORD OF MY HEART Jo Beverley
76784-8/$4.50 US/$5.50 Can

BLUE MOON BAYOU Katherine Compton
76412-1/$4.50 US/$5.50 Can

SILVER FLAME Hannah Howell
76504-7/$4.50 US/$5.50 Can

TAMING KATE Eugenia Riley
76475-X/$4.50 US/$5.50 Can

THE LION'S DAUGHTER Loretta Chase
76647-7/$4.50 US/$5.50 Can

CAPTAIN OF MY HEART Danelle Harmon
76676-0/$4.50 US/$5.50 Can

BELOVED INTRUDER Joan Van Nuys
76476-8/$4.50 US/$5.50 Can

SURRENDER TO THE FURY Cara Miles
76452-0/$4.50 US/$5.50 Can

Coming Soon

SCARLET KISSES Patricia Camden
76825-9/$4.50 US/$5.50 Can

WILDSTAR Nicole Jordan
76622-1/$4.50 US/$5.50 Can

The Incomparable

ELIZABETH LOWELL

"Lowell is great!"
Johanna Lindsey

ONLY YOU
76340-0/$4.99 US/$5.99 Can
"For smoldering sensuality and exceptional storytelling,
Elizabeth Lowell is incomparable."
Kathe Robin, *Romantic Times*

ONLY MINE
76339-7/$4.99 US/$5.99 Can
"Elizabeth Lowell is a law unto herself
in the world of romance."
Amanda Quick, author of SCANDAL

ONLY HIS
76338-9/$4.95 US/$5.95 Can
Like the land, he was wild, exciting…and dangerous
and he vowed she would be only his.

Avon Romantic Treasures

*Unforgettable, enthralling love stories,
sparkling with passion and adventure
from Romance's bestselling authors*

ONLY IN YOUR ARMS *by Lisa Kleypas*
76150-5/$4.50 US/$5.50 Can

LADY LEGEND *by Deborah Camp*
76735-X/$4.50 US/$5.50 Can

RAINBOWS AND RAPTURE *by Rebecca Paisley*
76565-9/$4.50 US/$5.50 Can

AWAKEN MY FIRE *by Jennifer Horsman*
76701-5/$4.50 US/$5.50 Can

ONLY BY YOUR TOUCH *by Stella Cameron*
76606-X/$4.50 US/$5.50 Can

FIRE AT MIDNIGHT *by Barbara Dawson Smith*
76275-7/$4.50 US/$5.50 Can

ONLY WITH YOUR LOVE *by Lisa Kleypas*
76151-3/$4.50 US/$5.50 Can

MY WILD ROSE *by Deborah Camp*
76738-4/$4.50 US/$5.50 Can

1 Out Of 5 Women Can't Read.

1 Out Of 5 Women Can't Read.

1 Out Of 5 Women Can't Read.

1 Xvz Xv 5 Xwywv Xvy'z Xvyz.

1 Out Of 5 Women Can't Read.

*As painful as it is to believe, it's true. And it's
time we all did something to help. Coors has committed $40
million to fight illiteracy in America. We hope
you'll join our efforts by volunteering your time. Giving just a
few hours a week to your local literacy center can
help teach a woman to read. For more information on literacy
volunteering, call* **1-800-626-4601.**